When she woke her first sensations were all of pain. She hurt all over. Something rough and hard pressed against her back, her hips, her head. The odor of incense was smothering, the light so dim she could barely see. She shut her eyes and a yawning blackness sucked her down.

A noise brought her back to consciousness. She opened her eyes and found the light a little brighter, not much. She blinked, waited for her sight to focus. Someone else was in the room. The floor creaked under slippered feet. Something rattled, bottles, perhaps. The light flickered. She heard a hiss; the smell of incense thickened.

Surreptitiously, she moved a hand. Her sword belt was gone. The hand moved again, and she froze. Demonfang was gone! She bit her lip, forced herself to remain still, though every nerve in her body screamed to get up and search for the dagger.

SKULL GATE

ROBIN W. BAILEY
SKULL GATE

A TOM DOHERTY ASSOCIATES BOOK

SKULL GATE

First printing: October 1985

A TOR Book

Published by Tom Doherty Associates
49 West 24 Street
New York, N.Y. 10010

Cover art by Kevin Eugene Johnson

ISBN: 0-812-53139-6
CAN. ED.: 0-812-53140-X

Printed in the United States of America

For Diana,
all the loves of all my lives.

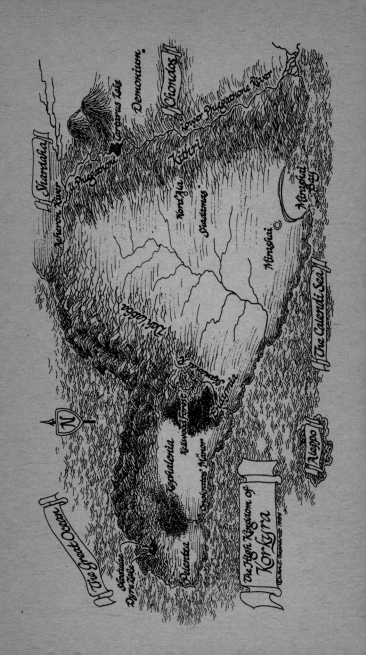

The Great Ocean

Shamakaj

Acheron River

Phlegethon

Tartarus Tide

Demoncium

Chondos

Lower Phlegethone River

Kitor

Hanija

Sanianus

Warulu

Staiamus

Warughai Bay

The Oriendi Sea

Dah Gobba

Tsatmu

Kalymuu

N

Cephalonia

Kanwod Forest

Onomawu's Manor

Pelortaa

Shantaia Devi Tule

Aleppo

The High Kingdom of Korsira

Chapter One

The barest sliver of a crescent moon floated peacefully over the sleeping city of Mirashai. Soft golden was its color, but it shed no light on the broad, paved streets or gloomy alleys that laced Korkyra's ancient capital. An enigmatic smile in the dark sky, it captured the eyes and imaginations of the usually alert palace sentries. They leaned on their pikes, inhaled the gentle salt breeze that blew inland from the Calendi Sea, and composed poems for each other.

They did not see the shadow that slipped over the palace walls. It dropped soundlessly into the royal courtyard and crouched behind the queen's favorite roses. It studied the garden, noting where the guards were, where a patch of gravel might turn noisily underfoot, where a tree or bush or shadow might provide cover as it made its way to the garden's far side.

It started off, moving phantomlike among the unwary sentries. As it ran, a stray moonbeam fell upon its face, lending glitter to dark eyes. A black mask hid any other features.

A guard coughed. The intruder snuggled in the shadow of an orange tree and peered around. He had not been spotted. He moved on, swiftly, silently, and came to a door.

Its cracked wooden surface and rusted hinges betrayed

the antiquity of Korkyra's palace. There was no lock; in troubled times it was barred on the inside with an oaken beam, his sources had warned. But finally, the nation was at peace. He expected no bar.

Putting his shoulder to the wood, he pushed. There came the faintest creak, inaudible to the sentries. Still, he took no chances but reached beneath his cloak, extracted a sealed pot of oil from the pouch on his belt. When the seal was broken, he carefully collected the wax fragments and returned them to the pouch, leaving no evidence of his passage.

He smeared the pot's thick contents around the edges of the door and into the rusty hinges. When he tried the door again, it eased open without complaint. He slipped inside.

There were no lighted sconces in these seldom traveled levels. Darkness was utter, intimidating. He took a breath, felt for the wall, and hurried on, counting his steps carefully.

Somewhere ahead he'd find a passage and a way to the western tower. His hand found a niche and a basin of water, once herb-scented, now quite torpid. He allowed a faint smile. Ten steps more to the passage.

He made his way stealthily. Most of the halls he traversed were dark, a few dimly lit by weak, slow-burning lamps. Once, a squad of soldiers passed; he heard their heavy footfalls and hid in a side passage until they were gone.

A winding stairway carried him to the next level and another black corridor. He crept along toward a distant brightness, the royal passage, illuminated by a hundred lamps and torches. There, he would find another stair ascending into the western tower.

He would also find a guard, so his sources informed him.

Several strides from the royal passage, he stretched flat on his stomach. The stone tiles were cold even through his tunic. He crawled to the end of the darkness. Face close to the floor, he peered into light.

A gleaming silver plate hung behind each lamp, reflecting the firelight, turning the hall into a place of burnished brilliance. The corridor was wider than he expected, the ceiling high and vaulted. Frescoes decorated the upper reaches. The floor was a chessboard of pink-and-white marble.

He glanced right. That way led to the throne room and other parts of the palace. He glanced left. At the hall's far end was a small, arched doorway and beyond, a stair mounting into darkness.

By the door a guard stood rigid, a veritable mountain of muscled flesh. His right hand gripped a huge iron-tipped lance; his left rested on the haft of a wicked double-bladed axe which hung from a strap on his weapon belt. Polished metal rings sewn to his leather armor shone brightly.

The intruder crept back into darkness and stood. He unlaced his cloak, let it slip to the floor, removed his mask. Gloved fists rubbed furiously at eyes until they burned. He opened his tunic to the waist. In a wrist-sheath, he wore a short, thin-bladed dagger; he reached up his sleeve and loosed its catch-strap.

Then, in a low and rasping voice he began to sing an old tavern song. He slurred the words, made a shambles of the proper melody. He sang softly at first, then louder.

He scuffled noisily into the brighter passage, set a weaving course for the stairway.

The guard snapped alert at first sight of him. The lance swung down. Two eyes glared suspiciously from beneath a helmet rim. "Who's there?"

The intruder flashed a big, disarming grin. He reached for the tapestried wall to steady himself and took another wobbly step. "Gon' sing for the queen," he announced boisterously. "Sing a little song for the queen, yessir!" He cracked out another verse, grinning, wobbling.

The sentry frowned with stern disapproval, leaned the lance against the wall, and bore down on him. "You're drunk, sir," the guard declared. "Find another place to sing before you wake Her Majesty."

"Gon' sing for the queen." The guard bent near. With feigned carelessness, the intruder tripped on his own heel and pretended to fall. Reacting by well-intentioned instinct, the unwary guard reached out to catch him.

The sleeved dagger lashed out, bit deep, straight into the guard's unprotected throat. The intruder twisted the blade and jerked, severing the windpipe. A gurgling rush of air was all that came of the man's attempt to scream. He crumpled, quickly dead.

Hastily, the intruder cut a strip from the dead man's cloak and stuffed it in the gaping wound to prevent more blood from spilling on the tiles. Too much of the telling crimson already stained the floor; he mopped it up with the rest of the cloak. Someone might happen by. A missing guard could be explained by a dozen things: drink, women, nature's necessities. Blood told a more chilling tale.

Seizing the body by the heels, he dragged it back into the dark passage he had emerged from. No one would come that way until morning. He recovered his own cloak and made for the stair.

Narrow stone steps wound higher and higher. He felt the wall constantly as he ascended. There were lamps on the walls, but no light in them. The only illumination came from two small windows whose wooden shutters had been left open. A faint, pale moon grinned as he passed them.

At the top of the stairs was a short corridor and a single door. On noiseless feet he crept to it, loosening the short sword in the sheath he wore strapped to his thigh. Slowly, he drew it out.

On the other side of the door the High Queen of Korkyra slept with her lone guardian. His gloved hand pushed on the smooth, polished wood. He had been paid well for this night's work.

It was time to earn his money.

Frost sat on the edge of the high window and stared at the moon. The stone was cool against her bare buttocks. An easy wind rustled the scant nightshirt, her only garment. She sighed, and her small breasts heaved gently under the thin material. She breathed the salt air, smelled the rich odor of flowers from the garden far below.

She closed her eyes. The night was full of ghosts and bad memories. She imagined she could hear the sea waves as they roared upon the shore and shook the vessels anchored in the harbor. The sound of breakers and thrashing foam played in her mind, and she thought of a little girl who once stood among the rocks at the ocean's edge calling in a tiny voice for the wind and tempest that came at her command.

She drew a deep breath and sighed again. It was on such nights as this she worked her wildest magics, bending the elements to her will. How she rejoiced in the energies that surged within her, forces that rose, bursting free like an arcane and potent song! She recalled all the sensations: the crackling on her skin, the immense gulf that opened in her mind, from whose dark depths sprang the power she wielded so effortlessly.

But that was long ago. Now, her witch-powers were gone. Her sorceress-mother had closed that gulf forever, cursed her daughter with a dying breath and stripped away all vestige of her eldritch talents.

Frost told herself it no longer mattered. She didn't miss the magic. She had been much younger in those days, a very different person, a little girl. Little girls were easily captivated by such things without seeing the dark price the soul had to pay. Still, she remembered. . . .

What had become of that little girl at the ocean's edge?

The Calendi Sea was only two miles away. She seldom went there anymore. The blue, crashing waters always brought back memories of Esgaria and the place where she grew up by the shore. She couldn't bear those memories or the nightmares they so often brought.

Tonight, though, it was no nightmare that kept her from sleeping.

She looked up at the pale moonlight and the dim silver stars that peppered the sky. A low, moaning wind chased a wisp of hair from her eyes. She cast her gaze over the towers and minarets of Mirashai. In a far-off window, a candle flickered and went out.

"Time to go," she whispered to herself. It was almost a

sigh. She looked across the room to the queen's silken draped bed. Aki no longer needed her. The war with Aleppo was over. Korkyra was at peace.

She had found friends, made a respectable place for herself here. Why it wasn't enough, she couldn't tell. But it wasn't.

"Time to go," she whispered again. The increasingly sedentary life of Aki's court left her too much time to think, too much time to brood.

What would Aki say? For over a year Frost had stood by the little queen's side as champion and guardian. Aki had given her authority not only over the palace elite guard, but over most of her personal advisors.

Frost shook her head and turned her gaze back to the night sky.

Aki was young. Too young to bear the responsibilities of a crown, Frost mused. She should have had a longer childhood, a chance to play and be a young girl. All that was lost now, thrown over for a golden circlet.

She remembered how the young queen had watched as her father's murderers, Aleppan spies, were put to death in the traditional Korkyran manner. Aki never flinched as the two men were hanged screaming by their feet and their wrists cut. Even as the dust soaked up the red blood, she set the crown on her own head, and all the armies hailed her as their rightful ruler.

Frost had been a soldier then, a common mercenary.

A cool gust fluttered her short nightshirt and startled her from her reverie. She yawned. Her own bed, less ornate than Aki's, waited in a corner near the door. The deep cushions beckoned. She was bone-tired, but not yet ready for sleep. She hugged her legs close, leaned her head on bent knees. A heavy strand of hair hid her face.

Time to go, she told herself again. She smiled faintly and closed her eyes.

A sudden stir in the air brought her out of a light doze, a gentle draft that brushed the wrong side of her body. She looked up and caught the dim flash of metal, heard the ripping of bedclothes. A shadow moved beside her bed.

She rose silently to a crouch on the windowsill and leaped.

To her dismay she remembered the moon behind her. Her shadow raced before her, alerting the intruder. He whirled, dodged her outstretched arms. With a bitter curse, she landed in a heap on the bed, sprawled among the thick blankets and cushions, her back an inviting target.

From the corner of her eye she saw the blade rise. She twisted furiously. The point bit deep in the mattress, barely missing her ribs. Again the weapon flashed. She threw herself aside, half-tangled in the shredded quilts, and lashed out with her feet.

Her foe grunted and crashed to the floor. She scrambled from the bed, listening in the dark, hoping for the clatter of his blade on the uncarpeted stone tiles.

That sound never came. She peered into the blackness; was the intruder invisible? Did he have some spell or charm that prevented her from seeing or hearing him? Or was he just good at his craft? She swore after this to keep a lamp lit, no matter what the hour. The damned darkness swallowed everything.

"Frost? I thought I heard something."

Frost barely made out the silhouette of Aki's head poking through the silken drapes of her bed. At the same time a swiftly moving shadow crossed by the window.

The intruder!

She lunged and cried out as a coverlet fallen from the bed caught her foot. She fell heavily and rolled to her feet. Too late.

A gloved hand seized Aki by the hair and jerked her through the veils. The little queen screamed once before the same hand released her hair and clamped brutally over her mouth. She struggled and twisted but clearly was no match for the strength of her captor. Suddenly, she froze. The point of a short sword hovered at her heart.

Frost's sword hung on a peg just above her pillow. She dived for it, snatched the scabbard, rolled over the bed, and came to her feet, blocking the only way into the

chamber. Her weapon came free with a hiss. The long
blade gleamed, catching the moonlight.

For a tense moment there was no sound but her own
breathing and a muffled whimper from Aki. The light
through the window drew a tenuous line across the room, a
line neither she nor the intruder seemed willing to brave.
She could not see him clearly, but his silhouette was target
enough for her sword.

"Drop it." The voice was a harsh whisper. "I'll kill her
if you don't."

She gripped her sword tightly in both hands, bastard-
style, and swayed ever so slightly on the balls of her feet.
When she answered there was a cold, challenging edge to
her words. "Then what will you hide behind?"

"Move from the door, or she's meat."

"She's dead anyway if I let you leave with her. You'll
cut her throat in one of the dark passages."

"You want to watch her die here and now?"

She kept her voice calm, but her palms were beginning
to sweat. "Yes," she answered. "Then, she'll be swiftly
avenged." She hesitated. The sword above Aki's heart did
not waver. "Or I can make you a bargain. Let her go, and
I'll give you fair time to get away before I call the guards."

The intruder didn't answer at once. "My terms," he
said at last. "Drop your sword out the window, and I'll
release her. You escort me from the palace."

Frost shook her head. "You found your way in alone,
and you can find your way out. I count my own life
valuable, too."

The sword moved to Aki's throat. For a dreadful moment Frost feared she had bargained too hard. Then, her
foe answered, and there was an undisguised note of mirth
in his voice.

"Capturing your opponent's queen is supposed to be an
enormous tactical advantage."

The metaphor was not lost on her. She had watched
many nights while her father had played the Game of
Kings with other nobles.

"Stalemate, this time," she said. "Worse, if you reject my offer."

A heavy silence settled on the room. Even Aki was still. Then, "They say you murdered your parents and a brother, too."

She stiffened. Even here. The story had followed her even to Korkyra. Her grip tightened on her sword until her fingers went cold and half-numb. "Then you know it will mean nothing for me to cut you down."

"No, I suppose not." The tension had left his voice. He seemed relaxed, even conversational. "I've heard other tales about you, too, in the taverns and among the rabble."

"Quit your chattering, magpie," she hissed, annoyed that he could sound so calm. She trembled from head to toe, and her cheeks burned. She longed for nothing more than a chance to carve him. Who was this fool that dared poke in the ashes of her past? She swallowed hard, striving for a measure of control. "What's it going to be? Aki has a long day tomorrow and needs her sleep."

A deep laugh echoed in the room. "Gods! The bitch dares to be impatient with me!" He laughed again. "Maybe you're a sorceress after all, as some say."

"If it were true," she answered, "I'd blast your soul to hell!"

Again, the room grew quiet. Again, the intruder broke the silence.

"All right," he said, "the game is yours, but we'll play again another time." He stepped forward into the light that spilled through the window with Aki locked tightly in the crook of his arm. The short sword still hovered near her throat. Even in the faint illumination she could not see his face.

"You'll give me a fair start, on your honor?"

"A fair start," she affirmed, "before I send the guards to hunt your carcass through the city."

He moved toward the door, keeping Aki between himself and the point of Frost's sword. She backed away, but not so far she couldn't reach him if his own blade wavered a hair.

He paused at the threshold.

"Let her go," Frost said.

His grip on Korkyra's child-queen did not lessen. "Not a night for assassins, it seems." He shrugged his shoulders. "Ah, well, had I succeeded, I was to leave this behind. Now, it's just extra weight to a running man." He sheathed his sword, though he still clung to Aki. The empty hand disappeared inside his tunic for a brief moment. Then, he tossed something that clattered at her feet. "It belongs to my employer. You may know him."

She glanced at the thing on the floor, barely visible in the gloom. "What—"

Aki's startled cry was scant warning as the intruder pushed the little queen straight at her sword's point. She twisted to avoid splitting her royal charge. Little queen and guardian fell in a tangle of arms and legs, and Frost felt the cold metal slice her shoulder. She had no time to think of the pain. In the doorway, the assassin balanced a dagger in his fingertips.

She reacted swiftly, tugging Aki's smaller body under her own. She heard a *thunk* and opened her eyes to see the quivering blade sprouting from the leg of a stool near her hand.

"It goes without saying"—the intruder laughed—"I could have put that in your heart at any time."

"Liar," she began, but there was no chance to ask him how he would have done that with a child in one hand and a sword in the other. He made a short bow and vanished in the outer gloom.

She let out a string of curses with a viciousness that surprised even her. She pulled Aki roughly to her feet. The youngling's arms went around her waist and locked. Aki trembled all over.

"It's all right now," Frost soothed. "He's gone, and we're both fine."

Tears misted in Aki's azure eyes. "Who was he?" she cried senselessly. The child part of her overwhelmed the queenly part. She buried her face in Frost's short nightshirt.

Frost separated herself from Aki's grasping arms and

retrieved the object the assassin had left behind. It was a medallion. Her fingers traced the device raised on its surface. She started, and slowly the fire rose in her cheeks again. No mistaking that emblem. She didn't need a light to recognize that seal.

"It wasn't your life he wanted, little one." She ran the tip of her tongue over her lips, tasting her own sweat. The assassin had not gone to the wrong bed, as she first thought. "He came for me."

Aki gave her a quizzical look. The mist began to clear from her eyes.

"An old enemy dogs my tracks," she explained. "I'd completely forgotten him, a nearly fatal mistake." She picked up her sword. "Stay here and wait until I come back. Lock the door."

"Where are you going?" Aki asked with wide, innocent eyes. "You gave your word he'd have time to escape. On your honor."

Frost gave her a stern look. "Honor is a precious thing, Majesty. Like an orient spice, learn to use it sparingly." She stepped into the blackness beyond the threshold, then whispered back, "I only promised not to alert the guards. I said nothing about following him myself."

She closed the door behind her with a soft thud and waited until she heard the bolt slide home. Her bare feet made no sound on the chill stones as she advanced. She listened for footsteps ahead. Nothing broke the eerie silence.

There's more light in the bowels of hell, she thought, wishing for a torch or a lamp. Could he have gotten away so quickly? Or was he crouched unseen somewhere ahead, ready to plunge his stubby sword into her vitals? She held her sword out before her, as a blind man might hold a stick.

Her right fist clutched the medallion, and the sigil of Lord Rholf. The old man governed a city called Shazad in Rholaroth near the border of her own Esgaria. Two years before she'd been forced to kill his two drunken sons. Rholf and his remaining sons chased her, bent on vengeance, but she thought she'd eluded them when she crossed into Chondos. Rholarothans feared that land with a super-stitious dread. Yet somehow he'd managed to find her.

I'll not be hunted, she swore. *I'll have to end this, though it means returning to Shazad.*

She came to the stairs and began a cautious descent, feeling for the edges with her toes. Near the bottom the darkness began to dissolve as she approached the bright royal passage. The passage was empty. No sign of the intruder or the guard who should be on duty. She kicked the wall and cursed again.

"Seems cursing is all I'm good for tonight." Her words echoed meaninglessly in the corridor and faded away. She turned to mount the stairs.

Sudden sounds of racing feet and rattling weapons made her stop. A squad of the palace guards spilled into the hall from one of the adjoining passages. Tras Sur'tian himself, commander of the elite force, led them, his aging face grim and creased with worry. Some of the worry seemed to disappear when he saw her.

"Aki sounded the alarm!" he called gruffly.

She held out a hand to halt them and nodded. There was a velvet cord by the queen's bed, and a bell attached to it in the guards' quarters. A faint smile lifted the corners of her mouth. Aki must have rung it the minute her guardian left the room, throwing "honor" to the winds.

"She's all right now."

Tras Sur'tian said something else, but she didn't catch all the words. Instead, she wondered why his men were grinning in such an idiotic fashion. Then, a light draft spilled down the stairway from the unshuttered windows above, and she remembered with a start that all she wore was a thin nightshirt she slept in. Embarrassed, she waved her sword. "I'll cut the lips off the next man who smiles." Their grins faded.

Tras Sur'tian glowered at his men and ripped the cloak from a young lieutenant's back. She murmured thanks as he draped it over her shoulders.

"You're hurt," he said, spying the blood that trickled down her arm.

"My own sword," she said as ungentle fingers probed
the wound. "I fell on its edge. Clumsy of me, but not
serious."

Hastily, she sketched the details of the intruder's surrep-
titious visit. Tras Sur'tian gave orders and half his men
sped away to seal the exits from the palace grounds. Too
late, she secretly feared.

"First thing in the morning I want to see every man on
duty tonight," he told the lieutenant. "I'll know who fell
asleep, or I'll hang the lot."

"Let's see to Aki," Frost said. "She's alone right now
and no doubt frightened." She hugged the cloak tighter
around her shoulders and hurried up the stairs. The lamps
borne by Tras Sur'tian and his squad lighted the way this
time, and passage was much quicker.

"Hell of a country that puts a child on its throne," she
muttered.

Tras Sur'tian agreed. "The choice was not mine or
yours to make."

"I can't stay with her any longer, Tras." She touched
her old friend's shoulder. "I was thinking of leaving anyway, but now my presence is a threat to her safety. Aki
mustn't be in the way if my enemies try again."

Tras Sur'tian nodded understanding. They moved quietly up the last of the stairs. When they reached the door
to Aki's bedchamber, Frost pushed. Locked from the inside, as she had instructed. She called out.

No answer.

Again she called, and a third time. Tras Sur'tian's hand
clamped on her shoulder. "Let me try," he said. One time
only he called Aki's name, his booming voice filling the
narrow corridor. Then he slammed his massive frame against
the wooden door. It shook on its hinges, but held. A
second assault broke the bolt; the door sprang open.

A sickening stench of brimstone and sulphur boiled into
the passage, filling her lungs with choking fumes. She
staggered back coughing, nearly tripping over a man who
had fainted behind her. Smoke stung her eyes. Someone
bumped roughly into her, gasping for breath: Tras Sur'tian.

She took a deep breath, covered her face with a corner of her cloak, and rushed into the room. No trace of Aki. The walls were scorched and blackened as if a fire had raged through. Wisps of thick smoke clung to everything. Yet despite the smoke, the walls, all evidence of fire, nothing was burned. Furnishings, carpets, tapestries were all intact.

Tras Sur'tian pointed to the silken sheets strewn upon the royal bed. The canopied veils were thrown back. Five long, charred streaks ruined the fine material. The sentries all pressed closer for a better view.

"It has the shape of a large handprint," one guard observed.

Indeed it did.

"Sorcery," whispered Tras Sur'tian. He made a hasty pass in the air. "The work of demons."

The soldiers imitated his passes, invoking the protection of the One Korkyran God.

Frost leaned on the windowsill and drew a clean, slow breath. The spires and minarets of the sleeping city made dark silhouettes on the star-speckled horizon. The sudden wind that stirred her hair did nothing to cool the flush of anger that ignited her heart. Her gaze swept the courtyard below, then the palace boundaries and beyond, as if from her high vantage she might penetrate the gloomy shadows that swallowed up the streets and alleys.

Tras Sur'tian came to her side. "Come away and let me tend your arm." His voice was low, thick with fear and sorrow. "There's nothing more to do here."

She shook him off. It had been her job to protect the child-queen. She had failed. The blame was hers. She gripped her sword-hilt until her knuckles went white and threatened to break the skin.

Where was Aki?

She looked up at the moon for an answer.

The pale crescent was still a smile in the night sky.

Chapter Two

There was no sleeping that night. She spent the time interviewing guards and combing the palace grounds for any clue to Aki's disappearance. Little hope, she told herself bitterly. Not by physical means had the little queen been stolen from under their noses.

As dawn began to unfold in the east, she made her way back to the tower and the chamber she shared with Aki. A pair of sentries stood watch at the door, set there by Tras Sur'tian. They saluted sharply as she passed between them.

A vague odor of brimstone still lingered in the room.

Beneath her bed she kept a chest containing her few possessions. She retrieved it and, kneeling, began to rummage through. There were traveling clothes of gray leather; she spread them on the bed. There was a silver circlet set with a polished, gleaming moonstone; she placed it on her head to hold back her hair.

"Very pretty."

She glanced over her shoulder. For a heavy man, Tras Sur'tian could move quietly. "A gift from an old friend," she said, and turned back to her rummaging.

"It becomes you," he answered. "And what's that?"

She gazed at the small silken-wrapped bundle in her hand and the three strips of leather that bound it. For a long time she hesitated, just staring at it. Then she drew a slow breath, closed the lid of the chest, and pushed it back under the bed. There was nothing else she needed.

"What is it?" Tras Sur'tian repeated. "It must be precious, you've wrapped it so carefully."

She almost smiled at that. Any Esgarian would have recognized the binding. White silk and leather were meant to contain a charm's magic power. If an object were wrapped so, its energies would not seep away, nor could it be contaminated by outside influences.

But this bundle contained no mere charm, and the binding was little more than hopeful caution on her part. She untied the leather strips one by one and laid them aside. Then she unrolled the silk.

Tras Sur'tian whistled softly and leaned closer.

It gleamed softly in the combined lamplight and light of dawn that spilled through the window. The sheath was pure polished silver and the belt a chain of shining silver discs. Three crimson bloodstones sparkled on the dagger's silver hilt.

"A finer-looking piece I've never seen!" Tras Sur'tian reached out to touch it.

"No!" She caught his hand. "No one touches Demonfang but me. Pray you never learn why." She pushed his hand away, rose, and set the dagger beside her riding clothes.

"Demonfang?"

She began to undress, casting off her soldier's garb. She thought nothing of Tras Sur'tian's presence. Men had seen her naked before. "A silly habit we Esgarians have of naming our weapons."

"What do you call your sword?"

She shrugged. "Sword." In truth, Demonfang had been named long before she'd possessed it.

She pulled on the riding outfit and tucked the trouser legs into her boots, buckled the dagger on her left hip, sword on her right.

"You're going to look for her, aren't you?"

"She was my charge," Frost answered coldly. "I let her be taken."

"What could you have done against sorcery?" he responded. "You're no witch."

She stiffened, then drew a careful breath and let it pass. "She was my charge," she repeated.

Two more guards appeared in the doorway. They called her name. "His Highness summons you," said one. "We are sent as escort."

Frost shot a look at Tras Sur'tian.

"It's what I came to tell you," he said. "Thogrin Sin'tell arrived less than an hour ago. He'll rule in Aki's place now. The coronation is three days away."

She was able to hide her anger from the guards at the door, but Tras Sur'tian knew her too well. "He has the right," he continued, "as Aki's first cousin and Baron of Endymia. Korkyra cannot be without a monarch."

"I'll be along shortly," she said to her escort, and she made to shut the door.

The guards did not budge. "We are to escort you."

"I'll escort her myself," said Tras Sur'tian. "You are dismissed." The two bowed, turned smartly, and disappeared. Frost closed the door.

"Endymia is on the other side of the kingdom," she hissed when they were alone. "How in the nine hells did Thogrin Sin'tell learn Aki was missing?"

Tras Sur'tian tried to calm her. "He didn't. He was coming to pay a visit, that's all."

"Traveling at night?" she pushed. "In all the two years I've served Aki, Thogrin Sin'tell has never shown his face at court. Why now, of all times?"

"Are you saying he's involved?"

She nearly laughed at his disbelieving countenance. "Right up to his coronet. You can't be so stupid. You have to see it."

He shook his head. "He's of royal blood."

She spat. "History is written with such blood, families butchering each other for a crown. The armies are loyal to Aki. Arrest this rat and wring some answers from him!"

Tras Sur'tian paced the room. "They won't do it. No army has ever rebelled against a monarch. They won't do it," he repeated. "I won't do it."

"He's not your monarch," she insisted.

His face purpled and one fist pounded the wall. "We have no proof that Aki lives," he roared, "or that Thogrin's involved in her disappearance!"

"A taste of the rack would gain you such proof, I'll warrant."

He straightened, striving for a measure of control again. For all her urging, Tras Sur'tian was a Korkyran commander, a soldier trained to loyal service. "It is not possible," he said finally.

She gave up. There was more to worry about. "Do you know why he has summoned me?"

Tras Sur'tian turned to face her; maybe her words had left a mark after all, for she read a sudden concern in his large brown eyes.

"I can only guess," he answered. "With Aki gone you have no status now. You're a common mercenary again, and your fate is in Thogrin's hands."

She frowned. "That's not terribly reassuring."

"Be wary of him, woman." Tras Sur'tian was suddenly animate again. He paced the floor and rubbed his hands as he spoke. "Thogrin does not look like much of a man. In fact, I doubt he has ever held a sword. But he is wily and has about him the look of a man who has waited a long time to be king. Say nothing about this quest of yours to find his cousin. He'll not look favorably on it, or on any action that would foster the belief that Aki still lives."

"Would he try to keep me from leaving?"

Tras Sur'tian nodded. "If he knows you plan to search for Aki."

She thought for a moment, realizing that time was slipping away and that Thogrin Sin'tell was waiting for her. "Then, Tras, if you hold our friendship of any worth, and if you ever loved Aki, you must do something for me." She removed her sword and wrapped it in the gray cloak that still lay on the bed. She pressed it into his arms. "My horse is in the royal stables. Bring him to the eastern gate. Don't try to saddle him, just bring the gear. Speak my name, and he'll follow you. Don't treat him roughly. And best you disguise yourself in some way so no one knows you gave me any aid.''

Tras Sur'tian looked disturbed, his brow furrowed. ''You'd ask me to disobey my king?''

''Has he already commanded that I'm not to leave?''

The old commander shook his head.

''Then you're not disobedient. And if you leave now, you'll never hear if such an order is given.''

He seemed unconvinced. She touched his arm and spoke softly. ''Tras, please? I'll need your help.''

At last he shrugged his huge shoulders. ''Damn if I ever thought I'd see the day a woman made me her puppet,'' he said, ''but you've done so, and handily.''

''Then I've one more thing to do.'' She unfastened Demonfang's belt, then her tunic, which she raised above her breasts. She rebuckled the dagger next to her skin. When she lowered her garment no trace of it showed.

She caught the look in Tras Sur'tian's eye. ''I'm no assassin,'' she assured him. ''But I can't leave this blade lying around or trust it even into your care. Neither can I wear it openly in Thogrin's presence, since he's of royal blood and I'm not sworn to him. This is the best way.'' She pulled a piece of velvet cord from the trimming on Aki's bed and tied it around her waist for a belt. ''See,'' she said, patting the dagger beneath her tunic, ''how difficult it would be to reach?''

Tras Sur'tian hugged her sword in its cloak wrapping. ''I'll be at the gate,'' he said, ''and look that you deal cautiously with Thogrin Sin'tell.''

''If I'm not there in an hour, look for me in prison.''

His eyes darkened at that, but he said no more. They opened the door and departed, leaving the two original sentries to guard an empty room.

Two more sentries stood rigidly outside the reception hall. They parted as she approached, but she hesitated between them. She knew the role she had to play, and a few moments to compose herself would ease her task. Slowly, the anger ebbed from her, and the tension in her muscles faded. She checked her appearance, making sure

Demonfang could not be detected under her clothes. Finally, she was ready to confront Thogrin Sin'tell.

The reception hall doors were massive carven oak. At her push they swung back on well-oiled hinges.

She had stood in this hall on countless occasions. It never failed to impress her. The ceiling was supported, not by columns, but on the heads of tall, slender sculptures of milk-white marble, men and women from the various Korkyran myths and legends. The ceiling and floor were painted with all manner of birds and animals and flowers. The walls were draped with tapestries. A light incense floated in the air.

At the far end of the hall twenty ivory steps led upward to the emerald throne. Above it, the ceiling rose in a deep bell. The merest whisper could be heard clearly throughout the entire chamber.

Sprawled on the cushioned seat, Thogrin Sin'tell spoke to her. "You've kept me waiting, woman."

She didn't miss the mocking note or the thinly veiled threat. Her footsteps echoed loudly on the painted tiles, and she bent one knee on the bottom stair. She averted her eyes.

"Pardons, Highness," she answered softly. "I was not attired when you summoned me."

He shrugged and held out a cup. A serving girl at his right hand produced a jug and poured for him. At his left sat a court clerk whose name Frost could not recall. He held up a document. Thogrin glanced at it and shook his head.

"No matter. As you can see, I have plenty to occupy my time. My little cousin was a sweet child and popular with the people, but it seems she had no head for state affairs."

Frost bit her lip and forced her hands to unclench. The liar! Aki was a conscientious leader. What she lacked in years and experience she made up for with the best tutors and advisors. Still, it would not be wise to say so.

Thogrin lifted his cup and drained it. He gestured for more. "You know, I can drink and drink and never get

drunk.'' He smiled and regarded her for a long time.
''You're some kind of warrior, I understand.'' His smile
broadened and he leaned forward, resting an elbow on a
knee. ''You don't look too fierce.''

It was not a question and required no response. She said
nothing. Her knees were beginning to ache.

Thogrin pressed her. ''They say you can best any man
with a sword. Is it true?''

She swallowed, choosing her words carefully. ''Highness, men are sometimes given to exaggeration.''

He raised an eyebrow. ''Are you saying my soldiers—my
Korkyran soldiers—are liars?''

She let her shoulders slump and pouted. ''No, Highness.''

''Ah, well''—Thogrin shrugged again—''whatever your
skill, you were my cousin's guardian.'' He paused, examined a paper the clerk held up for him, and nodded. The
clerk dropped a spot of candle wax on the paper. Thogrin
pressed his ring to it. He looked back at her. ''Why were
you not with her last night?''

''There was another intruder,'' she answered. ''I tried to
pursue him.''

Thogrin drank from his cup. ''I've heard that story,'' he
said, ''and yet, there's no proof to substantiate it.''

She met his eyes for the first time, feeling the heat rise
in her cheeks. ''The slashed bedcovers,'' she countered,
''my arm . . .''

He held up a hand. ''Not proof,'' he said. ''Your sword
could have done those things.''

She rose slowly to her feet, hating the creature who
dared look down on her. Let him read the act as defiance if
he would. She was no one's scapegoat. ''Are you accusing
me?''

He glared. ''Not yet. The circumstances are odd enough
that I doubt you were actually involved in the murder of
my cousin—''

''Murder?'' she interrupted.

His voice dropped a note. ''Don't take that tone with
me, woman.'' He hesitated, challenging her with his silence, then resumed. ''There's no doubt of Aki's death,

whether by your intruder or some clever sorcery, as some say. You may not have been involved, but you were certainly not at your appointed post, that is, at Aki's side. That's the same as desertion.''

Her defiance melted, and she looked away. No denying it, he was right. Her place was with Aki. Had she remembered that, the child might not be gone. The blame was hers.

She chewed her lip.

Thogrin continued. ''For now, though, I'm inclined to mercy.'' A subtle smile spread over his face and he stretched, gripping the jewel-encrusted arms of Korkyra's throne. ''I have to consider that it may have been your carelessness that has brought me to this great seat.'' He beckoned for the serving girl to refill his cup.

Frost regarded him, her eyes narrow slits, as he sipped the wine. She had to get away. This man did not trust her; his attitude, every word he spoke betrayed that fact. If he did not arrest her now, he had a reason. Probably to arrange more evidence against her, she considered. She had no doubt that Thogrin Sin'tell would lay blame at someone's feet. It would not do to leave Aki's disappearance unexplained. The people would always wonder.

He leaned forward again. ''However, mercy is not foolishness. There are still questions to be asked before this affair is solved.''

There it was. He intended to *solve* it. She calculated the time that had passed. Tras Sur'tian would be waiting at the eastern gate.

''So you are not to leave the palace for a few days,'' Thogrin went on. ''When this is cleared up, then we may negotiate your continued enlistment in the service of Korkyra.'' He paused, pursed his lips. ''But certainly not as a soldier. Trousers just don't become you.'' The serving girl leaned forward and whispered in his ear. Thogrin barked a short laugh and waved her away. ''Not pretty enough,'' he said over his shoulder. Then, back to Frost, ''You may keep your quarters for now, but you have no status in court. You are my guest.''

He dismissed her with a gesture.

She backed up a few steps, then turned and walked away. There was a fine film of sweat on her palms. She wiped her hands on her tunic, feeling Demonfang beneath. Tras Sur'tian was right. Thogrin Sin'tell was not a man to trifle with. His ambition made him dangerous.

But had he, in fact, arranged Aki's disappearance?

If she had any doubts, they vanished when, at the door, she turned for a final look at the man she'd already begun to think of as foe.

In the shadows behind the throne a figure stirred and came forward into the light. He was dark-robed, hooded. She could see no face. For a brief instant she thought it was last night's intruder. But this man was shorter, and the way he slouched spoke of age or infirmity.

He saw her then, stopped in midstep, and drew himself erect. They regarded each other across the hall. Still she could not see a face. Then the figure walked to the throne, took up a position behind Thogrin, and laid a withered hand on the emerald seat.

She nodded and left the hall.

Thogrin Sin'tell was not the sole possessor of Korkyra's crown. The old man had admitted it with his gesture. There was challenge in that gesture, and warning.

"Wizard," she muttered to herself, "or sorcerer or witch." Well, she'd known from a first glance at Aki's strangely scorched sheets that magic was involved. Yet her own witch-powers were gone forever. What could she do?

She took a deep breath. Whatever she had to do, she vowed. She had failed Aki once. If the little queen lived, it was her responsibility to find her. If she was dead, then the blood was on her hands.

She looked closely at her palms and rubbed them together, not liking the thought. Still, if it proved true, then only blood could wash away blood.

She started down the corridor at a casual pace that hid her real purpose. She was not safe in the palace, not even in Mirashai. She could do Aki no good at all if she were imprisoned. Nor was Thogrin her real enemy, she suspected. If that old man was truly a wizard, the eyes watching her might not be detectable.

She went to the kitchens and sampled the morning's fare with an approving nod. In the quarters of the palace guard, she inspected weapons and chastised an improperly clad sentry, all with barely concealed haste. In the courtyard, she sniffed the flowers. Two guards stood watch at a gate in the wall. She knew them and stopped to chat. Apparently, word of her confinement had not yet spread. They made no attempt to stop her when she wished them a good day and passed out into the street.

Beyond the wall, she dropped her pretense and headed at a brisk walk to where Tras Sur'tian was waiting. With each step she thanked her Esgarian gods that no guard accosted her. Her sharp ears were alert for a cry of "Halt!" or the marching bootsteps of an armored patrol.

The streets were full of people, merchants spreading their wares for the day's trade, beggars and urchins, the rare noble out for a morning's stroll. She pushed her way through them, making no apologies, speaking to no one.

She spied the eastern gate and looked around for sentries, saw none.

Just beyond it, an old man waited clad in the dirtiest of rags. A patch covered one eye. The disguise was good, but she knew Tras Sur'tian at once by the size and shape of his body and by the beautiful black beast that stood at his side.

The creature's name was Ashur, and Frost smiled when she saw him. His mane was thick and lustrous. His proud tail brushed the earth. But to Frost, his most beautiful features were the two eyes which were not eyes at all, but pools of unnatural flame which burned hotter according to the animal's temper, and the glistening horn, long as a man's arm, that sprouted from his forelock.

Ashur was a gift from the same wizard who had given her Demonfang. There was no other such creature on all the earth. To normal eyes Ashur appeared just a horse, although a big and unusually strong horse. Though his speed was no greater, no earthly steed could match his endurance.

But for the rare few who possessed the true-sight, the power to see through mere appearance, or for a man on the very brink of death, the illusion dissolved.

Wilder than the winds was Ashur. None but Frost could ride him.

Tras Sur'tian moved like a crippled old man. He stepped forward, waving a dirty bowl. She dropped a coin into it and moved past him to hug Ashur.

"Your sword and a few provisions," he whispered, "there by the wall. You're late. Trouble?"

She threw back a dusty blanket that covered her sword. She strapped the blade on her right hip. "I think so," she answered.

Tras Sur'tian frowned.

"There's an old man with Thogrin. Do you know him?"

"No, I saw him this morning for the first time."

She was grim as she fastened a cloak about her. "You may see more of him than you like. I tell you, he's the true power behind Thogrin Sin'tell. Together they're responsible for Aki's disappearance."

"Have you proof?" he whispered.

"I feel it in my heart of hearts," she answered.

"Not proof."

She shot him a look as he echoed Thogrin Sin'tell's words. Then she looked away and spat in the dust.

A group of merchants approached the gate headed for the city's bazaar. Mindful of his disguise, Tras Sur'tian slumped against the wall, squatted on his haunches, and extended his bowl. No coins came his way.

"May you sleep with diseased women!" he called after them as they passed. Then, to Frost, "If you truly believe that, then your search for Aki must begin here."

Her lips parted in a queer half smile. She shook her head slowly. "Thogrin's got to hang somebody for this, and since I was Aki's guardian that makes me the prime candidate. I'm not sticking around long enough to give him the chance."

He looked up at her with his one eye. "Are you coming back?"

She didn't answer, just swung a blanket over Ashur's back, then the saddle, and cinched it tight. That done, she lifted Tras Sur'tian's bag of provisions on her shoulder and turned to say good-bye.

A squad of guards stood in the gateway. She hadn't even heard them approach, nor had Tras, by his expression of surprise. She quickly counted their number.

Eight soldiers, all strangers to her. Thogrin Sin'tell's personal men, she guessed. Their weapons gleamed naked.

"Hold." A young lieutenant stepped smartly forward. "You have disobeyed the order of His Highness, Baron Endymia." A crooked grin suddenly poisoned his youthful features. "By attempting to leave Mirashai, you have proved your guilt in the murder of our beloved Queen Aki." He called to his men over a shoulder. "Take her sword."

One obedient guard came close and reached for her blade. She counted his steps, then swung the bag of provisions with her full strength. It caught him squarely in the face, knocking him off his feet. On the backswing she hurled it at the startled lieutenant. Apparently, he'd not expected resistance from a woman.

Her sword cleared sheath in one easy motion.

The guards were a young, untrained lot. Instead of trying to surround her, they charged her from the front, further proof they were Thogrin's men and not Korkyran regulars. Experienced soldiers knew better.

She swung, gripping her hilt with both hands, cleaving the nearest man nearly to the spine. She tugged, and her weapon reluctantly came free. Still, the others would have had her had she been alone.

Even as she slew the first one, Tras Sur'tian's booted foot smashed into the groin of another, and his massive fist took another out of the fight.

Then, a startling, unearthly cry sounded, mingled with the screams and shouts of four young men who suddenly beheld a monster in their midst. With a powerful lunge Ashur thrust his ebony horn through a fear-frozen sentry. He tossed his head, and the body smacked sickeningly against the wall, broken. He reared, and shining black hooves crashed down into the upturned faces of two more. The last man died as gnashing teeth clamped horribly on his neck and shoulder; he screamed once and no more.

The first guard who had fallen to the provisions bag made to rise, but a swing of Frost's foot spared his life, if not his nose. He hit the ground with a grunt, and if he wasn't unconscious, he wisely pretended to be.

"Tras?" She looked around for her old friend as she backed toward Ashur. She caught the unicorn's reins, still reluctant to sheathe her sword.

Tras Sur'tian bent over the body by the wall. His face crinkled as he traced the gaping hole in the dead man's chest.

"How?" There was genuine fear in those old eyes when he stared up at her. "No horse . . . "

She sighed. The illusion held; Tras Sur'tian would live to see another day. But there was no way she could explain, nor time.

A crowd began to gather; she had to leave. But Tras still knelt by the fallen sentry. Imperative he leave, too: he was well-known in Mirashai. Someone might penetrate his disguise.

"Run, beggar! Before I skewer you as well!" She raised her sword menacingly above his head.

A chilling mixture of fear and anger filled his gaze. He looked from her to her sword, measuring. For one tense moment she feared, in his confusion, he meant to attack her. But then his vision seemed to clear as he took notice of the mob and realized her intent. He cringed, threw up his hands as if to ward off a blow, ran, and disappeared into the crowd. A rich handful of coins scattered on the earth in his wake.

She smiled grimly as men and women scrambled for the bits of gold and silver, a clever gambit that gave them both time to get away. She swung quickly into the saddle and nudged Ashur's flanks with her bootheels.

Mirashai and its greedy populace receded in her dust.

Chapter Three

Frost stretched in the saddle. The sun neared noon, and the growl in her stomach reminded her she hadn't eaten. Too bad she'd left that bag of provisions behind. She was thirsty, too, and no waterskin.

Well, there wasn't much farther to go.

Ashur plodded along. She'd given up watching for signs of pursuit. It was clear none was coming. After the fight at the gate she'd run eastward to the rocky hills of the Kithri region, then doubled back to the west. Any followers would have a tough time picking up her trail.

She passed a farm. In the fields, a handful of workers rose over their hoes to watch her go by. They didn't wave. Without the armor and shield that marked her as Aki's champion she was just another stranger. And in these parts, as in all rural parts, strangers were not trusted.

Not far ahead she entered Shadamas, a small village with only a few ramshackle shops, a smithy, and an inn barely worthy of the name. A few pigs wandered the streets in search of garbage. A dirty little boy chased an even dirtier little girl across the only road. A hammer rang on an anvil.

The smith stopped his work as she rode by, and the children stopped playing. She felt the eyes peering out at her from behind the doors and windows. Here and there, someone came to the doorway long enough to watch her pass.

When she was through and the last building was behind
her, she let out a sigh. She hadn't realized she'd been
holding her breath. It had been tense. Yet word that she
was fugitive could not possibly have reached this far. Not
that it mattered. Shadamas was too small to warrant a
peace-keeping force of its own. Any trouble, and they sent
word to the garrison at Kord'Ala, and that was many miles
away.

A short distance beyond Shadamas she came to a shack.
It stood alone and isolated in the cleft of a low rise of hills.
A small garden flourished beside one wall. An old woman
bent between the neat rows, carefully pulling weeds from
the tender shoots.

"Oona!" Frost hailed her and dismounted.

The old woman looked up, squinting in the hot sunlight.
Her face was brown leather, her hair and the tufts of her
eyebrows gray as a winter morning. Her small blue eyes
seemed to work at focusing. Then a broad, toothy grin
brightened her features. "Oh, child!" she cried, rising as
quickly as her old joints could allow. "Samidar, my child!"
She stretched out her arms as she hurried toward Frost.
"You've come to visit!"

Frost met her embrace with a gentle hug, but a frown
creased her fine lips. "Please, I've asked you not to call
me that."

Oona pushed away and waved a hand between them.
"Oh, twaddle! That's your name, and don't bother me
with that other foolishness!" A gnarled brown hand reached
up and tickled Ashur's nose. He lowered his head closer,
appreciatively. "And you've brought your beautiful unicorn! My, this is a special day!"

"No pride!" Frost chided, half scolding her beast. "He'd
follow a Shardahani for a scratch on the nose!" She
reached out, too, to stroke his neck.

"Shardahanis aren't so bad once you get to know one,"
Oona said, quietly serious. "They're just people like us,
with a few odd customs." She grabbed Frost's arm and
pulled her toward the shack. "But you must be hungry.
It's a long way from Mirashai. Did you leave early?"

Frost nodded and let Oona lead her inside. She was hungry, no doubt of that, and a little saddle sore. She hadn't ridden in some time, and apparently the old calluses had gone away. They'd return soon enough.

The shack's roof was a sieve. Sunlight leaked through, casting little mote-filled beams all around. Frost took it all in. Nothing had changed. Shelves lined the walls, cluttered with dusty jars and bunches of dried herbs from Oona's garden. A pallet of grass and blankets made the old woman's bed in one corner. A rickety, weather-worn table and chair sat by one of the windows. A couple of stools were scattered here and there, a bundle of cloth and thread on one, more jars on the other. Dust on the floor was an inch thick.

Oona scuttled to the fireplace. A small iron caldron hung over the cold ashes. She lifted it with both hands, half bent with the effort. "You sit down over there in the chair. I'll be right back." She disappeared through another door in the shack's rear wall. When she reappeared a few minutes later, she wiped her hands on her skirts, brushed the bundle of cloth off one of the stools, and carried it to the table. "I told you now, sit down. There'll be some stew warm in a little bit. When it's hot like this, I keep a fire going out back so it doesn't get so warm inside. How about some water? No wine or milk, I'm afraid."

Frost took the chair and nodded. She leaned on her elbows as the old woman leaped up and went to a shelf, took down two earthen mugs, and ladled water into them from a bucket on the floor. She set one in front of her guest and drank from the other, taking careful, almost shy sips.

She watched the old woman and smiled inwardly. Oona was a jewel, one of the few people she truly called friend. They saw each other very rarely, but those were moments she treasured. She drank from her cup. The water was cool and sweet. "You've put something in it," she said, nodding.

Oona smiled. "Juice from some roots that grow near here," she admitted. "It keeps the water fresher so I don't have to go to the stream as often."

"Very good." Frost took another long drink. "Better than wine or milk."

Oona's smile widened. "Oh, the stew!" she said suddenly, and jumped up. She snatched a couple of earthen bowls from another shelf and went through the back door again. She returned with the bowls steaming. Frost stirred the contents of hers with a wooden spoon and blew on it. Chunks of meat in a rich broth. She could smell the herbs.

"Found the rabbit last night in one of my snares," Oona said proudly. She took a bite and chewed noisily. Oona still had her own teeth and never minded letting others know it. "Now, what brings you so far from the capital? Some trouble in Shadamas I don't know about?"

Frost swallowed. "Nothing happens in Shadamas you don't know about, you old keyhole-peeker." She took another bite. The stew was delicious, better than anything she could remember eating in Mirashai, for all those snobbish palace cooks.

She told the entire story, leaving nothing out. She couldn't have lied to Oona anyway. The old woman had the true-sight, the ability to see through lies or illusions, that rarest of all gifts that came only with age and wisdom.

"Then you're going to stay a few days," Oona announced. "Word will spread to Kord'Ala pretty quickly, if they haven't heard already. But knowing those lazy, overfed garrison toads, it'll be days before they spread the word this way."

That was one of the things she most appreciated about Oona: the old woman possessed a healthy disrespect for authority, learned from age and experience. She smiled and touched the gnarled, work-hardened hands. "Thanks, I hoped you'd let me stay awhile. I have to figure out what to do now, and I thought you might be able to help."

"Thogrin's mysterious ally?" Oona scratched her chin. "No help there, I'm afraid. I know of no wizards in these parts. Korkyrans don't go in for that sort of thing much. Even we few healers are a despised lot. They come to us when there's sickness and treat us like dogs the rest of the time. Take now"—her eyes hardened suddenly—"this poor

child I'm treating in the village. Got the root-fever bad, he
has. Only his father's half convinced I'm the cause, for he
and I had some harsh words recently.'' She sighed, and
her eyes softened again. ''If it wasn't that the child's such
a sweet one, and he sneaks me hill-flowers now and then,
I'd let the whole lot of them rot.''

''Not true,'' Frost said gently. ''You're a healer.''

Oona shrugged, rose, and went back to work in her
garden.

For two days Frost wandered the hills around Oona's
small shack, searching her mind for some clue she might
have overlooked, some hint that would tell her how to find
Aki. Was Lord Rholf involved, or had his assassin merely
chosen a coincident time to try for her life? Should she
return to Rholaroth to find an answer? What if he was not
involved? Rholf had never trafficked in sorcery before;
Rholarothans had an extreme fear of things arcane. Then
she would have wasted time. Days, weeks would pass, and
she would be no closer to Aki.

She returned to the shack to take meals with Oona and
to help with a few chores. She swept the floor, nearly
choking on the cloud of dust she raised. She cleaned the
shelves and carefully replaced each of Oona's mysterious
jars. The old woman kept lots of herbs and other things
Frost didn't know or recognize. She swept the ashes from
the cold fireplace.

And all the while, her mind worked. Not Rholf, she was
sure. Thogrin held the answers, and the figure in black
robes who so smugly leaned on Thogrin's throne. But who
was he, and was he wizard? She felt sure of it. The fire, or
whatever it was, that had scorched Aki's chamber had
certainly been magical. And she had sensed *something*
when that darkly hooded stare had reached across the
palace's reception hall to meet hers.

She returned to the hills at night to count the stars and
think some more. But the second night her thoughts were
endless puzzles, circles that left her dizzy until she collapsed and lay back on the cool grass. She closed her eyes

and opened them. The stars moved across the sky. Even the wind seemed to whisper *Aki*.

She didn't know how long she lay there, but suddenly she sat bolt upright. "You live too much in the mind!" she cursed herself, and slammed a fist into the earth. "Now act! Or count Aki damned and go marry a farmer!"

She got up and ran all the way back to the shack, threw open the door so it rattled the entire wall. The old woman was curled up asleep on her pallet in the dark corner.

"Oona!" she called. "Oona, wake up!"

The old healer stirred, rubbed her eyes, and peered uncertainly into the face that loomed so close in the gloom. "What?" she mumbled. "What is it?"

"I need clothes," Frost said. "Old clothes, anything you might have lying around. I need them now."

Oona sat up. "Why, child?"

"I'm going to Kord'Ala. I've got be outside the walls before sunrise. Don't dally." She bent down to help the old woman to her feet, cursing the darkness. She was overused to palace ways, where there was always a torch or lamp close at hand. Out here, when the sun was gone so was the light. She cursed again, but not so loud that Oona could hear.

Oona protested, but she moved to an old trunk, opened it, and began to rummage. "You can't go there. They'll be watching for you by now. All the big cities will and many of the smaller towns. They have a garrison, you know."

Frost held up the things Oona passed her, trying her best to see the garments that would make her disguise. "I know," she said. "That's why I need these. They'll be looking for someone else, not a farmer's wife or a beggar."

She began to strip off her own clothes. The back door opened and shut. Oona had gone out and returned with a small brand from the fires she kept going out back. With that light she found a stump of candle and set it on the table. The tiny flame set shadows dancing on the walls and ceiling as they moved around. Oona returned the brand to the outside fires.

"Don't like to do that inside," she said, closing the

door again. "Afraid the place might burn down. Poor as it is, it's mine." She rapped her knuckles on the door frame. The walls vibrated in response.

Frost smiled her appreciation as she dragged up another skirt, the third, and tied them all around her waist with a length of cord. Ages since she'd worn such things, and they felt strange. She pulled a tunic over her head, plain homespun that reached nearly to midthigh, and belted that with another cord. She rolled the sleeves halfway up her arms.

"Make sure you never touch that," Frost warned, pointing to Demonfang as she spread her weapons on the table. She couldn't take them with her; they'd make her too conspicuous. At last, she thought herself ready. She smoothed her skirts and patted back her hair. "Well?" she said, turning to Oona.

The old woman frowned, shook her head.

Too clean, Frost decided. She went outside, rubbed dirt on her face, in her hair. She rolled on the ground. Unused to the skirts, she tangled her legs, rose, tripped and fell, rose again. "Well, now?" she asked again, back inside.

"No good at all," the healer announced. "You're too healthy for a beggar, not lean or haggard enough. It shows."

"A farmer's wife, then."

"Not humble enough, not broken down from the work. That shows, too, in your bearing and in your walk; worse . . . in your eyes!"

Exasperated, Frost threw up her arms.

"Wait." Oona carried the candle stump to the trunk where she'd stored the clothes and bent over it, digging. When she straightened up she tossed something.

Frost caught it, curious. She sobered at once, recognizing the feel of silk with leather bindings. She motioned for the candle and sat down at the table. Oona brought the light and sat opposite her.

Yes, white silk and a thrice-wrapped leather binding. She looked across into the old woman's eyes as she untied the bundle. Dark shadows, a trick of the light, swallowed Oona's face. Her old hands rested quietly by the candle.

When the silk was removed a pile of cards spilled out. Frost turned one of them over, gazed at the crowned half skull that peered back at her. She turned another and another.

"A descroiyo?" She leaned forward. The candle flame was hot on her cheeks. "You want me to be a descroiyo?"

Oona leaned closer, too, until the shadows no longer hid her face. "What better?" she whispered. "No one seeks a fortune-teller but the bored or the desperate. And you are familiar with the cards. You know their ways."

"They won't work for me, you know that."

"You know their meaning. You can lie about the rest, make up stories." She shrugged, and her sigh set the flame to flickering. "All anyone wants to hear is how rich they're going to be or how many women they'll make love to. You can handle that."

Frost thought about it. Yes, it was good. The descroiyos occupied a special position in this land of the One God. No one believed in their power to tell the future, but most were afraid to disbelieve it. Hence, they came and went as they pleased, scorned but left alone. A good disguise, she decided. She gathered up the cards, retied them in the white silk, and placed them in a pouch that Oona gave her. She kissed the old woman.

"One more thing," Oona said. She went to the fireplace and reached up into the chimney. She came back, her finger smudged with soot.

"Bend down here." Frost obeyed and Oona made a dark crescent moon on her brow. "That's the sign," she said. "Everyone will know what you are."

Frost thanked the old woman and went outside. Ashur was nowhere in sight. She never tied or hobbled him but let the unicorn wander, munching grass or whatever he pleased.

"Do you call him?" Oona asked from the doorway.

Frost looked out toward the clustered silhouettes of hills. They rose, unevenly breaking the starry skyline. "No need," she answered. "He knows I need him now."

The sound of hooves followed her words, a racing

clip-clop in the night. "Look for his eyes," she said to Oona.

Two points of flame, small and far away, appeared in the direction of the hills. The thunder of hooves swelled on the breeze. The flames drew nearer, nearer, the thunder louder. The earth trembled faintly beneath their feet.

"I see him!" Oona gasped.

The flames danced furiously, part of the black shape that sped toward them. Frost smiled at the note in the old woman's voice. "Ashur," she whispered, half in awe herself.

The unicorn stopped its headlong rush several safe paces away, kicking up dust, came forward, and nuzzled Frost's hand. The long spike on its brow slid past her arm. The twin fires that served him for eyes cast pools of light about them, yet gave off no heat.

Oona crept closer, passed her hand near one of the flames, then through it. She stared at her palm. "When I saw him that first time you came," she said, "I thought I'd gone mad. What is he, child?"

"Magic," she answered simply, making no effort to hide the near rapture she felt when she and Ashur were together. "More than that, I don't need or want to know." She gathered her skirts over one arm and leaped onto the unicorn's broad back.

"No saddle?" said Oona.

"Not this time," she answered, and dropped her skirts. They spilled all around her and hung down Ashur's flanks. She grasped the thick and lustrous mane. "I'm not taking him into Kord'Ala. He can wander the hills while I do my work."

"You may need to depart quickly," Oona cautioned.

"He'll be near if I need him," Frost assured her. "I should return tonight or early tomorrow."

She waved to Oona and sped off toward Kord'Ala. Before the eastern sky flushed pink with the sun's dawning, she slid from Ashur's back, sent the unicorn away, and squatted in the dusty road to wait. At sunrise the gates of the city opened wide. She rose, brushed her skirts and pulled her long hair close about her face, then started inside. A pair of guards quietly watched her approach. She said nothing but gave each a hard, haughty look, making sure they saw the crescent charcoal marking she wore.

"Fortune, sir?" she said to one.

He spat and took a step away.

"You?" she asked the other.

He shook his head.

She looked inquiringly at each once more, then laughed and left them, swirling her skirts.

Oona trudged through the door, bent and weary. On her arm she carried a basket filled with jars and bits of dried herbs. A bit of cloth tied around her head kept the hair from falling in her eyes. She closed the door softly. Her feet scraped the old wood as she shuffled across the floor and set her basket in a corner. She sighed audibly and straightened, massaging a hip with one hand.

"Oona?"

The old woman jumped at the sound of her name and turned. Her wide eyes shone in the darkness. "Samidar?"

Frost lifted the earthen jar with which she'd hidden the small candlelight and leaned back in her seat at the table. "I got back hours ago. Where've you been?"

Oona took a seat opposite her and leaned on elbows. Then her head sank slowly into her hands. After a long moment she looked up again. "The boy in the village, remember?"

Frost nodded.

"He's worse, burning with root-fever." Exasperation filled her voice. Frost reached out and stroked her old friend's hair in sympathy. Oona sat up. "I've done everything I can think of!" she cried. "Nothing works."

"The father still blames you?"

Oona got up and paced the floor. "He's in a high rage for sure." Suddenly Oona noticed the cards that were spread across the table. She sat down again and drew a breath. "How did you fare in Kord'Ala?"

Frost couldn't hold back a frown. "I'm a wanted fugitive, but we knew that much," she answered. "Thogrin's offered my weight in silver to the man who finds me. Other than that . . ." She shrugged and got up, went to a small bundle that rested on the trunk where Oona kept her clothes. "I did turn a few cards, enough for coins to buy that new candle and a new paring knife and shawl for you." She held up the thin wrap.

Oona's face lighted. She pushed back her stool and rose excitedly. "Oh, child!" she exclaimed, grasping the shawl in her old fingers, carrying it toward the light to examine the delicate embroidery. "No one's bought me anything in years! It's beautiful!" She turned suddenly and threw her arms around her younger guest.

Frost felt awkward as the old woman hugged her. She'd never been much for letting others touch her, and she could feel scarlet heat rising in her cheeks. The hug was nearly a wrestling grip; her arms were pinned. Opponents had tried to grip her like that to throw her down or squeeze the breath from her. She inhaled deeply, feeling the old woman's breasts against her own. Well, for friendship's sake, she could endure.

Finally, Oona released her. "Did you say a knife? I have a good knife already, over in my basket."

Frost moved to the trunk again and leaned on it. The bundle minus the shawl lay close at hand. "Well, actually I needed it for something; I'm done with it now, and it's yours."

Oona's eyes narrowed. "Was there trouble?"

She picked up the bundle and began slowly unwrapping. The knife was hidden under the first layer. She set it on the trunk. "No, not trouble." She continued unwrapping. "Do you keep zimort in any of those jars, and any sisamy?"

Oona's face screwed up suspiciously. In the candle's dim light, her eyes appeared to darken and shrink far back into her head. "There's zimort, but no sisamy," she answered.

"Hellebore can substitute, you must have that?"

The old woman nodded slowly.

Frost finished her unwrapping but held the cloth so that

whatever was within remained concealed. "I have no answers, Oona." She spoke softly, slowly, but with intensity, locking the aged healer's gaze with her own. "I found none in Kord'Ala and none in the cards." She indicated the display on the table. "They don't work for me; you know my curse. Aki is still missing. If I'm going to find her, I've got to get back into Mirashai." She hesitated, knowing the gravity of what she must ask. "You're the only one who can help me do that, Oona."

She brushed away the cloth and held up her prize.

Oona gasped and stumbled back. "You don't realize what you're asking." She stared, pale even in the candlelight. Then fear vanished, replaced with dark suspicion. Oona drew up to her full height, eyes glittering, angry, accusing. "How did you get that?"

Frost kept her voice calm. "They hanged him at dusk outside the city gate."

"Who's they?" Oona demanded.

"The garrison, some soldiers at Kord'Ala." She was getting angry despite herself. She didn't like Oona's tone. Her voice dropped a note. There was an edge to it when she said, "I didn't murder him."

Oona sighed. She came closer and peered at the severed hand her guest held up. "No, he'd have to be hanged."

Frost was still petulant. "I had to go back and buy the knife. I didn't take one."

Oona seemed not to hear as she studied the member. She showed no desire to touch it, though. "It's the left one, good." She looked up suddenly, and her eyes gleamed. "He'd have to be guilty, though, or it wouldn't work. Was he guilty?"

She chewed her lip. "We won't know until we try it."

"That could put you in a bad spot."

Frost said nothing. She laid the hand on the table and backed away from it. Grisly work, cutting off a man's hand with only a knife. Hours dead, there was still plenty of blood in that limb. She'd gotten it all over the skirts Oona had loaned her. That's why she'd thought to buy the shawl, to make up for it. She'd used the bloodiest skirt as the wrapping to carry it in.

"I could read the cards for you," Oona said suddenly. "Maybe I can get answers to your questions."

She looked at Oona, knowing the reasons behind that offer. Oona was a healer. What she was asking of the old woman went far beyond that, though, deep into the realms of sorcery. A Hand of Glory was not an easy thing to make. She could direct, but Oona would have to do the actual work. Frost dared not touch it until after it was completed or the magic would be nullified. It might be already, since it was she who had done the cutting.

"Read," she said, then.

Oona restacked the cards on the table, shuffled them, and dealt. When they were all laid out, she frowned, reshuffled, and spread them again. Frost pulled up a stool and watched, a dull hope throbbing in her chest. She did not want to make a Hand if there was another way.

"How did you learn descroiyo?" she whispered.

The old woman shrugged, gathered the cards, and re-shuffled again. "How does one learn anything?" she answered cryptically. She touched the cards to her breast this time, then to her lips. She breathed on them. Then, one by one, she turned them up.

First card, the half skull crowned with gold; then, a rose with bloodied thorns.

"I can see!" Frost muttered tersely; she bent closer to see the casting. "I can see! Korkyra's monarch and that's the rose garden at the palace! But is it Aki or Thogrin, and is that Aki's blood?"

Oona said nothing but turned another card: the hermit, dark-robed and alone on a mountain.

"The dark-robed figure by the throne," Frost cried excitedly, then scratched her chin. "Or maybe the intruder."

Oona looked up from the cards. Her hand paused with the next one drawn, but not turned. "Samidar, child . . ."

Frost smiled weakly and leaned away from the table. Oona waited a needless moment for emphasis, then returned her smile and turned the next cards.

A sword; a magic staff of power; the wheel of fortune; the three stars; the ring of fire. Oona grunted. The lovers; the demon. Oona stopped and stared. "They don't fit," she said at last. She tapped the last card exposed. "This doesn't fit at all, the position is all wrong."

She swept the cards together and dealt them out again. Nine different ones, this time. Oona slammed her palm on the unfeeling wood and tried again.

"No," she said at last, her voice heavy with resignation. "A pattern starts to form, but then it breaks down."

"Maybe because I've handled the cards?" Frost offered nervously.

Oona shook her head. "You can handle magical things. Ashur and Demonfang, for instance. You just can't make magic." Her old eyes drew slowly to the hand still lying on a corner of the table. The flickering candlelight cast shadows of the upcurled fingers across the walls and ceiling. As the flame danced, the shadows seemed to beckon to them.

"I know *about* this thing you want"—she spoke slowly, her voice strangely muted—"but not how to make it."

"I'll guide you," Frost answered with a shiver. "I've lost my witch-powers, but not my memory."

Chapter Four

Frost leaned forward in the stirrups and rubbed her backside. She'd made good time, arriving in the middle of the night, though she couldn't tell it by the sky. The stars were hidden behind a dense curtain of gray clouds. Not even the moon peeked through. She lifted her hand, turned the palm in several directions. No wind, either.

Down below Mirashai lay, barely visible, seeming unchanged in the month she'd been gone. She'd ridden half the night, skirting Shadamas and all other towns to get here at this particular hour. Her work must be done between midnight and dawn. Certainly it was late enough. Her hand wandered to the cloth pouch that hung from her weapon belt. The outline of the contents showed through the thin material.

With a gasp, she jerked her hand away.

"No," she whispered firmly, getting a mental grip on her reaction. "You know what it is; you helped make it; it can't hurt you." But she had grown unused to arcane ways and the strains they sometimes demanded. Twice, Oona had nearly fainted at the instructions the younger woman had given her. From the beginning her old face had remained a pale, wrinkled mask of horror. Frost herself had had trouble keeping food down and had nearly quit the making. But once begun it could not be left unfinished.

She forced herself to touch the pouch again, to feel the

outline of the thing inside. Soon she would have to hold it in her own hand. Best get used to it now.

When she was rested, she urged Ashur down the low ridge and out onto the broad plain stretched all around the sleeping city. Her gaze combed the darkness, alert for any movement. Nothing, just the quiet.

She looked up at the sky again. At least there was no moon to give her away to watching eyes. The clouds hid everything, so low and oppressive.

Outside the city's wall stretched a collection of the dirtiest inns and taverns Frost had ever seen, places that prostitutes and criminals of all nationalities called home; where ancient sailors too old to ride the waves anymore littered the streets with their drunken bodies; where wealthy men with enemies in high places bought quick solutions to their problems. Aki had tried to rid Mirashai of this cess-pool and failed. So had her father and his father.

She touched the pouch at her side, then reconsidered. *Not yet*, she decided. *It must last*.

She passed the first tavern. The hand that touched the pouch now gripped her sword. She searched the windows and doorways as she rode by. No light, no noise, no faces peered out. She drew a breath and rode on. Two buildings stood clustered together. She watched them carefully, alert, ready.

No one stirred. It was late, yes, but would everyone be sleeping? She nudged Ashur on, releasing her sword long enough to wipe the sweat from her palm.

She might have sneaked in more quietly on foot, but she was going to need the unicorn's height.

The buildings were closer now, mostly dark. Here and there, a thin light flickered through cracked wooden shutters. She passed by as silently as possible.

A blast of laughter echoed from a tavern up ahead. She saw the door to the establishment push open. Quickly she turned her mount down a narrow alley and out of sight. She rode on through to the next street.

Someone stumbled toward her. She stopped. He stopped, too, and stared. A whimsical expression twisted his face.

He lurched against a wall suddenly, sank to the ground, and closed his eyes.

She hesitated. Should she kill him and shut his mouth, too? He might awaken and talk, later. She rode closer, drawing the sword from its sheath. She leaned down and nudged the man with the point. He didn't stir. She nudged him again, gasped, and drew back to thrust, but he merely fell over on his side and started to snore.

She put her sword away and moved on.

The next street was lighted with a reddish glow. Frost looked up and down. Candles encased in lanterns of scarlet cloth and paper hung from every door. She heard strange, muffled sounds from the windows above her and blushed. *The nighttime is theirs*, she thought. *No one sleeps on this street*. She turned to seek another way.

At last she came to the great gate in the city's western wall. It was shut, as she knew it would be, and barred on the inside with a mighty beam. But above the gate four posts stuck out from the masonry. She had remembered those, too.

If she stood on Ashur's back and jumped, she could just reach those posts. But first she reached into her saddlebag and took out a length of rope. A slender log was tied to one end. She slid the coil over her shoulders. It made a clumsy burden, but she would manage.

She stood carefully on the saddle. It wouldn't require much of a jump. Her fingers were only inches from the post she'd chosen. She pushed off and grabbed.

The weighted end of the rope began to slide. The fibers stung her bare neck as the rope rushed downward, tightening the coils around her. She grabbed for it, clinging to the post with one hand. That lasted all of two heartbeats before her grip gave way on the rough wood.

Ashur sidestepped away. She landed hard, tangled in the rope, the log pressing painfully on her spine.

"Gods damn!" she muttered, and kicked the stupid length of wood before she picked it up again. She could have hooked a grappling iron in her belt if she'd had one, but it was cursed hard to stick a log in your pants! Instead of slinging it over her shoulder again and risking a repeated incident, she placed the log under her arm against her side and hastily wound the rope around herself, binding it in place. Uncomfortable, but she only had to tolerate it a few minutes.

"Get over here!" she said to Ashur, who stood by watching. The unicorn meekly obeyed. "I think you're laughing at me! I ought to smack your nose!"

She climbed the saddle again, and this time gained the post without difficulty. It was wide enough to stand on if she was careful. She undid her rope. The top of the wall was about fifteen feet higher. She prayed she could reach it. She'd taken Oona's only rope, a short one, not daring to purchase another in Shadamas. Enough time had passed for the smallest towns to know she was fugitive.

She checked the knots to make sure the log was secure. It was stout enough to hold her weight if she could snag the parapets overhead. With a three- or four-pronged grapple, it would have been easy. With a log, she worried.

She listened. No sound of any sentry above. She knew they patrolled the wall but had no idea of their schedule. Her first toss missed. The log was heavier than she thought. She threw again.

Four attempts later, the log caught but made one hell of a clatter. She froze, expecting shouts and the rattle of weapons, soldiers bearing lances to appear over the wall, more soldiers to come charging through the gate below.

Nothing happened.

She'd stormed cities before amid the crash and clang of steel and the shouts of warriors and Gath's own chaos raging all around. Doing it silently was something quite different, and she cursed every little sound, every creak of the rope, every scrape of her boots on stone as she climbed. At last she gained the top, pulled herself over, and dropped in a deep crouch onto a broad walkway.

She touched the pouch on her belt to make sure she hadn't lost it.

Far down the walkway she spied a pair of torches. Sentries about their rounds, she guessed. She wasted no time but gathered up the log and the rope, coiled it tightly, and stashed it behind a rain barrel. In the darkness, she was sure no one would find it. The torches drew nearer. She could hear voices but distinguish none of the words. She moved quickly, found the stone stair that took her to street level, and dived for the nearest shadow.

She cowered there for long minutes, unmoving, listening. Her heart pounded in her chest. Her breath came quick and shallow.

Now, it was time.

She reached into the pouch and extracted the hand. The skin of it was dry and brittle to touch except for the fingers, which were slick with a fine oil. It exuded an awful odor of decaying meat and strange herbs. Even in the darkness, the bones and bloated veins showed. She shivered again, recalling the thing's making.

Her hand dipped into the pouch again, and she brought out a small vial of thin black powder. Before opening it, she rubbed her hands on her trousers, wiping away any traces of the oil that coated the dead fingers which might have spread to hers. Then she unstoppered it and sprinkled a small quantity on the tip of each digit.

A tiny flame ignited where powder and oil made contact, five fingers and five flames. Frost felt a tingle spread from the hand through her hand along her arm and all through her body to join with a different tingle which crept up her spine. The shadow where she crouched vanished. It no longer mattered.

She rose and stepped into the open, holding high her Hand of Glory.

The voices on the parapet continued for a moment, then ceased.

She bit her lip and stared at the five-fingered candle. The man was guilty, then. Of what? she wondered. Debt? Theft? Murder? She shifted the Hand of Glory to her right hand, laid her left on her sword's hilt. She wouldn't need the sword, though; it was just for reassurance.

She started down the street, walking slowly, using the Hand to light her way. Her heart thumped with every step, the blood pulsed in her veins. The flames danced and flickered, casting her shadow behind her, creating shadows before.

A window opened, a head poked out sleepily and stared at her. Her step faltered, then she passed on, watching the man over her shoulder. He didn't move at all, just stared, unseeing.

He would stare that way until the sun wakened him at dawn, as would anyone who gazed on the Hand's light. But that was only part of its power. Any who were already asleep would remain so, unable to waken for any reason until the first light of day. Some would awaken in mess and damp beds.

Only Frost and Oona, the Hand's makers, were immune, and the power of the Hand extended throughout the city. She set a straight course for the palace.

Another wall surrounded the palace, separating it from the rest of the city. It spanned half as high as the outer wall, but no sentry walked its narrow top. Only a north and south gate allowed entrance. The northern was reserved for ceremonials, such as visits by outland royalty or state ambassadors, or for the ritual entrances of the elite palace guard. It was an iron drop-gate and heavily patrolled. She chose the southern.

No drop-gate this, but two great oaken doors. She had no rope to scale this wall. Perhaps she would not need one. Two sentries stood constant guard inside this gate, she knew. There was a small, shuttered portal in one gate. She went to it and knocked softly.

"Who's there?"

The portal cracked slightly. She leaped back, holding the Hand well out of sight.

"Let me in!" she said, putting as much urgency as she could manage into her voice.

"On what business?"

She could not see the guard's face; the portal showed no sign of opening farther. What business could she have that would make him open the gate at so late an hour?

"The woman," she whispered, "the one who killed the queen? I have information!"

"Come back in the morning!" The portal shut.

She pounded on it until it opened again. Again she leaped out of sight, holding the Hand's light where it couldn't be seen. "I have to talk to Commander Sur'tian tonight! Let me in!"

"Let me see you," the guard said.

What to do now? The guard might recognize her even in the darkness. And if she got close, the Hand's power would see to it he never opened the gate.

"No!" she croaked. "Don't! Get away!" She slammed her weight against the massive doors, whipped out her sword, and brandished it before the portal. "I'm unarmed!" she screamed at her make-believe attacker. She swung the sword again, taking a chip from the old wood. "Aggghh! You've killed me! Help!"

Then silence. She waited, hidden. Moments passed and the gate did not open. Had her little drama failed to convince? The gate creaked open an inch, then more. A helmeted head poked out.

"Over here," she said.

The sentry turned to gaze on the Hand of Glory.

She heard a noise, then a voice. The other sentry, she remembered. There were two. She gave the first a push; he toppled over in a heap.

"Help him!" she called. "He's hurt!"

The second guard popped through the gate, nearly tripping on his comrade's body. Sword drawn, he'd also fetched a shield. It did him no good. He peered over its edge into the preternatural light and fell instantly asleep. She gave the shield a little shove and the two sprawled side by side.

Within the palace grounds, she made her way around to Aki's rose garden, taking no effort to conceal herself or move quietly. She wanted to be seen. More important, she wanted the Hand to be seen.

There were guards on duty in many parts of the grounds after dark. They were all statues by the time she got to their individual positions, for the Hand's light could be seen long before anyone got close enough to recognize her.

There was a door that led into the palace's lower levels. She had used it often with Aki when the little queen wanted to spend time among her flowers. It was not often used by anyone else, and it was away from the palace mainstream. Once inside, she needed to be more selective about who fell under the Hand's spell. Probably it was too late. If Tras Sur'tian were already asleep, nothing would wake him until morning. But if he were not, she wanted to see him. As for Thogrin Sin'tell, it would be nice if he were still awake. It would save her the trouble of carting his body out of the city, but she had no hope of that.

She found the door and stepped inside. The Hand lit the way for her like any common torch. She moved swiftly and quietly, maneuvering the narrow corridors with the precision of experience. When they joined to the main corridor, she hesitated. She was near the tower. There should be a guard at the foot of the stone steps.

She moved into the hall and faced the tower entrance. Yes, there he was. He regarded her down the long passage, proud in his polished armor, stiff of bearing, unblinking of eye.

"Good night," she whispered, and turned away.

She made it to the reception hall without encountering a soul. There were no sentries there this time of night, as no business was conducted at this hour. *Except my business,* she thought, and pushed back the doors.

The reception hall was ominous in the darkness. Even the light from the Hand seemed to cast only a tiny pool of amber, which was quickly swallowed by the chamber's vastness. She moved among the carven images of legend, suddenly feeling small and insignificant. Despite herself, she walked with a lighter tread, drew a softer breath.

One by one, she climbed the ivory stairs to the throne. The emeralds encrusted in the royal seat glittered and gleamed as she approached, catching and diffracting the Hand's light a thousand times. She moved past the throne to the tapestry that hung on the wall behind. Careful to keep the flames away from the ancient draperies, she pushed them aside and exposed the bare stone.

There it was, the chipped one. Aki had shown it to her only days after choosing her for champion and guardian. Frost laid her palm against it and pressed.

A section of the wall slid away. She stepped into the hidden tunnel, releasing the tapestries, and tripped the reversing mechanism which closed the secret door.

The tunnels were as old as the palace itself and smelled it. They led to all major parts of the palace, including the kitchens and the stables. More important, they led to all the private chambers, including the spacious royal suite, which all the rulers before Aki had occupied for hundreds of years. After becoming queen, Aki had kept her own private quarters in the tower rather than sleep in the same bed where Aleppan spies had murdered her father.

Frost gambled Thogrin Sin'tell would have no such qualms about the most luxurious rooms in Mirashai, indeed in all Korkyra.

She knew the way and moved surely, silently along, holding the Hand out for light and her sword to cleave the cobwebs strewn across her path. Inside the tunnels, the doors that were hidden on one side were easily identified. She paused at a couple of them and listened. Hearing nothing, she moved on.

She kept track of their number. When she came to the fourteenth she stopped.

She almost smiled at how easy it had been to get here. Yet the smile faded before it fully formed. Making the Hand had not been easy. It had exacted a great toll on her and a greater toll on Oona, who was no witch and had never dabbled in anything more dangerous than her own healing art. She would remember forever the look in the old woman's eyes when the making was over.

But the Hand had done its work. Now she had only to get Thogrin's body out of the city and to a private place where she could question him. He'd wake in chains, and

she'd make him talk if she had to strip every scrap of flesh
from his living body.

A small spy-hole was set conveniently in the door. She
placed her eye to it. The hole itself offered a very limited
field of vision, but a dressing mirror of highly polished
metal was cleverly mounted on the wall directly opposite
the hole, providing a view of the suite's central chamber.

She nearly gave a shout. Thogrin Sin'tell was awake!
Candles and lamps burned brightly in the room. Thogrin
himself sat at a great desk with documents piled high all
around him. He set his seal to a paper, picked up another,
and settled back to read.

If she was careful, she wouldn't have to bear the burden
of his fat carcass.

She set the Hand of Glory carefully on the floor. The
fingers were half-burned through. She might not be able to
use it escaping the city. As the flesh was consumed, the
power of the Hand began to wane. For now, though, it
was still quite potent, and Thogrin must not be allowed to
look on it. She turned away from it, satisfied there was
nothing around that the flames might ignite.

Her sword slid silently from the sheath. She found the
mechanism that opened the door, pressed it. Soundless
gears moved the stone. She sprang through and over the
carpeted floor. Quick as she moved, a draft of musty air
from the tunnels moved quicker. Thogrin sniffed and turned
to find the point of her sword hovering at his throat.

His eyes went wide and bright with fear, but the warning finger she pressed to her lips and the hard look she
gave him were enough to stifle any outcry. Half out of his
seat, he sat back and trembled.

The sword still at his throat, Frost reached past him for
a document and the quill pen. The tip was wet with ink,
and she wrote, *You have guards—send them away,* at the
top of the paper. She gestured for him to move to the door
that opened into the main corridor.

He got up slowly, his eyes never leaving hers. His
velvet-slippered feet made no sound on the thick carpets,
and she moved as quietly. As he reached for the iron ring

that opened the door, the blade jabbed him sharply in the ribs, not hard enough to wound. He understood her meaning, though. She flattened against the wall as he opened the door.

The guards turned. She heard the clink of their armor and weaponry.

"No, don't come in," Thogrin said. "You may retire for the evening. Guards are unnecessary at this hour in such a secure city. Find some wine, share a woman, enjoy yourselves."

Frost held her breath. When the sentries assented she allowed a tiny smile. Then she saw the way Thogrin rolled his eyes and the subtle gesture he made with his hand.

A snarl parted her lips, and she kicked Thogrin in the stomach and shouldered his folding bulk roughly away from the entrance. She jerked the door wide and her sword licked out twice. Two bodies fell, spilling blood on the floor-stones. She stepped over them to check the corridor. Only these two, no other witnesses.

She dragged them into the royal chambers and shut the door again. Thogrin groaned on the carpet and clutched his belly. She watched him, disgusted, as he struggled to rise, then kicked him in the face, shattering teeth.

He looked up at her, blood and tears streaming on his chin. Her incarnadined blade hovered near his left eye. "They didn't have to die!" she hissed. "You sold their lives for nothing!"

"S-soldiers . . ." he stuttered, spraying blood and bits of teeth as he spoke. "Duty to their k-king!"

"Damn their duty and damn you!" She seized a handful of his dark hair and wiped her weapon clean in it. Fear kept him from crying out against the pain. When the edge was bright again, she stood back and looked at the men she'd killed. She knew them both, good men who'd bought her drinks at the taverns when she'd been a common mercenary. The carpet drank up their life-fluids.

She turned back to Thogrin and indicated the chair at the desk. "Get up," she ordered. When he did not move fast enough she kicked him again—cracking ribs, she was

certain. His face contorted, the breath rasped from him.
"Move," she said.

With an effort he rose and struggled to the chair at the
desk. He eased very gingerly into it. After a moment, the
pain seemed to leave his features. A vague mockery of a
grin twisted his torn lips. "Pretty little wench," he managed. "You'll die very slowly."

She raised an eyebrow. "You're hardly in a position to
threaten."

His chest swelled. He wheezed as he drew a deep
breath. "I am High King of Korkyra."

"You're a man at the wrong end of a sword."

He thought about that. "I submit to your higher reason," he said at last. "How much do you want?"

Her hand twitched. How easy it would be to lean on her
sword and end this insulting pig's life now. She sucked her
lower lip. That would not get her what she wanted. "I
want Aki," she answered. "Where is she?"

Thogrin's grin spread into a full smile. "You killed her,
I have witnesses to prove it." He regarded her in a slow,
irritating manner, his gaze roaming up her blade, up her
arm to her face, down her body. "We thought you'd
escaped over the border or taken ship somewhere when we
couldn't find you to hang you."

She sat on the edge of the desk. The point of her sword
drew a thin crimson line upon his collarbone. To his
credit, he did not flinch this time. "No games, Thogrin
Sin'tell." She kept her voice calm, cold. "Look in my
eyes." He boldly complied. "I know you have Aki."

He shook his head. "It's all a game," he answered, "a
game called Power. Aki had it, and I wanted it. Korkyra
needs a man on the throne, not a child."

Her eyes narrowed. "Where is she?"

Thogrin lost his smile. "Look for her in hell."

His eyes taunted her, mocking, and the grin came back.
She spat in his face, and his head jerked away as if he'd
been hit again. He wiped the spittle with the back of his
hand. His look was purest hatred.

"You didn't kill her," Frost said. "You haven't the guts. Your kind never has the guts."

Thogrin Sin'tell shrugged. "Others have."

She considered that, recalling suddenly the man in the black robes. "It was he who put you on the throne," she said. "Wasn't it?"

He shrugged again.

"Who is he?"

Thogrin stared at his feet. "I don't think I'll tell you."

The flat of her blade cracked on his cheek. The impact reopened the cuts on his lips, which had just begun to clot. Blood poured down, spattering his gown. He dabbed it with a sleeve. "Bitch!" he mumbled. He tried to straighten in his chair, to draw himself up. A tongue licked out and collected the blood that threatened to run down. "I'll never tell you, no matter what you do!"

"You'll tell," she swore, "and eagerly. Get up." She'd make him tell, all right, and she knew just how to do it. But not here. If Thogrin was awake, it was possible others were, too. Someone might notice the guards away from their posts and come to investigate. She went to one of the bodies and cut a strip from a bloodied tunic.

"Turn around," she ordered when Thogrin was on his feet. He obeyed and she tied the cloth over his eyes.

"What good is this?" he asked. "I know every part of this castle. I've lusted for it long enough."

"I've no doubt of that part," she answered, taking his arm, "but you didn't know about the tunnels." And there was another reason for the blindfold. She didn't want him falling under the spell of the Hand when she was this close to the answer. She led him to the opening in the wall and into the tunnel, closing the secret door after her. The five-fingered candle still glowed brightly. She seized it and gave Thogrin Sin'tell a push.

"I can't see!" he protested.

"Feel with your hands," she said. "I'll tell you when to turn." The point of her sword prodded his ribs.

"Please!" He was almost whimpering. "Let me see! I don't like the dark!"

She nearly laughed at that. Some king, who feared the darkness like a child. "Tell me what you've done with Aki and the blindfold comes off." That would suit her. Once she had an answer, she'd whip off his blind, let him look on the Hand, and leave him to waken in the tunnels where even in daytime no light penetrated. He deserved nothing better.

But he reached out with his hands to feel the wall. "I'll tell you nothing," he said. "Do what you will."

"Then move, and quietly, too, or they'll find tunnel rats gnawing your flesh in the morning." *If anyone could find you in these tunnels at all*, she silently added. "To your left."

They made their way back along the tunnels to the reception hall. When she had opened the door, she took his arm again and led him to the throne. He sat slowly, in obvious pain, and tried to muster his dignity. On either side of the dais an iron brazier stood empty of flame. She moved to each and touched the lighted Hand to the oil within them. Bright as they burned, she could still not see the far end of the hall. There was plenty of light around the throne, though. The emeralds glittered with reflected fire. She placed the Hand on the floor safely behind the throne where Thogrin would not see its light, then pulled the cloth from his eyes.

He looked at her, his gaze unwavering, waiting.

But she ignored him for a moment, remembering instead something else, something that might help Oona. The emeralds sparkled, thousands of them encrusting Korkyra's royal seat. Gemstones were objects of power; every dabbler in the arts knew that. And emeralds, she knew, were especially potent, their color associated with the growth principle and the very life-essence of the earth from which they came. She considered, the germ of an idea growing. Kings and queens, rulers by divine right, were also said to have some healing ability. Then *royal* emeralds should be talismans indeed.

Talismans enough, perhaps, to help Oona cure a young boy's root-fever, if she showed the old woman how to use them. She dug a couple of the green stones free and dropped them in her pouch.

"Thief," Thogrin accused disgustedly.

"With these I may save a life even as I take one," she answered.

He folded his arms. Seated on his throne with the warm glow of the braziers surrounding him, he seemed to find his courage. "Mine, I assume?" His voice was light, mocking.

"Unless you tell me about Aki, your accomplices, everything I want to know."

He said nothing, just looked askance, resolute.

"I've no more time to play, Thogrin Sin'tell."

She sheathed her sword. A look of relief flickered over her captive's face until he saw her reach for the dagger on her hip. She hesitated, fixed him with her gaze, then yanked the smaller blade free.

A screaming filled the reception hall, thousands of voices joined in torment and despair. The sound filled her ears, swelled and echoed in the immense chamber. No matter how many times she heard it, the unearthly din shook her, beat at her senses.

The room spun dizzyingly. Demonfang trembled in her hand. Its shining blade shimmered in the braziers' light.

Thogrin stared wide-eyed in sudden terror, all color gone from his face as he cringed into a corner of his throne. His own screams added to the soul-twisting tumult even as he clapped hands over his ears to shut out the sounds.

Frost felt a shivering creep up her arm. She fought the sensation, knowing its meaning, knowing there could be no turning back. "Listen to the voices of hell, Thogrin," she shouted, straining to be heard, faces so close she could smell the fear on his breath, "and count yours among them unless you answer my questions!"

"No!" he cried, unable to tear his gaze from the arcane weapon she held.

The wailing grew louder. The tingle in her arm grew

more insistent. She had little time left. "Where's Aki?" she demanded. "Tell me, or embrace my blade!"

Demonfang shivered like a living thing in her hand. The tingle turned to fire and spread raging up her arm, her veins, into her blood.

"My crown!" Thogrin shrieked.

Something flickered in the corner of her eye, a flame. No, many torches, she realized, racing into the hall. The night watch had heard pandemonium. They raced to the dais.

There was no more time for answers. "Die, Thogrin Sin'tell!" She raised Demonfang to strike. "You cursed dog!"

"Onokratos has her!" He threw up his hands to stop the dagger's descent. He babbled, spittle drooling on his chin. "She may live yet! I don't know! Find Onokratos in Kephalenia, but spare me!"

From the moment she drew Demonfang from its silver sheath she knew she could not spare him. The dagger's commanding power coursed irresistibly through her. Demonfang rose, plunged, found his heart's blood.

In that instant all screaming ceased. A pall of silence closed over the chamber. She drew a breath, fingers still closed around the hilt. It was not finished yet.

Thogrin gagged on his last breath. His chest heaved, then collapsed. A moment's pause, then bluing lips parted, and the screams began again, all the souls in hell wailing with one dead man's mouth.

It lasted but a few heartbeats, then she tugged the dagger from his body. Thogrin's blood spurted on her fist, soaked his garments, stained the royal emeralds as it trickled on the throne.

It must taste blood—either your enemy's or your own. Once drawn, that was the power and the curse of Demonfang.

Did even Thogrin Sin'tell deserve such an end?

A rush of bootsteps and the clangor of steel snapped her alert. There was no more hell-noise to hold confused and faint-hearted soldiers back now. They had witnessed their king's murder. In shame and anger they surged forward to avenge him.

She sheathed the dagger before its power began to swell again, as it would in moments if left free of its scabbard. The soldiers reached the first of the ivory stairs, howling for her blood. Quickly she reached behind the throne for the Hand of Glory.

They froze in midrush, entranced by the five-fingered light. A spear clattered on the floor, then a sword. A shield fell, rolled on its rim in ever-smaller spirals until it was suddenly still. She looked down on them, a chill creeping along her spine. They stood, asleep on their feet, like statues, like the great pillars that supported the hall.

She descended half the stairs, using the Hand as a torch. She searched their faces one by one. Tras Sur'tian at the forefront of his men gripped his sword, eyes closed in peaceful repose. She looked at him and the Hand, wishing she had not used magic against him. She had forsaken that path years ago, unwillingly at first, later gladly. Now she seemed set on that path again.

"Join me, Tras," she whispered in his ear, unsure if he could hear. "Aki lives."

But was it true? Thogrin only told her a man named Onokratos had Aki. Was Onokratos that black-robe she had seen before with Thogrin the day after Aki's disappearance? Then he was surely a sorcerer, maybe a wizard. But what would a wizard want with a child? One answer dominated her thoughts, made her shiver with dread. She glanced back at Thogrin's sprawling form as it slipped from the throne to the floor of the dais.

Be patient, she promised his spirit. *If your Onokratos has harmed her, you'll soon have company.*

She set the Hand upright on its wrist on the top stair, wanting nothing more to do with the abomination. It would burn out soon, then everyone would waken at dawn. She could make her way out of the city without it.

Chapter Five

The next day's noon sun hung swollen in a perfect sky. Frost sat cross-legged by a rippling stream, leaned, and dipped her hand in the cool water, wiped it across her sweaty brow and neck. A few drops trickled down inside her tunic; they felt good, refreshing.

She squinted, peering out over the plain below to check the progress of the approaching rider.

From her vantage point on the hill she could see far to the west from where she'd come. Not that the hill was so high. An amused smile creased her lips. Mountains, the locals called these hills of the Kithri region. Overgrown anthills, maybe, big mounds of dirt with a smattering of grass, here and there a tree that pushed up from the rocky soil. But mountains? The Creel chain in Rholaroth, those were mountains. But not the Kithri.

The rider was closer now, hurrying at a gallop.

She'd made it easy enough, not bothering to hide her trail. He'd been following her since shortly after dawn, and she'd urged Ashur along just fast enough to beat him into the hills. It would be easy enough to lose a foe in the Kithri if she needed.

The unicorn munched noisily on a scraggly stand of wildflowers. "Glutton," she accused, pouting. "I've had no breakfast, either." He ignored her and chewed another mouthful.

She stretched out on the bank, leaned over the water, cupped her hands, and drank deeply. The water rushed down the hill, gurgling as loudly as her empty stomach. Another long drink would quiet her insistent gut. She wiped her lips and sat up.

The rider reached the foot of the hill. He saw her, hesitated, then started up. She nodded slowly, waited while his mount climbed the gentle slope. She didn't bother to rise but moved the scabbard of her sword so it rested in her lap.

He drew to a halt before her.

"Hello, Tras," she said evenly. "Fine day for an outing, is it not?"

The sun glinted on the metal rings sewn to his armor, on his shield, the hilt of his sword. The scarlet cloak he wore fluttered in a light breeze. His white beard fairly sparkled beneath the rim of his bronze helm.

His sword hissed out. "I arrest you for the crime of high regicide. Get up."

She remained seated. "Take off that helmet, Tras." She kept her voice calm. "In this heat your brains must be baking. Climb down awhile. The water's very good." She dipped her hand in the stream, raised it, spilling shining droplets between her fingers. "Its source is a spring at the summit."

He shifted nervously in the saddle. "Is it also bewitched? That's what you are, isn't it? A witch? That's how you killed Thogrin."

"That was sorcery," she corrected, "not witchcraft."

He removed his helm, cradled it in his shield arm. By the intensity of his gaze she knew his anger was genuine. But something else lurked there: fear. He was afraid of her.

"Sorcery, witchcraft! What's the difference!"

She dried her hand on her trousers. "A great difference," she replied. "A witch's power comes from within." She tapped her chest. "She doesn't need spells or talismans or potions. Those are the tools of the sorcerer. He finds power in objects or words and taps that power to work his magic. Now a wizard," she continued, "is something else. He chums up to a god or a demon, and when he needs a favor he just asks."

Tras Sur'tian raged. "Damnation! Who cares? You've killed my king, possibly my queen before him, and you've got to pay!" He leveled his sword as if he meant to run her through.

She got slowly to her feet, taking her scabbard in her right hand. "Thogrin Sin'tell was at least partly responsible for Aki's disappearance. He probably planned it."

"Liar!" he accused. "You killed Aki with your witchcraft or sorcery or whatever, and then you came back for Thogrin! I saw that *thing*, that hand with the burning fingers! And I heard those screams, like the nine hells had opened to suck my liege lord down! You've tried to destroy the very soul of Korkyra by striking at its monarchs!"

"You're an utter ass if you believe that!" Her own temper suddenly burst free. "Your precious Thogrin—and I spit on his name—needed Aki out of the way so he could seize the throne for himself! He confessed it before I stilled his wretched, evil heart! And there was an accomplice. I know his name and where to look for him. If you think you can stop me"—she fixed him with a cold stare—"don't. Or before this hour's done one of us will be shaking hands with Gath!"

"You dare speak the chaos god's name!" he shot back. "You've brought more chaos than any of your night-dwelling heathen deities! Stop you?" he thundered. "Woman, I mean to kill you if you don't surrender that sticker and return with me to Mirashai!"

Her blade whistled from the sheath. "Damn you, Tras Sur'tian!" she shouted, feeling the heat rise in her cheeks. "I called you friend!"

He brandished his own weapon. "You've killed my king!"

"Your king?" Her voice went shrill. "What of your queen? What of Aki? Did you hear nothing I said? She may yet live!"

His voice dropped a note. "Where?" With all the scorn
he could muster, he added, "Witch!"

"In Kephalenia," she answered, "there's a man named
Onokratos, Thogrin Sin'tell's ally."

"How do you know this?"

She shook her head angrily. "I told you, Thogrin confessed it before he died. Is it so hard to believe a Korkyran
noble could be as greedy and scheming as any other man?
To be king Thogrin would have killed." She paused,
thoughtful. "He may have."

Tras Sur'tian's features seemed suddenly to soften. His
shoulders sagged; the point of his sword wavered. "You
pose quite a problem," he said at last. "Do I believe you
and go off chasing a criminal who may not exist except in
your lies? Or do I settle for the murderess who committed
her crime before my very eyes?"

"Trust your heart," she advised guardedly.

He scoffed, but the anger was gone from his words.
"But the heart lies; you've told me so yourself. I would
not have believed a member of the royal family capable of
what you claim Thogrin Sin'tell has done."

The stern, threatening warrior of moments before was
no more than a dejected old man, filled with grief, pain,
confusion. His gaze flickered all around but did not fall on
her, as if he couldn't look on her face.

Her own anger melted; she sheathed her sword. "I'll
make a deal with you," she offered. "If by one of the
moon's cycles I haven't proved Thogrin's guilt, then I'll
come back to Mirashai to stand judgment. There are two
conditions to this."

He waited without speaking, his expression betraying
his interest.

She held up a finger. "First, if I go back and the
populace judges me guilty, you must promise not to let me
hang." She remembered too well the Hand of Glory and
the hanged man who had made its magic possible. "Kill
me any other way."

He nodded. "Second?"

"You're coming with me."

"That isn't your condition," he said. "It's mine."

She shrugged. "No matter. Evidence isn't always the kind you can carry back. I want your eyes so that I can have your voice in my defense. You'll clear my name when I've shown you what a dog your Thogrin Sin'tell really was."

"Speak no more ill of him," Tras Sur'tian warned. He swung stiffly from the saddle and dropped to the ground. "For all you accuse him, he still wore the crown of Korkyra."

She hooked her scabbard to her weapon belt. "So did the bedpost when he slept at night, but I owe it no respect."

Tras hung his shield on the saddle, removed his gloves, kneeled by the stream, and set his lips to the water. It splashed over his face, drenched his beard and the ends of his hair. When he rose, his dour features were more composed.

He came to her side. "It's a fair bargain," he said, "and we're friends again?" He extended his hand.

She stepped back. "No, you're my judge and jury, and I'll not clasp your hand while that remains so."

His brief smile faded, replaced by a look of deep hurt.

Unaffected, she met his gaze. "You demand a lot of your friends, Tras. Maybe too much. It's not out of any sense of duty or justice I made that bargain. I'm a paid mercenary—I owe no loyalty but what I give. If you returned to Mirashai without me, you would feel dishonored. I know what honor means to you." She paused, letting him feel the full weight of her words. "Or if we'd fought, one of us would be dead." She looked away, turning her gaze to the stream, where the sunlight danced on the water. She sighed. "You see, I'm caught two ways in the same trap. Because I let myself care for Aki, I'm suddenly plunged neck-deep into some terrible danger; I don't know what the danger is yet, but by all the gods I can feel it closing in! And because I let myself care for you, I'm sealed into a foolish bargain that could mean my life." She laughed suddenly, threw up her hands. "How much better off I was in younger days when I thought I could never love anyone!''

He came, opening his arms to embrace and console her.

She stepped back again, slapping his hands away. "No!" she shouted, then regained a measure of calm. "If I try very hard and apply myself to the task, maybe I can unlearn this habit of caring for others, and be damned to you all!''

Tras Sur'tian drifted back toward his steed, looking much like a whipped mongrel. He gathered his reins but didn't mount, just leaned his head against the hard leather of his saddle.

Frost made fists of her hands and stared at the ground, letting her anger ebb. At last she drew a deep breath. Nothing made sense right now. Perhaps she would think more clearly when she was in the saddle once more. There was a lot of road ahead before she reached Kephalenia.

She bent for one last drink from the stream's sweetness and noticed her reflection in a small pool that collected in the heel of one of her bootprints. Green eyes, deep as the Calendi Sea, regarded her with unshakable calm. Her only pretty feature, she thought. She dared not call them beautiful, quite; there was nothing of beauty about her. She leaned out and took her drink, wiped her mouth, and gazed once more at her image in the print. Abruptly, she smashed the image with her fist, splashing mud on her sleeve. But enough water still filled the depression, and when the murkiness cleared those green eyes still regarded her, calm, aloof, serenely uncaring.

Strive for that uncaring, she told herself, then rose and climbed into Ashur's saddle.

Tras mounted clumsily, his armor jingling. "Kephalenia, you say?''

"Shadamas." She fingered the emeralds in her pouch. "I've got an errand to complete.''

"More important than finding Aki?''

She shot him a look; he withered and said no more.

She felt the emeralds again. In the hands of a skilled healer like Oona they might have power to save another child's life. The old woman cared deeply for that suffering little village boy who brought her wildflowers. And Shadamas lay in the general direction, if not exactly on the road to Kephalenia.

She swore and cursed herself.

Care, care, care!

Who cared?

She clenched a fist and chewed her lip in exasperation.

Dusk had settled upon the world by the time they neared Oona's poor shack. Tras Sur'tian's mortal steed had not been able to keep Ashur's constant pace. Time after time the old captain had begged to rest his foam-flecked mount. Each time, she had reluctantly complied, and Tras had glared suspiciously at Ashur and scratched his head. No doubt he'd recalled how this strange *horse* that seemed to need no rest had impossibly gored a man to death outside Mirashai's walls. Once, when he'd thought her out of hearing, he'd muttered, "Witch-beast!" She'd hid a secret smile at that.

They reined up side by side at the shack's front door. No light shone through the window or the cracks in the old walls' boards, nor did any sound come from within.

She called the old woman's name.

"Maybe she's not home," Tras suggested when silence answered them.

Frost slid from the saddle. "Where would she go at this hour?" Even as she asked, she thought of a dozen possible answers. Oona had no fear of the dark. The hills loomed nearby, and many kinds of medicinal herbs could only be gathered by the light of the moon.

She looked up. A thin crescent hung golden overhead. *The same moon as when Aki disappeared,* she realized with a shiver. An omen? She pushed open the creaky door.

No light was required to discern the chaos inside. Jars were smashed, the contents scattered. Trunks and boxes were overturned. The old table and its only chair were broken, stools were broken. On the floor she found the new candle brought back from Kord'Ala.

"Tras!" she shouted. "Tras!" She ran out the back
door, flinging it wide. The small fire Oona kept always
alive was only smoldering coals. She stared toward the
hills and called Oona's name.

Tras Sur'tian came up behind her. "I found this in the
dust out front." He held the splintered head of a crude
wooden hay rake. "Looks like she had visitors."

"They've taken her," she said without further explanation. "The boy must have died. Gods damn them all, and I
wasn't here to protect her!" She spun and smashed her fist
through the bare plank wall, leaving a gaping hole. "I'm
never where I should be!"

She ran back through the shack, kicking rubble from her
path, through the front door.

"Where are you going?" Tras Sur'tian demanded as she
climbed into the saddle.

"To Shadamas or to hell!" she shouted over her shoulder.

"But we detoured around it because you didn't want the
villagers to know you were still in these parts!"

She didn't answer, just spurred Ashur into motion. Moments later, his voice rose over the rush of the wind as he
raced at her side. "Never believed in hell myself!"

You may soon, she thought. *Very soon.*

Shouting and laughter rode the air, reaching them as
they entered the village. A dozen bonfires lit the streets.
People reveled and reeled like drunken idiots, mostly men
and children, here and there a woman with her skirt slit to
the waist or blouse pulled low to expose sweat-sheened
breasts. A group of men called to the mounted newcomers,
offering bottles and broken-toothed leers. One wine-muddled
fool made the mistake of squeezing her thigh and offering
more than just drink. The toe of her boot connected with
his eye, sending him twitching in the dirt. His friends fell
away, no longer laughing.

Frost and Tras Sur'tian rode on, but now to the villagers
it was clear they hadn't come to celebrate. Like a ripple on
water the revelers became quiet until only the raging bonfires gave hint of the gaiety before.

At the center of the village Frost drew up. Her heart

went cold at the sight she saw there, the stake with bundles of wood piled high around it. Silently, she cursed the town, its people, their children, and all the children they should ever bear until the end of time.

Yet that fire, at least, had not been struck. Oona still lived, hidden somewhere, probably until that hour when the slender moon reached its zenith.

And longer, if I can help it, she swore.

The villagers began to press around her, their expressions sullen and suspicious. She regarded them coldly from the saddle, and when she spoke there was an edge to her voice that stopped the crowd in their tracks.

"Where is the old healer?" It was a command, no question.

"You mean the witch!" someone answered, and the mob took up the cry, shouting, "Witch! Burn the witch!"

She reached for her sword, but Tras Sur'tian caught her hand. Then he threw back his cloak. Perhaps no one could recognize its scarlet color in the shadows of the night, but the firelight glittered resplendently on the emblem of the royal guard that emblazoned his coat. "Bring out this woman called Oona." His voice boomed over their heads, crisp with authority. "You must surrender her to me. King Thogrin Sin'tell himself has ordered her arrest."

Frost raised an eyebrow at that. She'd never guessed lying was one of the old man's talents, but that one rolled off his tongue as glib as could be. Shouting gave way to a low mumbling and grumbling as the crowd wondered what to do.

One man, burly with hair and muscle, wearing a leather apron, stepped to the fore. Frost recognized the blacksmith she'd seen when she'd passed through Shadamas before.

"By all the nine hells we won't, bub!" he answered. "An' we're none impressed by yer pretty clothes, neither. A king's order is supposed to come on a fancy paper with a big seal on it. I seen 'em before. An' yer not wavin' one o' them." His voice was as deep and loud as Tras Sur'tian's, and its effect on the crowd was just as great. He turned to survey his friends and neighbors. When he looked back again his lips parted in a malicious smile. "So you better get outta here. We're not givin' up no child-murderin' witch!"

"We kin take care o' her ourselves!" someone shouted.

"Tell that to the king!" another added.

"Fire! That'll take care o' her!"

The sound rose like a tumult, the mob spoon-feeding courage to themselves with jeers and threats and insults. The blacksmith led them, shaking his fists.

"Where's the boy's parents?" Frost called over it all, repeating until they grew quiet enough to hear.

The blacksmith came close to her knee. His eyes burned redly in the firelight when he looked up at her. "Mournin' for their dead son, where parents should be!" he answered.

She rose in her stirrups, slowly slung a leg over the saddle, and slid to the ground. Not an arm's length separated her from the huge blacksmith. His gaze bore into her. She met it dispassionately. "You count yourself a man among all these people?"

"Huh?" he grunted.

She echoed. "Huh? That's an animal sound, not a man's."

"Frost," Tras Sur'tian tried to caution her. She silenced him with a casual wave.

"What'd'ya mean by that?" The blacksmith leaned forward, trying to intimidate her with his greater height.

She circled around him, showing him her back as she regarded the villagers one by one. "You don't sound like so much of a man to me," she said over her shoulder. "You sound like an animal." She imitated his grunt again, smiled for the gathering. When she turned back to the blacksmith the smile was gone. "In fact, you sound like an ass."

His face darkened, he puffed up his chest. "I'm more'n man enough for the likes o' you!" he roared.

She opened her arms invitingly, thrust her hips forward. "Prove it!"

His huge bearish arms reached out to engulf her, and that malicious grin returned. "I'll prove it all right, you

gutter-slut, here before the gods and everybody!'' He made
a grab for her.

She tilted her head, batted her eyes provocatively, pouted
her lips, and kicked him between his legs with all her
strength. The big blacksmith fell screaming, clutching his
groin with one hand, his kidney with the other.

''Maybe you were man enough *once* . . .'' She clucked
her tongue, pretended to brush dust from her hands. ''Now
I'll make the same fair offer to any other *men* among
you.''

But she had miscalculated. She'd grown too used to the
honorable men of Korkyra's elite guard, men whom she
could offer single combat in exchange for someone's life.
These were field rabble and farmers, drunk at that. What
did honor mean to them?

Hands reached for her; a cry went up for her blood.

She leaped back, sword hissing from the sheath. Tras
Sur'tian spurred his horse, forcing the crowd back for fear
of being trampled. But one brave soul grabbed for his
reins; the horse reared, throwing the guard captain.

Clubs materialized as if by magic in the villagers' hands,
rakes and hammers, knives, a few swords. Someone struck
at her. She gave no notice to the kind of weapon, just
blocked the blow and gutted the attacker. Blood spurted on
her tunic.

Tras Sur'tian was up and fighting. Wooden weapons
had little effect on his armored form, but his helmet was
suspended on a thong on his saddle, leaving his head
unprotected. For farmers and drunks, the villagers fought
like demons, fearless of steel, and the old man was sorely
pressed.

And she still had no idea where to find Oona.

A shrill scream rose behind her. She braved a quick
glance that way, expecting to find Ashur's ebon horn
bloodied. But no! A stranger's sword had saved her a
clubbing. The firelight and shadows made his face impossible to see. He worked his way to her side.

''The old woman's in there!'' she heard over the din.
The stranger pointed to the inn. A rake descended toward

his head. He caught it deftly in his free hand, gave a tug,
and kicked the wielder. He cast the implement as if it were
a lance, catching another man in the face with the pronged
end. "Come on," he urged.

"Tras!" she called, and the three made a bloody path
down the street. Still, the mob resisted them with an
insane fury. "Ashur!"

The unicorn reared; the flames of his eyes flared as
bright as the bonfires around. He charged into the villagers, scattering men everywhere. They broke suddenly in
all directions, screaming as the beast reared again, crushed
a skull with flashing hooves.

"I'll get Oona!" she told her two companions when
they reached the inn's door. "Keep them out." But the
two were rapt in the scene in the street, where Ashur
pranced back and forth. Most of the mob had leapt for any
door or window to avoid the black, snorting creature. Not
all of them were so quick or lucky.

Frost kicked in the door, sword ready, but the inn was
empty. Mugs and bottles sat on the tables, still half-full.
Customers must have rushed into the street to join the
melee. *Much to their regret*, she reflected. She mounted
the stairs that led to a set of upper rooms. The first two
were unoccupied. Oona was in the third.

Her hands were cruelly bound, and she was gagged and
blindfolded, presumably to prevent her from weaving any
spells, speaking incantations, or giving the evil eye. Frost
spat in disgust. Nothing so simplistic could have stopped a
real witch. She recalled how her hateful brother had once
bound her in a similar fashion. She'd nearly brought the
castle down on him.

She tore away the blindfold and gasped. They'd beaten
her! Black circles ringed both eyes, the cheeks were puffed
and bruised. The gag came away to reveal split and bleeding lips. Oona whimpered once when she saw her rescuer,
then closed her eyes again. "Wake up!" Frost urged,
struggling with the intricate knots that bound the old woman's fingers. If she was careless, those old fingers could

snap like dry twigs, she feared. "Wake up!" But Oona did
not move.

Frost shivered, fearing her friend was dead. Quickly she
reassured herself, pressing an ear to Oona's breast, finding
a heartbeat. She cast off the last cords and strained to lift
Oona's still form. With an effort, she made it to the door.
She took the stairs slowly, one at a time, her burden
seeming heavier with each breath. "Tras!" she called.
"Tras! Give me a hand!"

Tras rushed in, sheathing his sword, and took the limp
woman from her. "Hurry," he said. "That beast of yours
has damn well cleared the streets. Best get out of here
before someone finds a bow and starts shooting from a
window."

Outside the inn the stranger still kept guard. Ashur
paced up and down, snorting, kicking up road dirt. He
trotted over at Frost's call. "How did you ever train him to
do that?" the stranger exclaimed in a tense whisper. "Never
seen such a thing before."

Frost ignored him. "Once we're gone they'll find their
courage again and come after us." Her gaze swept around.
"Unless they've something more important to think about."

Tras Sur'tian frowned. "Like what?"

She strode to the nearest bonfire, alert for anyone hiding
in the darkened doorways. She seized a blazing brand in
each hand, crossed to the nearest building, threw one
through the open window, the other onto the roof.

The stranger ran to the far end of the street, grabbed
brands from another fire, sent them hurtling into the blacksmith shop, into a stable. Two men and a woman ran
shouting from the stable, dodged away from the stranger,
saw Frost standing with two more firebrands, and ducked
into another dwelling.

Tras Sur'tian watched it all, comforting Oona's head on
his broad shoulder.

When seven buildings were burning, Frost rejoined him.
The stranger was at his side. "They'll be too busy saving
their town to worry about us," she said grimly.

"A few belongings, maybe," the stranger observed.

"There'll be no saving the town." He shrugged. "I guess that makes me as much a criminal as you, queen-killer."

He said it quietly, and his eyes bored into hers as he spoke the words. An icy sky blue, those eyes, she could tell in the swelling fireglow. "You saved my skull back there," she remembered. "For bounty?"

He spat in the dust, then his gaze locked with hers again.

No time to pursue the matter now, she decided. Fire was spreading, people were rushing into the street. And Oona needed attention. "We'll talk later," she told him. "You have a horse?"

He nodded, ran down the street, and disappeared between two structures where the fire had not yet reached.

"He knows you," Tras said. "What do we do about him?"

She chewed her lip; then: "Nothing for now; Oona comes first. After that, we'll see."

She mounted Ashur, and Tras Sur'tian passed her old friend up into her arms. Ashur could carry the weight of two better, she explained, and they had need of speed. Tras's own steed waited where he'd dropped the reins, undisturbed by the fire or shouting. The stranger galloped into view and beckoned.

They rode, leaving Shadamas to burn.

"Where?" the stranger called.

"My shack!" Oona responded, awakened by the rush of wind. Her voice faltered, and only Frost heard her first words, but she gathered strength. "There're some things I can't leave behind."

Frost nodded and turned Ashur in the proper direction. They arrived breathless, the horses panting and lathered. Oona slid to the ground. Apparently recovered from the shock of her beating, she moved with sure quickness.

"My garden!" she moaned. Frost dismounted and went to her side. The little plot was ruined. The villagers had trampled the tender shoots flat and raked over the earth. Oona threw up her hands with a sigh and went inside. "I'll need some light," she said halfheartedly, and began rummaging in the dark, picking up things, squinting at them, casting them down with a clatter.

Frost went to the hearth, took Oona's apron from the nail where it always hung, wrapped it around a broken stool leg, and made her way through the rubble to the rear door. The coals, all that remained of Oona's fire, still glowed with a dull heat. By blowing on them, she produced enough flame to ignite her makeshift torch.

The two men were standing in the front entrance when she returned, watching Oona sift the debris. Tras looked up, shook his head, and shrugged. Frost shrugged, too, but held the torch higher.

The villagers had been thorough. Not a piece of furniture remained intact, not a jar unbroken. "Over here," Oona called. Frost moved closer with the light, tripped, nearly fell over part of the table. "Ouch, damnation!" she hissed, and scattered pieces of the poor board with a kick. Oona said nothing but took the torch and bent over the remains of her trunk. The lid was nearly ripped off; the hinges were badly twisted.

"I can't quite manage it," Oona finally admitted. The stranger hurried to her side, lifted the trunk, and set it upright. The lid groaned and lurched suddenly, pinching his fingers. He snatched his hand back without an oath.

Oona felt along the underside of the lid. Frost heard a click, and a section of the felt-lined interior popped out. Oona extracted a flat, narrow drawer. "My few treasures," she confessed.

There was the dagger Frost had given the old woman. Oona slipped it carefully down the front of her dress. There was a bracelet of gold; that went on her wrist. A couple of tiny vials filled with colored powders followed the dagger. Only a jewel remained in the drawer, crimson and shimmering in the torchlight. Oona passed it to her young friend.

"Beautiful," Frost said, admiring. "Has it a name?"

Oona scoffed. "Korkyrans never adopted that custom of naming inanimate objects. More important is what it does, not what it's called.'' The old healer rose, her knee joints creaking.

"What it does?" The stranger peered at the gem curiously. Even Tras Sur'tian leaned closer to view it.

Oona closed Frost's fingers around it, squeezing them into a tight fist. "Hold it so," she instructed, "and it will protect you from the evil things of the elements, the creatures born of earth, air, fire, and water."

"A talisman," Frost muttered.

"Magic!" Tras Sur'tian spat the word. "Get rid of it."

Oona kept hold of Frost's fist with the gem gripped inside. "Samidar, child, you've told me your suspicions about Aki's disappearance. Sorcery, you thought." The old hand trembled around hers. "We turned the cards together. Remember the gate of destruction? That card means an evil place. And the three stars?"

Frost nodded. "Mysterious influences," she interrupted, "and hidden enemies."

"And the demon," Oona pressed. "Danger to the mortal soul! Keep this stone, I beg you. It's only a shield against evil, but sometimes a shield is enough." She glared at Tras Sur'tian. "Tell this old fool to shut up. Keep the stone!"

Frost met Tras's gaze defiantly and slipped the ruby talisman into her belt pouch. The Korkyran captain scowled, turned on his heel, and strode from the shack into the night air.

"I'd better keep him company," the stranger said, and departed also.

Oona spotted the shawl Frost had brought back from Kord'Ala. It lay in a corner. She picked it up, shook the splinters and fragments of earthen pottery from the garment, and draped it around her shoulders. "Nothing more for me here," she announced, and headed for the door.

Frost caught her arm. "I'm sorry about the child," she said. "I know you did what you could, but root-fever . . ." Her voice dropped.

Oona's head dropped, a tremor racked her aged frame. When she turned, the gleam of a tear hung in one eye.

"You've got a child to save, too, Samidar, if you can."
An old hand reached out to caress her cheek, then Oona
grabbed her in a fierce hug as she had the first day Frost
had arrived. This time, though, Frost felt no embarrassment and returned the embrace wth all her heart.

"Go now," Oona said finally, stepping back. "Your
friends are waiting."

Frost straightened. "But you're coming with us," she
said. "We'll find you a safe town along the way."

Oona shook her head. "Avoid the towns. Ride straight
and hard until you find your child. I hope she lives."

Frost protested, "But what about you?"

"I've got a secret place in the hills," she confided,
"and a few stores to hold me over until I've rested a bit.
Then I'll head east toward the Chondite border until I find
someplace. There's always need for a healer. Not everybody is as foolish and backward as that bunch in Shadamas."
She shrugged. "I knew years ago it was a mistake to settle
here."

Frost remembered the emeralds in her pouch. "Take
these," she said. "You'll have expenses."

Oona declined. "I've everything I need in my secret
place. Always known I'd have to leave someday. I've
prepared for it." Then, on reconsideration, she took the
jewels. "On the other hand, I haven't prepared *that* well."

Frost smiled. "And I have your ruby jewel in exchange."

They went outside arm in arm. Oona pulled Frost's face
close and kissed the younger woman. "Take care, child,
and remember I love you." She turned, then, skirts aswirl,
and walked toward the looming hills.

Frost watched, trembling, silent, until the night swallowed the old woman. Tears threatened to spill on her
cheeks. She held herself stiffly, every muscle tense. *Why
did Oona say that? Why?*

She had memories of a mother who called her Samidar,
who hugged and kissed and said those words to her, who
consoled and protected her from the night, memories of
when she was younger. And memories of what followed,
dark memories. She choked back a sob for fear the men

would overhear. That mother was dead now with the rest of her family, murdered. And with her dying breath her mother had cursed her.

Frost squeezed her eyes tightly shut and forced the memory away. It would return, she knew. It always returned in her dreams and nightmares.

She exhaled slowly, then climbed into the saddle.

"She called you Samidar," Tras Sur'tian remarked when she had mounted. "Why?"

More than a hint of ice tinged her answer. "My name is Frost." She said no more, and her heels encouraged Ashur to a swift run.

Chapter Six

"You haven't told us your name."

Frost sat near the edge of the scarp staring at the midnight moon, chewing a piece of dried fruit from the stranger's saddlebag. Her back ached from long riding, and she felt bone-tired, though not ready for sleep. A horse nickered, probably Tras Sur'tian's. The Korkyran had gone to hobble his mount and not yet returned. Ashur and the stranger's horse wandered free.

"Kimon," he answered, and bit into his own ration.

She leaned back on her saddle and regarded the slender man. He sat with one leg drawn up, a lanky figure in comfortable repose. She had yet to see him in decent light, but he had that air of self-confidence and arrogant indifference that usually bespoke a seasoned warrior. Certainly he'd handled himself skillfully enough in Shadamas. "You're not Korkyran." She knew it by his accent, though she couldn't guess his true homeland.

"I'm from a lot of places," he admitted. "Trafyban, Keled-Zaram, Shagea, Emmidar—"

"Which do you call home?" she interrupted.

He chewed lazily and swallowed a bite before answering. "How much stock we put in that silly word," he said. "Home is where my horse is." He tapped the sword that leaned beside him against his saddle. "Where this is."

Tras Sur'tian strode out of the darkness with an armload

85

of dead wood and kindling. No wonder he'd been gone so long. He dropped his burden, arranged it neatly, and produced a flint box from the pouch on his belt.

Frost sat stiffly up. "No," she snapped. "No fire. From this high point even a little blaze will be visible far off."

"No one followed us," Tras Sur'tian grumbled. He took the flint in one hand, steel in the other.

"We've nothing to cook," she protested, "and the night air is warm. Why risk it?"

A bright spark illumined his face, gleamed on his armor, on the gold threads of his coat. His eyes shone momentarily. But the spark failed to take hold in the small dry nest he'd assembled. "The Shadamites are too busy burying their dead to worry about us." He prepared to strike tinder again.

"Did you wait to bury Thogrin Sin'tell?" she answered pointedly.

He shot her an angry look that even the darkness could not mask, and for a moment she feared she'd dared too much. Too often in the past her mouth had gotten her into trouble. But Tras Sur'tian rose finally, put the flint box away, and crawled to his own saddle. He stretched out on the hard ground, stared fixedly at the stars.

"Why don't you remove your armor?" she suggested, hoping to assuage him. "You'll be more comfortable."

He ignored her.

Kimon smacked loudly on his last bite as if to remind them he was present. "What did you say his name was?" he asked, putting on a broad smile of feigned innocence. She hadn't said, nor had Tras told him, though as long as the stubborn old soldier insisted on living in his uniform, it was no secret that he commanded the palace guard. The device emblazoned on his tunic proclaimed it to the world as surely as his scarlet cloak. She told him.

Kimon nodded in recognition and glanced casually at Tras's unmoving form. Apparently, the captain had fallen asleep at once. "I heard a minstrel sing about him once in a tavern back in Mirashai. Some adventure or other; the verses were endless.'' He rubbed his chin, leaned back. ''He must have been formidable in his day.''

Frost undid the tie that held her long hair back. It spilled around her shoulders as she shook her head. ''He's formidable now,'' she answered. ''Those aren't wrinkles in his face, but notches for the men who crossed his path and didn't live to regret it. Time carved them to warn away the foolish.''

Kimon crossed his ankles, regarded her over the toes of his boots. ''You should have been a minstrel yourself.''

She worked the tangles out of her hair with her fingers. A shrug was her only response to his comment.

Minutes passed before he spoke again. ''What makes a woman take up the sword?''

She stopped her combing, stared into the darkness beyond the scarp's edge. How many others had asked that? What answers had she given? In Korkyra none but Oona knew her secret. Not even Aki, who had comforted her on occasion when the nightmares had become too intense and she'd awakened screaming, shivering, drenched in sweat, fighting for breath.

She was silent for a long time. It always took time to shake off the memories. She looked up; the slight crescent moon was slowly descending, taking its faint light. Kimon was little more than a shape in the night, but she could feel his gaze upon her.

''What made you take it up?'' she countered.

''Money.'' He said it with a peculiar, offhanded kind of sigh. ''I decided to seek my fortune, being too restless to remain a farmer, too muddle-headed to become a merchant, and not nearly morbid enough for the priesthood.'' He slapped his thigh. ''So here I am.''

''Did you find it?''

''Several times,'' he affirmed. ''And, gods willing, I'll find and lose it several times more. After all, I'm still young.'' He rubbed his hands together. ''But you dodged my question.''

She thought about it. Why not tell him? This Kimon, this *stranger*, could do her no harm. There were others in

Esgaria, in Rholaroth, and in Chondos who knew. The story followed wherever she went, and one day it would come to Korkyra. Why not tell it now, let someone hear it straight without the embellishments and exaggeration that minstrels and storytellers would inevitably lend it?

"Money," she lied, "like you. I'm a mercenary."

"Not an assassin?"

The wind whistled suddenly around her, whipping her hair. When it calmed again, she answered. "I didn't kill Aki."

"I know."

She jerked around. "What?"

"By the three-eyed witch-goddess, woman! Most of the country knows Thogrin Sin'tell killed her. Most of Mirashai, anyway. They just don't talk about it. It offends their inflated senses of honor to admit their royal family can be as filthy and corrupt and greedy as the rest of us mortals."

She leaned over to make sure Tras Sur'tian still slept. "He'd slit your throat if he heard you say that," she whispered.

Kimon shrugged. "What I can't figure is why the two of you are out here together. Even if you're innocent, a palace captain is oath-bound to bring you back for public trial."

She was only innocent of killing Aki. Apparently, this stranger knew nothing of Thogrin's murder. She decided not to enlighten him. Word would spread fast enough that Korkyra's throne was empty again.

"We struck a bargain," she answered evasively. "I'll go back with him to Mirashai at month's end. First, there's business he's agreed to let me finish."

He yawned. "Looking for Aki?"

That brought her bolt upright. Her sheathed sword lay on the ground a quick grasp away. She glanced at it, then at him. "You're awfully well informed for a drifter."

He yawned again. "Come now." He stretched full length on the earth and rolled to his side. "A half-blind fool could guess. You were Aki's guardian, and Tras Sur'tian

her most trusted officer. What else could it mean but you
think she's alive and you're looking for her?"

She looked away. "It could mean we're planning to
avenge her."

"Which is it?"

She didn't answer. She wasn't sure herself.

"Well, maybe I'll just stick around to find out," he said
after a long silence.

She peered at his silhouette in the dark. "You don't
know what you're getting into."

"When did that ever stop me?" he answered. "Ignorance is the supreme gift of the gods."

"Then you're lavishly bestowed, friend." She hadn't
intended to call him that, but he was offering his sword
without questioning the risks. Harsh words or insults were
unfit pay for such service. She had been a wanderer herself and knew what it meant to find friends on the road,
someone to share supper with, stories or sometimes song,
even an adventure or two.

"I'm sorry," she said. "Ride with us as long as you
will, leave when you like, and no more questions. You
proved an ally in Shadamas and helped save my friend. I'll
share what I have with you as long as it lasts. But I'll also
warn you: none of us know what lies at the end of this
road."

He made a gesture, barely visible. "All roads are the
same, and we both know what lies at the end." She heard
a rustle, saw the partially exposed hilt of his sword. "This
is the coin of our passage." He lay back down and fell
immediately asleep.

She crossed her legs, folded her arms, yawned, but
sleep eluded her. She counted the stars, tossed from side to
side. She sat up, finally, and stared the way they had
come, imagining she could see a village burning, homes
crumbling to ashes, children crying. She closed her eyes,
but the vision remained. She was the cause. Her hands
were torches, Hands of Glory, and everything she touched
burned to ashes.

Was Oona sleeping? she wondered. Could she sleep?

*   *   *

Dawn broke slowly in the east. Streamers of carmine chased away the last of the night. The morning air was crisp and warm, promising a scorching day. Frost jerked the cinch tight around Ashur's underside.

"I don't like it," Tras Sur'tian grumbled.

"You don't have to like it," she answered, then turned to glance around, hands on hips. Kimon's mount had wandered a bit, and the youth had gone to fetch it.

The sun had brought that surprise. In the light she'd discovered Kimon was no older than she, possibly younger, though age was no measure of a man, she reminded herself. Yet he sounded, *acted*, older. She scratched her head and shrugged. Experience did that.

"We don't need him," Tras Sur'tian insisted. "He's a drifter, no loyalties. What does he care about finding Aki's killers?"

"He's a sword," she countered. Kimon came toward them, leading his horse. "Look, I won't argue. He proved his worth in Shadamas. That's enough for me. And he shared food with us. As long as he wants, he has a place beside me."

Kimon was close enough to catch that last. He drew up short, gazed from one to the other. "Am I a problem?"

"No," she lied, and shot Tras Sur'tian a look that threatened war if he contradicted her. "Get saddled. Kephalenia is a good week's ride, then who knows how many more days to find the man we seek." She licked her lips. "And I'm hungry for meat. We'll have to do some hunting along the way."

"With what?" Tras Sur'tian snapped, not looking at her.

She sighed. Leather creaked as she climbed into the saddle. "I didn't get a wink, and you wake up grumpy." She flashed a brief smile, then showed her teeth. "If you were a child, Tras, I'd spank you. As it is, just try to keep up, and maybe I'll teach an old dog a new trick."

Kimon laced his saddlebag in place, then his bedroll.

"Perhaps he's been a *palace* guard too long." He winked at her.

"You keep a civil tongue in your head," she ordered before the old Korkyran could defend himself. "Nobody's singing your deeds in the taverns, yet."

Kimon looked properly humbled as he mounted. "Sorry," he offered, and said no more.

Tras Sur'tian was last to mount. Frost gave them both a long look and sighed again. Maybe it was a mistake after all, letting this stranger ride along. She had enough on her mind without quarrels. Kimon had a quick tongue, and Tras a quicker temper, sure formula for trouble if she didn't keep an eye on them. Tras was a reliable friend and good right arm in a conflict. But Kimon was good company.

She rubbed her eyes. It would all work out. She'd make it work or break their necks.

The scarp sloped steeply downward to a broad, fertile plain. They rode the first few hours in silence. Then, of a sudden, Kimon began to sing. It startled her so, the strength of his voice, that she nearly fell from the saddle. The sound of him filled the air, rolled over the land. The words were old, the melody older, a song of beginnings and adventures, of marching to war against limitless enemies, a song of striving and greatness.

She studied him as he sang. In the sunlight he had a fair face, deeply tanned, clean-shaven but for a slight stubble. He sat his saddle well, broad-shouldered and straight of back, lean at the waist. His hair, raven-black as her own, touched his collar. Where she was dressed all in gray, black silk clothed his frame. His boots and gloves were black leather. No beggar, this wanderer. She watched him ride, watched the muscles in his neck and throat as he sang. Though slender, almost willowy, there was strength and power in his body.

The song ended and another began. A Rholarothan tune, she knew parts of it and joined in. He turned, smiling, as her voice harmonized with his, and she returned his smile. Only Tras Sur'tian would not sing. He glowered at them with a disapproving scowl that troubled her. She wished he would be joyous and share their mirth while there was opportunity. But the music rose in her, lightening her spirit. Tras would find his own peace in time, she hoped.

"You've been to Rholaroth?" she said when the second song ended. "Are you from there?"

"The ballad?" he acknowledged its origin. "I've been all around the Stormy Sea, even to Esgaria. By your accent, that's where you're from."

She winced but refused to yield to those memories. The morning was too nice, and the music had her feeling good. No morbid daydreaming, she promised herself. She was on the road again, the sun was high, the air fresh, and the company pleasant.

The next question slipped out. "How did you like Esgaria?" She clamped a hand to her mouth.

Kimon didn't see the gesture. "Friendly enough to travelers. Beautiful countrysides, too. The forests are fantastic, like none I've ever seen." He scratched his chin. "Strange customs, though." He twisted to face her. For the second time she noticed the sky blue of his eyes and the pupils that were like huge dark clouds. "I thought Esgarian women were forbidden to touch men's weapons? In fact, I heard they were killed for it. Yet, you must have trained since childhood; I saw your technique."

Tell him, an inner voice urged. *Tell him and be done with it. Purge yourself with one gushing confession and accept whatever scorn he decides to heap upon you. Then, maybe you'll be able to sleep nights once someone knows your sins.*

But she turned away, shaking her head. *Oona knows the truth, and the nightmares still come to haunt you.*

"I trained in secret under the best teacher in my homeland." That was truth, at least. The rest was evasion. "When I was old enough I decided to leave."

Kimon looked doubtful. "Just like that?"

"There was nothing to keep me." She changed the subject. "Tras, how about another song? Something from Korkyra, this time."

But Tras was as sullen as ever. "Not a time for singing,'' he grumbled. ''A queen is missing, a king is murdered, the country has no ruler . . .'' He hesitated and rubbed his belly. ''And I'm so hungry I could eat my horse if we didn't have so far to ride.''

She ignored his use of the word ''murder,'' but she did catch Kimon's expression. Well, she'd have to explain the past few days to him, but later. Right now, she spied the green darkness of a woodland glade. She'd been watching for such a place before the singing had made her forget her hunger. The evidence of the earth told her to expect such a place, for the grass was lush, the soil dark and spongy. That meant water, and water would mean game to hunt.

''I'm hungry, too,'' she answered with a cheerfulness she hoped would infect her old friend. ''Let's go eat.''

Tras was not so enthusiastic. ''What? Roots and tubers, leaves and grass and greens? I thought you wanted meat!''

She couldn't suppress a grin. There was something amusing in the griping grumping of this stiffly proper, almost starchy old warrior. Back at the palace he was so different, always so much in command of any situation, so dignified and disciplined, a soldier of true mettle. Now, he seemed much less. She wondered if Kimon's gibe were true. Perhaps Tras Sur'tian had grown too used to soft palace life.

''Just follow me, old dog,'' she called, half-teasing. ''I promised to teach you a new trick, and the lesson starts now.'' She spurred Ashur and headed for the distant forest. Kimon followed with a whoop, and when she glanced over her shoulder she was pleased to see Tras Sur'tian chasing right behind, crimson cloak aflutter in the wind.

She smiled to herself. It really wasn't a bad start they were off to.

The woodland was small, but dense with wild foliage. She reined up at the edge. Her comrades halted on either side of her. Kimon's face was alight with laughter. The youth seemed to have a limitless capacity for finding amusement in everything, even a swift ride overland. Tras Sur'tian was all frowns. She made a face to imitate his.

He rolled his eyes. "Now what?" he challenged. "The horse is all sweaty, and I'm still hungry."

She clucked her tongue, threw a leg over Ashur's head, and dropped to the ground. "Watch closely so you'll remember in the future." She took her rumpled cloak from her saddlebag and spread it over the unicorn's rump. "You see this section of the hem?" She pointed for them. "The thread, you may notice, is thicker." She slipped a fingernail under one loop, got a hold, and yanked. What came loose was a handsome length of waxed bowstring. "An old Esgarian precaution," she informed them. "Ruins the hem, but handy when you need it."

"Let me guess," Tras Sur'tian said sarcastically. "You pull the bow out of your boot. Or do you conjure it from air?"

She sighed. "Just bring your sword, Tras. Your brain isn't too keen today, so we'll test your muscle."

The men tied their reins to bushes. Frost never tied Ashur; he never wandered far. Then she led the way into the brush and soon found her bow: a stout young sapling, straight and strong and supple. "Cut it close to the ground," she told Tras Sur'tian, "and strip the branches from it." He drew his sword. She turned to Kimon. "Let's cut some arrows."

"What about tips?" he asked.

"Won't need them," she answered. "We're after small game. Carve the shafts to points, maybe leave a bit of a barb. That'll serve."

They got to work. Soon there were nine branches stripped and lying on the earth. Using Kimon's dagger, Frost made her points and cut notches for the string to fit. Tras Sur'tian waited with the denuded sapling in his hands, flexing, testing its strength. She tossed him the length of bowstring, instructed him how to tie the loops so they wouldn't come loose when the bow was bent, then checked his work.

He examined her arrows. "We could fire-harden the tips," he suggested.

She shook her head. "We'll have a fire when we've got something to cook over it."

"What about fletchings?"

Again, she shook her head. "I could spend the next week making perfect arrows, but I'm hungry now. I thought you were, too?" The look in his eyes told her she'd teased him enough. She raised on tiptoe and kissed his cheek. The impulsive act surprised her as much as it did him. She took the bow. "You prepare a good fire, and I'll bring back the rabbit. By the way, I only hunt; I don't skin the things." She faked a shudder and was rewarded with the faintest flicker of a grin from the Korkyran. "Come on, Kimon."

They plunged into the woodland, leaving Tras to gather kindling. The smell of moisture was rich in the air. From the spongy earth she knew there would be water nearby. Birds scattered as they moved through the underbrush. Patches of wildflowers blossomed everywhere. The trees stretched upward, weaving branches in a lacework that threatened to shut out the sun.

"Are you a good hunter?" Kimon inquired softly when they had wandered some distance and found no suitable game.

She peered left and right into the undergrowth. "I've never hunted in my life," she admitted. "But I learned the bow in the Aleppan War. I'm a good shot."

He stopped. "Better let me," he said, holding out his hand. "Shooting a nervous animal isn't the same as lobbing a shaft into an advancing army."

The half smile he wore irritated her, but she wouldn't let that show. She knew its meaning. Other men had made the mistake of underestimating her abilities. She'd taught them all hard lessons. She'd made the bow and arrows, not this smug young adventurer, nor the battle-wise career soldier. Without her, they'd be riding hungry a while longer.

He must have read her thoughts. "I mean no insult," he assured her. "But hunting is a different skill from soldiering. Would you waste all day finding food when you could be after Aki's killer?"

She winced at the ease with which he assumed the little queen's death. Aki might be dead, but Frost kept hope, a hope that Kimon's and Tras Sur'tian's doubt made ever more fragile. Her hunger lessened; her desire to get back on the road grew stronger.

Yet they must eat, reason told her. She passed the bow and bundle of arrows. "All right," she said, "I'll let you have the first shot." She tossed her hair back. "But if you miss, I promise to laugh so hard Tras Sur'tian will hear."

Kimon took the bow. "If you do, you'll scare away any other game that might be lurking." He cocked his head and grinned. "Then we'll all go hungry."

He moved out in front, letting her follow. She wished she had kept one of the arrows so she might jab his rump with the sharpened point. That prospect brought a mischievous smile. It was such a nice rump, too. A slow warmth spread through her. She watched as he moved, admiring his grace, the easy way he walked without making a sound, the way his gaze swept from side to side, the way he clutched the bow with the arrow notched and ready on the string. Yes, there was much about Kimon she liked.

They found a broad, lazy stream. Fat mushrooms grew all along the grassy bank. Frost bent down to study them. Edible, but full of insects. She wanted meat, anyway. If they didn't find any, they could come back for these.

"Tracks," Kimon announced. "Several kinds of animals drank here." He looked up at the sky, searched for the sun through the leafy canopy. "Wrong time of day now, but if we hide in a blind, something may come along." He spotted a browning thicket. "There."

They crawled behind it and sat quietly, bow at the ready. Kimon stuck the other shafts point first in the ground near at hand, easy to reach. They had a fairly unobstructed view of the place where the tracks were found.

Time crept by. Her legs began to stiffen and cramp. Worse, the sound of water so near made her thirsty. She licked her lips. An ant crawled on her hand; she slapped it off. Flies buzzed her nose. She tried to keep still, but all the annoyances! She leaned back, trying to relieve the incessant tingling in her calves. A twig snapped as she shifted her weight.

"Quiet!" Kimon whispered.

She stood up. "I've had enough," she announced. "This is boring. We came to hunt, and so far all we've caught are flies. Not my idea of a tasty meal, nor Tras's either, I'll warrant. I'm hot and dirty and thirsty, and I'll not spend another instant crouched in these dusty bushes." She pushed through the thicket, headed for the stream. The cool sweet water would quench her thirst.

"Just a little longer," he called.

"Forget it."

She kneeled and touched her lips to the water, drank deeply, washing the dust from her parched throat. If she didn't get anything to eat, the water would stop her stomach's grumbling. Kimon dropped beside her and drank, too. She sat up and watched him.

He bent far over, his tail high as any bitch dog's. Suddenly she recalled an earlier impulse. A small, tight smile flickered on her face. The bow lay between them on the ground, the arrows, too. She picked one up and felt the point with a finger. Wonderfully sharp.

Kimon gave a choked yelp, grabbed his backside, tried to leap up, but lost his balance on the slick bank, fell headfirst into the stream. She roared with laughter, clapped her hands gleefully.

Kimon sputtered, glowered at her, waist deep in the drink. "What was that for?" he shouted.

"Because you're so smug," she answered exultantly. "And because you needed a bath. The only thing worse than the flies in that thicket was sitting so close to your stink. You must have been on the road for days before we met you!"

"You're no rose from the queen's garden, either!" He launched a barrage of water, drenching her.

She got up, dripping. "You're right, we both need a bath." She unfastened her sword belt, then the belt that held Demonfang's silver sheath. She placed them carefully on the grass. Kimon tossed his own weapon belt on the bank, then peeled off his soaked tunic, wadded it, and threw. She ducked barely in time.

Her garments came off. Her bare breasts shone, small and palely piquant in the daylight. Other women would have wished for bigger ones, she knew, but she was satisfied, even glad at those times when she needed to pass for a man. She tugged off her boots and breeches and jumped in. The cool water sent an immediate tingle through her. She shivered, but it felt so good!

Kimon turned at the sound of her splash. He had waded out into the middle of the stream. Stream? It was really a small river. The water that rose to the tops of her shoulders lapped gently at the brown nipples on his chest. His arms treaded water, though she was sure he was touching bottom. She wrapped her own arms about herself for warmth and met his gaze. Another shiver passed through her, though not caused by the water's chill. He came closer. She backed away.

"Frost," he said softly. The breeze stirred the branches overhead. A ray of sunlight fell on him, igniting his face with a shining luster, making the drops in his dark hair gleam. The water diamond-dazzled around him. She caught her breath, bit down on her lip.

She had never wanted a man before! There hadn't been time, going from city to city, looking for food or a place to sleep, just trying to keep alive. Other men had sought her favors, but she'd scorned them or fought them off.

She knew that look in Kimon's eye; she'd invited it by her brazenness. No matter that the water came to her shoulders. He knew she was naked, had seen her strip on the shore. She felt fires rise in her cheeks. Her muscles tensed, ready to fight or flee.

Yet, by all the nine hells, she wanted Kimon! Whatever the confusion she felt, she wanted to touch him.

His sky-blue gaze was soothing as he wrapped her in his arms. She trembled, no matter how hard she tried not to. He pressed her close; she could feel his strength, the heat of his body next to hers. She gave a little, laid her head against his chest. ''I'm afraid,'' she admitted softly, almost to herself.

It was true. She thought she'd conquered fear, squeezed it out little by little and replaced it with a kind of fatalism that said nothing worse than death could happen to her.

But this was different; she knew it, and was afraid.

She was supposed to be cold, distant, detached from everything and everyone. People believed she was that; the songs about her sang of it. *Frost,* that was her name. But lately, people were getting through her walls, penetrating all the defenses she'd so carefully erected and maintained over the years. Aki, Tras Sur'tian, Oona, they'd all touched her somehow, sparked some dormant part of her she'd tried to shut away. Now, there was Kimon. She felt his lips in her hair, his bare chest against her breasts.

A sudden anger smoldered in a corner of her mind. She opened herself to these people, and they were all demanding things! Aki demanded rescue or vengeance; Tras Sur'tian demanded the bargain that meant her life if Aki couldn't be found. Oona had also demanded rescue. Not by word, of course, not one of them, but by the strengths of the bonds she had allowed to form. And now, if she permitted this new bond, what would Kimon demand?

She moaned with resignation and desire. It didn't matter; she didn't care. His lips came down against hers. She kissed him back clumsily, fiercely, begging, daring, challenging herself to do less, knowing she could not.

He lifted her and carried her to shore, placed her gently on the pile of her garments, and rose to remove the rest of his own. She had seen naked men before; it was impossible not to on the battlefield. But she remembered none so beautiful as Kimon seemed, with sunshine pouring through the swaying limbs, weaving patterns of shadow and light on his rampant form. He bent over, embraced her, showered kisses on her until she quivered and burned. At the first touch of his maleness, though, she nearly stopped. Her hands clenched his hips. Again, fear rose strong in her, and she wondered: If she shared this with Kimon, what else would he require of her? Then she forced the thought away. That fear was born of her nightmares, not of this moment. She closed her eyes and arched her body to take all of Kimon.

Afterward, Kimon returned to the stream to wash himself. A strange, rare warmth flooded him, but his brow furrowed. He turned away from the woman who sat watching him on the bank.

He thought about a fat purse of gold coins, Rholarothan klugats, back in his saddlebags. Payment, he reminded himself. He was an assassin, and the woman was his mark. He'd missed her once in Mirashai and then she'd vanished. Instinct alone had led him to follow the tracks of the palace's guard captain the morning after Thogrin Sin'tell was murdered.

There had been opportunities to complete his task. Yet there was something about the woman that fascinated—no, excited—him. He'd never known a female who could handle a sword, let alone face him down in a dark, private chamber. What a stroke of genius, he'd thought when he'd come to her aid during that trouble in Shadamas and had thus won her confidence. How easy, he'd reasoned then, it would be to kill her at his leisure.

But he had tricked himself. What had seemed a clever plan was becoming something else. He had won her trust all right. And her friendship and more.

He laved water over his chest absently, stared into the distance, seeing nothing and everything, reflecting.

He had known whores before, but they had never loved him so fiercely. He might have strangled her and earned Rholf's pay, and yet passion was all that had fired his thoughts. Even now, he felt his body stirring again.

Trust, friendship, love.

When had he known such things before? When had anyone ever offered him so much? He shook his head; it didn't make sense!

What was Rholf to him, anyway? An employer, certainly nothing more. A user and a coward who hired others to dig the dirt. Well, what if he chose not to dig for once?

He looked back at the woman on the shore, watched as she dressed, smiling at him. Could all the water in the stream ever wash his hands clean?

Gods, she made his blood burn!

As they made their way back to where they'd left Tras Sur'tian, Frost noticed a decidedly pleasant odor in the air. Her mouth began to water, and her pace quickened. Kimon hurried along beside her. Neither spoke of what had transpired.

They found Tras curled up against a tree trunk. A fire at his feet sizzled as grease drippings fell into the flames. He wore a contented expression, and his hands were folded across his stomach. Half a rabbit had made him jovial.

"Have some." He indicated the remains on a spit. "It's getting a little bit overdone, though, so hurry."

Frost looked at Kimon. Kimon looked at Frost. They both looked at the bow and arrows they carried, then at Tras's catch. They'd brought back nothing at all.

"Some hunters." The old soldier grinned. "I waited until my gut threatened to break out and go hunting on its own, then I took some rope and made a snare." He nodded to Kimon, who had gone to his saddlebags and was rummaging. "You'll find some of that dried fruit missing. I used it for bait." He waved a hand encouragingly. "Go on, help yourselves. Fattest rabbit I ever saw."

Frost moved toward the fire, but suddenly Kimon stood up and threw something deep into the woods. There were several brief flashes among the branches, as of sunlight on metal.

"What was that?"

Kimon shrugged and moved toward the rabbit, tying a nearly empty pouch to his belt. "Nothing," he answered. "Something I no longer wanted."

Chapter Seven

The sun slipped toward late afternoon. Frost threw a last handful of dirt on the embers; a wisp of smoke rose, dissipated. They'd wasted too much time in this glade, she chided herself. That meant riding late into the night to make it up. Yet, was it really time wasted? She felt more at peace with herself than she could ever remember. She stood slowly and stretched.

Kimon had removed the bowstring from the makeshift weapon. He carried it to her, made a loop of it, and placed it around her neck, tucked it inside her tunic. "Never know when you might need it again," he said. His hands lingered on her shoulders, saying more. They caressed with their gazes.

"Never know when I might need it again," she echoed softly.

His smile was answer enough. She longed to throw her arms around him, to feel his strength and warmth again. All the walls were down, now. Whatever the price, she was willing to pay. How had she lived in solitude so long, shutting herself away from the joys and passions that others allowed themselves? Kimon brushed her cheek. She pressed his hand more firmly to her face, kissed his palm.

Then she noticed Tras Sur'tian. He stood watching, looking over his saddle as he prepared to mount. She released Kimon's hand and took a hasty step back. *Don't look at me like that*, she pleaded silently. *I've done nothing wrong, don't accuse me*. But she could see the doubt in her old friend's eyes, the sudden suspicion, the subtle flare of anger that glinted there. Kimon saw, too; defiantly, he reached out to touch her again.

She caught his hand and took another step away. Maybe all the walls weren't gone after all. Did it matter what Tras Sur'tian thought? She knew that answer before the thought was even completed. Tras was her friend; they had shared much together. Nothing was more important than that.

But she and Kimon had shared much as well. That was important, too.

Tras said nothing, but climbed into the saddle. His eyes never left her, those eyes that said more than words. Then he turned his horse and rode slowly off. She stared disbelieving at his back.

Kimon touched her shoulders. "Forget him," he whispered close. "Let's go someplace together, someplace away from Korkyra and dead queens and kings and meaningless quests. We're good together, and we can be better."

She shook her head, went to Ashur, and gathered his reins. "I can't," she said simply, sadly.

"Why not, what's that old man to you?" He came behind her and caught her shoulders again. For a moment she allowed herself to lean on his chest. Then she straightened.

"A friend." There was a note of pain in her voice as she spoke. "I made a promise to him, and I can't break it."

"Just a friend?" The cold edge of his scorn was an icicle in her heart. "Well, what am I?"

She turned before he could continue; her hand covered his lips. "A friend," she answered quickly. "Be my friend. Lovers are a thing of the moment. We were lovers by the river, and maybe we'll be lovers again. I hope so, with all my heart. But I won't desert Tras Sur'tian now, and I won't desert Aki. She's my friend, too. I *owe* them for that friendship. Don't you know there's a price on everything?"

He stared, saying nothing. There was hurt in his eyes, laced with anger or bitterness or both. She looked away. Tras Sur'tian was still visible in the distance.

"They're my friends!" she pleaded.

Kimon rubbed a hand along his cheek, collecting a bead of sweat that trickled there. His lips drew in a tight line. Then he said, "Guess we'd better mount up before he gets too much of a start."

She threw her arms around his neck. "Thank you," she whispered urgently in his ear. "Thank you, friend!" She kissed him long and hard as he'd only recently taught her to kiss.

He pulled back suddenly. "Hey, do you want to follow him or not?" He was grinning again, that grin she was coming to love so much.

She leaped, caught a stirrup, swung a leg over, and mounted Ashur before Kimon even moved. "For someone who moves so fast you're awfully slow," she said, laughing. "Last one there . . ." Ashur sped off, raising dust.

Tras Sur'tian kept his gaze straight ahead as she rode up beside him. She could hear Kimon's hoofbeats close behind. Moments later he joined them, taking position at her left hand. "We're still with you, old dog," she told the Korkyran. He said nothing but nodded and pursed his lips.

Kimon began to sing.

Night found them deep in the hill country of the Dah'labba region. They'd made better time than Frost dared hope, but now they were forced to stop and rest. The treacherous terrain shifted and dipped underfoot. If they continued without light to show the way, it would only be a matter of time before a horse broke a leg.

Kimon dismounted first and rubbed his backside. Tras Sur'tian followed, his armor creaking. Frost rose in her stirrups, stretched, but gave no indication of getting down.

"Need some help?" Kimon offered his hand.

She shook her head. "No, I'm not too tired, yet. Think I'll scout ahead just a way."

Tras Sur'tian cast down his cloak. "We're a long way

from Kephalenia," he said. "These hills go on for miles with nothing in them but animals and insects and a hermit woodsman or two."

"Don't go," Kimon asked, soft-voiced. "It's too dark."

"I'll be all right," she assured him. But his concern sent a rush of warmth surging through her.

"I was thinking of your horse. He could get injured."

She smiled at his lie. If Kimon only knew: Ashur could take care of himself. Darkness meant nothing to his bizarre eyes. "I'll be fine." She bent to touch his cheek. "Don't worry. Tras, take care of him. I'm growing fond of his black, curly head."

"I've noticed," the Korkyran answered with a smirk. "But I doubt that's all you're fond of."

Kimon grasped her hand. "I'm coming with you, then."

She put a foot on his chest. The gesture said more than words. She was used to doing things on her own. However she felt about Kimon, she didn't need his protection. Right now, what she needed was some time alone to think about things.

"Just make a fire so I can find my way back," she instructed. Not that she needed that. Ashur wouldn't get lost. But maybe Kimon would feel better if he thought there was a beacon to guide her. She looked for the moon, but trees and hills hid much of the sky.

Tras touched Kimon's shoulder. "You have a lot to learn about women," he said, "especially this one." To Frost: "Go on, I know your moods. You've put up with ours enough to earn a respite from our company."

"Make a fire," she said. "I won't be gone long."

She rode into the night, down a long slope, into a small valley. Trees rose on either side of her. The grass sparkled with dew. Despite a light chill, she left her cloak tossed back from her shoulders, enjoying the breeze that kissed her throat and face. Insects chirruped in the branches; a night owl flew across her path. Ashur moved surefooted, avoiding the ruts and holes and loose rocks. The pools of flame that served him for eyes flickered, cast an amber glow on the earth.

There was no path; she rode where she pleased. The ground began to steepen. She climbed a hill. At its summit no trees grew. She gazed back the way she'd come and thought she could just make out a small fire in the far distance. The wind blew hair in her eyes.

She dismounted, started to walk. Ashur followed on her heels, the huge ebony spike that sprouted from his forelock bobbing near her back. *So quiet,* she reflected. *Kimon's songs were a joy on the road, but there is pleasure in silence, too.*

She spied the moon low in the eastern sky. It hung over the peak of a hill, a pale teardrop striving toward fullness. She recalled another night when she'd regarded the moon. Aki had disappeared that night.

Let her be alive, she prayed to her gods. *Tak, patron of witches, let her live! Skraal, whose name means vengeance, deliver me her murderer if she is dead!*

She closed her eyes, let the anger ebb from her. If only it were that easy, to pray to the gods and have your prayers answered. But gods did nothing for men who did nothing for themselves. And if you did for yourself, then there was no need for gods and praying was a waste of time.

She needed a plan, but none came to mind. Nothing to do but ride to Kephalenia, seek out Onokratos, and beat the truth from him. But where in Kephalenia would she find the man? She sat down on the grass. The dew dampness soon penetrated her garment, but she paid no mind. She rested her head on her knees. The stars floated above dark silhouettes of distant hills. Some claimed there were answers in the stars to all the questions men could ask. She regarded them, beautiful, but cold and silent. If they had answers, they said nothing to her. She sighed.

Suddenly, a bright, cyan ball streaked across the night, trailing sparks and streamers of green and golden fire. Frost leaped up, twisted to keep it in sight as long as she could before it disappeared over the horizon.

Beautiful! In all her experience she'd seen nothing like it! An omen, surely. Perhaps there were answers in the stars after all. But what did it mean, this strange comet?

An omen could be for good as well as evil. Did it foretell
failure or success?

She contemplated that, then shrugged. What did it matter if there were answers in the stars? She didn't speak
their language.

Ashur nuzzled her shoulder, his horn gliding past her
cheek, breaking her reverie. She stretched, yawned. Time
to return to camp before the men got worried. She reached
out and scratched the unicorn's nose; Ashur endured it
calmly. "I love you," she whispered, "and I love Kimon,
Tras Sur'tian, and Aki." She stepped back, regarded the
beast wryly, and repeated it. "Why does it sound so
foolish when I say it out loud?" Pondering that, she
gathered the reins, climbed into the saddle, and rode back
down the hill.

As she retraced her course across the valley, a sudden
warm rush of wind set the leaves to rustling. She glanced
skyward. Another fireball sizzled through the heavens,
brighter and closer than the first. She watched until it was
gone from sight, scratched her chin, brushed hair from her
eyes, and rode on.

The hairs rose on her neck when the comet appeared a
third time. She watched through the shivering latticework
of branches. Its trajectory was different. The first had
traversed west to east, the second north to south. This
traveled northwest to southeast.

Sorcery, for sure. Was she under attack? When she'd
first glimpsed Onokratos's shrouded figure in Thogrin
Sin'tell's grand reception hall, she'd thought he might be a
sorcerer. All her instincts screamed it, just as they now
screamed that these fireballs were manifestations. She
spurred Ashur. The unicorn raced through the darkness,
dodging trees and hidden obstacles that would have tripped
a common horse. Frost hugged the saddle tightly with her
knees and fought to keep her balance, ducking low limbs
that threatened to sweep her down. She had to reach
Kimon and Tras Sur'tian. Knowing nothing of magic, they
were in danger. Only she might protect them.

Yet without her witch-powers, what could she do?

Ashur thundered into camp, kicking grass and dirt in the small fire as he slid to a halt. Frost jumped down. Tras Sur'tian hurried to her side, but his stare remained directed through the trees at the sky. Kimon was nowhere in sight.

"Did you see it?" the old soldier exclaimed. "Incredible!"

"Where's Kimon?" she demanded.

"In the woods," he answered excitedly. "Private business. I wonder if he saw it? Did you see it?"

"I saw it." But she didn't share his enthusiasm. She wanted to extinguish the campfire, but would Kimon find his way back without it? She cupped hands to her lips. "Kimon!" she called urgently. "Kimon, get back here!"

Tras Sur'tian whirled at her shout. The firelight cast patterns of shadow and ruddy glow on his face but couldn't mask the puzzlement she saw there.

"We're under attack," she told him before he could ask the question. "I don't know how, but I can guess who. Onokratos, I'll bet the last tooth in my grandmother's head! That's no natural comet. How many times did you see it?"

"Just once," he answered. His right hand drifted toward his sword hilt.

"I saw it three times, traveling a different direction each time."

"What do we do?"

"About what?" Kimon hurried into camp, emerging from the shadows. "Did you see that thing in the sky?"

"We saw!" they answered together.

Frost scooped dirt as quickly as she could to douse the campfire. Smoke rose, dissipated as it curled in the branches.

"Hey, it took some effort to get that going!"

"Shut up!" Tras ordered. "She knows what she's doing."

"Quiet!" Frost insisted. She listened intently, searching the starlit skies.

"Look!" Tras pointed suddenly.

A *whoosh*ing noise filled their ears. Trees bent under a great gusting wind. It buffeted them, whipped their cloaks. The grasses rolled like waves as another fireball flashed above them, skimming the tallest branches, igniting the darkness with a cerulean radiance, trailing sparks like bright, dying stars. It swerved, soared high, swerved again, and plunged straight downward. They drew steel and shielded their eyes. Frost called on her gods, sure death was upon her. Her right hand closed on Kimon's arm. Her fingers curled in the silken sleeve.

But no explosion came, no impact. The fireball hovered just above the ground, giving light, but not heat. Disbelieving, Frost shot a hasty glance around. The trees did not scorch and blacken; the grasses did not wither.

Inside the fireball lurked a dark, vaguely human shape. Its face had no features she could see, but she could feel its dispassionate gaze.

Then a tingling started deep in her head. The tingling became an itch, unscratchable. She grabbed the side of her head, massaged her temples. Nothing eased it. Dimly, she discerned that Tras Sur'tian and Kimon were experiencing the same queer sensation.

Words began to form in her brain.

Thee searches for the child-queen. Well it is thee are close. Make speed and thee may yet save her soul.

Frost fought back the pain, glared at the fireball and the being within. Magic power of a fantastic order radiated from it. Behind her, Ashur stamped and snorted. The unicorn's flame-eyes blazed with startling intensity, flickering, dancing on his face. This could not be Onokratos. She would have sensed this kind of power when she'd first glimpsed him. She concentrated, sending her thoughts to the creature that confronted them, unaware that she vocalized them.

"What are you?" she questioned. "How do we find Aki?"

The pain of mind-speech intensified. Her eyes felt as if they were popping from her head. A muscle began to twitch in her neck.

Look to the west each evening at dusk. I will guide thee each night until the coming of dawn. The fireball crackled with new energy and shot, sizzling, into the sky.

"Wait!" she cried, but it was already high above the

trees and climbing swiftly. She strained to keep it in sight; the branches were too thick. But through a gap in the leaves she spied a luminous emerald star winking on the horizon.

"It means for us to follow," Tras Sur'tian pronounced, plainly shaken, but with a fatalistic strength in his words. He would go anywhere, dare anything to find his queen.

"What was it?" Kimon exclaimed. The effects of mind-speech seemed to have dampened none of his exuberance. He paced around camp, trying to find the best place to view the sky.

"I don't know," she answered. "But if it can lead us to Aki, then we're going to follow it."

She went to Ashur. The unicorn's eyes still blazed as they did in the presence of magic; she wondered how her friends could fail to see his true nature. She looked for the star again, set a foot in the stirrup, and swung into the saddle.

"This reeks of a trap," Kimon warned, "and stinking sorcery."

Tras Sur'tian went to his horse. "Then go home, Kimon," he said. "Without clues we could search for weeks and not find Aki. Kephalenia is a big region." He pointed to the twinkling star where Frost was looking. "Now we've more than a clue, we've an invitation." He laid a hand on Frost's thigh and gazed up at her. "It said we could save her. That means she's alive!" He bowed his head. "I release you from the vow you made in the Kithri hills and offer my deep apology."

She smiled gently and nodded, then gazed back at the star that would be their guide. *Can we trust it?* she wondered. But let Tras keep his hope. "It also said to hurry," she said to Kimon. "So put that sticker back in its sheath and mount up. It's still dark, so pick your path carefully. A horse with a broken leg means someone gets left behind."

For two nights they rode. The rough terrain was soon behind them; the ground leveled and they could see some distance in all directions. At night the swelling moon

stretched their shadows far before them. By day they slept
without shelter while the blistering sun beat down. There
was no game to hunt, and they quickly finished the last of
Kimon's dried fruit. Their bellies grumbled for real food.
Fortunately, the waterskins were full.

"Doesn't that beast of yours ever tire?" Kimon asked
once. His own mount plodded along, head low, lathered,
weary. She only shrugged and rode on.

Each day at twilight they waited, mounted, for the last
rays of the sun to fade and the evening gloom to deepen.
The green star appeared, flickering, beckoning, brighter
than the other stars. While the rest of the heavens rolled
across the night sky it held its place fixed in darkness.

Shortly after dawn of the third day they arrived at the
bank of a great river. Their celestial guide had vanished,
but they continued on in the direction it had led them.
Frost smelled water, heard its rushing, and remembered
her hunger.

"Do either of you fish?" she asked. "I'm ravenous."

Tras Sur'tian paid her no attention but rose in his stirrups, looked out. "This must be the Skamandi River," he
reported. "On the other side lies Endymia."

"Thogrin Sin'tell's baronial holdings?"

He nodded. "As far as you can see."

"Then there will be a town or village close where we
can eat and find a good bed for a change," Kimon suggested hopefully.

"We'll sleep out here," Frost corrected him. "Then, in
the afternoon you can scout alone for a village and, maybe,
bring back a few supplies."

"Why alone?" Kimon said with thinly disguised suspicion.

"Why not me?" Tras Sur'tian put in. "I don't know
this region well, but these are still my people. They respect a royal uniform."

Frost slid from the saddle. "I'm still wanted for Aki's
murder, remember? And though we've wasted little time
on the trail, there's the chance Thogrin's subjects might
know of his death. They certainly have my description for

the first charge, in any case.'' She winked at Tras Sur'tian. ''And you're too well known across the kingdom, old friend. If someone should see you in these parts, they'd surely guess you were following me. It's much better if nobody has a clue where I am. I'll be no good to Aki at the end of a rope.''

''Then let's avoid the towns and just keep riding,'' Tras said.

She shook her head vigorously. ''I'm too hungry,'' she insisted, rubbing her stomach. ''Let Kimon bring back food for a good meal, and maybe some real wine; gods, I'm tired of water.'' She wiped sweat from her face. ''If I remember, Endymia is not a very wide land.''

''Long, but not wide,'' Tras agreed. ''We should reach Kephalenia tomorrow night.''

She sighed. ''Let's get some sleep. I'm so tired I can't tell the difference between my saddle and the calluses it's worn on my rump.'' She patted her backside.

''I can,'' Kimon said, grinning, as he got down.

They unsaddled their mounts. The two men pulled hobbles from saddlebags and fitted them to the horses' legs. There was plenty of grass for grazing, so Ashur was allowed to wander.

They spread their bedrolls in the shade of the large trees that grew along the Skamandi's banks. Tras Sur'tian quickly fell asleep. Frost stretched on her back and shut her eyes, feeling the delicious warm sun on her lids. But sleep never came easily to her, and this time was no different. Finally, she cracked one eye, pleased to find that Kimon was also awake. She rolled over next to him and curled in the crook of his arm. His body was warm like sunshine, firm and secure. She felt good lying next to him.

For a long time they said nothing. Then Kimon spoke, but softly, so as not to disturb their companion. ''I've been wondering why the old woman called you Samidar.'' His fingers crawled slowly up her spine, his breath blew gently on her cheek.

She stiffened, but the nearness of him and the comfort of his arms, the gentleness of his voice, made her relax again. She looked into his eyes, those blue eyes that seemed to swallow her. "Because it's my name," she confessed in a tight whisper. She squeezed her eyes shut. Oona knew only because it was impossible to lie to her. Frost had not spoken that name for a long time. *Samidar*. Her father had given her that name. She had always liked the sound of it.

"I thought Frost was your name."

How much could she tell him? Would he still want her if he knew her past, what she'd done? Perhaps she had suffered enough penance. It would be good to share the secret with someone she cared for. Oona knew the truth, and Oona hadn't rejected her. Yet Oona was old and lonely, the kind who took in anyone. Kimon was a proud man. He might leave if he knew her shame.

"You're right," she answered after a long silence. She blinked back threatening tears. "My name is Frost."

"But it wasn't always?"

She rolled over so her back was against his chest. His arm draped over her breasts, and she could feel his breathing sweet on her neck. "Another time for those stories," she told him wistfully. "Now I want to sleep."

He kissed the back of her head and moved up against her. Shortly, he began to snore. Only then did she release the tears she had fought to hold in check.

She awoke with a start, grabbed for her sword.

"The dreams again?" Tras Sur'tian regarded her from nearby, where he sat against a tree. He rubbed the edge of his blade with the whetstone he kept in his saddlebag. For the first time in days he was out of that hot armor.

"Where's Kimon?"

"Do you love him very much?"

She leaned back on her elbows. "I don't know," she said truthfully. "What do I know about love?"

The old warrior shrugged. "He rode out to find a village. We decided to let you sleep; you seemed tired."

She patted her stomach in anticipation. "Hope he gets back soon."

Tras Sur'tian measured the sun's journey in the sky. "It's only midafternoon. It may be a while. No telling how far he'll have to go. But Endymia is a populous land. He'll find something."

She got to her feet and stretched. Her skin felt clammy; the nightmares always brought a cold sweat. Her hair was filthy with road dust, too. She could smell herself. Tras Sur'tian had already bathed, she could tell by the damp ringlets in his beard that hadn't quite dried.

"I'm going down to the river," she announced. "Could you do that for my sword, too?" He nodded. She unbuckled her belt, tossed him the scabbarded blade. "Water's cold," he warned, returning to his work. A fine gray powder covered his hands as he slid the stone up the weapon's length.

She walked down to the bank, out onto a broad sandbar. She pulled off her boots, laid them aside, and removed the rest of her clothing. The sand toasted her toes and the soles of her feet. A light breeze blew her hair, caressed her skin. She waded in until the water reached her knees.

Tras had told her. The water was frigid, no doubt fed by underground springs. The Skamandi flowed with moderate swiftness; the water churned around her legs. She shivered despite the sun on her shoulders and grit her teeth, walked farther in. When the water touched her waist, she stopped. The sand underfoot had turned to mud. She could feel the tug of the current; it could be dangerous to stray farther from the shore.

She scrubbed as quickly as she could, immersing herself and rubbing until the flesh turned ruddy. Her hair hung in wet ropes plastered to her skin, shining with sunlight as droplets ran down her back.

A peculiar cry from the bank made her turn. She grinned. Other men mistook that sound for a horse's whinny; she knew better.

Ashur watched from the shore. She called to him, "Come on in, coward!" The unicorn tossed his head, then came down to the sandbar, dipped a front leg up to the fetlock joint, and cautiously drank. His long, shaggy mane floated on the surface, but he ventured no deeper. "Coward!" she repeated, and used her hand to launch a curtain of water. The huge animal danced lithely away, avoiding her attack, then returned calmly to drink again.

She smiled, full of pride and affection for the creature. She waded toward him. Too late, she saw Ashur's horn dip and jerk upward. A pitiful attempt, but she laughed at the few drops that actually splashed her. "If that's the best you can do with that thing, we'd better saw it off, make you a common horse," she chided, "maybe a gelding, too. How'd you like that?"

Ashur nodded his great head excitedly as she approached.

"Oh, you think you'd like it?" She reached out to put her arms around his neck, but the unicorn stepped aside and suddenly shook himself vigorously. The wet mane lashed out, showering her.

She leaped back, open-mouthed. "I'll get you for that!" she shouted. But Ashur turned and fled over the sandbar, up the bank, and out of sight. "Sooner or later," she added, grinning.

She climbed out of the water, shook the sand from her clothes, and pulled them over wet flesh. Tras Sur'tian had worked a bright, shining edge on her blade by the time she returned from her bath. He continued with an oil-soaked cloth, polishing the length of steel to a fine gleam, working with a professional's respect for a good tool. He hefted it in one hand. Sunlight rippled along the metal.

He nodded approvingly. "It's as heavy as mine," he said.

She found a leather thong in her saddlebag and tied back her hair. Her moonstone circlet lay in the bottom of the bag; she set it on her head also to hold back her long hair.

"I trained with a heavier one," she told him, recalling long nights in the dark lower levels of her father's castle, and a man as dear to her as kin. "He taught me two-handed techniques seldom seen in this part of the world, how to use speed and momentum to make up for what I lack in sheer muscle." She bit her lip. Her weapons master was dead now. "Before his death he had that one made specially for me."

He lowered the blade, looked at her over the point. "You look about to cry."

"Nonsense!" She forced a smile and waved at the sky. Not a cloud spoiled the deep blue. "Too beautiful a day for crying." She pushed her memories away, an easy thing to do in the daylight. If only her nightmares could be banished so easily.

But Tras Sur'tian was persistent. "What happened to him?" he probed.

"I don't want to talk about it." She started to walk away, but he reached up, caught her hand, pulled her to a seat on the ground beside him.

"I've been pretty grumpy, haven't I?" he said, changing the subject.

She peered quizzically at him, then took the smile he wore as a sign it was all right for her to agree.

"I've been afraid," he confessed, and set a finger against her lips before she could say anything. "I've been a palace guard so long I was afraid I might not be much good in real battle." His smile wavered, returned. "I still might not be; nothing's proven, yet. I'm old. I've kept the rust off my sword, but not off my bones."

She hugged her legs to her chest, rested chin on knees. "You're as good as any ten men," she assured him.

"That's flattery," he chided her good-naturedly. "Truth is, I'm not sure what I'm worth anymore. But this morning I finally decided to put my fear aside." He gestured at the pile of his belongings. "It lies there, somewhere, with my armor."

He was silent then, his keen gaze piercing, unflinching. She licked her lips. "You're trying to tell me something."

He nodded. "Take off your armor."

His meaning was clear. She wanted to open up to someone. She'd thought about it, nearly opened to Kimon, but couldn't. Why not Tras Sur'tian? The old soldier had always been kind to her, called her friend, looked after her in almost a fatherly manner. In fact, he was much like her real father; his physical appearance alone had caused her no little pain during her first days at Mirashai.

She opened the gate to her memories, let them out one by one. Each brought pain, guilt, refused to be studied dispassionately. They rushed upon her, images from her nightmares, visions that haunted her every waking moment. She tried to control them, and when she couldn't she tried to dispel them as she had earlier. This time, they would not be banished. She began to tremble; the air no longer felt warm.

Could she ever tell? Could she describe those images and nightmares? Or would the tongue rot in her mouth and fall out before the words formed?

Tras's eyes never left her. She saw the concern in them and the love. Even more than Kimon, she knew she could trust this old man. Yet he loved her in ignorance, not knowing what she was, what she had done! He'd run away when he knew the truth. Her sin would taint him. She shivered again. A drum throbbed in her skull; her heart raced.

Tras had been truthful with her. *Afraid*, he'd confessed. *Afraid*. Keeping her secret now would shame them both. Despite her past, she had found a home and warm, good friends in Korkyra; she didn't want to lose them. Suddenly, her secret seemed an immense hammer poised to shatter everything and everyone who meant anything to her.

Tras had taken off his armor and invited her to do the same. She shook visibly, felt shame for it. "What do you really know about me?" She hated the whine in her voice when she said that. It just slipped out. She bit a nail. Maybe he would say nothing and just let the conversation drift away.

"You call yourself Frost," he answered, "but your name is Samidar. You come from Esgaria. You're born of a noble family."

She looked up sharply. "How do you know all that?"

"The old woman spoke your name. Your accent betrays your nationality, and you speak a variety of languages.

Commoners get no such education. You also mentioned a weapons master; that indicates your father kept a garrison of household soldiers as Esgarian nobles are known to do.''

She licked her lips. ''What else do you know?'' she challenged.

''You're a fugitive from your homeland.'' He ticked them off on his fingers. ''You're a witch, or used to be. You've honorless enemies who would seek revenge through assassination.'' He listed a few more obvious facts, looked thoughtful, then held up one more finger. ''And I think I know what haunts your sleep.'' He spoke slowly, as if asking her permission to say more.

She hugged herself; a cold dread crept through her. Could he possibly know? It distressed her how much of her secret she had given away to him. What of the others she'd spent time with? How much had Aki gleaned about her? Aki's councilors? The palace guards?

Tras Sur'tian took her silence for approval. He swallowed. ''You murdered your family,'' he said, ''or caused them to be murdered.''

She leaped to her feet, reached for the sword she wasn't wearing. Blood pounded in her ears, her vision refused to focus. She couldn't get a breath. Tras caught her hand, but she jerked free, stared horrified at the stranger who spoke her name, at the accuser who knew her deepest secret.

''No!'' she shrieked. Hysteria wormed its dark way through her; she fought to control it, a battle she sensed she was desperately in danger of losing. ''How could you know?''

Tras Sur'tian kept his seat on the carpet of grass. His expression stayed calm, steady, his voice soothing. But there was sadness and sympathy, too. She didn't trust his sympathy.

''It's no secret, Samidar,'' he said gently. ''It never was to anyone who knew you or knew Esgaria.'' He met her gaze evenly. ''Esgarian law decrees that a woman who touches men's weapons must be put to death by her family. Something dark, terrible, has tormented you from your first day as a mercenary in the Korkyran regulars—and long before that, I surmise. I've seen it in your eyes, and men in the barracks heard you cry out in your sleep at night, screams that threatened to wake the dead. Only by Aki's direct order did we let you sleep in her chamber when she named you her champion.'' He hesitated, swallowed before going on. ''I've seen your swordwork, woman. Your technique is unearthly strange, deadly. You're no piece of meat to just lay down and be butchered.'' He looked her up and down. ''Was it your father?''

Her spine turned to ice. She stood stiffly, shivering all over, staring and seeing nothing but images and visions. Voices called to her, accusing, ugly voices that cursed her. She couldn't shut them out, refused to shut them out. This was the time; they had come to claim her. Let death take her and end it forever.

Yet she knew she wouldn't die. Visions didn't kill, just tormented, tortured, haunted, maddened.

''My brother, first.'' Her mouth formed the words; she could not stop herself. ''He found me practicing, tried to kill me. It was his right, by law. There was no love between us, and I really felt nothing when my blade slipped under his ribs and punctured his jealous heart.'' She saw the scene in her mind, that night in the dark bowels of the castle as she stood over him, blood dripping from her sword, spattered on her sleeve. ''My father heard his scream and came. My mother, too.'' She clenched her eyes shut; the chimera would not fade. Her voice sounded mechanical, empty of emotion. She no longer resisted the images. ''I was his favorite child. I might have stood there under his sword and done nothing to save myself, I loved him so.'' She rubbed at tearless eyes as she spoke. ''He couldn't carry out the law, couldn't avenge his son, couldn't kill his daughter. In shame, he threw himself on his own blade. My mother looked at me in grief and sudden hatred, disowned and cursed me. My sword had stolen her husband and her son. She stole my witch-powers and my name.''

''She was a witch, too?'' Tras Sur'tian interrupted.

"A sorceress, the most potent in a land where all women studied the arcane arts."

"Then, you fled."

The first tears began to slide down her cheeks. "No, there was another," she answered. "My weapons master. He trained me in secret, flaunting the law because he loved me. But he was my father's friend, too. He blamed himself." She sank to her knees. Tears flowed freely now, unchecked. Her body shook with the force of her sobs. "I didn't want to fight him! I tried not to! But he came after me, and something just possessed me!"

She collapsed into his arms, buried her face against his chest. He held her tight, stroked her hair, rocked her while tears stained his tunic. "The will to live," he told her. "We all want to live."

"It was just a game, my training, something to pass the dull hours!" she wailed. "I never expected to kill!"

He said nothing, just held her close.

After a while, her crying ended. She sat up, wiped her face. There was a hollow place inside her where the nightmares once had nestled. She felt drained. "I'm sorry," she muttered softly.

"We all cry," Tras Sur'tian said. "Tears are as much a part of us as blood."

"Even old soldiers?" she asked, forcing a weak smile.

"Especially old soldiers."

She hugged him around the neck and laid her head on his shoulder, the way she used to embrace her father. "I guess the armor is off," she whispered.

"I guess it is," he agreed. "Now, you'd better sit up. If Kimon is the jealous type, he may get the wrong impression."

She got up. Her gaze followed where Tras Sur'tian pointed. Kimon rode toward them, a bag bouncing on his horse's shoulder. His tunic was opened to the waist and a breeze rumpled his dark hair. A sudden warmth rushed through her, chasing away the last chill of her confession. She was pleased to see him.

"Food!" he shouted brightly, riding up, passing the bag to her. "Cheese, sausages, bread, and wine."

"You found a village?" Tras Sur'tian said.

"A farmhouse," he answered. "The farmer's purse is fatter by twice what all this is worth, but I was hungry and had spare coins. No dried fruit, I'm afraid."

"What a shame," Frost said sarcastically. Opening the bag, she extracted a large cheese. "Hobble your horse, but leave him saddled. After we eat we'll start out."

Kimon swung to the ground as she spread the bag's contents on Tras Sur'tian's cloak. When his mount was hobbled he came close, bent over her, and frowned. "You've been crying."

She looked at Tras, then at Kimon. "Nothing to talk about now," she assured him. "Someday soon, I'll tell you everything." His frown remained, but he straightened. His gaze flickered over each of them. "I promise," she added, giving his hand a squeeze. "Now sit down. You can cut the cheese. Tras, you carve the sausages."

Food had never tasted so good. They ate with relish, licking crumbs from fingers, leaving only a bit of cheese and some bread. A jug of wine shared among them washed it all down. Not a droplet remained. Tras rolled back, rubbed his stomach. "Your farmer was well paid," he informed them. "The best cooks in Mirashai would be envious."

Kimon grinned. "Then, at your leisure, you may reimburse me for your share of the meal."

The Korkyran flipped him an imaginary coin. Kimon pretended to catch and pocket it. "My thanks," he said, and Tras nodded. "And you, lady," Kimon added, turning. "What of your payment?"

She winked. "What would you ask?"

He scratched his chin. "Let's walk down by the river and discuss it."

She laughed and got to her feet. "We'll just have to defer your payment to another day. It's time we were moving out."

"But it's not yet dusk!" Kimon protested.

"No matter," she answered, patting his cheek teasingly. "We can be nearly across Endymia by full nightfall.

We know we're going into Kephalenia; we don't need a star to guide us to the border.''

"But—"

She wagged a finger. "No buts . . . or no payment later.''

Tras Sur'tian got up, lifted his saddle from his pile of belongings, slung it over a shoulder. "Give up, friend," he advised. "No one wins an argument with her." His horse was some distance away, hobbled, grazing. He started for it.

She didn't need to look around for Ashur, just cupped her hands and called. The unicorn's weird cry echoed in her ears. She turned. Ashur raced over the earth, an ebon streak, streamers of flame trailing from his face, mingling with the thick mane that lashed the air.

"A fine horse," Kimon commented admiringly, unwittingly. "I've never seen his like."

You certainly haven't, she thought, smiling inwardly. She took his hand in hers. He was special, too; she'd never met his like. "Look at Ashur closely," she said, "and tell me what you see."

He squinted, shrugged. "A magnificent piece of horse-flesh," he answered. "Strong, fast, well trained . . ."

She sighed. Ashur thundered to a stop before her, kicking dust. The mane was a tangle, and she tried to smooth it. She stroked him along the withers, down the broad forehead, passed her hand between those bizarre and beautiful eyes. The flames shimmered near her skin, but she was not burned, for they gave off no heat.

If only Kimon could see him and know how rare a creature he truly was! A horse? That was like comparing the stars to coals in a half-dead firepit. She sighed again and lifted her saddle.

Chapter Eight

Midnight brought them to the edge of a vast forest. The moon glinted on the beaten road, on the tops of swaying trees. Leaves shivered and rattled. The rasping of crickets echoed from the shadowed depths. Their own shadows stretched far behind them, as if reluctant to enter the wood.

A sharp wind had risen early in the evening. Frost's hair whipped her face. She hugged her cloak tight around her shoulders and glanced upward. The green star seemed to have changed position, though she had not seen it move.

"But the road goes that way," Kimon protested when she mentioned the shift. They brought their mounts to a stop. The wind whistled shrilly around them.

"Then that's the way we're going," she decided finally. "I'm not plunging into that unknown in this dark. Gods know what we might find."

"Or what might find us," Tras Sur'tian added.

"Maybe we should wait for morning, then," Kimon suggested.

She nudged Ashur into motion again. "No," she said. "If I remember my maps, this forest separates Endymia and Kephalenia."

Tras nodded. "A kind of no-man's-land, claimed by neither province according to an old treaty. It grows larger and deeper every year."

"While the provinces shrink," Kimon observed. "That can only lead to war one day."

Tras Sur'tian answered with stiff formality. "There are no internal conflicts in Korkyra."

Kimon snorted. "What do you call it when cousin murders cousin for a throne?"

Frost interrupted before an argument could brew. Tras's mood had improved immeasurably since their talk in the afternoon. Yet Kimon's sharp tongue might yet provoke her old friend into his customary sourness. She needed no more gripes or complaints. "This place has a name," she said, "but I can't recall it."

Tras Sur'tian's retort to Kimon was cut short. He looked thoughtful. "Kellwood, I think."

The wind wailed a higher note and set their cloaks flapping. The trees bent, leaves rippled like waves on a stormy sea. Low in the west the bloating moon sent the forest's shadows yawning toward them as they entered Kellwood. Young saplings and scrub rose like gnarled hands clawing up through the earth. Huge, ancient trees, moss-dripping, swept the skies with twisted limbs.

Kimon's horse whinnied pitifully, fought the reins.

"Damn!"

Frost jerked on her own reins, turned in the saddle, sword half-free of her sheath. "What is it?" she whispered tensely.

Tras Sur'tian answered normal-voiced. "Nothing. Cloak caught on a bramble is all. Thought something had me!" She heard material rip as he gave a pull.

They pushed on, following the narrow road. The chirping of insects was frequently drowned as violent gusts savaged through the branches overhead. Frost scrambled for something scratchy that blew down her neck, a dead leaf. The luminous eyes of an owl peered down at them, but the bird kept silent. A few spears of moonlight penetrated the forest canopy, some on the road, more in the dense foliage to either side. Frost glimpsed a patch of flowers, a scampering nocturnal rodent, a serpent crossing the road, all in shades of black and gray.

The green star was the only hint of color. Somehow, it seemed always to hover in a gap between the trees, never out of sight for long, as if insisting they return to the course it prescribed for them.

But she would not plunge through the underbrush in darkness. She stuck stubbornly to the path, convinced she was right to choose the safer way. The leaves grew thicker, obscured the sky and the star. When the road took a sudden turn and the branches parted, it floated bright, twinkling, unobstructed, calling them down the trail.

"I'd feel a hell of a lot better if I knew what that thing was," Kimon said.

"Or where it was leading us." Tras hugged his cloak tighter.

Frost kept her silence. There was nothing to gain by conjecture. She had her suspicions about the creature who was guiding them, but Tras Sur'tian, like most Korkyrans, dreaded the supernatural. She didn't know Kimon well enough yet to judge his reactions.

But this she knew. The thing in the fireball was not human, nor wizard, witch, or sorcerer. Its power was far too great. She had dealt with gods before and learned that even gods had gods to worship and be manipulated by, hierarchy on hierarchy. Perhaps this being was a god. She couldn't be sure. But its motives were unguessable.

It claimed it could lead her to Aki. That was enough to make her follow, but not trust. There would come a time later, she felt sure, when it would exact a price.

Her backside began to ache from too much riding. She leaned back on Ashur's rump, tried to stretch. "Tras, how far do you think we've come?"

His saddle creaked as he shifted his weight. "I don't know," he admitted. "In this cursed dark the wood seems to go on and on without end. I thought surely we'd be through by now."

She caught her breath as something draped over her face, a spider's web suspended from a low-hanging branch. Frantically she wiped the sticky, clinging strands away, cursing and fuming, shivering, praying the thing wasn't occupied. Even after she was sure the silken threads were gone, she continued to rub at her face. Damn! but she could still feel it on her skin. She knew it was imagination, but that didn't quell the sensation, and every now and then she swatted her neck, half-certain she'd felt something crawling there.

"It's gone!"

Startled by Kimon's shout, she twisted around, missed seeing another low limb across the road. It smacked her in the face, evoking a string of profanities. "What's—"

Then she saw.

There was no sign of the green star. It had vanished from the sky. The other stars winked down at her, mysterious, icy cool in their velvet setting.

They stopped again. "What does it mean?" Kimon asked.

She bit her lip. "It promised to lead us to Aki," she told him. She peered into the darkness on either side of the road. "I don't see her here. We ride on."

"Maybe it'll come back," Tras Sur'tian suggested.

She moved down the trail. Desire to be clear of Kellwood was strong within her. The trees seemed to press in on her like the walls of a too small room. Her nostrils were full of a damp odor, her ears with the grating sounds of unseen creatures and rustling leaves. The hackles rose on her neck, and she wished for the clean light of day.

"Maybe we should wait," Tras Sur'tian insisted, "to see if it returns."

"Wait if you want," she said, "but the road's plainly marked. I'm riding on. I'll meet you at the end of it."

Both men came after her.

"Are you all right?" Kimon inquired, directing his mount abreast of hers.

She forced a smile, but it quickly vanished. "I've never been afraid of a forest before," she answered. "Gods know we grow them bigger in Esgaria. But this place gives me gooseflesh."

He peered around and agreed. "I know what you mean."

But she did wonder about the green star's absence.

They'd followed a crooked road; taken more time than they had anticipated. Had the star tried to lead them a shorter course and at last given up? Or had they arrived where it planned to lead them? Answers, she needed answers. All she had was wind and cricket songs.

At last, the forest began to thin. Old trees gave way to younger ones, and they gave way to saplings and brush. When they were free of Kellwood and it was no more than a vast shadow behind them, they halted. Frost breathed a deep sigh of relief.

"Better?" Kimon asked.

She could see his grin. "Much," she answered honestly.

Tras Sur'tian climbed wearily out of the saddle. "The horses could use a walk," he pronounced, wrapping his reins around a gloved hand. The others dismounted, too. Ashur, of course, needed no rest, but her legs were stiff and sore; stretching would do them good.

She peered ahead, squinting to penetrate the night's gloom. The plain extended far, broad and featureless. Only a few twinkling stars revealed where the horizon ended and the sky began.

"We could make camp now," Tras Sur'tian suggested. "The moon is down; dawn's only a few hours away."

Kimon surveyed the heavens. "I wonder where it goes?"

Frost also wondered about the green star. It had promised to lead them to Aki, but it seemed they were on their own now. "I'm not as curious about *where* as *why*," she said. "It's supposed to stay visible until sunrise." She followed his gaze skyward, shrugged, and kept walking until the long, monotonous strides began to work a merciful magic, draining her mind of all thought or care.

Kimon called suddenly. "Look!"

A new light climbed rapidly from the horizon, a bright red star, splendid and mysterious as the emerald star. It sailed in a great arc, hesitated, descended.

"It's coming straight at us!" Tras Sur'tian shouted. His mount began to panic. He caught his reins tightly in both hands as the beast reared, stamped earth, whinnied pitifully. Kimon's horse behaved just as wildly. Even Ashur

began to snort and tear at the ground. The flames that
met his eyes raged, flashed, crackled with energy.

A crimson glow suffused the land. Frost whipped out
her sword, denying the fear that gnawed at her gut. Kimon
and Tras Sur'tian let go their reins, freeing their mounts,
drew their weapons, too. Gone were the shadows of night;
the earth blazed the color of shimmering effulgent blood.
She grit her teeth, braced herself as she stared into the
thing's burning core. A memory triggered. She grabbed
for the strings of her purse.

A white flash tinged scarlet lanced from the fireball,
blinding her. The screams of her comrades filled her ears,
mercifully brief. She heard them fall. She alone remained
to fight, but barely. One knee gave way, and she collapsed. The sword fell from her grip. Her other hand was
thrust halfway into her small leather purse.

Her fingers just brushed Oona's jewel.

Another flash stabbed her; she cried out in agony. Nee-
dles seemed to prick every part of her flesh. Her bones
smoldered with some strange, inner fire. Yet it did not
consume her. Her dazzled vision began to clear. The sky
was one huge fireball of sizzling radiance. She sensed its
conscious, malignant force, all directed at her. If she could
not make her fingers move, that force would smash her
down.

She pushed her hand deeper inside her purse. So many
coins! She closed her fist on the contents and jerked it out.
Bits of gold and silver scattered, but she had the jewel!

Her hand began to shine with its own crimson light. The
bones and veins within the flesh showed plainly through.
For a fearful moment she thought it the work of the
fireball, but there was no pain, no fire in her body.

Another flash speared toward her. She raised her hand
instinctively to ward it off. To her great surprise, the beam
shattered, splintered, dissipated before it touched her. The
fireball attacked again, then a third time, with the same
results.

She held her fist like a shield before her. "Begone!"
she commanded, and her throat went raw with the force of

her shout. "Back to hell, and leave us alone!" She looked around for her friends. They lay side by side, appeared dead, though she prayed not. Keeping her fist between herself and the fireball, she crawled to them. Kimon was physically the slighter of the two. She grabbed his arm with her free hand, dragged him closer to Tras Sur'tian. Their faces were twisted with pain; eyes open, they stared at some terror beyond this life. She threw herself across them, raised her fist higher. "Gods take you straight to damnation!" she screamed. "Begone!"

Slowly, the fireball climbed higher in the sky, paused, hovered uncertainly, then sped off the direction it had come, discharging a final, ineffectual bolt. She watched, on guard, until it disappeared from sight.

The crimson umbra that surrounded her fist paled, faded.

She bent over Kimon. The night was once again a pattern of blacks and grays, but she could see his ghastly face. She tried to close his eyes, but the lids would not budge. His flesh was cold, unnaturally rigid. Tras Sur'tian was the same. Never again would the Korkyran greet his beloved little queen, unless it was in the netherworld.

She wrapped her arms around Kimon's still form, hugged him to her, suddenly filled with a vast emptiness. Alone again, after such brief, sweet closeness. *Sing to me,* she urged, running a finger over his icy lips. *I need to hear you sing.* But there was no music, no merriment dancing in his eyes, just terror. *Hold me,* she begged, *please hold me.* But his arms were still, stiff.

She stretched out beside him, put her lips on his. Hot tears scalded her cheeks, fell streaming onto Kimon's marble face. *Don't cry,* she told herself, *never cry.* But her grief would not be checked.

Then, Kimon's lip twitched. She blinked, disbelieving. His flesh was still cold, glassy eyes still stared blankly. Yet his lips twitched again; the tip of his tongue protruded slightly and collected one of her tears. A hand gripped her thigh. He saw her, then, and a weak, confused smile blossomed where a mask of fear had been.

She trembled and jumped away from him. Kimon was

dead, she knew it. What could this thing in Kimon's body be but some demon come to renew the attack? Yet it didn't threaten, just lay there, too feeble to rise. But the eyes followed her. Did she know those eyes?

"Kimon?"

He nodded, too weak to form words. She knelt quickly beside him, felt his face. The cold ebbed from his skin. She lifted his head from the dirt, kissed his eyes, hugged his head to her breast, and gave fervent thanks to all her gods.

She remembered Tras Sur'tian. The old Korkyran was unmoving, silent. What was different? Kimon lived and Tras was dead. Why? The gods owed her no favors. She thought back over all she had done.

Kimon's lips had moved first, lips moistened by her tears. His tongue had sought out the salty fluid. Could that be the cure? Magic killed her friends, but she knew of no special power in human tears to counter potent sorcery.

Still, there was no time to question. She was no longer crying; Kimon's resurrection had startled the grief from her. She touched her cheeks gingerly. They were still damp. She gathered moisture on her fingertips, pressed them to Tras Sur'tian's lips.

Moments dragged by; she feared she'd guessed wrong. She lifted Kimon, cradled him in her lap. He seemed drained of all strength. Rocking him, childlike, she watched her other friend, prayed, and waited.

Ashur plodded softly to her side; the other mounts were nowhere to be seen. She spied her sword, leaned over to claim it. Though it had been of little use against the fireball, she laid it protectively on Kimon's chest.

Tras Sur'tian gave no warning when he awoke, just turned his head, met her gaze. He said nothing. Like Kimon, he seemed drained of strength. She shifted position so she could hold both men, wishing she could pour her own strength into them.

She sat with them like that all through the night. When dawn trickled over the horizon they began to speak a little, as if the sun gave them the vitality she could not. As the light grew stronger so did they. By the time the sun cleared the distant low hills they were able to stand on shaky legs.

Frost embraced Kimon tenderly, laid her head on his shoulder, closed her eyes. The empty feeling was gone with his arms tight around her. Tears threatened, but she held them back. This was a happy time, not a time for crying.

"I think I was dead," he whispered strangely. "I was dead. I don't understand." He gazed into her eyes, seeking answers.

"Never mind," she urged him with gentleness. "Don't think about it." She extracted herself from the embrace and went to Tras Sur'tian, touched his sleeve. "Tras, are you all right?"

He pulled away, found his sword on the grass, sheathed it. Suddenly, he shivered all over. "I don't . . . I can't . . ." He hid his face in his hands. "I was : . . in hell!"

She wrapped her arms around him. "It's all right," she assured him. "You don't have to talk about it."

"But I want to!" Kimon exclaimed. His face was a twisted mask of confusion and fear. "I was dead, but I'm alive!"

She cut him off with a gesture. "No!" she insisted. "Say no more! It may all have been some magical illusion. Tras doesn't want to talk about it, and I don't, either. If it wasn't an illusion, if it was really hell you saw, then keep the vision to yourself. No man needs a description before his time. We'll all see it soon enough."

Tras Sur'tian shrugged free when she tried to grip his hand. She could read the disturbance in his soul. His One Korkyran God preached of no hell, but of a paradise for all good men, oblivion for all others. His faith was deeply shaken. "I'll try to find the horses," he said. "That beast of yours didn't run off." He indicated Ashur. "Wish ours were as steadfast."

Kimon laid hands on her shoulders as the old captain trudged away. She sank back against him, glad for his warmth. "Sorry I snapped at you," she murmured. He nuzzled her ear, his breath soft on her neck. She gazed at the far horizon, at the blue morning sky, at the huge golden fireball that was the sun.

She stiffened.

They didn't know where to find Onokratos. *But Onokratos had found them.* It couldn't have been the wizard himself who attacked them; she wouldn't believe a mortal could possess such power. One of his agents, then, a powerful demon at his command. It boded ill for them if he could conjure such a creature.

"What's this?" Kimon's fingers curled around her right fist and lifted it. She'd clung to the jewel all night until it seemed a part of her hand and she'd forgotten it. She opened her fingers and showed him the stone. "Oona's parting gift," he said, recognizing it. "She said it would protect you." His face darkened. "I was dead. I don't understand."

She drew a breath and bit her lip. She didn't understand, either. She'd been a witch once. She'd had experience with the arcane. Yet this brush had shaken her badly, more than she wanted to admit.

"You don't have to continue." Her own voice sounded distant, alien. "Aki isn't your responsibility."

His hand tangled in her hair, pulled her head back. His lips came down on hers. When the kiss ended, he held her out to arm's length, looked her over with mock seriousness, drew her close again. "I can't desert you, Samidar. I love you."

She laid her head against the hollow of his shoulder, a place that was becoming familiar, comfortable. She knew she should answer, but she couldn't speak. Her mouth wouldn't form words. She hugged him instead, letting her body answer. Maybe he would know without saying.

"Frost!"

She pushed free of Kimon. She'd not even heard Tras Sur'tian's approach. "What is that creature of yours?" He ignored their embarrassment and pointed to the unicorn. Ashur followed behind him, leading the missing horses. "I couldn't find hide nor hair of those worthless fleabags. Then he came along herding them like a four-legged shepherd!''

Ashur whinnied a high, unnatural note.

She couldn't help but smile. Even the unicorn's cry sounded natural to her friends. ''He's special,'' she said proudly. She brushed back a few strands of hair from her face, righted the circlet that held it all back. The longer locks had come loose from the thong she'd once tied it all back with. ''This place has lost its charm,'' she decided with a last glance around. ''Let's get out of here.''

They didn't ride far. Noon found them on a high, barren ridge. The green grasses had turned brown and scraggly. Once dark, spongy earth took on a sandy texture. A few withered trees grew stark, leafless, bent, and knotty on either side of the rutted road they followed.

Far below sprawled an ancient manor estate. The fields lay fallow, untended, dotted here and there with ramshackle sheds once used for the storage of grains. The roofs had fallen; the walls were worm-rotted. Surrounded by its fields was the manor house, bleak and gray-toned, squat with two stories and wings that wandered designless, without apparent planning.

Frost started Ashur down the long slope, alert for signs of life about the old place. Kimon and Tras Sur'tian rode to either side, guiding their mounts carefully down the eroded terrain. Tras clutched nervously at the hilt of his sword. His gaze swept all around.

They passed the ruins of a log fence hidden in the high, dusty grass. The rails were rotted and fell off rusted nails as they rode by, causing them to stop, their hearts to quicken, until they were sure it was only a rotten log that had startled them. The road led up through the fields straight to the manor's main gate. A wall of smooth, unmortared stones surrounded the manor. Moss and lichen dripped from cracks, and bees buzzed around the wider fissures where they had made their homes. The gates hung open on rusted hinges, oaken surfaces split and pitted from time and weather.

They rode through, stopped. Frost dismounted.

"Looks deserted to me," Tras Sur'tian said, sounding more hopeful than sure.

She didn't answer. Something about the place, perhaps its age, weighed on her, demanded silence. She crept forward. *Crept,* so that her footsteps would not crunch too loudly on the graveled way. The green star had shown them the road, she told herself, and the road led here to this very door. She couldn't banish that thought. Yet there was no sign of life, no indication that anyone had lived here for years.

The main doors were tall, wooden, intricately carved and once beautifully painted. A few flakes were all that remained of the paint. She reached for the knocker, a tarnished brass bull's head with a heavy ring through its nose. She hesitated, looked back to her companions. Kimon remained by the gate. Tras Sur'tian rode up to a shuttered window, tried to peer in through the cracks.

She lifted the knocker, slammed it once, twice. The sound reverberated hollowly. She waited, knocked again. Was that a scuffle she heard so swift and faint? Rats, maybe. A place like this, abandoned, surrounded by old fields, would be infested with the rodents. She gripped the brass ring with both hands and strained. The doors gave reluctantly outward.

A shriek ripped from the darkness within. A shadow flew out, struck her in the middle, bore her down to the earth. Claws raked at her eyes, and she threw up an arm to defend her sight. Multiple blows pummeled her face and body. Her flesh tore, began to bleed. Frost rolled frantically, but the thing clung to her, biting, scratching, pulling her hair until a scream bubbled in her own throat.

Suddenly the blows stopped; she was free of the creature, though its wails still echoed in her ears. Kimon bent over her worriedly, using the edge of his cloak to dab blood from an oozing cut on her cheek. She sat up painfully, dazed, angry, heart racing. Her clothing had protected her from the worst of the scratches, but her bones and muscles ached from a terrific beating.

The air tingled with a new series of screams, a hissing

and snarling of savage intensity. For the first time, she got
a look at her attacker.

"A girl-child!"

Tras Sur'tian sat on her chest. A pair of small, dirty
knees drummed furiously on his spine to no avail. She
cursed the Korkyran, showered him with spittle while he
pinned her tiny hands in one of his big fists. The child was
completely naked. Small, nascent breasts jutted from her
chest. Her face was nearly hidden in a tangled mat of
black hair.

"A hell-cat if there ever was one!" Tras Sur'tian snapped.
A pair of dark, fathomless eyes glared at him through that
wild mane. Once again, she spat in his face. This time his
free hand drew back, dealt her a vicious, stinging slap. It
only made her shriek louder, struggle harder. "Crazy little
animal!"

"She's only a child," Frost reminded him. "Don't hurt
her!"

"Then you sit on her," Tras barked. "She nearly ripped
my throat out before I got her off you."

"I said don't hurt her." Frost knelt slowly, tried to
stroke the girl's sweaty brow. The child seemed to calm
for a moment, then her eyes rolled up and gleamed with
atavistic fury. Frost snatched her hand back barely in time
to avoid flashing teeth. "She's about Aki's age," she
observed. "Cleaned up, she'd make a pretty child."

"What made her this way?" Tras Sur'tian asked through
gritted teeth.

"What are we going to do with her?" Kimon asked.

A voice boomed behind them. "You'll do nothing with
her! Get off my daughter, oaf!"

Frost whirled, her sword coming half-free in the sheath.
The exposed steel glinted in the sunlight. Equally swift,
Kimon whipped out the dirk he wore on his belt. Yet
before either could do or say more, there came a grunt and
a sharp curse. Tras Sur'tian, by reaching for his own
weapon, had relaxed his grip on his young captive's hands.
She struck him uncomfortably close to the groin, twisted,
unseated him, leaped up, and ran a short distance. She

turned. A low, bitter howling rose from her lips, a keening
that chilled mortal bones. Then she fled into the tall grassy
fields and disappeared.

"Stop her!" cried the old man who had appeared in the
doorway. "Kalynda! Come back!" It was too late. The
girl was gone.

Frost let her sword fall back into the sheath. Clearly,
such an old man posed no threat. His face, what could be
seen of it through the grizzled white beard, contorted with
grief and torment as he stared over the fields for some sign
of his daughter. His eyes misted; he wrung his hands.

"Who are you, sir?" she asked. "Lord of this place?"
She phrased it politely in deference to his age and because
she shared some small part of his concern for the vanished
child, so ragged, so disturbed.

She regarded him critically. His garments were only a
little better than his child's. If he were indeed lord of the
manor, then he had declined to a miserable state. She
repeated her question.

Grief changed to fury. His eyes shone, mouth twisted in
wordless cursing. Clenched fists raised as if he intended to
strike her. "This is your fault!" he exploded, finally
finding his voice. "She's gone, and you're to blame!"
With surprising speed he lunged; hands locked on her
throat, began to squeeze.

She gasped and jabbed him in the gut with her fist. He
gave a *whuff* but clung with all his anger-driven strength.
Yet his grip had loosened. She swung her arm up in a wide
arc, breaking his hold, shoved him backward. Tras Sur'tian
caught him in a massive hug, pinning his arms, lifting him
off the ground.

She rubbed her throat. "Don't hurt him, Tras," she
croaked. "He's an old man."

Kimon waved his dirk suggestively. "And if he wants
to get older, he'll mind his manners."

The old man ceased his struggles. A deadly intensity
replaced the manic rage in his mouthings. "You've let
Kalynda get free. My daughter may harm herself." His

eyes pinched shut tightly, then snapped open. "Why didn't you just leave us alone! I didn't want to hurt any of you!"

Tras Sur'tian gave his captive a shake that was only half-playful. "I wouldn't worry about hurting us if I were in your place."

But something about his expression, his tone, the sudden calm he exuded, sent a warning shiver creeping up Frost's spine. "Tras . . ."

"You're as crazy as your hell-cat daughter," the Korkyran added, and gave the old man another shake.

"I really didn't want to hurt you!" he repeated. "But I have to find my daughter. I can't let you delay me." His eyes rolled up inside his head; the lids closed. His body went tense until the frail muscles and veins bulged along his neck and bare arms. Lips curled back, revealing teeth.

"What in all the hells—" Kimon started.

"Tras, let him go," Frost ordered.

The old man's eyes popped open suddenly; his mouth opened. He screamed one word. "Gel!"

A wind exploded from the bowels of the manor, blasting the wooden door off its hinges. A sharp edge struck Tras Sur'tian on the head. He groaned, released his prisoner, fell like a puppet whose strings had been severed.

Gale force buffeted them. Frost fought to hold her ground, but it pushed her back. Kimon cried out. She saw him blown backward. He tumbled head over heels, arms and legs flopping. Tras Sur'tian followed him, unconscious, rolling. Her garments made angry, whipping sounds; they threatened to rip free of her body. Dust and grass, small stones rose up, pelted her with stinging fury. She shielded her eyes with an upraised arm, but pieces of wind-borne matter smashed her, drawing blood where they found unprotected flesh. She stumbled back, giving ground, and with that first retreating step, when for one instant all her weight balanced on one foot, the wind snatched her up and over. Lights burst in her head as she hit the earth; air rushed from her lungs. The wind tossed her, tumbled her along the ground. She clawed for handfuls of grass to stop herself, and the grass tore away.

At the gate's threshold her ordeal ended. She ached all over as if she'd been beaten. Someone pulled on her arm; a voice shouted insistently in her ear.

"Get up!" the voice said. "It isn't over yet. Get up!" It was Kimon, but what was he saying? The ringing in her ears was much too loud. Why was he tugging on her arm when it hurt so much? If only her vision would clear.

Suddenly, the ringing in her ears was replaced with a roaring louder than anything she'd ever heard, drowning all other sound. She felt a deep vibration in her very bones, knew that if she didn't rise, she might never get up again. She struggled to her knees. Kimon locked his arms around her, dragged her to her feet. She nearly fell; he caught her and held on. His lips moved, but she heard nothing over the rushing tempest. Her eyes began to focus. Except for Kimon and Tras Sur'tian at their feet, the world was a rapidly diminishing blur.

They stood at the calm center of a vast maelstrom. Rocks, dust, and chaff from the fields flew tightening circles around them at dizzying speed. Beyond the vortex, she could barely see the outline of the manor house. The old man stood by the door. Another shadowy figure stood beside him.

She knew him now.

Her lips formed the name, but she couldn't seem to speak or, indeed, make any sound. Her lungs burned. She drew a deep breath, but no air rushed in to ease the fire in her chest. *I can't breathe,* she realized. She fought a cloying panic and tried to warn Kimon. It was clear he already knew. They stared, gasping, clinging to each other.

The rich color of his eyes was the last thing she saw before she passed out. *Blue,* she noted with a strange serenity, *blue like the old man's eyes.*

Chapter Nine

When she woke her first sensations were all of pain. She hurt all over. Something rough and hard pressed against her back, her hips, her head. The odor of incense was smothering, the light so dim she could barely see. She shut her eyes and a yawning blackness sucked her down.

A noise brought her back to consciousness. She opened her eyes and found the light a little brighter, not much. She blinked, waited for her sight to focus. Someone else was in the room. The floor creaked under slippered feet. Something rattled, bottles, perhaps. The light flickered. She heard a hiss; the smell of incense thickened.

Surreptitiously, she moved a hand. Her sword belt was gone. The hand moved again, and she froze. Demonfang was gone! She bit her lip, forced herself to remain still, though every nerve in her body screamed to get up and search for the dagger.

The room was suddenly quiet again. She had that peculiar feeling of eyes upon her. She held her breath, waited for those eyes to turn away. Some instinct, though, told her they did not, would not. At last, she let out her breath and sat slowly, painfully up.

A red-glowing brazier burned charcoal and incense, casting black-and-crimson shadows around the room. She could make out a few pieces of furniture, some shelves. In a far corner a dark figure hunched over a table, peered at her, shielding the small flame of a candle with his hand. The wavering fire cast strange lightplay on his features as he leaned over it.

"Onokratos?"

He nodded somberly and pushed back the book he had been reading. "I was afraid the light might wake you," he said. "I'm glad you were not hurt too much."

Her aches and bruises were mute contradiction. *On the other hand,* she reflected, *I'm alive.* "You're not exactly what I expected," she admitted, swinging her legs over the edge of a bare wooden bed frame.

"You're just as I remember you," he said with the faintest of smiles, "that first time I saw you in the reception hall at the palace. You played your part well for Thogrin Sin'tell. I saw his murder in a dream. Did you kill him?"

"Did you kill Aki for him?"

He ignored her question. "It must have been you. You certainly had a motive, and you knew the palace well enough to slip by the guards undetected." He scratched his chin and nodded. "I sensed that moment when I saw you that you were unusually resourceful, someone to be reckoned with. I read that in your aura." He reached out, marked a page, closed his book. "And I've not been proven wrong. That's good."

That caught her off-guard. She didn't expect compliments from enemies. She got to her feet, but a muscle in her thigh twinged, and she leaned on the bed frame for support. "Good?" she said. "Yes, I killed Thogrin, and you know damn well that I came to kill you, at the very least to beat some answers out of your treacherous hide."

He waved a nonchalant hand. "Thogrin Sin'tell was no friend of mine. I owe him no grief and seek no revenge. I used him because, at the time, there was no other person who could fill my need."

This is not a harmless old man, she reminded herself. He had a certain disarming charm that made it easy for her to relax with him. But he was a wizard of considerable power. She had experienced that power and fallen. Now, she faced him weaponless.

"Where are my comrades?"

"Safe and well," he assured her. "The old soldier took quite a bump on the head, I'm afraid, and he's still sleeping. The other one awoke some time ago and is taking food at this moment. He eats like a horse, you know."

She bit her lip again. It was not a good sign that Tras Sur'tian was still unconscious. She wasn't sure how much time had passed since their quick defeat in the manor yard, but she sensed it was considerable. It was daylight then. If it was still daytime, Onokratos would be reading near an unshuttered window, not by candlelight. Tras Sur'tian was tough in a fight, but age took an invisible toll. Could that bump be anything serious?

"I'd like to see them."

"Let's talk about my daughter, first." He went to a shelf, gathered a bundle of new candles, dipped their virgin wicks in the flame of the lighted one. He placed them variously around the room. "Better to see each other's eyes and know when truth is spoken," he said, fixing the last candle in a pool of its own dripping.

"Kalynda," she said, recalling his daughter's name. She was glad for the extra light. It made the chamber less eerie, drove away most of the shadows and the crimson glow that reminded her so of tales of the ninth hell. She looked around, saw that many of the shelves contained books and jars of powders. The bed frame on which she leaned was lavishly carved but without a mattress. She knew some mystics disdained unnecessary comfort and surmised Onokratos was such. She returned her attention to her host. "Did you find the child?"

The old man nodded. "She's safe again," he acknowledged. "I refuse to lock her up. Despite appearances, she's not an animal. I give her the run of the house and use special enchantments to seal doors and windows against her opening them. You broke those seals when you opened the main door."

She shrugged. "Sorry." She wasn't, terribly.

"My oversight," he admitted. "But no matter, Gel found her."

That word, she'd heard it before, thought it part of a spell or a word of power. Apparently, it was a name. "Who's Gel?"

Onokratos laid a hand on the book he'd been reading. "You'll meet him," he said, "tomorrow."

She pursed her lips. He'd answered with a bit too much mystery for her comfort. "But your daughter is well?"

With so many candles it was easy to read his expression. Pain flickered over his face, eyes gleamed with sudden wetness, shoulders sagged as if a great weight had fallen on them. His hands disappeared up voluminous sleeves, and he hugged himself.

"No, she's not well," he answered. "And I don't know how to make her well, not with all my power." He looked up at her, drew a breath, and straightened, regaining some composure. "You came looking for the child-queen." He beckoned. "I'll take you to her now."

He took up two of the candles and passed her one. Then he opened the door, led the way into a dark corridor. She could see sconces on the walls, but no torches or oil lamps burned in them. The hall was dusty and smelled of mildew. They passed other doors, but it was clear from the dust and cobwebs on their thresholds they hadn't been opened in a very long time.

They turned down another unlighted corridor. Conditions appeared no better. The manor seemed as ruinous inside as out. A long web draped from the ceiling; Frost's candle illuminated its plump occupant. Onokratos saw it, too. Bending quickly, he snatched off a thin felt slipper and smashed the spider against the wall. With a wild hand he destroyed its home, leaving not a strand. Then, staring hatefully at the pulped remains of the arachnid, he mouthed a torrent of blasphemous curses.

Frost watched it all in stunned silence and shuddered.

They came to a stairway. She had not considered where in the two-level manor she might be, upper floor or main. She lifted her light higher, followed her unpredictable guide. His candle cast an amber glow against the darkness, but she could not see the stair's bottom. She took the first step, grabbing the banister to feel her way, then snatching back her hand. The rail was covered with a pale, chalky powder, ancient dust. She brushed her palm on her tunic and swallowed.

Down they went, with no end in sight. It had not occurred to Frost that the manor might have levels hidden below the earth, but certainly that was the case. The way wound down and down. The air grew chill, moldy. Onokratos led, head bowed. She saw only his back and the hand with which he clutched his candle. Could it still be a man hunched so in that heavy robe? She felt for her sword's hilt and remembered it was not there.

"Old man?"

Only an echo answered, no other sound. They descended lower, deeper into the earth, the stairs winding tight, ever around and around. *It's like a tower,* she thought to herself, *built in the wrong direction, down instead of up.*

A low growl rose out of the ebon depths, freezing the blood in her veins. She stopped. It came again, a snarling that sent shivers racing up her spine. She peered over the edge of the stairs into an abyss, a blackness that her small candle failed to penetrate. She looked back the way she had come, darkness that way, too. Onokratos did not stop; the gap between his light and hers widened. She hurried to close it up.

The growling continued with intermittent pauses. Then came a shriek so loud, so soul-shriveling, she nearly dropped her candle. Hot wax splattered on her hand, it trembled so. For one terrifying moment she feared someone had unleashed Demonfang. But the sound degenerated once more into a series of low, animal snarls. A fine sweat broke out on her forehead and palms. She wiped her hands.

"I thought you were leading me to Aki," she said. The passage flung back her words. She waited for the echo to subside. "You said you were taking me to Aki," she repeated. But Onokratos kept his silence, and only the sounds of whatever lived below answered her.

An odor of filth and stale urine wafted in the air. It grew stronger with each step until she wrinkled her nose against it. Then the stairs ended. They walked a short distance down a narrow passage and stopped. The light from Onokratos's candle fell on a lonely door.

From behind that door issued the growls and a bestial scratching. The terrible stench had become a foul, pungent taste in her throat. She studied the old man's face, wary of a trap. She had seen such doors as this, with their shuttered portals, in prisons and dungeons. A hot anger began to blossom in her heart.

"Is this where you're keeping a child?" she accused icily. "In a fetid cell?"

He returned her stare impassively, reached up, seized a small wooden peg on the peephole's shutter, and slid it open. He beckoned for her to look inside.

She cried out and staggered back. "Oh, gods!" she moaned, and sagged against a wall for support. "You beast, you devil!" She shut her eyes, but the vision remained to sting her eyes. With an effort of will she forced herself to look a second time through the portal.

It was Aki, barely recognizable, but certainly the child. Her once lustrous hair was a black mass, tangled and wild. She was naked, her flesh smeared with her own excrement. Her eyes, once so full of mirth, gleamed ferinely in the light of Frost's upraised candle. Her small fingers were cut and bleeding from scraping at the walls and floor. In one hand she clutched the half-chewed carcass of a rat. She peered at her guardian from a corner of the cell, then, lips curled back over teeth, she howled. When the echo faded, she pressed the rat's flesh to her mouth and bit deeply. Blood dribbled on her chin.

Frost whirled away, seized Onokratos by his robe, slammed him against the cell door. "Devil!" she screamed. The back of her hand crashed into his head, sending him in a heap to the floor. "What have you done?" She bore down on him, fist ready to strike.

The old man rolled over, pointed one ringed finger. "Stop," he whispered.

She loomed over him, wanting with all her heart and soul to smash him, to pound him into the stone, to sink her fingers in his soft throat, to rip out his black heart and squeeze it in her hands until it beat no more. But she had seen his power, knew what he could do. It would not help Aki to get blasted to ashes. She had to wait, bide her time, then find a way to help the child.

Onokratos got his feet shakily under him. "She's no better or worse off than my daughter," he said. "Only I can't let this one run free in my house. They would fight like the animals they've become."

Frost struggled to quell her temper. "Why not lock them both up?"

He sneered, a startling change from his usual passivity. "Kalynda is my child, my flesh and blood," he said. "Should I lock her up in her own home, or this one"—he jerked a thumb at the cell door—"who is nothing to me, nothing but a pawn?"

She almost hit him again. Such callousness toward any child filled her with loathing. Later, she would make this man pay dearly for his cruelty. Now, she bit her lip, kept her tongue under tight check.

Abruptly, he turned and led the long way back up the stairs. The stench was left behind; the animal noises faded. Her heart cried out not to leave the young queen, but reason told her there was little she could do without consideration. She had already encountered Kalynda; Aki seemed every bit as savage, as feral.

"Isn't there some danger that your daughter will attack us if she's free to roam the manor?"

The old man shook his head. "I am protected," he answered. "But because you and your friends are my guests, I've confined her activities to the western wing of the manor. She won't hurt you."

Rather, I was concerned with hurting her, Frost thought. *Aki is my charge. Your daughter means no more to me.*

Finally, they arrived back at the room where she had awakened. Onokratos extinguished the stubs of their candles. The other candles still burned, but the rich light did nothing to drive the chill from her bones. That would take much time, she figured, as long as her mind retained an image of Aki gnawing that rat.

She strode to the bare bed frame but was too agitated to sit or lie down. She paced back and forth, arms folded, head lowered as she thought. Onokratos watched, sitting on the edge of his table. She could feel his eyes upon her. On his lap he cradled the book he had been reading earlier.

"What happened?" she demanded when it was clear he would offer no explanation.

"Kalynda was playing and fell—"

Frost waved a hand impatiently. "I mean, what happened to Aki? Your daughter's problems are not mine."

He set the book aside, regarded her evenly. "One story requires the telling of the other."

She glowered, then drew a deep breath, forced herself to sit on the old bed frame. When she was as comfortable as she thought herself likely to become, she nodded and waited for him to continue.

"We are not Korkyrans, Kalynda and I."

Frost sighed. The old man was determined to weave a tale when she only wanted facts. She knew by his accent he was not of Tras Sur'tian's people.

"Keled-Zaram is our home, far to the east."

"I know the land," she informed him, hoping it would speed him up.

"When Kalynda's mother died I could no longer bear to live there. Every tree, every hill reminded me of her. The birds and smallest squirrels reminded me of her. I saw her face in every cloud. So, I sold my small business, took my daughter, and began to wander. Kalynda had seemed like a miracle to me, born in the lateness of my years and of her mother's. We had been childless through our long years and long since resigned ourselves to barrenness until her birth. She was our gift from the gods." His eyes misted over and took on a faraway look. "At length, our grief lessened and the desire to see new lands left us. We found this old manor abandoned, but thought we might once again breathe life into its fallow fields with only a little honest sweat. We had been here less than the lifespan of one moon when Kalynda—'' Onokratos choked suddenly, unable to get his words out. His whole body sagged. He swallowed hard. Two tears rolled thickly down his face. ''She was playing in the fields. There was an old well we knew nothing of, and she fell in.''

Frost shook her head, confused. ''Was it some injury to her head that made her mad?''

''A moment,'' he begged, holding up a hand to end her questions. ''This is very hard for a father.''

She regarded him with considerable frustration. She had come to confront an evil man, another Thogrin Sin'tell, when she'd begun her quest for Aki's captor. She thought she had found him in the heartless creature who had dispassionately caused her charge's fearful condition.

And yet this man's pain was real, his concern for his daughter genuine. Men did strange things, she knew, for love of family. Was her own history not tainted with that fact? Suddenly, she wanted very much to hear all the story.

''It was not such a deep well,'' he began slowly, ''and there was no water. The fall did not hurt her, but . . .'' He shook all over and clutched himself as if to still his quivering flesh. ''There were spiders, so many fat, blood-sucking, chaos-spawned spiders!''

A cold hand gripped her heart, and she remembered the old man's unsettling, violent reaction to the unlucky web dweller her light had chanced to fall upon in the corridor. She had no love for the horrid things, either. As a small child they had terrified her; as an adult she had learned to live with that fear. Still, the fear remained, lurking in some shadowed corner of her mind.

Onokratos's face streamed wetly, though he wiped a sleeve over his eyes. ''They stung her, not once, but many times, until she was swollen and paralyzed with their poison.'' He sobbed like a lost child; great shudders racked his aged frame. ''She screamed, but the well was far from the manor, and my joints are old. By the time I got to her there was little I could do.''

Frost caught her breath. "Are you saying the poison drove her mad?"

His head snapped up. His face contorted with rage and contempt. "Ignorant Esgarian whore! I'm trying to tell you she died! She died!"

Frost leaped up, crossed the room in three strides, seized the front of his robe. A finger's breadth separated their noses as she shouted at him. "She lives, you shriveled old vulture! I've seen her myself. Look where I bear her scratches!" She stabbed a finger at the wound on her cheek. It was scabbed, still sore. "What game are you playing with me that requires such lies?"

He knocked her arms away and rose, stumbling back. "She died, I tell you! But I prayed to Gath, chaos master and lord of spiders, to give her back to me. I prayed to that monster for the soul of my beloved, dearest Kalynda!"

She froze even as she reached for him. "The spider god?" She would not believe that anyone, no matter how desperate, would dare invoke that forbidden deity. What utter, terrible foolishness! Gath was chaos itself, and all the universe was no more than a fly in his subtle web. Not even the other gods, though their strength be his equal, held converse with him.

"For Kalynda, yes!" His fist smashed down on the wooden table as he worked his way around it, putting it between them. "I dared even that to gain her back!" Then his anger deserted him; his gaze sought hers. "But that treacherous god betrayed me," he confessed in bleak despair.

Her rage had not subsided. It boiled within her. "What did you expect? That such a power would deal fairly with you?"

He turned his back to her, unable to meet her accusing gaze. "I bargained with him, expecting to see my Kalynda play and laugh and sing again, to see her happy, to hold her in my arms as she slept, to hear her sweet voice, to have her bring me flowers still kissed with morning dew as she used to." Tears came again unbidden, dripped to the table, splashed on the book.

"And Gath answered your prayer," she urged him, when he didn't continue. "But not as you expected."

He shook his head. "Not immediately," he answered. "First, there was a price."

He told her of a dream that came the night Kalynda died. The chaos lord, night's master, the thousand-named, dark and awesome in his terrible beauty, spoke, and his voice was the voice of the earth and air, a rumble and a whisper all at once. The ransom of Kalynda's life was a small price: one pure and uncorrupted soul to take his daughter's place, not in the land of the dead, but in the abyss of chaos that was Gath's realm. When such a soul was offered, Kalynda might again walk the earth at her father's side. So promised the voice of the spider god. Then the dream melted into the common nightmares of mortal sleep.

"But it was a true vision," he insisted, "a visitation from the leveler of all."

To meet Gath's price, though, he needed more than the simple acumen his small business required of him. He needed the special knowledge that only a few special books contained, that only a select few individuals could teach him. He sought out the wise elders of the villages for miles around. Some saw through the lies he told and turned him away. Others not so perceptive embraced him as a student, taught him the secrets of element and ether. He learned fast and left his teachers when they could teach him no more.

Years passed. Onokratos sought out ancient libraries and rare books in all the civilized nations, learning mysteries, vile esotery. His soul hovered on the brink of damnation.

"Who's to say if I went too far." He paused, looked thoughtful, and sighed. "Then, I learned of a large private library practically under my nose in nearby Endymia. I'd heard of Thogrin Sin'tell, of course. I knew he was related to the royal family. But of his collection I knew nothing."

He went to Endymia, to Thogrin's castle, as a common prestidigitator, an entertainer. Thogrin Sin'tell lived alone with only his retainers for companionship. Any new diversion was welcome, and the baron invited Onokratos to stay awhile as a guest. As the days went by it proved easy to win the nobleman's friendship, an accomplishment made easier with a few simple, subtle spells.

Though the library was impressive, it offered none of the knowledge Onokratos thirsted for. Still, the journey was not wasted. It was Thogrin who opened his eyes, convinced him the purest, most uncorrupted soul in the kingdom must belong to the young Korkyran queen. Did a monarch not rule by divine right? And would not a spark of godly divinity burn in Aki's soul? It couldn't be coincidence that Aki and Kalynda were the same age. She *must* be Gath's intended ransom. It was so plain.

"We laid plans, Thogrin Sin'tell and I. Oh, he was a great schemer. On the first night of the Horned Moon, with Thogrin's help, I raised the demon, Gel, and commanded him to steal the little queen." He looked up and their eyes locked. His grief was gone, and his anger. A hard calmness shone in his unwavering gaze. "When she was ours, I called the thousand-named, and he came and ripped the spirit from her living body, leaving only the husk, the shell, *the animal essence.*"

No, she was wrong. Grief had not yet left him. She felt the saw-edge of his pain when he spoke. His words had been meant only to hurt her, to make her feel like pain.

And it did hurt. Knowing Aki's soul writhed in the cold grasp of the chaos lord stabbed her to the heart. Again, she wanted to lash out, smash the frail figure hunched before her. He was to blame; the fault was his, Aki's bestial ravings still echoed in the dark corners of her mind, the smells of the little queen's prison filled her nostrils.

Breath hissed through clenched teeth. "And in return for your efforts you won, not your true daughter, but another *animal.*" She sneered. "You fool! The dark deceiver kept his promise exactly as he spoke it in your dream. Kalynda walks the earth again! But it's only the soulless flesh. Gath still possesses her spirit. And without the soul the flesh only offers the primal instincts. She and Aki are two alike: human in shape only."

"Gath betrayed me!" he shouted furiously.

"Stupid old man!" Her temper exploded. She slammed fists against the table between them; then, seizing its edge, she flung it aside, grabbed his lapels, slapped him twice rapidly, and propelled him forcefully into his chair so that it nearly toppled backward. "You think the gods are common alley merchants that you can bargain with, coin for goods, in equal value? You pitiful pawn! They move us about for amusement like pieces in the Game of Kings, at whim or fancy." She spat at his feet. "You flattered yourself you were a player when you were never more than a piece on the gameboard."

His face reddened where her blows had stung. He clenched his fists, the veins stood out on his hands, throbbed on his temples. "You don't know so much, spiteful witch!" He jumped up, went to a shelf in a corner, and lifted a bundle. In better light she saw he held a bedroll.

He flung it at her feet. "Arrogant bitch! You don't even know the company you keep! Look to yourself before you play haughty with me or call me fool!" He pointed accusingly. "Look at it, if you dare!"

She touched the bundle with a booted toe. She recognized it now as Kimon's bedroll. The blanket had a distinctive border she couldn't mistake. She looked at her host again, suspicion eating wormholes in her sudden resolution. Could this be some trick? His eyes burned with a queer, furious light; his finger stabbed again at the bundle.

Cautiously, she bent and untied the thin leather thongs that bound it at either end. She could feel something hidden in the cloth as she worked. Something hard, long, and flat. She unrolled the blanket. The candle fire glittered on a beautifully crafted blade, a fine short sword.

"He's been right at your side," Onokratos taunted. He barked a harsh laugh. "No doubt waiting for another chance to murder your precious child-queen."

Her jaw dropped. The assassin she'd fought in Aki's chamber had used such a weapon. Only, Onokratos was mistaken. *It wasn't Aki he'd come to kill!*

"Liar!" she shouted. Her senses reeled. She'd given her

body to Kimon, her trust, maybe her love. He'd had a dozen opportunities to slay her if he was the assassin. "Not Kimon!"

He loomed over her, merciless, as she kneeled over the blade. "Yes, Kimon!" He shook his fists. "I took that from his horse myself, and other tools of his despicable trade." He touched his temples. "Why, if you had any sensitivity, any *psychic* sensitivity at all, you could just touch that steel and hear the screams of all the murders that've been done with it." He glared, eyes full of reflected flames. "And it's hired to murder a child, your charge. How dare you scorn me for trying to save my daughter? Look to yourself!"

She picked up the sword, ran a finger down its keen edge. If she was still the witch he called her, she might sense the truth, know the weapon's history as she held it. But she had no power, now. The sword was silent in her hand.

"Liar!" she hissed. But Onokratos only grinned. "Liar!" she screamed again, rising. He backed away, but his grin broadened, became mocking laughter. Her grip tightened on the hilt until her knuckles were white and bloodless. She struggled for control even as she raised the blade. "I don't believe you! I won't!" She smashed the sword down, taking a slice from the lip of the overturned table. He could stop her; he had the power. She didn't care. She raised the sword again, advancing.

But the blade caught the candles' gleaming, and in its flashing, steely brightness, she remembered that night in Mirashai when this, or another such blade, had lured her into darkness away from Aki's side. She froze. Could she desert Aki again by throwing away her life so intemperately? Gods of Esgaria, what could she do?

"Get out!" she raged. The cold point of the blade, so hungry for his heart, thrust at the door instead. "Get out, or I'll gut you! I swear! Leave me alone!"

He puffed himself up, tensed as if he might respond to her hinted challenge. Then a cruel smile split his face, and he moved toward the threshold, never taking his eyes from her. "All right," he agreed, his voice under control again. "We both can use a rest." He indicated the wooden bed frame. "That's as comfortable as anything I can offer. I'll wake you in the morning." He took one of the several candles, then the door closed gently behind him.

She ran to it, jerked it open, fearing he might have locked her in. Already he was some distance down the corridor, holding his small light like a shield against the gloom. He turned into a branching passage and was gone. She slammed the door.

A low shudder began at the center of her being, spread through her. Her hands trembled. She bit her lip to still her chattering teeth. Yet it was not fear alone that caused the trembling, but anger, frustration, indecision.

Her gaze fell on the shining length of steel that blossomed from her fist.

Kimon had appeared from the shadows and saved her a nasty clubbing in Shadamas. He'd fought beside her to rescue Oona. He'd stayed with her afterward, rode hard, shared food. Why should she believe Onokratos, a monster who'd damned an innocent child to an unthinkable fate?

She judged the sword, keen-edged, balanced to perfection, a professional's weapon. Kimon could be a professional. She'd observed his technique in Shadamas. *But was he an assassin?* She kicked at the blanket on the floor. That was Kimon's, yes. *But was the blade?* Onokratos could be lying for some purpose. He could have planted it in the bedroll. Aki's chamber had been dark that night. She recalled her attacker. The size and height could be right, but . . .

A shout ripped from her. The sword hurtled across the room. The point bit deeply into the wall, the haft a vibrating blur that made a soft, short humming.

Hot tears streaked her face. She hugged herself and sank down on the bed frame. It creaked with the intensity of her sobbing.

After a while, there were no tears left. She tried, prayed, to slip into the blissful oblivion of sleep, but it wouldn't come.

Onokratos's book lay forgotten on the floor. There was enough light to read by, though most of the candles had burned to stubs. She opened the tome, scanned a few pages, and barked a short laugh. A grimoire, very basic, full of inaccuracies and ineffective spells. She'd read it as a child at her mother's knee, or a copy of it. More likely, this very book.

She sank back in the room's only chair and sighed. Sorcerer and wizard. Onokratos had learned too much too fast. He possessed power, but no wisdom; courage, but not good judgment. To strike a bargain with chaos . . .

She sighed again.

What was she going to do about Kimon?

Chapter Ten

A gentle shaking woke her. Her neck throbbed with a dull pain; her back felt stiff. One arm tingled numbly where her head rested on it. She opened her eyes slowly . . . to gaze directly into Onokratos's eyes.

She didn't flinch or even look away. She'd had time to think; sleep had calmed her. *Eyes are windows to the soul*, her mother had taught her. She peered long and deeply, seeking for his soul, if he had one, searching for some insight into this strange old man, unable to ignore the expression of almost fatherly tenderness as he leaned over her. What she saw brought only confusion.

"I don't believe what you said about Kimon," she said.

"I spoke out of anger last night," he answered. "It's not important." He turned to the table; he must have set it upright while she'd slept. There was a bottle of wine and two earthen cups. He poured careful measures. "That chair wasn't very comfortable, was it?" He smiled, passed her one of the vessels. "I should apologize for the lack of luxuries. I've never entertained guests here before."

She rose slowly from the hard chair, stretched, feeling joints pop, cramped muscles ease, sensation return gradually to her limbs. If only the ache in her neck would fade . . .

"I'd like to see them."

"Kimon and your other friend?" He regarded her over

155

the rim of his cup. "Of course, they're waiting for us at breakfast." That smile flashed briefly again. "You're not prisoners here."

She sipped her own wine. It was sweet, fruity, very good, not a Korkyran vintage, though she couldn't place its origin. Mention of breakfast made her realize how hungry she was. But her host seemed in no hurry; he held the bottle to refill her cup.

"What are we, if not prisoners?"

"Guests, certainly," he responded, setting the bottle aside. "I only acted at the gate to defend myself. You were understandably irate." He winked. "That's behind us now. We have business to discuss."

She arched an eyebrow. "Oh?"

He nodded. "I want to save Kalynda, and you want to rescue Aki. I think I can assume she's no good to you in her present condition. So, we work together for both children."

She felt her temper surge and forced it back down with another sip of wine. "You're responsible for Aki's condition," she reminded him pointedly.

He dismissed that with a wave of his arm. "To help my daughter I'd sacrifice ten like Aki, or a hundred. I'll not pretend otherwise. I love my daughter that much. I nearly sacrificed you."

She set her cup aside, refused more when he offered. "Two nights ago on the forest edge. The fireball. That was you?"

"Gel," he answered bluntly, "acting on my orders. You were able to nullify his power, and you knew how to waken your friends from the doom-sleep. That demonstrates to me that you have some power and knowledge yourself. So, we may be able to help each other."

She digested that. Gel, then, was the demon that had attacked them, and Onokratos's familiar. How powerful could the old man's sorcery be? Powerful enough to breach hell and bind one of its denizens. Powerful enough to make himself a wizard.

"Why should I help you?" She sat back down in the chair.

He sat on the edge of the table, folded his arms. "Because Aki means as much to you as Kalynda does to me. The only reason you're not at my throat right now is because you harbor some small hope that what I've done I can undo."

She drew a deep breath. "Can you?"

He met her gaze evenly. A moment's silence passed, then he finished off his wine and turned the cup upside down. "I don't know," he answered. "Not without help."

"I'm not the kind of help you need," she snapped suddenly. "The chaos god is a first-order deity; there are lesser gods who pray to him."

Onokratos came and took her arm, urged her to her feet with a gentle but firm tug. "We'll discuss it over breakfast. I'm hungry, and I'm sure you are, too. Your friends are waiting for us." He grinned disarmingly. "There hasn't been such a meal prepared in this place since the previous landlords lived here. I don't know when that was."

She hesitated, turned, and her gaze fell on the short sword where it sprouted from the wall. She hadn't touched it or looked at it all night.

"I could send him away, if you want."

She shivered suddenly, aware of all the things that could mean to a man of Onokratos's abilities. "I told you, I don't believe what you said about Kimon." But she crossed the room, seized the haft, and worked the blade free.

Her host leaned over her shoulder, rubbed a finger across the splintered woodwork, and shrugged. "Ah, well," he said with a sigh, "gives it character." Then he turned back toward the door. "Coming?"

She scooped Kimon's blanket from the floor, crumpled it into an untidy bundle, and thrust the sword deep into its folds. She put it all snugly under one arm.

"Since we're not prisoners, may we have our weapons?"

He closed the door behind as they stepped over the threshold. "Of course, I'll have them brought to the dining hall."

He led the way through a series of corridors. All the shutters had been thrown wide. Morning sunlight poured in. The air still smelled musty and old, but a mild draft blowing through·the halls promised to change that.

The last passage made her stop and catch her breath. At an earlier time it must have been beautiful indeed. Even now it was awesome. Dusty busts of forgotten heroes stood mutely in niches carved in the walls. Larger niches housed whole sculptures, stone figures now draped in lacy cobwebs and blackened with sulfate. Ornate frescoes rivaling those in Mirashai's great reception hall decorated the ceiling. Beneath a thick carpet of grime, the floor was plainly of fine marble.

A large set of oaken doors loomed at corridor's end. Onokratos leaned on them. They flung back with surprising ease.

The dining hall was as lavish as the corridor, with an important difference: it was clean. A long table ran the length of the chamber with board seating for, perhaps, fifty. The far end of the table was piled with fruits, raw vegetables. She smelled roast meat, and her mouth watered.

Tras Sur'tian and Kimon sat in secret conversation, heads close, ignoring the platters and bottles of wine and water. They wore glum expressions that brightened when they saw her.

"Samidar!" Kimon leaped up, ran to her, nearly swept her up in his eager hug. She returned his embrace, and their lips met with sweet brevity. "I worried about you," he breathed.

She answered softly, glad for his warmth. "It's all right, now." She looked beyond him. Tras Sur'tian watched, too gracious to interrupt a lovers' reunion, but his face told her he was relieved to see her. She detached herself from Kimon and went to him. He clasped her forearm as he would another Korkyran soldier. "We've grown past that," she whispered, raised on tiptoe, and kissed his cheek.

"We didn't know what happened to you," he said, pitching his voice low, eyeing Onokratos suspiciously. Frost wondered how much to tell him: nothing about

Aki, yet. But he'd have to know sooner or later. She
repressed a shudder. Coming up behind her, Kimon's
hands settled on her shoulders. They stood close together.
"Relax," she assured them. "There's so much you don't
know."

"We can jump him," the Korkyran suggested.

She thumped a finger on his chest. "I said relax." She
read the questions in her old friend's eyes, but now wasn't
the time to answer them. "We'll talk later. Right now"—
she gestured to the table—"I'm starved. This looks great."

Onokratos had kept a polite distance during their brief
talk. Now he came forward, smiling, indicating the benches.
"Please, be seated and help yourself. I'm sure you'll find
everything to your taste."

"Our weapons," Frost reminded him.

He nodded. "Right after breakfast. First, let's eat while
everything is still hot." He took a place at her right side.
Tras Sur'tian gave her a peculiar glance, then sat opposite
the wizard; plainly, none of his suspicions had been averted.
Kimon sat close by her left.

They lifted chunks of steaming pork onto trenchers made
of hardened slices of bread hollowed to contain the vict-
uals. Mixed with the meat was some kind of cooked grain
she couldn't identify, salty but very appealing. She took an
apple from a bowl of fresh fruit, filled her cup with water
instead of wine. It occurred to her to wonder where all the
food came from. She'd seen neither livestock nor orchards
on their approach, and the fields were fallow.

"Gel provides," Onokratos answered, "whatever I need."

Frost hesitated, a bite of meat slipped from her fingers.
Was it real food or some substance magically conjured?
Tras and Kimon looked strangely at her. The Korkyran
had eaten only sparingly at first, suspecting poison, then
with relish when nobody dropped dead. "Is anything
wrong?" he asked her, taking note of her reaction.

She forced a smile. Whatever, the food was tasty and
filling. No telling when she and her friends might eat again if
they refused this fare. She scooped up the bite she'd dropped

on the table and swallowed it. "Just a bit of gristle," she lied, "nearly went down wrong."

Kimon turned to their host. "Who is Gel?" he said.

A deep, booming voice answered. "I am Gel."

They all turned at the sound. For the briefest instant, Frost had the impression of a huge, fire-eyed crow perched in the entrance. She blinked, clearing her vision, and stared at the largest man she had ever seen. Nearly a head taller than Tras Sur'tian, Gel's gleaming black body rippled with sinewy muscle; midnight-colored hair flowed over neck and shoulders; eyes dark and hard as onyx glistened with an unwavering gaze. Frost felt a warm flush as their eyes met.

Kimon leaned forward, insouciant, and grinned. "Tell me, Gel," he said, "don't they wear clothes where you come from?" Frost nudged him in the ribs. Clearly, Onokratos had told her comrades nothing of the demon.

Gel strode forward. In one huge hand he grasped all their weapons. "Your concept of morals means nothing to me," the creature rumbled. "If nudity offends thee, then be offended. I am unconcerned." He deposited their possessions at the table's opposite end, sat, and rested his hand on them.

Tras Sur'tian was obviously intrigued by Onokratos's servant. "What is your homeland?" he asked not unpolitely. "I've not seen your like before."

The demon barked a short answer.

Tras reddened. "Hell, indeed. You repay civility with insult, like a dog that nips a poor wanderer's heels. Then back to hell with you, I say." He returned his attention to eating and looked no more at Gel.

Yet Frost could not help but look at him. Her gaze roamed the stern angles of his features, the marble smoothness of his throat, the broad expanse of his heaving chest. Again she experienced a rush of heat. The demon was not at all what she'd expected. *Beautiful*. He was beautiful.

She glanced at Kimon. He was beautiful, too. On the bench between Onokratos and herself lay the bundle she had brought with her. She'd hidden it behind her back when she'd seen Kimon and had thrust it out of sight when she'd sat down.

She swallowed a draft of water from her cup. "Sorry you decided to ride with us?" she said to her lover.

"Not at all," he answered, regarding the demon over a meaty morsel. "It's been . . . most unusual."

Onokratos leaned forward, wearing a crooked smile. "But all this hardly compares to the pleasures you found in Mirashai, eh?"

Kimon swallowed his food. "I was only there a short time. Didn't see much of the city." He drank his wine.

Her hands trembled ever so slightly. She hid them in her lap. "But you did see the rose garden. You told me so."

Kimon sat his cup aside. She could feel his eyes on her. "Yes," he answered finally. "I glimpsed it over the wall as I rode near the palace one afternoon."

"But it's a very high wall." She bit her lip. Why was she playing this game? There was no purpose to these questions. She should concentrate on finding help for Aki. She looked up, found Tras regarding her strangely. Her trembling grew. The Korkyran knew the events of the night Aki disappeared. Had her questions awakened suspicion in the old guard captain?

Kimon gave her knee a squeeze beneath the table. "I confess," he said, winking, "I stood on my saddle to see. I'd heard of its beauty and of the little queen." His fingers found her chin, turned her head so she had to look at him. He smiled broadly. "And of the queen's guardian."

But his flattery was no reassurance. She reached for her cup, drank deeply, and set it aside, wished she'd filled it with wine after all. But Kimon saw how her hand faltered and caught it between his own. Her flesh felt cold next to his. His features creased with sudden concern.

"Samidar?"

She pulled away, no longer able to hide her shivering. A numbness settled over her, a chill that penetrated her bones. Her hand fell on the bundle at her side. She didn't believe Onokratos, she didn't! She dug among the blanket's folds. Her fingers curled around the haft of the short sword. She squeezed her eyes shut, unable to deny what she felt: doubt that rose like a wall between her and Kimon.

She placed the blade on the table. Light shimmered on its keen edge. Tras Sur'tian stared questions at her, but she ignored them. "Is this yours?"

A range of emotions danced over Kimon's face. Then he went as impassive as stone, as if the life had drained from him. His hand hovered near the hilt, then retreated to his lap.

Onokratos rose from his seat. "Give them their weapons," he said to Gel. The demon stood. The swords and belts clattered as he gathered them.

"I love you, Samidar," Kimon said weakly, forlorn.

"Frost?" Tras Sur'tian looked from one to the other, aware something had passed he was not part of. Yet, he suspected. A darkness clouded his features; his eyes bored into her.

A massive arm reached over her shoulder. Her sword belt fell on the board with her pouch and the silver-link belt with the scabbarded Demonfang. Another hand caught hers before she could claim them.

"Assassin!" Tras Sur'tian leaped to his feet, kicking back his bench seat. With a hoarse shout he reached across the table, seized Kimon by his tunic. The hand that had trapped Frost's wrist opened and closed again on the hilt of the arcane dagger.

Kimon flailed, off-balance, as Tras Sur'tian dragged him through the scattering meats, vegetables, cups. "Murdering bastard! You must be the one who came skulking like a cur in darkness!" He jerked the blade free of its sheath.

Demonfang's high-pitched wail filled the hall. Frost shouted too late. Kimon stared wide-eyed at the shining blade and redoubled his effort to free himself from the crushing grip that pinned him by the throat to the table.

Tras Sur'tian also stared in horror at the thing he held. He groaned, unable to relax his fingers and let it fall. His hand began its plunge, but he caught it with his other hand, releasing his intended victim. The dagger shrilled a higher, urgent note.

Frost witnessed the battle Tras Sur'tian waged within himself, one hand fighting the other. It was a war fought in the span of heartbeats. Tras's will began to fade as unholy screams assailed his ears. No man was strong enough to resist: once drawn, Demonfang must taste blood.

Yet she couldn't stand by and let either friend die on that hell-whetted point. In a bound, she cleared the table, caught her old friend's arm. Her momentum sent them crashing to the floor. Tras fell on top of her, his weight crushing the breath from her. Demonfang, still clutched tight in his fist, descended toward her heart. Desperately, she trapped his wrist in both her hands, strained against his formidable strength.

Then Kimon was behind him, grabbing the Korkyran, dragging him off her. She gulped air, lashed out with a foot. Tras Sur'tian went sprawling. Kimon, moving lithely, pulled her to her feet. They whirled as one, crouched to fight.

The expected attack never came. Tras Sur'tian stared, blank-eyed, at Demonfang, the point aimed at his own heart. *It must taste blood,* a voice roared in Frost's brain, *either your enemy's or your own.* She leaped again, moving without thinking.

There was no resistance in his arm when she grabbed it, and that surprised her. Overbalanced, she nearly fell, recovered, spun, expecting to find a gleaming point whistling toward her breast. Tras Sur'tian moved with dreamlike slowness. She seized his hand, fought him for the dagger, tried to uncurl his fingers from its hilt. He glared, eyes full of fear.

Demonfang shrieked, a long, piercing wail like a banshee dying. It swelled, reverberating in the chamber, a series of deafening echoes, then began to fade until it was silent.

Frost didn't understand, but she acted. With all her strength she tried again to unwrap Tras Sur'tian's fingers. They were rigid, unbending.

"Gel's enchantment," Onokratos explained. He crept cautiously to her side, face pale. He paced a wide circle around the Korkyran, ready to bolt, studiously observing.

Kimon touched her shoulder, pointed. Gel stood as immobile as Tras Sur'tian, transfixed, hands outstretched, straining. His huge black body glistened with a fine sweat. As she watched, fresh beads popped out on his brow, ran in rivulets down his face.

A new solution hit her. Swiftly, she snatched up the dagger's sheath and clapped it over the blade.

"No!" Gel's voice was a barely audible whisper. He shook all over, great muscles corded with effort. "B-blood!" he stammered.

She knew his meaning and bared the blade again.

"What are you doing?" Kimon shouted, trying to prevent her.

She pushed him away and jerked her tunic sleeve high, exposing her forearm.

"You can't!" Kimon's arms encircled her. An elbow smashed against the side of his head. His grip loosened, she grabbed his wrist, twisted, throwing him to the floor.

She raked her forearm over Demonfang's edge. It gleamed, incarnadined. She slammed the sheath back in place.

The demon let out a groan, sagged against the wall, lungs pumping laboriously. Tras Sur'tian blinked, stared, wordless. When his knees started to buckle, Onokratos caught him around the waist. Bruised but unhurt, Kimon flung his belt around Frost's arm just above the cut, began to twist it tight.

She stopped him. "Not serious," she murmured. Their eyes locked just for a moment. Then, remembering the cause of the argument, she slipped her arm free and turned from him. Blood ran down over her palm, past her fingers, fell in heavy drops to stain the floor, but she reached out and took the silent, sated Demonfang from Tras Sur'tian's lax grip.

The Korkyran regarded them all uncertainly, then stumbled to a seat at the table. He grabbed the nearest bottle of wine and slugged down the contents. A trickle spilled over his chin, spoiling his tunic.

Kimon took another bottle, poured a cupful, and offered it to Frost. She accepted it noncommittally and sipped. Onokratos came to her side. "A fascinating weapon," he remarked. He tugged on his earlobe, looking unpleasantly thoughtful. She strapped the dagger to her waist, set a hand on its hilt, and moved away from him.

Gel had not stirred. He leaned on the wall, half-standing, half-crouched. His immense chest heaved. For the third time, she felt a warm, disturbing rush, but with it mingled a genuine concern. The demon had saved her friends. Despite what he was, what he'd done in the past, she owed him a debt. She went around the long dining table toward him.

His eyes followed her, though he seemed too weak for speech. When she was close, he reached out with a slow, languid motion. Clawed fingers brushed at the streaming wound on her arm.

She jumped back, an involuntary reaction. Kimon, seeing, scrambled over the table, sword drawn, to her defense. She turned on him, glowering, his aid unasked. His expression betrayed his hurt as he stopped in his tracks. Then, shaking his head, he sheathed his weapon, went back to his place at the table.

"Sorry," she apologized, facing Gel again. "You startled me." That was true enough. She'd never touched a demon before or let one touch her. The sight of his claws had unnerved her momentarily. She chided herself for the foolish reaction as she glanced at her wound.

She gasped. "By the nine hells!" she swore, and watched disbelieving as the gash healed at a greatly accelerated rate: blood staunched, flesh melded, a scar formed and disappeared. Only a dried trail of crusty blood betrayed where the cut had been.

At her exclamation Kimon came running again. He leaned over her shoulder, mouth gaping, and rubbed a finger over the unblemished skin to convince himself of what he'd witnessed. "It's not possible," he whispered tersely. "This is some kind of illusion."

"It is possible." Tras Sur'tian had also come unnoticed behind her. He clutched another bottle in his hand and swilled from it, gulping noisily. "It's all clear to me, now." He gestured toward Gel. "He said he came from hell, didn't he?"

Tras stumbled back to his seat and raised the bottle for another drink. Frost prevented him. All color had gone from his face; his eyes were reddened. Wine had stained his beard, and his hands shook visibly. She tried to pry the bottle from his grip, but he jerked it back.

"Leave it!" he bellowed. "By the One God, woman, I've earned a good drunk! That business with the burning hand in Mirashai; those fire things flying at us in the wood trying to do us in." He shuddered, took a drink, swallowed hard. "When that bolt hit I thought I was dead." A strange look came into his eyes; his face turned impassive for just a moment, then reanimated. "But I'm alive. Then that damned dagger of yours . . ." He looked up at her, and she could see his anger and terror. "I felt it in my mind, like a thing alive, controlling me! Is it that way for you when you use it?" He waited for an answer. When she gave none, he turned his attention back to the wine. "Yes, by hell, I need this." He started to drink.

She slapped the bottle to the floor. Tras Sur'tian rose in a dark rage. The back of his huge fist crashed down on her cheek, sending her sprawling. Pain exploded in her skull as it impacted on the tiles. Then she heard a sound, a savage growl and a struggle. Something was happening, but her eyes were full of stars and intricate swirling lights. She shook her head to clear it, telling herself to get up, willing rebellious legs to move.

Suddenly, hands pulled at her, Kimon's hands. The demon's claws were fisted in Tras's tunic. The Korkyran kicked air; Gel hoisted him with one hand. The claws of his free hand prepared to rip.

"No!" She barely recognized her own voice. Was it some spell that brought this madness down on them? Or

just the strain of all that had happened? No matter, it had
to end, now, before they destroyed each other. "Let him
go, Gel." She forced authority into her words. Every eye
turned. The demon set Tras Sur'tian back on his feet.
Kimon stood guard at her side, clutching his sheathed
sword sternly, ready to enforce her will. Onokratos, standing a safe distance from the near brawl, watched coolly,
unruffled. He arched one brow when her gaze locked with
his. "Now, everyone sit down," she ordered.

Onokratos sat, then Kimon. Gel drifted to his master's
side and stood just behind him. Tras Sur'tian regarded the
demon hatefully, spat, and took a similar position next to
Frost. *Like two fighters squaring off*, she observed, and
cursed silently.

She planted a foot on one of the benches, leaned forward. "Did you have anything to do with that?" She
wiggled her fingers suggestively.

The wizard understood her meaning. "No," he answered, pouring himself a dollop of water into one of the
few cups that hadn't been kicked over or smashed. He
lifted it in a mock toast. "No magic needed. Human
nature will out."

"Nothing human about that," Tras Sur'tian mumbled,
pointing. Gel showed his teeth in response. The demon
betrayed no hint of weakness now.

"Tras," she said quietly, "shut up."

He glowered, looked about to say more, then thought
better.

Frost drew a deep breath, chewed her lower lip as she
had a habit of doing. An apple from the overturned fruit
bowl rested in front of her. She picked it up, studied it
casually, tossed it a couple of times, then took a small,
crisp bite. She looked around the room at all the staring
faces, enjoying the moment's respite.

"Well, gentlemen?" She spoke with a calmness she
really didn't feel and forced a smile. "What now?"

Onokratos tapped his fingers on the wooden surface and
set down his water cup. He pursed his lips. Then he
announced, "I think I have a plan."

Chapter Eleven

In her room, Frost paced impatiently, waiting for Onokratos. There were things the wizard claimed he must do before explaining his plan. The floor creaked under every footstep. She sat down, but the chair was uncomfortable and she resumed her pacing.

Tras Sur'tian was somewhere outside trying to chase down their horses. She didn't worry about Ashur; the unicorn would come running when she called. Could the same be said of Kimon? she wondered. He'd drifted off alone after the argument, long-faced, his thoughts veiled from her. She hadn't seen him since.

She hugged herself, wishing for company, anyone to talk to.

Perhaps she should check on Aki. Onokratos assured her the child-queen had been fed and bathed as she'd requested. Still, it wouldn't hurt to pay her charge a visit. Maybe, deep down inside, some human part of Aki would appreciate a companion.

No, she knew that wasn't true. No part of Aki was human now. Aki was an animal, soulless. Frost wasn't even sure she could find the way to Aki's cell. The corridors seemed to shift like colors in a kaleidoscope, no passage ever leading to the place it did when she'd last traversed it.

Yet there was no harm in trying, and it was something to do.

Her mind at last made up, she turned to the door only to see it open. The demon, Gel, ducked his head ever so slightly and stepped over the threshold, barely squeezing his great ebon bulk through the frame. She caught her breath. His size had impressed her when she'd first seen him in the spacious dining hall. In the cramped confines of her room, he seemed half again as large as she remembered.

He drew himself erect, stared down on her. The hard gleam in those dark eyes made her shiver. She was no stranger to the supernatural, yet something about this creature unnerved her, repelled and at the same time attracted her. Unconsciously, she felt for her purse and the ruby jewel within.

"Thee will not need the talisman." His voice thundered, rich, sonorous, vaguely alien. "I offer thee no harm."

She swallowed, blushed, realizing how tightly she clasped the small purse. She fought against the odd quiverings he stirred inside her and tried to appear nonplussed. "Don't you feel a bit of a draft?" she said, folding arms over her chest.

He glanced at his body. "Are thee offended by my nakedness?"

"Well . . . no." She swallowed again. He really *was* enormous.

"Good." He stretched, deliberately sensuous, she thought, curling his arms to avoid the ceiling. Then he came toward her. She took a quick, reflexive step back and bumped into the table at her back. She bent nearly over it as the demon loomed above her. She could feel the heat that radiated from his body; his hot breath brushed her cheek.

She struggled to regain her balance, but two massive arms on either side of her kept her from straightening. Finally, she said flatly, "If you intend to break my back, you've chosen a particularly inefficient way to go about it."

He didn't answer. His eyes roamed over her. A great

hand moved to caress her shoulder. She saw it coming and steeled herself for his touch. Once before she'd recoiled from him; she refused to show him fear a second time. The hand slid along her arm with surprising gentleness. His fingers played on the back of her hand. Then Gel stepped back.

"Onokratos summons," he said. "He is waiting."

She stood up, tossed her hair back, and headed for the door. "What in hell does he think I've been doing?" she called over her shoulder with a calm she didn't really feel. "This isn't exactly a pleasure palace."

"I could give thee pleasure."

She didn't turn around; she could feel those eyes on her. A chill raced up her spine, but she mastered herself. "I doubt that," she informed him bluntly.

She waited in the corridor for the demon to squeeze through the door, then followed him along the maze of passages. From the outside the manor had seemed such a simple, almost plain structure. She scratched her chin in puzzlement; the interior was quite the opposite, a frustrating exercise in confusion even in daylight. She wondered that anyone found their way about.

They stopped before a door banded with three thick strips of cold silver, each engraved with glyphs and symbols of unknown origin. She sniffed a faint odor of incense, knew the nature of the room on the other side. The demon rapped on the door. Footsteps echoed within, then the door swung open.

Onokratos looked past her and spoke with his familiar. "Bring her friends," he ordered. "Everything is ready." He beckoned to her. "Of your own will, enter." The door closed behind her.

She was not surprised by what she saw. On the inside, the door was a solid sheet of the argent metal; silver had power to contain magical forces. The walls, the ceiling, and two silver-shuttered windows were all emblazoned with unreadable glyphs and strange sigils.

A rack of candles seven shelves high blazed on the north and south walls. In the four corners braziers burned redly, pouring smoky incense into the unventilated air. There was no furniture, but a lone wood stand supported an open grimoire. Painted on the floor was a large triangle, a seal of conjuration most commonly used in the neighboring kingdom of Chondos. Its outline sparkled in the firelight with a fine layer of silverdust. Within the triangle, more symbols and a circle at its heart.

She had often stood in such rooms when she was younger. "Our philosophies are similar," she said, gazing about. She pointed to the shutters; opened, they would give a western view. "The direction of the unknown, therefore, magic," she noted. "Silver for binding. The triangle, one corner each for conjuring the gods of light, the gods of darkness, and the neutrals." A few of the glyphs were familiar. "Those are Esgarian."

"I've been to Esgaria," he admitted. "I stole some books there. Men are forbidden to study the dark arts in your land, as you well know."

She bit her lip. It seemed the memories were not completely exorcised after all, nor the pain. It was true. In her country only women studied the secret ways, and only men were permitted the use of weapons. She had violated that law, taken up the sword, lost her family and her name for her disobedience.

She let out a long sigh and dismissed the past. For the present there were more immediate problems, and Onokratos was still talking.

". . . the Chondites were even less cooperative. I had to sneak over their border. They promptly expelled me when they discovered I'd milked one of the neophyte sorcerers for every bit of information money could extract from him."

She shook her head impatiently. "The plan, wizard. Explain your plan."

Onokratos paced around the triangle. Suddenly, he avoided looking at her. A brooding suspicion began to grow in her; a slow, heavy tension began to wring her muscles.

At last, he spoke. "I had to discuss the premise with

Gel. His perceptions are naturally much sharper than ours, and he had a direct psychic contact with the dagger."

"Hold it." She grasped the blade's hilt protectively, eyes narrowed. "If this brilliant scheme involves Demonfang, forget it."

His features hardened to a cruelty that startled her. His voice rasped. "If you want help for that precious little bitch below us, you'll do as I say!"

She bit back a sharp retort. Nothing would be gained by arguing until she knew what he had in mind. But Demonfang was hers. No one wielded it but her, and woe to anyone who tried to take it by force. She leaned against the wall, resting her hand casually on the dagger's butt, prepared to listen.

"It will take all your courage," he said smugly, folding hands into his sleeves, "and more. You actually gave me the idea when you pointed out that none of us, not even Gel, possessed the power to challenge the thousand-named one." He beamed suddenly, obviously pleased with himself, and resumed his pacing around the triangle. "What we need then is an alliance with a first-order power."

Her jaw dropped. "You're insane," she said simply.

"Gel agrees." He thrust a bony finger at the sheathed dagger. "That most amazing artifact provides a means of gaining such an ally." His smile flickered, faded, returned. "Or at least of getting to the negotiating table."

She repressed a shudder as the old man unveiled the true horror of his plan. The dagger's screaming had been the clue, he told her. The sound came not from the dagger, but through it. Gel confirmed that. So he believed, and the demon agreed, that Demonfang might actually become a gateway.

Her throat was dry. "A gateway to where?"

His smile vanished utterly. "To hell," he answered, "where all souls spend eternity." Then, with caustic bitterness, he added, "Except Kalynda, who writhes in Gath's evil web."

"Or Aki, whom you condemned to the same fate." They both fell silent, thoughtful. She considered Aki's soul, food for the spider god's gross appetites. She squeezed her eyes shut to expel the image. "You're suggesting a journey into hell?"

"We must strike a bargain with Orchos, lord of the dead," he affirmed. "That god has been cheated of two souls who never will enlarge his realm unless he aids us. And he is as jealous, as hungry and insatiable as the lord of chaos."

A heavy knock resounded on the door. Onokratos crossed the chamber, opened it, and admitted Gel, Kimon, and Tras Sur'tian, admonishing them to move carefully and not disturb the silverdust outlining the triangle.

The Korkyran was tired, but surly. He glanced around the room disapprovingly, wrinkled his nose at the incense. When his gaze fell on Kimon he gritted his teeth. She could feel his hatred for the younger man like a tangible force. Fortunately, Gel stood between them to prevent trouble.

He faced her across the triangle, the shadows of the candlelight masking his features as his dark eyes reflected their glow. "I caught the horses," he reported stonily, as if by assuming a formal attitude he could ignore the trappings of Onokratos's sanctum sanctorum. She knew how the elements of conjuration frightened him and all Korkyrans. Their belief in an indifferent One God was as much an insulation against the unsettling realities of a magical universe as it was a true conviction of faith.

He mastered his fear magnificently. "But not that big black of yours," he continued. "He's out there, though, strutting as though he ruled the countryside."

Kimon interrupted. "It's bright and sunny outside," he declared a trifle too cheerily, betraying his own unease. He, too, had been exposed to more than he could readily comprehend in the last few days. "Why not open the shutters and blow out these smoky candles. It smells like the whore-goddess's temple."

She felt pity for both men. "Hush, Kimon," she ordered gently. The demon closed the door, barred it with a silver bar. He turned back, and his eyes roamed over her again in that way that gave her gooseflesh. With five, the chamber felt as close as a tomb. She sucked her lower lip, hoping the analogy didn't prove prophetic.

"Samidar?"

She found both her comrades looking at her, seeking reassurance. Both were out of place here, plainly uncomfortable. And suddenly, the atmosphere of the room overwhelmed her, too. The unreadable glyphs swam on the walls; the candles danced, dazzling her vision; smoke stung her eyes; she clenched her fists until the nails dug into her palms.

"So many times I've stood in places like this," she muttered, "not rooms, but caves burrowed deep in the cliffs and mountains where one could listen and hear the dark things eating at the earth. I've commanded the winds, made the ground tremble, the sea rage, all at my whim. I've raised the lightning and worse." She turned slowly, not seeing Onokratos's room, but stalactites and stalagmites burning with lichen sheen; seeing the sweaty, naked bodies of sister-witches cavorting around fires that seemed so tiny, insignificant, against the gloom of the earth's bowels; seeing her mother's face, encouraging her, instructing.

The room came back into focus. "And I turned my back on all of it." She clapped her hands suddenly, a sharp crack that seemed out of place in the chamber's solemnity. "This is crazy. I'm getting out of here." She headed for the door.

"Coward!" Onokratos accused. "You're afraid!"

"Yes, I'm afraid!" she hissed, whirling on him. "Any fool would be. First, you invoked the chaos god and damned an innocent child. Now, you would bargain with death's master!" She barked a harsh laugh. "Your plan is not insane! You are!"

Kimon's eyebrows shot up. "You speak of Orchos?"

Tras Sur'tian snapped, "There's no other but the One God."

Frost gave the Korkyran a hard look. "You speak out of habit or ignorance," she informed him. She aimed a finger at Gel. "Look at the creature beside you. Is that a product of your One God?"

Onokratos planted himself between her and the door. "Do you fear for your own soul, woman? Do you value it more than Aki's?" He purpled with rage. "There are nine hells, paradise to perdition, according to your just due. You may aspire to any of them. But think of Aki cocooned in Gath's wretched web, dangling by a single glistening strand, feeding his vile lusts until she merges and becomes lost forever in the immoral vileness of chaos itself! Then think again of your cowardice!"

At mention of Aki, Tras gripped her shoulder. "What's this madman raving about?" he demanded.

"Nothing," she answered icily. "The moon has eaten his brain."

Tras Sur'tian was not convinced. "You speak of my queen." He addressed the wizard forthrightly. "You want to bargain?" He advanced toward Onokratos. "I know you've endangered her, damn your soul, but I'll do what I must to win her back."

Frost grabbed his arm. "Tras, shut up!"

He shook her off. "My life is dedicated to her; the duty is mine. You're nothing but a mercenary trying to earn your pay."

"You don't understand!"

"I'll do whatever I have to!"

"Let the fool!" Kimon spat, his eyes gleaming.

Her hand went for her sword, clasped the hilt . . . and froze. She suddenly realized how deep a rift had split their fellowship. It seemed only yesterday they had shared food and sung songs as they'd traveled the road.

What was happening to them?

Onokratos's long, thin finger stabbed at her. "Only she can go," he said. "No other."

Kimon took three quick strides, caught the wizard's wrist, and twisted, forcing the old man's back to the wall. "No, she goes nowhere for you! Send the Korkyran or that black beast of yours getting ready to pounce on me." Frost marveled at that. Kimon wasn't in a position to see the demon; he must have sensed Gel's movement. "Better yet," he continued, "go yourself, and take them both for company."

Neither Kimon nor Tras understood. "He intends a quest to hell itself!" she snapped.

Kimon released Onokratos and stepped back. "Then I'll stand by my last idea."

"Why not send the demon?" she said to Onokratos. "Let him bear your messages. Hell is his homeland, after all." That seemed reasonable, and it wouldn't require the use of Demonfang. In fact, why hadn't Onokratos thought of that first?

"Gel stays. That is not debatable." Onokratos glanced quickly at the demon. Frost thought he made some silent assurance, just a blink, a subtle nod. He looked back at her and went on. "You have the best chance for success. I can't go myself; I must remain here to command Gel, who is crucial to the plan." He turned a contemptuous gaze on Kimon and Tras. "These two are inexperienced for such an arcane journey. And you're more clever than they. That may count for something."

She locked eyes with the wizard and surprised herself to find she was weighing possibilities.

"Samidar?"

She shut Kimon out.

"I can do it," she heard Tras Sur'tian say. Her old friend would grasp any straw, even sacrifice himself to save Aki. He had pledged his life, he said. If she didn't go, he would.

"All right."

A look of pain flashed over Kimon's features. "Samidar, don't."

She reached out to reassure him with a touch, then snatched her hand back. Could he try to kill her for money and instead fall in love with her? The pleading in his eyes seemed real. She could sense his longing. Fair or false, how could she judge?

Now was not the time to ponder it. She had no choice but to accept this task Onokratos set for her. She swore to find Aki, to rescue or avenge her. So far, she had only found the child. That was not enough. Later, she would settle with Kimon.

She faced Onokratos. "What must be done?"

The wizard straightened his robes. "It shouldn't be complicated," he said. "Gel expects the sending to be easy."

"The sending," she repeated. "What about the return?"

Onokratos drew a handful of powder from a hidden pocket, tossed it on each of the braziers. Malodorous clouds roiled up, filling the chamber with a new, heavy smell. "That's why your friends are present. The strength of our combined wills, intensified by their affections for you, should be enough to guide you back."

"Are you certain?" Kimon demanded, his brow deeply wrinkled.

"This is wizardry," came the answer. "We deal with gods and demons; nothing can be certain."

Kimon's eyes blazed. He touched his sword's hilt and leaned close to Onokratos. "If she doesn't come back," he said, "I'll send you to join her."

The threat hung in the air, and no one spoke. Onokratos cleared his throat, finally, and pointed to Tras Sur'tian. "You stand at the southeast corner of the triangle; do not disturb the silverdust." To Kimon he assigned the northeast corner with the same admonishment. He took up position at the western corner. To Frost, he said, "Now you, in the circle at the center. That's right, you know how this goes."

"What of Gel? You said he was crucial."

"He'll be right behind you inside the triangle, but outside your circle." He drew his foot along one axis, causing a gap in the silverdust barrier, allowing the demon to pass within. Then he sealed the triangle again with more shimmering dust from a pouch in another pocket.

The old man stood up. "A small demonstration," he announced softly. "Gel, strangle the Korkyran."

The demon attacked. Tras Sur'tian leaped away, grabbing for his weapon, but long before those great, sinewy arms reached him, Gel roared in pain. Sparks flashed where his fists smashed against some invisible barrier. Obedient to the wizard's command, he reached again for the soldier captain's throat. His black face contorted with agony. Scintillant blue fire, appearing magically from the air, raced crackling up his arms.

"Enough, faithful servant." Onokratos clapped his hands, and the demon was calm once more. Tras Sur'tian glared darkly, barely controlling his rage.

Onokratos wagged a finger. "Don't be so touchy!" he chided. "I knew he couldn't harm you. I wanted you to see that nothing that is not human can escape the triangle." He looked to Frost. She shrugged, stepped out of her circle, walked between Tras and Kimon, then returned to her assigned place. Onokratos continued, "You must understand that as long as you do what I say, you'll be safe. No matter what transpires inside the triangle. No matter what you see. But if you disturb the silverdust and break the seal . . ." He drew a thumb across his throat, made a face. "Ugly, very ugly."

"Let's get on with it," Frost insisted. "They'll do their part."

Onokratos harrumphed. "You must be just as careful," he warned. "Even though you're inside it, if you misstep or thrash around, you could break the binding."

She waved a hand. "I know all this," she reminded him. "Now, the longer I stand here, the more convinced I become that this is the most stupid—"

Onokratos folded his hands into his sleeves again. "Then we won't delay longer." He spoke to Gel in a language she didn't understand, then asked him, "Ready?"

Gel nodded.

The wizard closed his eyes, said to Frost, "Draw the dagger."

"What?" Kimon and Tras Sur'tian shouted simultaneously and started for her.

"Stop!" Her voice was a thunderclap that echoed loudly in the sanctum. She fixed them with her gaze. "Don't interfere. Just do what he tells you." She glared at Tras. "You want to save Aki? Then obey him." She shifted her attention to Kimon. "If you value my life, obey. Nothing else."

Both men looked properly chastened. She called over her shoulder to Onokratos, "Let's get on with it."

The demon's hand touched the nape of her neck. His taloned fingers made brief, gentle, massaging strokes. He bent close and whispered so only she could hear, "Thee has my admiration, woman."

"I could care less," she answered, not bothering to pitch her voice low. Sweat beaded in her palms as the worms of doubt and fear ate away her resolve. "It's your insanity that's made this necessary."

"Not mine," whispered the demon. "I am but a tool for Onokratos to use." He took his hand away. "But it is necessary if thee wishes to save the children. I see no other course."

Nor did she, and that embittered her. She could taste her own anger like a black, choking bile. The demon claimed he was a tool, but he was not the only one. Onokratos was using them all, using them to save his Kalynda. She gripped the hilt of her sword and swore. However this adventure turned out, she would make him pay. If she had to come back from hell, back from the pit of darkness, she would make him pay.

Her grip shifted to Demonfang. She heard the breathing of her comrades pause, saw Tras Sur'tian's eyes widen ever so slightly. They knew the dagger's power and feared it. She shared that fear. But there was no turning back. She gritted her teeth and jerked the blade free.

Shrieking filled the chamber, long, horrible screams that froze the blood in her veins, made her skin crawl. Never had the sound seemed so shrill, so chilling. Demonfang shivered in her grasp, demanding its due.

"The point!" she heard the wizard call, his words barely distinguishable over the din. "Turn it toward you! Look at it!"

A new sound rose faintly amid the screaming, and she realized it was herself, whimpering and moaning like a frightened child. She bit hard on her lip to stop it. The

salty warm taste of blood filled her mouth. Slowly she
rotated the dagger, holding it at arm's length. The point
glittered wickedly in the candlelight.

The dagger writhed. Its screeching rang louder, more
intense. She'd never felt its power so strong before! Something flowed into her mind, dominating her will.

Blood! It senses my blood! She licked the crimson trickle
that ran down her lip.

A red glaze descended over her vision. Through it, she
saw a bearded, aging soldier. His chest offered an inviting
target. Dimly, she perceived she must be turning, for next
she looked on the wizard, the cause of all her troubles.
And the demon; his inhuman blood would make a feast for
Demonfang. Finally, she faced Kimon, the insolent whelp
who'd come like a shadow in the night to kill her.

So much blood! So much blood to quench the dagger's
thirst!

Demonfang turned in her hand, rose high to strike. She
no longer controlled her movements, but part of her mind
knew what must happen. With the last of her fading will,
she cried out, barely aware of her streaming tears, "Kra-
tos!"

The wizard's voice exploded over the dagger's screaming: one word, the demon's name.

A new power surged through her. She could see energy,
like a nimbus of scarlet radiance rushing around her, freeing
her from Demonfang's entrancement. Her will was her
own again. The shrieking diminished, faded, unsatisfied.
The room was silent except for the raspy breathing of her
uneasy friends and the pulsing blood that roared in her
ears.

She turned to face Onokratos, was pleased to find him
pale and sweating as much as she. He swallowed hard.
"Gel has control of it," he announced. She smiled at the
trepidation in his voice. "Now, gaze at the point. Turn it
toward you."

She turned it toward him, and her smile broadened. But
Gel was there between them.

She recalled the first time the demon had stilled her

unholy weapon. The effort had taken a toll on him. How long would he hold out this time before the dagger's power reasserted itself?

A thousand doubts and fears tormented her. All too late. There was nothing but to go on. The dagger was drawn. It must be used. It turned, this time at her willing. Firelight danced along its keen edge.

"Gel will release the blade's power very gradually until an equilibrium is struck between its magic and his." Onokratos spoke rapidly. A sign of his own fear? Or his own doubt in the demon's ability? "You'll hear the screaming again, the dagger demanding blood. But Gel won't let you strike. It should happen then."

"What should happen?" Kimon questioned.

"Your presence is all that's needed," the wizard chided harshly. "That, and your silence."

The first scream, faint and far-sounding, touched her ears. She shivered, or was it the slightest tingle from Demonfang? The scream sounded again, not one but many voices of souls in torment. Yes, it was Demonfang that trembled in her hand. She felt it slowly trying to bend her will. Suddenly the shrieking swelled louder than she had ever heard it; a scarlet haze blocked her sight, and she feared Gel had failed completely. Black thoughts crept to the fore of her mind, and she measured again the dagger's potential victims.

But she did not strike. The point remained hovering before her eyes. It swayed rhythmically, a steel serpent mesmerizing its prey. It commanded, begged for satiation, but was denied.

She was caught in a vise: ordered to kill, but unable to obey. She cried out. It was tearing her apart. Pain racked every part of her. Tears scalded her cheeks, ran in rivulets down face and throat.

Then, the pain ended.

She stared at her own body. Her face still contorted with the agony of soul separation. The knuckles were white and bloodless from clutching Demonfang. Veins and muscles showed livid beneath the flesh, straining, sweat-drenched.

She studied her new body, identical to her mortal case-ment, but surrounded by a silvery glow. A slender thread of purest light stretched from her new navel to her old one, linking body and soul.

She had experienced this marvel once before. She had achieved astral form and was ready for travel where human flesh could never go.

She looked at the dagger's point, sensing something there. A tiny ebon gleam rippled, caused by no earthly light. It grew as she watched, became an oval of shining darkness. From that darkness came the screaming.

This was the gate Onokratos had hoped for and she had dreaded. The screams were the tortured souls of the damned calling to her. Beyond, Orchos waited. She could feel his presence in the dark.

She knew the gate would close when Gel's strength began to wane. She turned to her friends to bid them a silent farewell. They did not move. Some spell held them suspended in time.

There was no time to waste.

She leaped into the void.

Chapter Twelve

She flew through an infinite night, trailing the tenuous silvery band, the lifeline to her mortal body. Its elasticity seemed as limitless as the darkness. She flew aimlessly, without reference points, guided by some preternatural instinct. Sometimes she felt a piercing cold; sometimes incredible heat seared her astral form. Neither radiated from an obvious source. Once, she thought she felt the leathery brush of unseen wings that paralleled her flight.

Most of all, she felt a growing loneliness. She would glance over her shoulder to reassure herself the soul-thread remained unsevered. She would strain for a glimpse of the dimly perceived portal through which she'd come.

Then, she saw him waiting. Enormous beyond imagining, his eyes shone like furious emeralds in a dispassionate face. His hand reached out to enclose her. She swerved, but the hand was there, fingers opening, engulfing her in a mighty fist.

She expected the fingers to squeeze, crush out her life. Instead, they began to glow. Tiny flames sprang up, swelled, licked at her. She felt the heat, though her astral body seemed immune to pain. She heard a scream, then more screams, long and protracted shrieks of despair that grew louder and more anguished as the moments passed.

Demonfang was in another world, she realized. She knew where these sounds originated.

Something solid materialized beneath her feet. Through the fire images began to form. Sulfurous rocks near at hand; in the distance, black mountains reared rebelliously against a burning sky. All she could hear was screaming. It rose around her like a wave of despondency. She couldn't shut it out. It bombarded her senses. She stared frantically left and right, trying to penetrate the fiery veil that blurred her vision.

When her sight cleared, she clapped a hand to her mouth to stifle the cry that bubbled in her throat. The mountains she glimpsed were twisted, fantastic shapes, unearthly. Far worse sights assailed her eyes.

She stood on a narrow, stony path. On either side stretched vast shallows of liquid flame, dotted by small islands and stalagmite formations. Horrible, malformed creatures splashed and thrashed. Dark smoke whirled in eddies over the surface, choking them. Fumaroles erupted with sudden, explosive power, spewing steam and lava.

They saw her, those execrable souls of once living men. They began to lurch, wade, swim toward her, arms outstretched and begging, blackened fingers grasping and dripping, eyes imploring.

The eyes were unbearable, filled with suffering, haunting and ghastly, reflecting things and visions she could not dream of or imagine. She tried to avoid them, but wherever she turned she met those eyes.

She ran, following the only path, a low and treacherous ridge made more dangerous by streams and puddles of fire. She leaped each obstacle as she encountered it and ran. Everywhere, the creatures looked up and saw her and followed, screaming, tears of fire burning their charred faces. She heard the sloughing of the scalding lake as they pursued, the scrape and rasp of scorched and crusted meat as they dragged themselves over incandescent rock, around steaming boulders, always reaching for her. She grabbed for a sword that wasn't there, bit her lip, and ran.

In frustration, some of the creatures seized the shining thread of her lifeline. They pulled, trying to break it; when that failed they chewed it.

She felt no pain. Yet, could she take the chance they might damage the cord and doom her to this place forever? Though swordless, she was not without skills. They repulsed her, and she feared to touch them, but fear of spending eternity among them drove her. She spun, determined to combat.

Turn not away.

She whirled again at the sound of another voice. She knew him at once. Orchos, death god, huntsman, lord of the nine hells. He stood on the path, blocking her way. His green eyes flickered with hints of fire. They held her with hypnotic power.

Welcome, daughter.

His lips did not move when he spoke, yet she heard him. He gestured to the creatures closing around. *My minions work to no avail. They would sever thy soul-thread and keep thee here to share their suffering.*

She found herself in control of her body once more. "Can they break it?"

The closing of yon portal may snap it. Naught else.

She swallowed, recalling her reason for traveling here, searching for words to win a god to her cause. "Lord Orchos—"

He interrupted. *The athame thee calls Demonfang brought thee to this lowest, most vile of all hells. Thee need not remain where only the worst of man must dwell.*

From his eyes a thick mist exuded, swirling around her. The lake of fire and its miserable denizens vanished. Streaming damp fog, cold and cloying, obscured everything. She checked the soul-thread. She could no longer see its end or the portal to her world.

Orchos stepped out of the mist. No longer did flames twinkle in the green of his eyes. They were smoky jade.

"Lord of worms, where are we?"

His thoughts were gentle in her head, so unlike what she'd expected from the dread deity. *Thee numbers it hell's third level. Above are the levels of reward. Below, of punishment. To this plane only I occasionally hold court for selected souls from other regions of my kingdom.* He bowed deeply; mist eddied around his arm as he made a grandiose gesture. *And daughter, thee has done me such honor, heaped souls on my altar of steel, that I am bound to honor thee with pageantry!*

At Orchos's beckoning, another figure emerged from the mist. She peered as the newcomer drew nearer. Suddenly, she cried out.

"Burdrak!" She flung her arms wide to embrace her friend and weapons master.

Daughter, nay! Thunder in her brain. Her muscles locked; she couldn't move. *Thee are yet living, but they are dead. They may not answer thy speech; thee may not touch them.* Her body was her own again.

Burdrak's shade bowed, moved on, disappearing in the mist as another took his place.

Her heart broke. Astral tears spilled from astral eyes. "Oh, gods, my father!" A trembling seized her as she gazed on those familiar, grizzled features and the sword wound that still gaped in his chest. She clenched her hands tightly against her sides, yearning to feel those arms holding her once more, to kiss those lips that used to smile and tell her stories. "Father, forgive me!" she implored him. Like Burdrak, he bowed and stepped wordlessly past her, vanished.

The shrouding mist parted for a third time. She knew even before she saw the face. "What game is this, corpsemaker?" she called bitterly as she regarded her brother's spirit. A sword wound also scarred his chest. She'd carved it there.

No game, daughter. Orchos's voice was a soft whisper, a distant echo of a dying wind. *Thee it was dispatched these souls to hell. Their greatest torment is to see thee lives after. Only a small part; not all suffer alike.*

"What of my suffering?" she shot back. "To see but not touch them?"

The god shrugged.

She met her brother's gaze. Her heart was ice, unrepentant. "I pray you suffer most of all," she said.

Orchos bent a finger. Her brother bowed stiffly and the mist swallowed him up.

"How great were the sins of my father," she demanded, "and Burdrak?"

His eyes crackled with lightning. He moved, and his shadow fell over her. She shivered in the umbra of his power and remembered a day when, as a child, she'd stood on the cliffs of Esgaria and watched a storm approach over the Calendi Sea, wondering with that tingling, innocent thrill if it would blow her away. Orchos was such a storm, beautiful and awesome.

Thy father came unbidden, a suicide, to my kingdom, he said sternly. *Thee needs no more answer. As for Burdrak . . .* His countenance softened somewhat. *Not all hells are for suffering.*

She bit her lip. If her father suffered, it was her fault. Fresh tears filled her eyes. If only she had not come to this dismal place.

"I journeyed here to seek your help." She brushed the wetness from her face. "I've found your cruelty."

Orchos nodded, and the parade continued. She stiffened her spine, prepared to endure it, determined to show no more weakness.

Some faces she remembered: Than and Chavi, the sons of Lord Rholf, who dwelled in Rholaroth. In a tavern brawl she'd killed one, wounded the other. Apparently, he had died later. For that, Rholf had sent Kimon to exact vengeance. There were few others she recognized. Men slain in battle, she guessed. Each performed the ritual bow and passed on.

The number surprised her. Still they came. Surprise turned to unease. So much done with a mere length of steel. When a small boy stepped from the fog, she protested angrily.

"I never harmed a child!"

Daughter, but thee harmed many children! The pride in his voice filled her with loathing. *Thee slew fathers aplenty in thy wars. Wives and little ones starved with no one to provide for them.*

"Carrion-eater! They would have slain me!" She flushed with rage and shame. The little boy bowed, departed.

Thee are my true daughter, sowing doom, cutting a crimson wake where thee wanders. Transported by thy sword these souls were, or by orders thee gave, plans thee made, or by consequences of thy actions. His eyes gleamed; he folded arms over his massive chest. *Thee makes me proud.*

She waited stiffly, silently, for the last shade to pass into the infinite mist. Then an odd thing struck her. An icy chill raised the hairs on her neck. She turned sharply to the lord of the nine hells.

"Where is my mother?"

Orchos blinked, said nothing.

"She died by her own hand," she pressed, "after my father!"

His tone was chiding. *A witch of such power as thee once possessed knows that to a great sorceress death is but another experience, a new source of knowledge, a wellspring of eldritch vigor.*

She clenched her fists to still their trembling. "She lives?"

His face was an impassive mask. *Thee came seeking help,* he said, abruptly changing the subject. *But thee has seriously failed me in an enterprise.*

"What?" He was rejecting her plea before she made it. That wasn't fair. She had traveled too far, seen too much to be refused without a chance. "To judge by this court of yours—held in my honor, as you put it—I have failed you in nothing!"

The demon, Gel, he answered, the mist suddenly swirling around him like a maelstrom. *In the guise of a green star I guided thee to his conjurer, expecting you to dispatch the misbegotten human. Thee knows it not, but the wizard has made a pact to set the demon free upon the earth.*

She was barely interested, shaken by the twin ideas that her mother still lived and that Orchos was refusing to aid Aki's salvation. "So slay him yourself," she snapped, then scornfully: "Are you not lord of hell and death's master?"

Yet I am bound by cosmic law, and this was lawful conjuration. I granted that Gel should serve the human.

She shook her head, not understanding. "But if Onokratos entered into a pact with you, then he is bound by those same magical laws."

Thunder crackled in his voice. *The fool is human! He has broken our pact by making a new one with Gel.*

"If the pact is broken, then why keep your part of it?" she argued sensibly. "Do what you will. Kill Onokratos and reclaim your demon."

His speech was no longer gentle; it throbbed in her skull, causing pain. *I am Orchos!* he raged. *My word is bond and must be kept, even to the mortal spawn who seeks to cheat me, even to a rebel demon who would escape hell.* He thrust a finger at her. Again, she remembered that storm she'd witnessed on the Calendi cliffs. It had blown inland, ravaging crops and homes, taking lives. *Thee must slay the wizard. Then Gel will be mine to claim.*

"I can't!" she shouted, clapping hands to her aching head. "I need him!" Hastily, she explained about Aki and Kalynda, how the chaos-bringer held their souls in bondage, how she hoped to rescue them.

"For one reason of itself you should help us," she pleaded. "Gath has stolen two souls that rightfully are yours."

Only one, daughter, the death lord answered. *Spiders are sacred to Gath. The Kalynda-child died from the venom of those creatures; her soul is rightfully his. As for the Aki-child: I will not war with chaos for the possession of one soul.* He waved a hand. *Speak no more of this matter.*

She felt a tingle in the soul-thread. She looked behind in alarm, but the cord soon disappeared in the fog. She could not see the portal. Desperation gripped her. Time was short.

"Would you risk it for five?" she challenged. "And for the return of your demon?"

The god's eyebrows shot upward, a curiously human sight. *Explain what thee proposes.*

That echoed softly, painlessly. She knew she'd caught his interest. But the soul-thread jangled now, sending shocks through her astral form.

"A contest!" she shouted. "If you win, you claim our souls instantly to punish as you will . . ."

And if thee wins? He was scoffing, mocking her. His amusement was a tangible sensation in her brain.

The soul-thread vibrated insistently. She rushed to spit the words out. "You agree to fight Gath for the girls' souls! To free them to live the natural span of their lives!"

His laughter nearly overwhelmed her. Her senses whirled, and for a moment the jangling of the soul-thread was forgotten. She covered her ears uselessly.

But who will fight? he inquired through his laughter.

"I will fight!" she answered fiercely through her disorientation. "And Tras Sur'tian and Kimon, Onokratos, and Gel!" She felt the soul-thread again, stronger, insistent. "I must go!"

He waved his hand again. The mists of hell's third level faded. The fires of the ninth and lowest hell licked harmlessly at her silvery flesh. The cries of the tormented assailed her. Far above, she spied the portal, a yawning hole in the blazing sky. She leaped, feeling the soul-thread contract, pulling her toward home.

Whom shall I send against thee? Orchos's mocking laughter resounded in her skull.

The portal grew rapidly as she sped toward it. The jangling in her lifeline did not ease; it spread through her. She flew as swiftly as she could, terror-stricken that the portal might close before she reached it. Would her soulless body become like Aki's, then, animalistic?

Whom? The question echoed again.

"The hordes of hell!" she screamed. "Or anybody!"

Heat and fire dissolved. She raced through inky blackness, the same void she had traversed before, following the shining, glistening soul-thread.

A vast image of the lord of death suddenly blocked her

path, limbs stretched to the four corners of infinity. *Daughter,* he hailed her. *Such audacity rivals the gods'. It deserves opportunity, which I grant.* His immense brow furrowed. *But be warned—thy sins have been great and many.*

The threat was not lost on her. Not all hells were for punishment, the god had told her. But most were. She pushed the thought away and flew faster. The warning of her soul-thread was more immediate, demanding her attention.

I am proud of thee, he proclaimed with a sage nod. *We meet again at Skull Gate.*

The image faded, leaving her way to the portal clear.

It was a dim light in the void. Drawing near it, she could see, as if through a window, the room where her body stood entranced. Gel loomed over it. The dagger—Orchos had called it an athame—trembled in her out-stretched hands.

She achieved the portal, passed through, went straight to her body, and merged.

A scream ripped from her lips. Demonfang's energy rippled through her mind, gripping her will with undeniable strength. She screamed again. Gel's control over the dagger was nearly gone. She could feel its hunger. Too long had it gone unsated. It would feed soon, feast on her heart. Through blurred vision she could barely see Tras Sur'tian. Didn't he know she was back in her body? She gathered what little strength she had left.

"Help . . ." she croaked unintelligibly. Could they have heard that pitiful sound? Hadn't they heard her screams?

Then Kimon's face was next to hers. His hands closed around hers. He nearly jumped on the blade as he jerked it toward his chest. "No!" she cried, though no word came out.

Desperately, she pushed against Demonfang's power, resisted, and managed to divert the blade ever so slightly. The point missed his heart, sank half to the hilt through the muscle of his chest. His mouth twisted in a noiseless shriek, eyes widened with sudden terror, and he fell.

Blood fountained on his tunic. He stared upward, seeking her gaze; his face convulsed with pain. Frost fell to her knees beside him and wrenched the dagger free. He gripped her sleeve. His features clouded over, and his head lolled abruptly to the side. Then, his lids closed.

"He loves thee greatly, daughter. . . ."

Frost clapped a hand to her mouth and recoiled. Kimon's lips moved with speech, but the voice belonged to the lord of the nine hells.

"His sins are blackest of all, yet he braves this death for thee. Remember thee in thy songs, then, how his father spurned him as a bastard son and his mother reviled him for the shame of his birth, how that father trained and used him as murderer and assassin, and how he walked all his days on the rivers of blood." The voice of Orchos paused, and a crimson froth boiled from Kimon's lips.

Death's master continued. "Thee alone, daughter, of all that he has ever known showed him trust and freely gave him heart-love. He saw the caring thee shared with comrades and thought to share it, too. Once, he might have killed thee for a coin. Instead, he fled his past and reached for a greater treasure."

Again, Orchos paused. Frost trembled, despairing, unable to move. Kimon's lips stirred. "I may have him this time," the god said. "I see his soul approaching. Like thee, he has served me well, and I am proud of him. Remember, daughter, in thy songs."

There was no more. Frost rose slowly, numb. The silent, sated dagger clattered on the floor. Her hand, bright and sticky with Kimon's life-fluid, shook uncontrollably. She stared at it, deep in horror, unable to accept that it was hers.

There was a noise barely perceived, a heavy thud as Gel collapsed, exhausted. Onokratos leaped inside the triangle of silverdust and swiftly snatched up Demonfang.

"No!" she shrilled, kicking it from his grasp.

Hands grabbed her gently but firmly by the shoulders. She felt breath warm on her neck; soft words, calming words whispered in her ear.

"Tras!" she cried, turning in his arms. Her thoughts
rushed in chaotic, disjointed fragments. "Help me!" she
begged. But then she pushed him away. "No, don't touch
me!" She stared at her incarnadined hand, at Demonfang
on the chamber floor, at Kimon, at the candles and braziers that smoked and glowed like the fires of hell. "Tras?"
Gel curled up weakly at her feet, and the demon glared at
her. "Tras!"

The Korkyran reached out again to soothe and hold her,
but she backed away from them all until the wall pressed
against her spine. Her shoulder brushed the shutter of the
western window. She whirled and flung off the latch,
threw it wide. The sun, a fat and dusky ruby, squatted on
the purpling horizon, tugged on the first strings of night.

Her mouth opened then. She screamed and screamed
until blackness swallowed everything.

Chapter Thirteen

From every side the demons attacked. She whipped out her sword, too late. It melted magically; molten metal seared her hands. Claws rent her flesh. Fangs dripping with ichorous saliva sank into her throat. The hordes of hell bore her helplessly down. The tattered end of her soul-thread lashed the scorching air. Her screams turned to frantic gurgles as they pushed her head beneath the steaming, boiling surface of the lake of fire. The skin dissolved from her skull.

Suddenly, they released her. She gasped for breath, looked up as the demons fell away, and gave a little cry of joyous relief. Orchos filled the sky with his presence; his laughter filled her ears. She lifted her arms suppliantly, thinking herself saved. But laughter ceased; his smile turned to a leer. His huge foot rose over her. She screamed as it came squashing down, down, down . . .

She sat up suddenly, drenched in sweat, shivering. Her hair hung in ropes about her face; the blanket that covered her nakedness was clammy and damp. Nightmare images still burned in her brain. She rubbed her hands nervously, sucked deep breaths.

Something moved in the shadows at the foot of her bed. She threw up her arms in a defensive posture; a sharp, raspy noise rattled in her throat. Then the figure shambled into the dim amber glow of the room's lonely candle, and she recognized the grizzled white beard.

Tras Sur'tian leaned over her. She flung her arms around his neck, dragged him down beside her on the hard bed, and buried her face in his chest to hide her sudden tears.

"Tras!" she cried. "I've made such a fearful, stupid bargain! I tried to be brave!" The words gushed out, uncontrolled. "But when I felt the soul-thread's pull, I panicked. I didn't think!" She pushed him back abruptly. "Tras, we should have made a plan! You can't imagine what it was like there!" She pounded her eyes with fists. "I can't get it out of my mind, Tras! I see it everywhere!"

He caught her fists, drew her close once more, pressed her cheek to his, and rocked her consolingly. "It's over now," he soothed. "It's done."

Their shadows rippled over the floor, climbed up the wall, brushed the low ceiling. She stared at the flickering, shifting shapes, so seemingly blessed or cursed with peculiar, independent movement, and bit her lip. "It's not over," she whispered tersely. "It's just begun."

Tears ran their course. When her eyes were dry she disentangled herself from him. "I want light," she said firmly. "As much light as possible."

Tras got up and opened the only shutter. The sky bled crimson and indigo on the spears of approaching night. Already, a pale wisp of a moon rode the horizon. The old soldier lit two more candles from the burning taper. "There are more on that shelf," she told him, recalling where Onokratos's store of candles lay.

She hugged the blanket around her shoulders while he set fire to three fresh wicks, but the light brought no cheer. She felt shamed. She thought she had toughened herself, hammered out all the womanish instincts, forged herself into a soldier, a mercenary to whom fighting and struggle and death were the natural way. Never before had she acknowledged fear, never surrendered to its sickening, sweet fever.

Yet now she was afraid, no denying it, and the sense of it crept up her spine like an itch she could not scratch.

"More candles," she urged, hating the strained sound of her voice. "Lamps, anything! Get some light!" But there were no more candles in the room, and when Tras hurried for the door a new dread stole upon her. "No!" she shouted. "Tras, enough light. Just stay with me, please."

Deep furrows creased his brow as he returned and sat down by her side. He brushed the hair back from her face with fatherly concern. But his eyes avoided hers.

"Please," she begged. "I just don't want to be alone yet." She laid her head on his shoulder, but his arms remained limp at his sides. She couldn't help but notice.

Abruptly uncomfortable, she changed the subject. "How's Kimon?"

He shook his head. "He lost a lot of blood. Might have died, but Onokratos's hell-spawned pet somehow found strength to repair the wound."

She tried to catch his eye and failed. "Then, he's well?"

He said nothing for a long moment, then breath hissed slowly between his pursed lips. "He's unconscious," he answered wearily. "Hasn't stirred, not even twitched." He got up and paced to the room's far side, arms folded over his chest, head hanging. Finally, he crossed to the open window, stared out. "I tried to hate him," he confessed after a while. "I did hate him. For his part in Aki's kidnapping I should still hate him."

"But you don't?" she ventured when he hesitated.

"How can I, after the way he tried to sacrifice himself on that demon blade of yours?" He turned on her suddenly, his face burning with anger. "Now you repay such devotion by whining and bellowing and putting on these cowardly airs!"

The force of his accusations struck her like a physical blow.

"Any other man might dismiss it as the womanish part of you!" he railed, shaking a fist. "But I know you better!"

"You know nothing!" she shouted defensively. "You still don't know the terrible deal I've made with Orchos."

"I don't need to know!" he answered crisply. In three quick strides he loomed over her. "Woman, I've had my share of frights on this journey, seen and done things that would damn my soul if I still believed in Korkyra's One God." He stabbed a finger at her. "You showed me how to keep my courage in the face of the unknown. Now show me you can do the same!"

"B-but you don't—" she stammered.

"Don't tell me I don't understand," he interrupted. "You've shaken the very roots of my soul, shattered the faith of my ancestors, the beliefs that sustained me, with the wonders and terrors you've led me to see. You were inside the circle but a short moment—"

"A moment!" she shrieked.

"A few heartbeats," he continued, "before Gel lost control of your dagger. Next, you're screaming like a soul in torment, Kimon's bleeding nearly to death, and that big, black devil is out colder than last week's cheese." He paused, swallowed. "All right, maybe you were frightened, then. But that's an unaffordable luxury now. We've got to pull together and get on with it."

"But you don't know," she whispered dejectedly.

He was unrelenting. "All I know," he insisted, "is that you're the only one with experience and skill to lead us through this. I don't trust our host or his vile pet. If you've lost your nerve now, then we've suffered for nothing, and Aki is lost to us for all time."

His words stung. She looked to him for some comfort, but his demeanor was unbending steel. Tears welled again in her eyes, but under his withering gaze she fought them back. Slowly, she rose from the bed, hugging the blanket around her shoulders.

"Where are my clothes?" she said finally.

Tras Sur'tian let out a long sigh. Then a grin spread over his features; he cocked his head sheepishly. "Wet," he answered. "I washed them. You"—he paused, licked his lips thoughtfully, embarrassed—"befouled yourself in your sleep."

She blushed, feeling the warmth in her cheeks. "What about my weapons?"

He pointed to the table. "Your sword is there. That other thing, too." She knew he meant Demonfang. "Onokratos wanted to examine it after you fainted. I nearly had to break his arm to get it away from him. Without the demon to back him up, he's not much."

She buckled on Demonfang's silver belt, then her sword belt over that. The metal was cool on her skin, the leather rough. She wore the blanket like a cloak. "Don't underestimate him," she warned. "He's not just a wizard. He has sorcerous powers." She gathered back her hair. Her moonstone circlet also lay on the table. She set it on her head to hold back her tangled mane. "Now, I'm thoroughly hungry. Let's find something to eat; then I want to see Kimon." She gripped her old friend's shoulder. A stray beam of moonlight made her ivory flesh shine where the blanket gaped open. The hilt of her sword glittered. "But first," she said gently, "there's something I'd better show you. I think, now, you can handle the truth."

She took one of the candles and motioned for him to do the same. She led him out the door, into the maze of corridors, and down through the murky darkness to the cell where the High Queen of Korkyra squatted on her haunches and pawed through the straw-littered floor searching for insects to squash and eat.

Frost entered Kimon's room quietly, and Tras followed. Gel, completely recovered from his part in the ordeal, stood over the bed in apparent study of the slumbering human. He nodded a stiff greeting.

"White beard," the demon addressed the Korkyran. "Thee looks pale as a slug's belly."

Tras didn't answer. He hadn't spoken at all since leaving Aki's cell. But he met the demon's mocking gaze coldly, and to Frost's surprise it was Gel who turned away.

She went to Kimon's bedside. It was a bare frame like her own, but someone had cushioned his head with extra blankets. "How is he?"

Gel shrugged. "I do not know. The wound is healed.

The human should be well." His black eyes roamed over her slowly as he answered. "What of thee?"

She ignored the question and sat on the bed, taking Kimon's hand. It was warm, at least. She raised each eyelid as she had seen the chirurgeons do on the battle-fields. She pulled back the coverlet to examine his chest. No trace of a wound, not the smallest scar where the dagger had entered.

"It was a mortal wound."

She turned at the new voice. Onokratos pushed the door shut behind him. "If Gel had not recovered in time, your young friend would be quite dead." He pointed to the dagger on her hip. In her carelessness the blanket she wore had slipped open. She tugged it tighter around herself. "If I understand the nature of that weapon, it sucks the souls of its victims straight to the ninth level of hell, regardless of whether or not they deserve that severest of punishments." He struck a scholarly pose with expression to match. "I suspect in that brief moment between life and death, Kimon glimpsed that fate. Unable to accept what he saw, his mind has shut down."

She shuddered, visions suddenly rushing upon her of the lake of fire and the creatures condemned to dwell there. Yet on her journey she had been insulated by the knowledge that she could leave, that she wasn't dead, and that the soul-thread would pull her back to the world of the living when she wished.

Had Kimon faced hell without that assurance? She shuddered again and laid a hand on his cheek. "Come back to us," she urged in a tense whisper. "It's all right. Come back."

She got up, cursing the blade Demonfang, swearing as she had so many times in the past to destroy it at the first opportunity. "Is it safe to leave him alone?" she asked Onokratos when her anger abated.

He cocked his head at an angle. "Why not? We can do nothing to help him. He'll have to climb out of this darkness by himself."

She headed for the door. "We've got to talk," she said.

"All of us. Now." After a brief hesitation, she added, "It's time you learned what lies ahead." She stepped into the passage and stopped. Frowning, she peered in either direction. Though she was beginning to learn some of the corridors, the manor was still a confusing maze of halls that never seemed to lead to the same place twice. She threw up her hands in disgust. "Would someone please lead the way out of here?"

Onokratos guided them to the dining chamber. She remembered suddenly how hungry she was and rubbed her stomach. A broken stool, evidence of the earlier struggle, blocked her path. She kicked it away, righted the overturned benches, and sat down at the table. She leaned forward on her elbows and regarded them as they each took a place. She looked at her host. "Anything in the cupboard?"

Onokratos crooked a finger and nodded to Gel. The demon went back through the large double doors and vanished up the passage. He returned moments later bearing a platter of cold meats and a tightly rolled bundle.

"What is that?" Onokratos inquired, pointing.

The demon placed the platter on the smoothly worn tabletop and set the bundle in front of Frost. His eyes met hers. "Nudity offends her," he answered with a twinkle. It was the closest thing to humor she'd heard him attempt.

"No, it doesn't." With a brazen toss she threw off her blanket cloak and took her time unrolling the package. She nodded appreciatively. The garments were of the finest black leather: tunic, trousers, belt, the softest boots imaginable. When she held them up, though, she feared they were too large. No matter, she decided. Oversized clothing was better than none. She unbuckled her weapons.

To her surprise, everything fit. "They're perfect!" she exclaimed. Tras Sur'tian ran a finger down one sleeve with an approving smile.

"That was stupid."

The sharpness in the wizard's voice startled her, but it was Gel he addressed. Onokratos's face contorted with another of those rages that seemed to possess him without

warning. She reached cautiously for her sword belt and
fastened it in place.

The demon turned a cold gaze on his master. Frost
thought he actually grew bigger as he bent over the old
man. She blinked, and the illusion passed. Then Gel turned
up his nose, gave his back to Onokratos, and smiled a
strange, twisted leer at her.

But Onokratos would not be ignored. "Cursed beast of
the pit!" he stormed, coming around, planting himself in
the demon's path, wagging a finger chidingly in the air.
"We cannot afford that kind of useless waste. Mark what I
say!"

Frost's brow furrowed. What waste did he rail about?
She felt her own wrath rising, and she drew deep breaths
to calm herself. Yet, clearly Onokratos was still keeping
secrets.

She picked up Demonfang, fastened the belt's silver
clasp, and rested her hand on its pommel. She strode up
to the demon, practically shouldering the wizard aside.
"He's hiding something," she said, carefully measuring
her boldness. "What?"

"Be silent!" Onokratos shouted, and stamped his foot.

Gel studied her for a long moment, rubbing his chin.
Then he gave the wizard a sidelong glance and answered.
"I am gradually—"

His master was livid. "Shut up!" he raged.

The demon ignored him. "—losing my powers." He
said it without batting an eyelash.

She caught her breath. "Oh, gods!"

Onokratos snatched a cup from the table near his hand
and flung it with all his force. It bounced harmlessly off
Gel's shoulder. "Disobedience! Our pact . . ."

Gel fixed him with a passionless stare. "Requires that I
aid thee in regaining the Kalynda-child. No more."

Onokratos's voice dropped to a barely audible pitch.
"You're like a pitcher, now, that contains only so much
water! Every time you use your powers they get weaker.
Conjuring nourishment is one thing, but providing clothing
when she has garments . . ."

"Those are her garments." The demon turned a gleaming eye on her, and she felt that weird flush of heat once more. "I have only transformed them to a more flattering material and style. Is she not pleasing dressed thus?" He made a short nod and grinned. "I can see that she is pleased."

Onokratos would have continued the argument, but she broke in. "Explain why your powers are failing."

Gel's face darkened; wrinkles lined his brow, and he looked pensive. "I believe thee are corrupting me," he answered thickly. "The longer I walk this mortal plane, the more I experience human emotion." His gaze did not waver from hers. "I lust for thee," he admitted, then pointed to Onokratos, "and I am learning disgust for this one." The wizard raised a threatening fist, but the demon ignored him. "The more I feel these emotions, the weaker my powers become."

Tras Sur'tian crept closer. "Is that why you collapsed in the sanctum?"

Gel nodded. "The effect seems cumulative. Each passing day I am weaker, and if I use my magic, I grow weaker still. The Kimon-human nearly died before I found strength to heal his wound."

Frost sagged against the table's edge and hung her head. "Nothing can be done to stop it?"

He shrugged. "I am infected already. The longer I am around thee, the more I share human emotion, and the weaker I grow."

She pondered her options while Tras Sur'tian questioned Gel nearly to distraction. Onokratos slumped onto a bench and spoke no more, but glared sullenly at all three.

Finally, she drew erect. "We've got to move fast." She pointed to the meats. "Eat while I explain. You won't like what you hear, but don't interrupt." When Onokratos didn't move, she snapped, "That means you. No telling when you'll feed again. You're going to need your strength."

When she finished her tale they stared, aghast.

Onokratos spat out a mouthful and shouted, "You mean

the five of us must fight an equal number of Orchos's demons?'' He slammed a fist on the board. ''Was that the best bargain you could drive?''

Tras Sur'tian kept his voice calm, yet could not hide his doubt. ''If we win, Orchos will fight for the children's souls.'' He pursed his lips, jerked a thumb at Gel. ''Even weakened, he may have some chance''—he looked around— ''but what weapons have you and I against champions from hell?''

''My powers are fast diminishing,'' Gel insisted.

''But not yet gone,'' Frost answered quickly. ''And we've got this''—she clapped Demonfang's hilt—''and this.'' She removed the jewel talisman Oona had given her.

Onokratos sneered at the jewel. ''That offers you some protection, but you need an offensive weapon. A draw is not good enough. You must win the contest.''

''You're a sorcerer as well as a wizard,'' she countered. ''You must have some skills to call on.'' She returned to Tras. ''And we also have these.'' She gripped the hilt of her sword. ''Orchos's demons must take solid form to harm us, and whatever is solid can be harmed in kind.''

Onokratos turned up his nose, barked a short, contemptuous laugh.

''You're forgetting the mathematics, woman.'' Tras leaned his chin on a fist. ''You've sworn for five of us. I'll go for Aki's sake. They, of course, for Kalynda's. But what about Kimon? If he should die or decide not to fight, what of that?''

''If Kimon is able, he will fight. For me, if no other reason.'' She looked to the demon. ''And you will not let him die.'' It was not a question.

Gel blinked. ''I can keep him alive, but I cannot animate his limbs.''

''He'll come around!'' she cried. ''If we must bear him to Skull Gate on our backs, he'll be ready when we need him. He must be.'' She was startled by her own intensity and rued it for its obvious effect on her companions. She sought to lighten the mood somewhat. "Speaking of Skull Gate," she said with a roll of the eyes, "who knows where it lies?"

The evening passed in a wash of amethyst and mauve. Frost watched the last of the sun's rays as she scattered straw and soft blankets over the wagon bed. A low whinny drew her attention from the shading sky. Tras Sur'tian groomed and fed his horse and Kimon's. Gel worked beside him, readying Onokratos's big bay mare and the pair of matched ash-colored palfreys that would pull the wagon. She returned to her task, preparing the place where Kimon and the girls would ride, making it plush. Near the front behind the driver's seat she stored waterskins and salted rations. Everything had to be ready for the morning's departure.

It was dark when they returned to the manor house with torches to light the way. Onokratos had excused himself earlier; they had not seen him since. Frost went straight to her room, leading Tras Sur'tian. She lit candles and turned to face him. Her shadow engulfed him, swelled upon the wall.

"Our work is not yet done." She spoke softly, almost a whisper.

He made a face. "Food is packed, horses ready, weapons clean and sharp. What remains?"

She put a finger to her lips, warning him to use a lower voice. "Metal weapons aren't enough." She closed her eyes, dreading what she knew must be done. "We need more."

He began to pace. "If you mean sorcery, say so. I'm not the ignorant One God worshiper I used to be."

She nodded. "All right, then. Sorcery."

He made a curt gesture. "Leave me out of it. That's work for our host and his pet."

"No, it's not!" she hissed stridently. "Would you trust someone else to sharpen your sword?" She moved around the room's small desk and leaned on it. Her shadow hulked on the wall behind her. "We see to our own weapons, you and I. That's how we were trained. Then we know they're ready when we need them."

He regarded her cagily. "You said you weren't a witch anymore, that you couldn't work magic."

She tapped her temple. "My witchcraft is gone, but not my knowledge." A sly wink. "Remember Mirashai and the Hand of Glory? Well, I instructed Oona in its making. Just as I'll instruct you."

He sat up, suddenly interested. "Will the Hand affect Orchos's demons?" He rubbed his hands. "That would be a weapon indeed!"

She shook her head; hair lashed her cheeks. "Unfortunately, no. Nor would there be time to create such a complex abomination. I also doubt you would have the heart for that task."

He frowned. "Then what?"

"Something much simpler, but possibly just as effective." She allowed a small grin. "Your Korkyran priests would call it holy water."

He arched his eyebrows in mild surprise. "Can you make this holy water?" he asked. "The priests say it is sacred, secret."

"Fie on all priests." She mimed spitting. "I can't, but you can with my instruction."

He hooked thumbs in his sword belt, drew a breath. "If it will help Aki, when do we begin?"

"As soon as we gain entrance to Onokratos's sanctum."

"Won't he object?"

She picked up the candle and opened the door to the darkened hall, peered both ways, and beckoned. "I don't even want him to know," she whispered.

Chapter Fourteen

The bright morning sun caused her to blink as she stepped out of the gloomy manor and breathed the fresh clean air. Droplets of dew clung to the clumped, withered grass; the day's warmth would soon evaporate them.

Onokratos waited by the wagon. Three horses stood tethered to one wheel. The wizard shielded his eyes and hailed her. "We have plenty of water already," he said, pointing to the two waterskins that hung on straps from her shoulders.

Frost feigned disinterest. "A little surplus never hurts," she remarked, gazing around. "Where are the others?"

She heard the scuffle of boots before he could answer. Gel carried Kalynda in his huge arms. Tras Sur'tian bore Aki. Both children appeared fast asleep. They were placed gingerly on the soft straw pallet in the wagon.

Frost peered over the side at them, then laid a hand on Tras's shoulder. "They look too still," she said.

The demon answered. "A simple spell to keep them quiet and manageable on the journey. They could not be left behind untended."

She admitted she hadn't thought of sedating them. It made things simpler. She studied the two small reclining forms. "It will be crowded with Kimon," she said.

"He says he will ride," Tras Sur'tian informed her, grinning.

She closed her eyes, uttered a short prayer of thanks to her Esgarian gods. "When did he awaken?"

The Korkyran rubbed his bearded chin. "He was sitting up when I checked on him at first light."

She leaned closer, whispered confidentially. "Is he all right?"

Tras Sur'tian's answer was loud, meant for all ears. "Why not ask him?" His gaze flickered beyond her shoulder. She turned.

"Samidar!" Kimon wore a weak grin as he came to her side. He appeared pale yet, and he'd lost weight during his three-day ordeal. Still, he bore himself proudly, lifted her hand and kissed it.

A disturbing tightness gripped her chest. She realized, with some personal consternation, that she still hadn't sorted out her feelings about Kimon. In fact, she'd actively sought other matters to occupy her time. Not that she'd had to seek far.

She looked up into those deep blue eyes, discovering again how easy it was to lose her heart in the warmth of his gaze.

He started to speak, but her fingers stopped his lips. Her arms went around him, pulled his face down. Their cheeks brushed; the warmth of his flesh seemed to ignite her with tingling fire. Then she gave him a hasty kiss and backed away. "There are more important matters right now," she told him, "but later, we must talk alone."

"Excuse me for interrupting this tender moment." There was a note of annoyance in the wizard's voice. "Everyone has a mount but you, woman. Do you intend to walk?"

She gave Kimon a last sidelong glance, then turned away and put two fingers to the corners of her mouth. A long, high note whistled on the air.

Onokratos sneered. "I'm impressed," he said, "but I've never seen a whistle saddled before. Do you mount it on the left side or the right?"

Tras Sur'tian came to her defense. "Shut your mouth and open your eyes, old man."

Onokratos flushed, raised a furious fist to strike. Tras

Sur'tian's cold expression silently dared. Then, as quickly as it had flared, the wizard's temper faded. Finally, he looked outward where the Korkyran directed him.

A black speck appeared in the distance, taking recognizable shape as it raced toward them. Frost whistled a second time, a piercing note.

"Ashur," Tras Sur'tian informed the wizard. "Her mount."

"How could it hear her that far away?" It was Kimon who spoke, awed.

"He hears," Tras Sur'tian answered. "He always hears."

Frost smiled at her old friend. He was learning. He had performed without qualm or sqeamishness last night, the perfect apprentice, trusting her implicitly, obeying instructions no matter how they contradicted his old philosophies. He was not the same man she had known in Mirashai.

"Onokratos? With your abilities, have you the true-sight?"

He shrugged, not bothering to answer her query. She assumed he didn't.

She wondered about Tras Sur'tian. The Korkyran had learned much in the last weeks. How much had his understanding deepened? "Tras, look carefully. What do you see?"

He squinted as he watched Ashur approach. "I'm not sure," he answered. "I know your Ashur. I've groomed him myself. But sometimes there's a shadow of something more when I look at him." He shaded his eyes against the sun's glare. "I keep remembering the hole in that soldier's chest outside Mirashai's gate. It's disconcerting, weird."

She turned to the demon. "Gel, what do you see?"

"I see what I see," was his cryptic reply. But she noticed his gaze did not waver from her speeding steed, and his lips parted slightly, damp with moisture. So, even demons knew amazement.

"Can you let them see, too?" she asked him, coming to his side.

Those dark, penetrating orbs slid over her. Yet again she experienced a warm rush, now familiar when she stood near him. With some effort, she ignored the sensation and repeated her question.

"It requires an expenditure of power," he answered slowly.

She considered carefully and reached a decision. "How much of an expenditure?"

The demon shrugged. With a quickness that belied his great bulk, he touched Onokratos's eyes, then Tras Sur'tian's. But Kimon, misunderstanding, ducked lithely under Gel's reach and leaped back. His sword whisked out.

"Kimon!" She stepped between them. He looked from her to the demon hesitantly. She laid a hand on the point of his blade and pushed it down. He didn't resist, realizing he'd embarrassed himself somehow. "Let him touch you," Frost urged. He nodded. Gel gently placed thumb and forefinger over his lids. "Now, look at Ashur. Most of all, I wanted you to see."

He gasped, stared, just as Tras Sur'tian and Onokratos stared, oblivious to all else. Ashur trotted to her side. The beast nuzzled against her, passing its great horn under her arm, pushing her playfully backward. She smacked him on the nose, a playful rebuke. "Behave!" she ordered. "Show-off!"

"His eyes!" Onokratos exclaimed. "Are they really—"

She waved him to silence. "I wanted you all to see," she said, "and take hope. There are some small powers on our side. If we use them properly, perhaps we stand a chance against Orchos." She stroked Ashur's withers. "For now, no more questions. Onokratos, show the way."

The wizard swallowed, regained his composure. He pointed westward. "Skodulac is an island in the waters of Dyre Lake. There, you'll find Skull Gate." He wiped a trace of spittle from his lips. "I'll tell you no more, but wait for you to see it." His gaze snapped back to Ashur. "I think you took a special joy from this revelation."

She gave no answer but swung up astride Ashur's bare back.

"What happened to your saddle?" Tras Sur'tian wondered aloud. "And your bridle? He was wearing them last I recall. The cinch might have given way on the saddle. But how did he lose the bit?"

She gave no thought to such things. It was enough to ride the unicorn, to call such a creature hers. She was a proficient rider. The lack of proper tack meant nothing to her. She scratched Ashur between the ears with one hand, tangled the other in his rich, wild mane.

They rode the first part of the morning in silence. The withered fields of the ancient manor gave way to a rocky, blighted expanse and that, in turn, to a distant rise of rolling hillocks. There was no road; they made their own.

A light wind rose, stirred her hair around her face. The steady fall of the horses' hooves and the creaking of the wagon were the only sounds. She contrasted that with the first part of her journey, when she and Kimon had filled the air with song and verse. Privately, she wished Kimon would break out with a joyful tune now, but his attention seemed elsewhere; his gaze swept the far horizon left to right.

When the sun reached its zenith they paused to rest the horses, allowing them to drink a little, not much, from a small stream that purled across their path. Tras Sur'tian assumed charge of the animals, taking care they did not overindulge, either on the water or the plush grass.

Frost went to the wagon to fetch a drink from the stored skins and to check on the children. They slept unmoving under sweet enchantment, but the hot sun had turned their small, serene faces a tender pink. "Is there some way we can shade them?" she inquired of Onokratos.

"I'll rig something," he answered curtly, and he began to experiment with ways to drape his cloak tentlike over the wagon's sides.

As she tipped the waterskin for a second cool drink, she noticed how Kimon stood off to one side away from the others. She carried the skin to him, offered it. When he turned, she saw how one hand rubbed his chest.

Her brows knitted in concern. "Does the wound hurt?" she whispered. "I thought Gel healed it?"

A tight frown. "It is healed," he answered. "Yet, I feel something, not pain, but an *awareness*. The way a bone break tingles when the air is damp. You know?"

She nodded and surprised herself by reaching out to touch the place where Demonfang had drunk his blood. Her finger traced a small circle on the rough material of his jerkin. Regret and shame stilled her tongue. Words would not come.

"I had such visions," he confessed suddenly. His eyes burned into hers. "Except they weren't visions." He squeezed his eyes shut, trembled all over, the knuckles showing whitely through the taut skin of his clenched fists. "Terrible, dark things grabbing, clawing at me, dragging me down!" He ground those fists against his closed lids. "Fire! Fire everywhere! It seared!"

She grabbed his wrists, pulled them down, flung her arms around him. She pulled him close, pressing his face down to her shoulder. His body shivered; she felt his heart beating swiftly so near that vicious wound. A desperate longing filled her. "I know!" she comforted him. "I saw it, too!" She smoothed his hair. Her hand trailed over the tight muscles of his neck.

"There was blackness, an immense, unending void," he hissed, his breath hot in her ear. "I didn't see or feel anything. I couldn't move." His arms locked around her waist, nearly crushing her with the strength he exerted. "Then, I heard you calling. 'Come back, Kimon,' you said. 'Come back.' " He released her suddenly and stood back. Terrible storms raged in the clear blue of his eyes. "And I did come back," he said furiously. "I heard you, and I came."

She blinked, unable to find her voice.

His trembling ceased; he was in control of himself again. He scooped up the waterskin she'd dropped. Fortunately, the stopper had held firm, preventing any spillage. He slung it over his shoulder in the manner of the two special skins she still wore.

He regarded her evenly, the tempest gone from his gaze. "Samidar, I've done what I've had to do to get by in this world. Sometimes, I've murdered. I'm not ashamed of it."

"You tried to kill me," she reminded him. "How can I forget that?"

He shook his head sadly. "I'm glad I failed," he answered. "I've never failed before." He cast a glance back toward the wagon. "I'm sorry Aki became involved."

She drew a long breath. "You're not really to blame," she admitted. "I see that now. Though Gel claims his power is diminishing, he must have been much stronger a month ago. I doubt I could have prevented him from stealing the child."

He took a step closer; his fingers brushed her cheek. "I love you, Samidar. When I was . . ." He swallowed. "In hell I screamed your name over and over. I didn't want to leave you." His hand wandered over her shoulder, down her arm. His fingers interlocked with hers. "I don't want to lose you," he said fiercely. "I love you."

She didn't let herself think, just flowed into his arms and kissed him, forgetting everything else. She clung to him with all her might, and there was no space between them.

"You give me warmth," she whispered, pressing his face to hers, "and strength to fill me for the rest of my days. So often I've denied my feelings. I've passed down the streets of red candles, seen figures holding each other in the cold and the shadows; I've ridden by hovels and farm huts late at night and seen old wives clinging to their husbands in the fireglow. Always, I pulled my cloak tighter and hurried on in silence." She pulled back a little, trapped his head between her palms, stared into his eyes with intensity. "Never let me be cold again," she said. "Let me live and die by your side. I don't care what you've done. I've done worse."

His lips came down on hers. They stood for a long time holding each other.

A loud *crack!* interrupted them. Reflexively, Frost jumped

away from Kimon, whirled, left hand gripping her sword's hilt.

Gel's dark shape leaned against the trunk of an old tree. He regarded them with a bemused smirk. In his hands he clutched a dead branch as long as his arm, nearly as thick. With startling ease he broke a piece of it and cast it aside. "She loves me." *Snap*. He broke another piece. It fell at his feet. "She loves me not." *Snap*. The crisp sound mocked the natural quiet of the forest. He destroyed the branch casually, a little at a time, an impressive display of muscular strength.

Yet the demon was not as amused as he would have Frost believe. Fire smoldered in his eyes; a dark mood underlay his words. No matter how she tried to hide it, he frightened her. Worse, she suspected he knew that.

"We've rested long enough," she announced, cursing the quaver in her voice. She headed for the wagon. As she passed close to Gel she felt the heat radiating from his flesh, smelled his strange, musky odor. She set her gaze on the wagon and quickened her step.

Onokratos had found a way to shade the sleeping girls with his cloak. They would not burn in the bright sun. She saw him with Tras Sur'tian and the horses near the stream's bank. The two were engaged in animate conversation. Ashur stood patiently nearby. She went to the unicorn, grabbed a handful of his mane, and swung up. "Let's go!" she called. "We've wasted too much time. Move!"

Tras Sur'tian looked up, his eyebrows knotting quizzically. He hurried toward her, leaving the horses to the wizard's care. Gel and Kimon were also approaching. Before they were within earshot, the Korkyran touched her knee and inquired, "Some problem has arisen?"

She gave no answer but glared at him. After a moment, he just shrugged, used to her moods. Onokratos, leading their mounts, looked about to say something, but a wink and a headshake from Tras warned him to silence. Kimon and Gel climbed into their saddles while the older men quickly harnessed the palfreys.

By midafternoon they were through the forest and out of

the hill country. A rich green carpet of land stretched before them. The wild grass was not too high to impede the wagon, and they made steady progress. By nightfall they were quite weary, except for the demon, who seemed immune to fatigue.

Trees were scarce; there was little to use for firewood. Instead, they gathered bunches of the dry, wheatlike stalks that grew among the other grasses and burned that. When the little bit of cooking was done, Frost extinguished the flames entirely with water from the regular skins.

Onokratos complained.

"Ever see a grass fire?" she asked him. "We could die in our sleep if the merest coal remained for the wind to fan."

But as she unrolled her blankets she began to wish for a fire. Korkyran nights were naturally cool, and a slowly rising breeze that rippled the ocean of grass promised to lend a sharp bite to the air before morning. She stretched on her back, cast her cloak over her legs and lower torso.

The stars gleamed above like slivers of ice. Far to the north she spotted the familiar serpent constellation with shinning Thubanr in the center of its body. The heavens revolved slowly around that bright star.

For a time, then, she was homesick. Thubanr reminded her of mariners who navigated by its light, and they reminded her of the sea and her home high on the cliffs above the raging Calendi.

Suddenly, she sat upright. She was remembering home, and for the first time in years, the memories were good. She lay back down. Were the nightmares behind her forever?

After a while, the increasing chill convinced her to seek out Kimon. She dragged her bedroll closer to his. He was already fast asleep but stirred and threw an embracing arm across her middle, effectively pinning her. She sighed and snuggled up to his warmth.

The last thing she remembered before sleep claimed her was a falling star trailing scintillant emerald sparks as it cleaved the darkness.

*   *   *

She rose with the sun. Kimon had rolled away during the night, and the cold had crept into her bones. She stretched until the stiffness in her muscles eased, then woke the others. Nobody mentioned breakfast; supplies were limited. Gel could conjure food as needed, but that would waste the demon's fading powers, powers that would be needed for the contest at Skull Gate.

The children still slept entranced in the wagon's soft hay bed. They required no food, no water. A strand of hair had strayed over Aki's eyes. Frost brushed it away. On an impulse, she kissed the ball of her thumb and pressed it to the young queen's brow.

The morning passed uneventfully. The sun followed them as it crossed the sky. Conversation flowed more freely than before as they settled into the journey's dull routine. The plain gave way to woodland again. For a while their course paralleled a small river. They took a short rest and watered their horses. Shortly after midday, the woods began to thin, and they discovered a well-cut road.

"The main road, by the look of it," Tras Sur'tian observed. "Somewhere, we crossed the regional border into Pelentea province."

"Then we've made good time." Onokratos took advantage of the moment and reached for a waterskin. Frost watched him drink, suddenly aware of the uncomfortable weight of the two special skins she bore. The straps had chafed flesh beneath her tunic. She considered placing them in the wagon but feared someone might drink from them when she was not looking or that they might be confused with the other skins. She unslung them and rubbed her muscles and the tender places. Then, making a decision, she gave the skins to Tras Sur'tian, who tied them to the pommel of his saddle.

"We'll make even better time on a decent road," Frost commented. They started off again.

Kimon began a song, his voice soaring on the quiet air. Surprisingly, Tras Sur'tian joined him on the chorus. It was a frivolous tune, as bawdy as ever she'd heard. More than once a particular lyric caused Onokratos to raise an eyebrow. Only Gel rode in silence, and his gaze raked the horizons.

Frost dropped back to ride beside him. "You have a hungry look, demon," she said quietly.

With dreamlike slowness his attention turned to her; his eyes locked with hers. Again, she felt that weird, disconcerting flush, and wondered why. "I am hungry," he admitted, "to make this world and everything in it mine." The demon blinked; she'd never seen him do that before. "My pact with Onokratos binds me to him until the Kalynda-child is free from the spider god's grasp. Then shall I fly, no longer slave to hell or Onokratos, finally to exercise my will upon earth." His huge, taloned hands curled into fists. An angry gleam flickered in his dark pupils, then died. "No, I shall not fly. My power is fading. Soon, all my magic will be gone. What shall it matter then if I am free?"

"Once, I was a witch," she reminded him, "and I lost my powers. There's life beyond that if you've courage to look. Your life is a bright diamond; every time you turn, a new facet shines—"

A scornful laugh swallowed her next words. "Little fool! So puny and insignificant! Would thee measure us by the same rule? Thee are human. Lose thy witchcraft and only a small part of thee is gone. But I am a creature of magic! If I lose my power, I lose my heart. What shall become of me then?" He barked another laugh, darkly rich with evil. "Human emotion! Hear me shout and rail? See how contact with humans has corrupted me? Emotion! What would thee call this one?"

"Bitterness," she provided; then, meeting his gaze with a certain smug pleasure, she added, "And fear."

"I could have ruled this miserable world," he muttered under his breath.

She shrugged. "All dreams are small ones in the end," she said, and set Ashur to a gallop until she caught up to

Kimon at the fore of their party. His mood was much more agreeable. "Sing me a song, sir," she requested.

He smiled. "I've a song for you indeed, composed of snippets I've heard in taverns and camps, some tidbits Tras Sur'tian let slip, and my own imagination."

"Will you sing it, or just explain it?" she gibed.

He sang.

"From a land where the trees grow tall as they please
And a diamond dew covers the earth;
Where the night wind sings to magical things
That laugh with fantastical mirth

Came a child with a sword all incarnadined, red
With blood of her family,
And she rides from the dreams that torment her sleep
And her witch-mother's last prophecy.

From Esgaria fair to Etai Calan
She rode through a sorcerous storm.
There, a Tool of Light brought her safe through the night
To witness his death on the morn.

But she took up his task, an old book that he stole,
Called the Last Battle 'Twixt Light and Dark,
And she rode like the wind on his great unicorn
O'er a landscape turned barren and stark.

Through fire and trial she came to a land,
By legends, a dark evil place,
To seek for a sorcerer, Kregan by name,
A lord of the cruel Chondite race.

But she found there a people to help with her quest
And a love to fill her young heart.
With an army to guide, they swept like a tide,
Bearing weapons of sorcerous art.

So they rode like the wind to Demonium Gate
Where their magical power would be strong.
Every stone glowed bright with the colors of fire
In a night supernaturally long.

And the eye of their foe, Zarad-Krul he was called,
Appeared with a cold, rheumy stare
To demand the book for the dark gods he served,
Or his magic and armies beware!

Well, that child with a sword and her sorcerous love
And her army prepared to make war,
And they met Zarad-Krul on the edge of a field
Till the night reeked of carnage and gore.

Oh, they battled each other with magic and sword
Till the dark gods themselves took a hand.
And three sent thousands to hell with a shrug,
And three shadows fell long on the land.

But next to her heart the child had the book,
And by witchcraft she opened it wide,
And there found a spell that would triumph o'er hell
If the lords of light fought at her side.

So she sang out the words and a whirlwind appeared
Bearing gods from the heavens to earth,
And they forced back the night with the power of their
    light,
Driving evil's three sons from the earth.

But when it was over and victory won,
Kregan, her lover, lay dead,
Lifted high by that whirlwind and smashed on a stone—
And her mother's words rang in her head:
(Prophecy from the lips of the dead!)

'Oh, you are a creature of fire and frost,
So Frost shall your name ever be,

And you'll never give your heart to a man
Unless death is his quick destiny.' ''

He finished and looked to her for approval. When she
said nothing after long moments, he reached for her hand
and squeezed. "Well?" he prodded.

She licked her lips. "Very fanciful," she conceded
softly, unwilling to meet his eyes. "Mark well that last
verse. Sing it often. Each time you think you love me."
She tugged on Ashur's mane, turned the unicorn about,
and rode to Tras Sur'tian's side.

"You had no right to tell him so much," she whispered.

He frowned. "I told him almost nothing, woman. Your
secrets have never been secret. I've heard a similar song
before, a score of versions in as many taverns."

The sun descended the afternoon sky.

Frost mopped the sweat from her brow and folded one
leg over Ashur's withers. The insides of her thighs were
saturated with the unicorn's lather. She rode with an easy
rocking motion, in no danger of falling, but idly she
wished for a saddle.

A word from Tras Sur'tian snapped her out of her quiet
reverie. The wagon creaked to a halt. They looked where
the Korkyran pointed.

A dozen men rode down a long slope on their left. She
shot a look behind. They'd passed through the woodland
country without her notice. There was no immediate shelter. She returned her attention to the riders. Bandits, she
figured. No hope of outrunning them with the wagon. Her
hand fell to the hilt of her sword.

Tras Sur'tian recognized them first: not bandits, but a
squad of Korkyran regulars on patrol. "We've got trouble," he murmured, and loosened his own blade in its
sheath. Frost, Kimon, Tras, and Gel fanned out before the
wagon. Onokratos sat nervously on the hard wooden seat
and watched.

The soldiers cut across their course, blocking the road.

Frost remembered the distinctive livery Tras Sur'tian

wore sewn to his tunic. Surreptitiously, she tapped her chest. "Maybe you'd better take charge," she whispered.

Tras Sur'tian rode a little forward to address the patrol's commander. "Ho, Captain! We nearly mistook you for bandits." He gave the traditional Korkyran salute. "We have met no other travelers on these lonely roads."

A warrior not much less than Tras Sur'tian's years urged his mount a few steps ahead of his troops. He sat his saddle stiffly, no hint of friendliness on his stony features. "You are Captain Tras Sur'tian, commander of the palace guard at Mirashai." It was not a question, but an identification.

Tras Sur'tian abandoned his amicable approach and adopted the other man's hostile tone. "We're on royal business. You're blocking our way."

The other captain was unruffled. He made a gesture; his soldiers spread out into a semicircle to his left and right. He spoke again. "You are under arrest for complicity in the murders of Aki, High Queen of Korkyra, and of Thogrin Sin'tell, Baron Endymia, heir designate." He paused, looked past Tras Sur'tian, and glared with hate-filled eyes at Frost. "You are also charged with harboring a wanted criminal and with willful desertion of your duty post." He rattled off other charges without benefit of a document. "For a month you've eluded us. To my everlasting glory, I have stumbled upon you."

Tras Sur'tian lied coolly, "You have your facts wrong. I've captured the murderess. And I've conscripted these men to help guard her." He cast a glance over his shoulder. "She's a tricky bitch."

The barest smirk stole over the other captain's face. "The evidence calls you liar, sir. You've not even bothered to take her weapons. And Mirashai lies in the opposite direction, so your falsehood is compounded." He indicated Kimon, Gel, and Onokratos. "These are most probably co-conspirators. You'll surrender your weapons at once."

Frost could no longer hold her tongue. She rode to Tras Sur'tian's side. "You know me, Captain?"

He nodded. "I saw you once at the declaration of peace between Korkyra and Aleppo. Queen Aki named you her champion."

She played her only card, her last hope of preventing a confrontation. "What if I told you Aki is alive?"

His mouth twitched, but plainly he didn't believe her.

Frost pushed. "She's in the wagon, but she's ill. I'm trying to save her life." She made a gesture, and Onokratos drew back the cloak he'd draped to shade the children. "Look for yourself," she offered.

The captain hesitated; then, laying hand to sword's hilt, he rode cautiously past Frost and peered into the wagon. His eyes narrowed. He looked up, then back into the wagon. He leaned down from his saddle and placed a hand on Aki's cheek. Then he resumed his place with his men.

"The first charge may be reduced to abduction," he announced. "But the other charges stand. You must come with us."

Frost barely kept her temper. "You pompous fool! Get out of our way, or there's no hope at all for Aki. Bring your men, if you must, and join us. But don't delay us longer!"

The captain raised a hand. His men drew their blades. Frost, Kimon, and Tras Sur'tian responded, showing steel. "Don't be stupid," the captain advised. "You've three swords to twelve."

Onokratos spoke for the first time, rising to stand on the boards, the reins draped lazily in his hands. "You've neglected to count me, sir," he chided. "Your mistake."

The captain openly scoffed. "My apologies, grandfather. I saw no blade at your belt. Have you some other weapon I should allow to your credit?"

A broad, mocking smile spread over the wizard's face; the corners of his mouth strained toward his ears. He pointed to Gel. "Him."

The captain pursed his lips in consideration. "The black brute doesn't wear steel, either, grandfather."

The huge smile disappeared. "He needs no weapon, fool," he answered darkly. "He is a demon."

Frost studied the effect of his words on the men before her. A few eyes darted nervously to Gel, reevaluating him. A few grinned at what they considered an old man's madness. The captain himself barked a short laugh and spat in the dust.

Gel twisted in his saddle to face his master. "They do not believe thee," he said.

Once again, that mocking smile returned. "Show them."

A blood-chilling yell boiled from the demon's throat, no human sound. Weaponless, he sprang over his horse's head. His massive arms lashed out as he leaped, knocking the two nearest soldiers from their saddles before they could lift swords to defend themselves.

Frost stared open-mouthed. Such a tremendous leap! And right out of the stirrups! But that feat paled beside the demon's next action.

Gel disappeared momentarily beneath one of the riderless mounts. Suddenly, the beast rose into the air, whinnying pitifully, hooves thrashing. The demon heaved; the screaming animal flew through the air, crashing into men and horses. The captain of the patrol saved himself by diving into the dirt. He rose, pale, shaken, but not yet ready to give up.

He snatched his blade from the roadside where it had fallen. "Get him!" he ordered his men. "Get them all!"

Blindly obedient, a young recruit scrambled to his feet and ran at Gel. The demon brushed aside the artless sword thrust. One huge hand closed on the soldier's leather-helmed skull and squeezed. An agonized cry choked, half-uttered, in the man's throat. Frost heard the crack of splintering bone and clenched her eyes shut, forcing down the bile that threatened to rise. When she opened them, fresh crimson stained the demon's hand. He kicked the body aside and laughed.

"Enough!" Onokratos's shout rang over the demon's terrible mirth. All eyes turned to the old wizard. His expression was hard and cruel as he glared down on the unfortunate captain. "Does he have to kill all of you? Or will you leave us alone?"

The captain shook his fist even as the color drained from his face. "I have my duty!" he cried.

"Think of your men!" Onokratos snapped. "What's left of them! Look around, man. See what your *duty* has wrought!"

Of the twelve, Gel had killed three with his hands. The horse he had flung into their midst had claimed another; Frost could see the unmoving form pinned beneath the beast's wriggling, broken bulk. Two more lives were uncertain. They lay on the ground, perhaps merely unconscious. Only now did she see what a young bunch they were. Farmers' sons, probably, products of the local villages. None but the captain, an older and more experienced warrior, seemed willing to fight on.

"Go home," Onokratos urged with surprising gentleness.

The captain seized his hilt with both hands, gripped it until his knuckles were white and the bone showed through. "There can be no going home!" he cried desperately. "Not while you have my queen!" He sliced the air twice, sunlight rippling along his blade, then leaped for the nearest foe.

Frost brought her sword around.

Gel moved, caught him by the neck before his feet touched the earth. Bone snapped. The demon looked up at Frost, holding the dangling corpse in one hand. A trace of a grin stretched his hideous lips. "Thee owes me thy life," he said.

"You flatter yourself," she answered coldly, disturbed by his cruelty and his insult. She'd been in no danger from the captain's clumsy attack.

The demon shrugged, dropped the lifeless hulk, turned to glare at the remains of the terror-stricken patrol.

"Go home!" Onokratos repeated. There was no captain to halt them this time. Three men, still mounted, spurred for the ridge where they'd first appeared. The rest ran or limped after them on foot.

Tras Sur'tian turned back to the wagon. "Thank you for your mercy," he said to Onokratos.

The wizard nodded and sat down with a sigh. "They

were your people. You would have fought them, I know, for the sake of your queen. But you would not have felt good about it." He scratched his beardless chin. "It was better my way."

Tras Sur'tian pursed his lips thoughtfully. "We should bury them," he said. "As men, they deserve that."

"There isn't time," Onokratos said reasonably. "Some of their comrades will return when their fear lessens. They'll do that work. I've learned that much of Korkyran honor."

"I think we need a drink," Frost said, reaching into the wagon for the waterskins. They all drank, even Gel. Frost noted that with some concern. Thirst was a human weakness; before, the demon had refused all food or drink.

They decided to abandon the road for fear of another chance encounter. They set off cross-country toward the waning sun. In the early evening they entered yet another woodland. The going was rough for the wagon and they made slow progress. A little way farther they found a clearing and decided to make camp. The first stars winked in the gathering gloom, barely visible through the leaves.

Frost helped Tras Sur'tian water the horses from a small pool. "Am I wrong," she said softly as they trudged back to camp, "or have you made a friend?"

"Onokratos? A friend?" He wrinkled his nose in a curious way. "I wouldn't call him that. But we have talked along the way." He looked thoughtful. For a while he didn't say anything; then he spoke again. "He's not so different from us, really." A wry smile flickered over his mouth. "He's got your temper. But he loves his daughter. He'll do anything to help her." He stopped and looked her straight in the eye. "Just as you and I will do anything to save Aki." He shook his head and resumed walking. "No, we're not so different at all."

She considered that, not sure she liked what it implied. The more she thought about it, the more it bothered her. She didn't like Onokratos. She didn't trust him. If they were so similar, what did that say about her?

She peered upward at the sky, full of a vague dissatisfaction. The leaves rustled in a gentle breeze. Through a gap in the branches, a swift flash of color caught her attention. "You know, that's odd," she muttered. "I saw a shooting star last night, too."

Tras Sur'tian followed her gaze, but the star was gone.

Chapter Fifteen

Another night on the hard ground. No matter how she tossed and turned, Frost couldn't get comfortable. Her muscles ached from the chill; her joints complained. She longed to curl up next to Kimon but feared her restlessness would wake him. She envied his every snore. The others slept as soundly as he, but try as she might sleep eluded her.

A scuffle in the darkness made her sit up. Her hand closed on the hilt of her sword, which lay sheathed at the edge of her blanket. The ashes of the campfire glowed dull red. Gel squatted near the remains and regarded her through the pale wisps of smoke that curled up from the last embers.

His whisper drifted across the space. "We're much alike, thee and me."

"I'm tired of hearing that," she answered, reclining again. "Go to sleep."

"I do not sleep."

She ignored him, shutting her eyes and reaching once more for much desired slumber.

But the demon's sibilant whisper reached into her mind. "What sees thee in that pathetic human male?"

With an uneasy start she realized he spoke of Kimon. Slowly, she sat up and glowered. "None of your business," she hissed. "Leave him alone." He said nothing and she lay back down, inwardly fuming. Fatigue made her irritable. If only she could sleep.

The wind rose loud through the leaves. The chirping insects seemed to roar. Her blanket rustled with every movement of her restive body.

"He has no bulk." Gel's whisper came again. "I could snap him like a dry twig."

She bolted upright, all thought of discomfort cast off. Her blade sighed from the sheath. She leveled the point in the demon's direction. The steel reflected the dying coal's ruddy sheen. "Can you die, demon?" The words scraped through her teeth.

His face became a patchwork of shadows and umber highlights as he leaned closer to the firebed. "Not in the sense thee means, woman."

"In any sense," she pressed.

Gel shrugged. "I do not know. It may be possible."

Her voice came out a tense rasp. "I'll make it possible," she warned. "If you ever harm Kimon, I swear I will. If I must make a pact with all the gods of darkness. *If I must pledge my soul to Gath!*"

She saw his grin, his fanged teeth tinged orange from the coal-light. "That is what I like most about thee!" he answered gleefully. "Thee are full of fire and spirit."

Tras Sur'tian stirred, a black lump beneath his cloak and blanket, but he did not awaken.

"You're going to rouse everyone," she hissed. "If you don't sleep, at least let them!"

She sheathed her sword, fatigue quenching her temper. "Remember what I've sworn," she whispered to Gel. Then she stretched out, determined this time to sleep.

But she heard footsteps. Gel's huge form loomed over her, blotting out the leaves and stars. He seized her arm, hauled her effortlessly to her feet. "Thee will not choose the human over me."

She opened her mouth to call for help, but his other hand clamped it shut. Her sword lay on the ground out of reach. Demonfang was her only hope.

Yet before she could draw the weapon, Gel's gaze

locked with hers. A cold fire grew in the black depths of
his pupils, filled his eyes, consumed his face. She tried
uselessly to scream. The unnatural fire swelled, engulfing
them both in a raging embrace.

Suddenly, she was airborne. The earth dropped away
with dizzying speed. The tops of trees churned in the wake
of their passage. A trail of flames streamed behind, lit the
landscape, spawned bizarre shadows that raced in all
directions.

She was transformed. All sense of body was gone. Yet
she was not alone. She felt the demon's mind close to her
own. Gel exulted in his power!

A hill rose ahead, its summit capped with a small grove
of trees. They flew toward it, losing none of their fantastic
speed. She cried out, fearing they would crash, but at the
last possible instant, momentum ceased. They drifted down,
a blazing fireball, not even scorching the grass. She felt
solid ground beneath her feet. The flames vanished.

Gel leered, his face close to hers. "Do not resist me."

She slammed her fist against his chin. The shock tingled
up her arm. Her knuckles felt broken; they throbbed with
pain.

His grin widened. Lust shone in his eyes. "I cannot be
harmed by the likes of thee," he boasted. His hand touched
her shoulder.

She caught his wrist, twisted. The demon made a startled squawk as he tumbled over her shoulder. She grabbed
for Demonfang's hilt but didn't draw the blade. "You can
be hurt by the likes of this!" she threatened.

He stood slowly, seeming to grow from the soil as she
watched. Ebon skin rippled over flexing muscle that gleamed
with sweat-sheen. Limbs lengthened and his chest swelled
as an evil laugh rumbled low in his throat. He challenged:
"Can I?"

She hesitated. Gel could control the dagger's hunger.
She backed away from him, fear eating its way into her
heart.

"I will be good to thee." Starlight glinted on his naked-

ness. His sex protruded hugely from his thighs. He gestured invitingly. "Come, the grass is soft."

"No!" she managed. "I won't!"

"Thee will."

A mighty wind rose from nowhere, forced her stumbling
forward. She threw up a hand to protect her eyes from her
hair. It lashed her face, turned into thousands of tiny whips
by the gale. Though she resisted, it pushed her toward the
demon. Something caught her toe; she tripped, fell to the
ground. Her fingers dug deep into the grass and earth,
seeking purchase.

"Thee will!"

The words rang in her head, not a voice anymore, but a
compelling sensation that screamed inside her skull. She
fought with all her strength to silence the voice, but the
demon advanced on her, his reaching arms blocking out
the starlight, closing around her as they transformed, became the wings of a giant raven. He swept her up, lifted
her into the sky.

Talons raked away her garments; cold air stung her
flesh. The world spun below. With a despairing cry she
saw her belt fall, taking her last weapon. Feathers, not
flesh, pressed against her body. One pair of massive pinions beat the night. Another pair effortlessly cradled her
weight. Her fists pummeled ineffectually against the bird-
thing that bore her.

Something pressed against her loins, radiating heat.

"I'll kill you!" she shrieked. "I swear!" She screamed
again, searing pain ripping through her, then she bit her lip
until blood ran down her cheek.

The demon began to move inside her.

When he was finished, Gel spiraled lazily down to the
hill where their flight had begun. He deposited her gently
on the soft grass. She lay limply, burning with shame and
anger, letting the stars revolve maddeningly above, praying
for the fire in her belly to subside. She rolled agonizingly
to her side in time to see Gel's raven-shape disappear. In
his human guise the demon took a step and suddenly
faltered.

"How's it feel?" An incoherent half laugh gurgled in her throat. "Soon, your power will be gone forever." She curled her fingers into a weak fist. "Then you'll be mine!"

"My power will live on," the demon answered. "Already my seed begins to grow in your body."

She shook her head, ran a hand over her abdomen. "No!" Fear took hold of her again; she smashed her stomach with her fist in a vain attempt to destroy whatever might be there. "No!"

His clawed hands clutched at the sky. He shouted to the heavens, "I was a commander in hell's legions! In all the ranks of demons, none surpassed my power. Not one! But Orchos ruled! Curse his name! His word was law, and I could never be more than a servant to his will, a slave to be ordered like any other insignificant creature.

"So, when Onokratos summoned me, I saw my way to freedom. I rebelled, and convinced the stupid human to make a new pact with me and break his bond with night's master. If I could not rule in hell, then I could rule this feeble world. It is no more than chaff among the jewels of the cosmos, yet it would be mine!

"Yet, my ignorance betrayed me, and I am undone! Corrupted by exposure to the human maggots! My magic wanes. Soon, I will be little more than a human myself."

His attention returned to her. No longer did he rage at the uncaring sky. His gaze burned with fervor. "But I will not lose all! Thee shall bear a child, spawn of demon and mortal. It shall have my magic. But because it is of thy flesh, it shall not be corrupted. It shall grow and mature, and someday it will rule what I cannot!"

She rose shakily to her feet, clutching her belly. "I won't let that happen!" she shouted defiantly.

The demon trembled in his weakness, but his voice answered with strength. "It has already started. Can thee feel it? It grows within thee."

She advanced on him, at last empty of all fear, full of a terrible hatred. "I will stop it!" she swore. "If I have to kill it!"

"Thee will not." His dark countenance glared at her.

"For two years my seed will ferment in thy body. When that time is past, thee will feel only love for something that is part of thee."

"Never!" She spied a large rock in the grass, bent, and lifted it. She heaved it over her head with both hands, strained, and flung it with all her strength at the demon.

Gel pointed one finger. The huge missile stopped, hung motionless in the air. "I was the most powerful demon of them all," he boasted. The rock exploded in a white, powdery shower. She fell back, shielding her eyes. His taunting voice echoed in her ears. "I cannot be harmed by the likes of thee."

In the far distance a strange trumpeting sounded. Gel looked around, startled. Frost cupped her ear, uncertain of what she thought she heard.

"You're weakening," she observed, regaining his attention. "It shows in your eyes, in the way you hold yourself, the way you suck for breath."

The unearthly sound came again, nearer. The demon stared suspiciously over his shoulder. Frost hid an inward surge of hope behind a sneering visage. She knew that sound; she had not imagined it. Perhaps there was vengeance after all!

"I'll never bear your monster." She poured all her rage into words. "You're still a slave! And you'll serve me well at Skull Gate, or you'll never win your freedom from Onokratos." Scorn twisted her features as she mocked him. "You thought you could rule humans? Fool, you'll serve us, instead!"

The trumpeting split her ears, drowning her mouthings. Gel whirled about and stared wide-eyed down the hill. A loud crashing in the underbrush punctuated the staccato drumming of charging hoofbeats.

"What is that?" he shouted, uncertainty tinting his question.

She threw back her head and laughed, a hysterical sound. "Does the darkness hamper your vision, now?" she exulted. "How like a human! Every heartbeat, every breath you draw makes you weaker. Are you weak enough to hurt, demon? Are you weak enough to die?'' She ran at him.

The force of his blow smashed her to the ground. Lights exploded behind her eyes, the air rushed from her lungs. She willed herself to rise, but muscles would not respond. Gel stood over her, fists doubled in fury.

''Thee dares too much, female!'' He seized a handful of her hair, dragged her to her feet, ignoring her screams. ''Thee shall not speak so—''

He did not finish. Once more that trumpeting cry shivered the air. She hit the earth hard as Gel dropped her. She lay limp, trying to make her eyes focus.

The demon turned, slack-jawed as a fiery-eyed Ashur charged to the summit. Barely in time, Gel leaped aside to avoid the lowered ebony horn that sought his heart. Dirt and grass flew from hooves as the unicorn stopped his rush and turned.

Frost rolled to her side, her body shrieking with pain from the effort. One side of her face felt numb where Gel had hit her. ''Kill him!'' she urged the beast, but the words came out a bloody, frothy bubble. ''Kill him!''

Gel crouched to meet the unicorn's next charge, but his face betrayed his fear. Suddenly, he straightened. The man-shape dissolved. Four immense black pinions spread, blocking out stars. Familiar red eyes shone with evil and hatred. The raven-thing answered Ashur's trumpeting with a raucous, ugly cawing. Then, it took to the sky and was quickly lost from sight.

Frost struggled to her feet, shouting curses after the demon, but the world spun crazily around her, and she fell. Pain and humiliation and anger overcame her senses.

Ashur's soft, wet tongue licked her to wakefulness. Her eyelids peeled slowly back. It was still night. The stars twinkled icily in the heavens, mocking her with their mute serenity.

After a while, she tried to sit up. Nausea was her reward. The grass felt cool, damp with dew beneath her bare skin. She was only vaguely aware of the cold. Every bone, every joint and muscle cried with its own silent voice. She lay back down, awake, but unable or unwilling to move, hoping the stillness of the world might heal her hurt.

Ashur nickered in sympathy. The unicorn paced worried circles, encouraging her to rise. Something else succeeded where he could not.

Another shooting star blazed a path across the firmament and disappeared below the far western horizon.

Realization crawled through the fog that filled her head. "I know you," she muttered with growing coherence. "I know who and what you are. Are you waiting for me?" She half expected an answer, but none came. Languidly, she eased onto her side, then to her knees. Ashur stopped his pacing and came close. She grabbed a handful of the creature's long, tangled mane and pulled herself to her feet. For long, painful moments she just leaned on the unicorn, fighting down sickness until she found strength to climb astride him. She bit her lip until the trembling that seized her subsided. Then she looked at the point on the horizon where the shooting star had fallen. "I'm coming," she promised.

Ashur carried her down the hill, through the woods, going where he would. She made no attempt to guide him. She had no idea where she was or how she would find camp and her friends. The unicorn had found her as he always did when she needed him. Let him find the way back. She rode, slouched forward, sliding in and out of consciousness, insensitive to the branches and brambles that scratched her naked flesh.

Yet as she rode, her heart began to harden. A good thing Ashur hadn't killed Gel, she reflected. She still required him at Skull Gate. She didn't wonder if the demon was already back at camp. Onokratos had only to speak his name and he was constrained by pact to answer the summons. She grinned bitterly to herself. Gel wasn't free, yet. He was still slave to the humans he detested.

The rose of morning was blossoming through the leafy foliage when she arrived in camp. Onokratos saw her first and called to the others. Tras Sur'tian and Kimon rushed to meet her. The strain showed on their faces, told they'd been awake long enough to miss her and feared the worst.

Kimon reached up to help her dismount. She hesitated an instant, struggling between logic and the revulsion she felt at his nearness. She looked into the deep sea blue of his eyes, read his concern and confusion. She sighed. After all, it was no *man* who had hurt her.

His arms encircled her waist, and he eased her down. He removed the cloak he wore against the morning chill and draped it around her shoulders. Someone had built up the fire, and they seated her next to it.

"Your face!" Kimon exclaimed suddenly. "Gods, what happened?"

She touched her right cheek gingerly and winced. It must be horribly bruised from Gel's blow. There would be other bruises, too. She began to take stock of her injuries. How could she explain?

She decided she could not. She pushed through them and went to her bedroll. Her few belongings lay where she had left them. She bent and picked up her sword, unsheathed the blade, and hugged it to her breast. She kissed the hilt, closed her eyes, shutting out everything.

Tras Sur'tian tapped her shoulder. She gratefully accepted the waterskin he offered. The liquid tasted clean, good, and when her thirst was quenched she raised it higher and squirted a stream over her face.

Onokratos asked the next question.

She gave the skin back to Tras. "Call him," she answered the wizard. "He's bound to your service. He must appear."

"I've tried that," he replied sharply, "but he doesn't obey. Something's happened."

She lacked the energy to make a show of concern. But the news disturbed her. Gel was an essential part of her bargain with Orchos. Would the master of worms accept another arrangement if the demon did not return? She gave a mental shrug. No point in worrying about it until they reached Skull Gate. If necessary, someone would fight twice, and she would be that someone.

"Get ready to move out," she told them. There was an edge to her voice that startled them. She read its effect on their faces and softened her tone. "Gel will join us when he's able." But to herself, she added, *if he's able*.

Onokratos's brows knitted together. He folded his arms stubbornly. "Something has happened to him. I think you know what."

"He . . ." She started to snap at him, then thought better of it. It wasn't his fault—at least, not all his fault. She considered her words carefully. "He expended a goodly amount of power last night. It may be that he's too weak to answer your summons right now." That sounded good to her. She added hopefully, "It may take him some time to regain his strength."

They all had the same questions. "What in your nine hells happened last night?" Tras Sur'tian pressed. "Where are your clothes?"

Again, she walked away from them. "We'll talk no more of it," she said with finality. "Get the wagon ready and saddle the horses. We've got a way to go yet."

Tras Sur'tian and Onokratos gave up and departed. Only Kimon lingered. When the others were out of earshot he came up behind and touched her shoulders.

"I'll ask no more," he whispered. "Not about your nakedness, not about the bruises and scratches, not about where you've been or what transpired." He paused. When she didn't speak, he continued. "Tell me in your own time if you wish. Or don't tell me. But I've been around, Samidar, enough to guess some of the answers." The hands drifted up her shoulders, massaged the soreness of her neck. "I'm glad you're safe."

He started to go.

"Kimon, wait!" She sheathed her blade. The sword belt dangled, and on the belt hung her pouch of coins. She loosened the strings and extracted Oona's ruby talisman.

She balanced the stone on her palm, regarded it with a sense of sad irony. Sunlight touched it, spilled diffracted fire over her hand. It alone of all her weapons might have spared her Gel's embrace. Too late now, she told herself.

But the demon had scorned Kimon and threatened him, spoken of him as a rival.

She pressed the jewel into his hand. "Keep this with you," she implored him, "and always in easy reach. You know how it works. Just close your fingers around it like this." She curled his fingers into a fist.

He urged it back upon her. "It was the old woman's gift to you. She said it would protect you."

Frost refused to take it back. "I want it to protect you!"

"But I've no place to carry it."

She gave him the pouch. "Take this, then," she said. "But don't wear it on your belt." She opened it again and scattered the few coins inside to the woods. "We'll tie the strings around your neck." She tied the ends for him. "And wear it inside your jerkin."

He traced the outline of the pouch next to his heart. His eyes were full of questions, and more. Unease and worry threatened to carve permanent niches in his face.

She squeezed his hand. "I'm glad I'm back."

He managed a faint smile and nodded. "I'd better help with the horses."

She wouldn't let him go. "They can do it," she said. "You can help me, instead. I seem to be in need of something to wear." She grabbed up her blanket. "Nothing stylish. Just cut a hole for my head and trim the length so I can ride and fight. I'll belt it with a strip."

He grinned and drew his dagger.

It was quickly done. She threw it over her shoulders, tied a length of the material around her waist, and belted on her sword. She held out her arms and turned for approval.

"I wouldn't go to court in it," Kimon said with a smirk.

"Neither would I," she agreed. She turned once more, then stiffened suddenly and clutched her belly.

Kimon was beside her at once, catching her elbow. "What's wrong?" he said. "Samidar, what is it?"

She waited for the wave of nausea to subside and sidled away. "Nothing," she lied, putting on a false smile.

"I'm afraid for you."

She touched his cheek tenderly. *So am I,* she admitted secretly, careful not to let it show. "Go see if you can hurry Tras along. We should be on our way." He frowned but did as she asked.

Alone, she ran a hand over her abdomen, probing for another sign of the hated life within. *I won't let you out,* she swore. *I won't let you out. I'll find a way.*

The three men had their mounts ready, the wagon hitched. Tras Sur'tian stole over to her. "I went into the woods for some privacy," he said delicately. "I found this caught in the branches of a tree." He slipped something from his tunic. There was a tinkle of metallic links, and Demonfang swung like a pendulum from its silver belt.

There were no more questions in Tras Sur'tian's eyes. "Apparently, you didn't get a chance to use it. Too bad, I say. Will the demon return?"

She hesitated, thinking how often she had wished to be rid of the dagger. Then she remembered the battle ahead and the powers aligned against her. She strapped the arcane blade over her left hip. She was beginning to feel herself again.

"Return?" she said with a malicious smile. "It's my most fervent prayer."

Kimon called out from the wagon's side. "What about the bay?"

She had forgotten about Gel's mount. "Put the saddle on Ashur," she decided, "and try to find something to lash him to the back of the wagon. If you can't"—she looked at Onokratos, thought of the demon, and shrugged—"set him free."

Chapter Sixteen

Skodulac. Hump-shaped, like the back of an ominous, scaly beast, the island rose out of the murky water of Dyre Lake. The sun squatted on the harsh, jutting isle, tinting the sky and the rocky beach a bloody cochineal. No tree or blade of grass showed along the shoreline, no sign of living creature. A flock of geese veered around the southern tip.

"Even the birds avoid it," Tras Sur'tian said reverently.

Frost wrinkled her nose. Two days and a good night's sleep had eased her aches and pains, but the stench of the lake threatened to make her sick again. The water was stagnant; the stream that once fed it had long ago dried up. She looked with disdain at the slime that lapped the bank near her bare feet.

A hot breeze stirred her limp hair. An insect lighted on her neck; she swatted it, wiped the rich, red smear on her makeshift garment. "Well, we've made it this far," she said, shielding her eyes against the glare of the setting sun. "Now, how do we get across?"

Kimon made a wry face. "I wouldn't like to swim in that muck."

"What about the children?" Onokratos reminded them. "They can't swim."

Frost was too tired to think. She turned to Tras Sur'tian.

"This is your country. You knew the way here. Tell us what to do."

The Korkyran looked up and down the bank, frowning. "I only know from hearsay," he defended himself. "Troops stationed in the nearby provinces used to tell tales. There used to be a ferry. I don't know what condition it's in. People generally avoid this place."

She gazed out at Skodulac again. Not a difficult swim, she figured. But she was so weary. And there were weapons to think of; they should not get wet. They had to take the girls.

"All right, let's ride around the shore," she decided, "and keep a watch out for the ferry. If we don't find it, we'll camp on this side for the night and seek another way in the morning."

"We could split up," Onokratos suggested. "You and Kimon go that way. Tras and I will ride north."

She shook her head. "We stay together."

The wizard opened his mouth to protest, but she cut him off. "We take no chances," she said firmly. "We've come this far together. Why change our luck?" She looked to the others for support. Kimon agreed wholeheartedly; Tras Sur'tian kept quiet but didn't challenge her judgment. "There's still some sunlight," she continued. "We should make it around the shoreline before dark. If there's a ferry, we'll find it."

Only a quarter of the way around the lake the land turned into a quagmire. A vulgar assortment of reeds and swamp grasses thrived in the stinking morass that blocked their way. Flies buzzed in a thick cloud; a water viper swam a crooked course among a crop of tigertails and vanished.

But Frost's attention was drawn to a tall and rotund tree that grew in the very heart of the bog, its trunk and lower branches dripping with slick moss. Just under the lowest limb a vine-twisted rope as thick as her wrist stretched out over the water and disappeared. Somewhere on Skodulac, she knew, the other end was anchored.

"Some ferry," Onokratos sneered. "The boat must be on the far side. Nor do I see a bell to summon it."

It was her turn to sneer. "What ghost would you expect to pole it? Look how far the swamp extends; it's had some time to grow. No ferry's operated here for quite a long time."

"We can still use the rope to get across," Tras Sur'tian insisted.

"With the children?" Onokratos looked doubtful.

Frost allowed a slight smile and wiped sweat from her brow. The moonstone circlet that held most of her hair back from her face was beginning to chafe. She removed it, rubbed the skin with thumb and forefinger. "It'll be hard work," she admitted. "But I see no other way. Let's get to it."

Kimon and Tras Sur'tian unloaded the wagon. They placed the sleeping children on the spongy earth, unhitched the pair of palfreys, removed the wheels. With concerted effort, they kicked loose the three upright sides, managed without tools to unbolt and discard the hitching shaft.

Onokratos, as instructed, gathered the blankets and cloaks, cut them into thick strips, and tied the ends securely together.

Frost waited for Onokratos to finish his task, then gathered the makeshift line over her shoulder. Mounting Ashur, she rode into the bog. The mud gurgled and churned, rising sometimes to the unicorn's knees. She rode slowly, cautiously, alert for hidden quicksand. When the ferry rope was directly above her, she stopped.

The rope was higher than she thought.

She pursed her lips, considering how best to accomplish her part. Carefully, she removed her feet from the stirrups and stood precariously on her saddle. She drew her sword, made a few experimental swings at the rope. The tip of the blade made contact but not sufficiently to cut. She cursed her luck and her gods as she sheathed her sword.

To the unicorn, she said: "If you twitch or make a

sudden move . . .'' She let the threat hang. Then, flexing
her knees, she leaped.

Both hands locked around the old rope. She swung her
feet up, crossed her ankles over the rough, scratchy line.
For a frantic moment Onokratos's hand-twisted cord began
to slip from her shoulder, but she trapped it with her chin.
Like a fly with its wings pinched off, she thought of
herself, suspended in her peculiar position. A splashing
caught her attention; Ashur slogged back to firmer land.
She glanced at the mire below and frowned. *And this is the
pleasant part.*

She inched up the rope until she touched the huge,
complicated knots that anchored it to the tree. They would
afford her a perch from which to do her work. She tightened her thighs and wrenched herself into a sitting posture
on the rope, crawled forward until she straddled the knot-
ted section. It was uncomfortable, clumsy, but allowed the
best possible seat. She leaned back against the trunk of the
tree.

"Are you all right?"

She looked down on Kimon as he rode out toward her.
"So far," she answered, and tossed him the end of
Onokratos's line. "But this damn thing is made of thin,
braided vines, and they've gotten kind of coarse with
age." She adjusted her seat ever so delicately. "And you
know how little I'm wearing."

"Afraid of splinters?" he teased.

"With all the time we've spent in the saddle?" she
replied. "I doubt if I'd feel them." She tied her end of the
cloth line securely around the larger ferry rope, hoping her
knots would hold. "Make sure you don't lose your end,"
she called to Kimon. "There's a lot of tension on this
thing. When I cut it free, it's going to snap out into the
water. If you let go, or my knots aren't good enough"
—she made a face—"then it's going to be a long and
messy swim for everyone."

"Tras Sur'tian is just about finished with the raft," he
informed her. "But the sun's nearly gone. Think we'll
make it?"

She studied the sky. The sun's fading rays cast a shimmering path of liquid fire over the water, pointing the way to Skodulac. "We'll make it."

Her blade hissed free of the sheath, and she began hacking at the rope. The vibrations her blows caused nearly unseated her. She gripped tighter with her thighs, placed one hand on the tree trunk to steady herself, and chopped away.

Kimon backed off a bit. "This is going to be so funny!" he called up to her, grinning.

Tras Sur'tian and Onokratos were watching as well. She spied them safe and dry on the solid land. The raft they had made from the wagon's bed lay near the edge of the murky swamp water. She could see the mirthful smirks they wore.

"One laugh out of any of you!" she warned. Hack, hack, hack. "And I'll cut your tongues out, I swear—Oh!"

The old rope parted more easily than she'd expected. Down she fell, *splash!* in the mire. She scrambled to get her footing, sputtering and spitting mud, soaked with filth and slime.

All three men doubled with laughter. She cursed them, brandishing the sword she had remembered to keep hold of. The guffaws only increased; they clapped each other on the backs.

She waded toward them, wiping the muck from her arms, face, and chest. "I'll get even!" she promised.

"Not too close!" Tras Sur'tian shouted, pinching his nose. "By the One God, you smell like a charnel pit!"

She snapped at Kimon, "Did you hang on to that line?" He held it up to show he had.

"Then get Aki and Kalynda before we lose the sun." She squeezed water and mud from her long hair.

Kimon and Onokratos hurried back for the children while Frost and Tras Sur'tian lifted the raft, which was really no more than the bottom of the wagon, and set it gently into the water among the reeds. They stepped onto it. Water seeped up through the boards.

"Tras?" she cried, feigning alarm. The Korkyran noted the seepage and took a hasty step back toward shore. She hooked his foot with hers. With an awkward shout, he plunged headlong into the clammy brink. He clambered out, flecked with slime, mouthing Korkyran expletives, ready to drink her blood.

She put on a mask of innocence. "Now, how could that have happened?" Her eyelashes fluttered, head tilted, lips pouted sweetly. She stepped lightly ashore. "You have to be so careful on these things," she advised. Then she gave a look of smug satisfaction. *Laugh again, old hyena,* she thought.

The other two returned with the children in their arms. Kimon took note of Tras Sur'tian's condition and clucked. "No time for a swim, sir," he said smartly.

Frost interrupted the Korkyran's sharp retort. "You're going to take a swim yourself, sir. Our combined weight proves too much for these few boards."

Onokratos frowned. "Then what good is all our work?"

"I never *really* expected us all to ride across," she assured him. "The raft was necessary for Aki and Kalynda. You'll ride it, too."

His frown deepened. "I see."

She took notice of his dour expression. "You object?"

He drew his shoulders back, straightened his spine. "Do you think I'm too old to swim? Why should I stay safe and dry? You're a woman; you ride with the children!"

She laid a hand on his arm. "No insult was meant." In fact, she doubted he could make the swim, but best to hide that thought. "You'll have the tough job of hauling the raft over on the rope." She indicated the other two. "But we're warriors, and we're stiff and sore from too much time in the saddle. A swim, even in this malodorous brine, will loosen us up for the contest ahead."

His old temper flickered briefly, then subsided. He mocked her habit of biting her lip, then said: "You're quite a liar, my dear." He hesitated, and his features darkened with an unvoiced fear. "Gel could carry us over on a whirlwind," he added wistfully.

She clucked her tongue. "At what expense of power?" She turned back to the raft. "We're doing fine on our own. When we reach Skull Gate, then you can summon him."

"What if he doesn't come?"

She gazed out toward Skodulac, feeling a chill dread close around her heart. Like Onokratos, she had kept that fear under guard for the past few days. "I made the first bargain, didn't I?" she answered with false bravado. "If he doesn't come, I'll just have to strike another."

She didn't want to discuss it further. There were still things to do, and she gave orders. Kimon and Tras Sur'tian placed the children on the raft, then all their weapons, their boots, and the two special waterskins. Onokratos hobbled the horses and left them to wander along the bank. But Ashur fled when he approached, refusing such an indignity.

When he finished he stepped carefully onto the raft, kneeled near the center between the sleeping girls, and clasped the line of shredded blankets firmly in his hands.

They watched water seep up through the boards. The riders would get wet, but the raft would float. Frost waded out into the bog. "We'll push you out as far as we can. If you pull too hard, some of those knots in the blanket strips might slip before we find the ferry rope."

Kimon and Tras Sur'tian looked on dubiously from the shore.

"Do I have to push by myself?" she added with a trace of caustic humor. She stared at Tras and winked. "You already stink from your first bath. Come on, make it squish between your toes."

They looked at each other, shrugged, and joined her. The murky water lapped at their thighs. The mud indeed squished between their toes. The reeds and swamp grass parted reluctantly as they forced the raft through.

As the swamp gave way to open lake, the bottom dropped away unexpectedly. Kimon yelped and went under, surfaced with a wild thrashing and splashing. As he treaded the water to stay afloat, he gave Frost a look to burn stone, then forced a sheepish grin. She and Tras shifted easily to a kicking motion, still pushing the raft.

Then, a loud splash far to their right: all stopped, seeking the source. "There!" Onokratos cried, pointing.

Frost slapped the water, exasperated, amused, proud. "Ashur!" she shouted as the animal swam for Skodulac. "You stubborn half cousin to a plow mare!" She looked at her comrades, rolled her eyes in relief. "For a moment," she confessed, "I thought someone or some*thing* had us,"

"This is no place for a fight," Tras agreed.

They redoubled their efforts to reach the island. Onokratos strained with all his aged might, hauling on the rope, making a growing coil between his knees. He uttered no complaint and wore an expression of earnest determination.

A familiar trumpeting made her look up. Ashur waited impatiently on Skodulac's shore.

There was barely a hint of sunlight remaining when they dragged the raft up on the rocky beach into the shadow of a high, stout tripod of old logs where the secured end of the ferry rope was anchored. They donned boots and buckled on weapons. Frost strapped Demonfang over her left hip, sword upon her right. Tras Sur'tian had only his broadsword and a dirk. Kimon donned his long sword, then for the first time since she'd returned it to him at the manor house, he unwrapped the cloth that concealed the beautifully wrought short sword. He held it up, and the sun's last rays rippled along its gleaming edge. He had no sheath for it but eased it inside his belt.

Ashur trotted over and nuzzled Frost, his great horn sliding just past her shoulders. She pretended to ignore him, then relented and gave him a playful scratch on the nose. The unicorn nickered and ran down along the shoreline, kicking up mud and small stones.

"I'll never get used to those eyes!" Kimon exclaimed, staring after Ashur.

"What about the children?" Tras Sur'tian said.

"They come with us," Onokratos insisted, "at least my Kalynda." He scooped up his slumbering daughter in his arms, allowing no debate. "I'll not leave her alone for a moment in this place." His gaze raked the inland skyline. "Do you feel it, woman? The very earth tingles with evil."

"You have a talent for the dramatic," Frost scoffed. But she repressed a shudder. She *could* feel it. And now that she opened herself to it, the air fairly sang, an indescribable sensation that made her instincts scream, made her want to run back into the water where it seemed not to reach. Kimon and Tras were not aware of it, but Ashur was. She saw the creature's restless pacing for what it truly was. The unicorn sensed the island's special nature.

Skodulac was a locus, one of those very rare places where the natural energies of the earth magnified to supernatural levels.

"It's not evil," she said, not bothering to explain to her friends, "but it is power, raw and primitive. Can you shape it?"

"I dare not try," Onokratos answered, pressing Kalynda's head into the soft part of his shoulder. "It's too wild; I couldn't control it. I'm a wizard. My sorcerous skills are quite limited."

It *was* wild. She could feel it prickling the soles of her feet, aquiver in the air she breathed, a rippling wave on her skin.

She could have shaped such power once, or at least tried. But she was a witch no longer. Onokratos was right to shut himself against this force. Even an adept might well fear to bend such energy to his will.

"The first bright stars," Kimon said, disturbing her reverie. Darkness was upon them.

Tras Sur'tian slung the waterskins over his shoulder. Kimon gathered Aki in his arms. "Which way?" Frost inquired.

"Inland," answered the Korkyran. "Skull Gate lies at the island's heart."

They trudged slowly up a rise and down between the yawning walls of a narrow canyon. Dyre Lake was quickly lost from sight, but its smell remained in the air. The terrain was rugged; stones turned treacherously underfoot as the seeing grew harder. Night swallowed them. Still, they kept moving.

"Wish we had a torch," Tras Sur'tian grumbled once.

"Save your wishes," chided Onokratos. "Or spend them on important things, like the souls of our children or the contest to come."

"Wish we had a torch," Tras repeated.

Frost didn't know how long they walked. It seemed like forever, though the island hadn't appeared that large in the daylight. She began to fear they wandered in circles and made an effort to remember strange shapes in the darkness that she could call landmarks.

An outcropping of rocks and boulders rose on her right. The course took them near, and as they approached she realized it was not a natural formation. The largest stones were chiseled smooth. Strange characters were chipped into the surfaces. She traced each glyph with her fingertips, trying to make some sense of them in the darkness. She counted the stones: three monoliths with smaller boulders piled around for support. Farther on, she thought she glimpsed a similar construction.

"This must mark the outer perimeter," Tras Sur'tian said suddenly. "According to tales, these things form a ring. The characters are probably warnings. No outsiders were allowed closer to Skull Gate than we are right now."

They moved out upon a broad mesa. No grass grew, nor weeds or trees of any kind. The land had a blasted look. They walked unhampered by roots or loose stones. The stars burned with uncanny brilliance in the vast expanse of sky.

They passed another of the stone constructions. Like the first, the individual boulders had been sculpted flat and engraved with runic figures.

"This would mark the inner perimeter," Tras Sur'tian claimed, running a hand over the stones. "The old stories must be true. These characters, if we could read them, would tell the histories of the people who lived here, their births, marriages, deaths, complete genealogies. Women would bring their babies here while priests carved their names. Beyond this point, only the men were allowed.''

Frost spat and promptly stepped past the marker. "So much for another taboo," she said stiffly.

"How much farther?" Kimon asked, shifting Aki's weight to his other shoulder.

Tras Sur'tian shrugged, offered to take the child, but Kimon declined.

They came to an abrupt halt on the jagged lip of an immense crater. Frost muttered an Esgarian expletive as she peered over the edge, thanking her gods for sharp eyes and a cautious nature. In the darkness a careless man might have fallen. "Why didn't you tell us?" she said to Tras Sur'tian.

"The legends refer to a valley," he replied, shaking his head. "Nothing like this."

"The legends are wrong, then," Onokratós interjected. "Do you feel it?" He looked at Frost. "The power radiates from here. This is the island's heart."

Frost swallowed and peered downward again. How far? she wondered. There was no stone to drop, no echo to help her judge. "I do feel it," she answered soberly, and hugged herself.

"Legend claims that Skodulac is haunted," Tras Sur'tian said to fill the sudden silence. "Long ago, when Korkyra was a much smaller kingdom, this corner of the nation was dominated by a tribe of flesh-eating savages. During our expansionist period we sought to wipe them out with the blessings of the priests of the One God, to whom such an act was abomination. We nearly succeeded, though rumor has it some escaped and dwell today in the Creel Mountains of distant Rholaroth. I don't know the truth of that.

"But Skodulac was special to them. It was a temple to their primitive gods, a training camp for their warriors, their last refuge, and finally their funeral pyre.

"The histories say that when our forces finally breached the island's defenses, the savages threw themselves into a huge firepit of unnatural origin." He paused, gazed thoughtfully into the blackness of the crater. "But all that was long ago."

Frost turned to Onokratos. "When we started out, you spoke as if you knew this place. Yet you've said little since we set foot on the island, and this crater surprised you as much as the rest of us."

The wizard stroked his daughter's hair, held her face close to his. "Gel told me the direction," he answered. "He showed me a vision of Skull Gate. It's a vast arena unlike anything you've seen. A shame the night is so thick; I had hoped to see your expression when you gazed on it." He shrugged. "Of the land itself, I know nothing; the demon did not enlighten me."

Kimon shifted his burden again, careful not to be too rough with the little queen, but plainly impatient. "Well, if it's at the bottom, there must be a road down. Let's get on with it."

Frost led them on a search around the crater's rim. The way down was, indeed, a road, wide-cut and smooth, excavated from the solid rock and earth. She marveled at its construction, knowing the great effort it must have taken to move such tonnage. She fancied she could hear the grunts and moans of the laborers, the cracking of the whips, the lumbering and creaking carts and wagons.

Tras Sur'tian had called these people savages. She laughed silently at that smug judgment. There was nothing primitive about their artifacts. The carvings on the stone markers they had passed required considerable skill and artistry, not to mention patience; this road, like the gently sloping spout of a dark, bottomless bowl, rivaled the best Korkyran highways.

If only there were more moonlight, she wished to herself as they descended into the deeper blackness. The earth formed increasingly higher walls on either side of them as the road led downward. The sky became a narrow, star-sprinkled ribbon. *Maybe we should have waited for the dawn.*

"Why do the gods always prefer the dark?" Tras Sur'tian wondered aloud, echoing her thoughts.

"If they do," Kimon muttered, "then Orchos chose well. This must be the anus of the world."

"That's in Keled-Zaram," Onokratos contradicted. "There's a cave, huge bats like you've never beheld—"

"Onokratos." She brought them to a halt. The lower end of the road was still nowhere in sight. A cloying fear ate away little pieces of her courage. The night was like a strangling thing; she had never feared it before. Now, it overpowered her, swallowed her up. It made her feel small and weak.

She had been about to snap at the old man, stifle his silly, useless patter. Now, she thought better of it. "Why don't you try to summon your demon."

He didn't answer for a long moment. "I have tried to call him several times. Twice since we left the upper edge."

She uttered a quick, silent prayer. Orchos had bargained for five contestants. What would he do when only four showed up? She clutched her sword's hilt, finding no real measure of security in the contact. *I've bargained badly and doomed my friends,* she cursed herself hopelessly. *I've bungled through this from the first. I've had no plan, no real course of action. Without Gel we may be lost. Orchos wanted the demon most of all.*

"By the One God!"

She started as Tras Sur'tian's hand clapped her shoulder. Deep in private thought, she had missed the fact that the road had leveled and they had reached the crater bottom. She looked up, stared wide-eyed at the massive gate and wall that loomed before them.

"Is it real," she gasped, "or carven?"

"It is the skull of the giant, Yahwei, whose footsteps were thunder on the earth when Man climbed down from the trees," Onokratos said reverently. "It is quite real."

"How do you know that?" Frost persisted.

"I told you before, Gel showed me this place in a vision. How could I gaze on that and not wonder the same things you do?"

The stars twinkled through the huge empty eye sockets

and the place where once a nose had been. The arena's entrance was the gaping mouth itself. The lower teeth were gone and the jawbone thrust deep into the earth. The walls, extending far beyond the range of sight, held Yahwei's skull upright.

"The walls, too, are made of skulls and bones," Onokratos informed them. "Both human and animal mortared together. I can well believe Tras Sur'tian's charge that the builders were flesh-eaters."

"I'm not sure I'd feel any better about this place in the brightest daylight," Frost admitted softly, peering through the mouth into the arena's liquid blackness. Ashur nickered, and she smiled halfheartedly. She'd nearly forgotten the unicorn, he'd been so quiet since sunset. "He isn't sure, either," she added.

She gave the unicorn a couple of loving strokes, then she walked through Skull Gate into the arena.

Ashur's warning cry came too late. She saw the flames that were his eyes swell to raging fury, then pain exploded in the back of her head; she bounced helplessly off the unicorn's shoulder as the ground rushed up to meet her and the air deserted her lungs.

From the corner of her eye as she lay facedown in the dust she perceived a great, scaly *thing* as it bent over her, slavering, one taloned fist poised to rake the life from her body. Its drool splashed on her bare neck, icy cold and slimy. Its breath came harsh and rasping, and a malignant evil gleamed in its only eye. It reeked of all the charnel in hell.

She struggled to draw a breath, to reach her sword as the razored claw flashed down. Old reflexes took over and she rolled, found her feet, tugged her blade free . . . and swallowed hard.

Moving on goat legs, her foe closed for a second blow, thrashing a spiked, reptilian tail. Half again as tall as she, its great arms reached for her. She fell into a fighter's stance, terror making tight fists of her hands around the sword's hilt. If it could hit her, she tried to reason calmly, then she could hit back. And what she could hit, she could hurt. She braced herself, raising the sword.

But the creature stopped suddenly, let out a howl, an inhuman cry that was more than mere agony. It rose, erect, talons ripping at the sky, tail whipping spasmodically. It wailed again, and steam began to ooze from its saurian flesh, then a creamy foam that sizzled and popped.

She jumped away as the monster toppled. It writhed, shrieking in the throes of death, kicking up the fine, powdery ash that covered the arena's floor. Within moments, the steam and crackling foam obscured its form. Frost could feel the terrible heat generated by its dissolution. A reeking stench filled the air. She watched until nothing remained but a damp, ichorous puddle.

Tras Sur'tian stood just inside the gate, the last drops of the specially purified water pouring from the two ruptured waterskins that hung tellingly from his grasp. "I didn't think," he said lamely, mouth agape. "I just hit it."

"Don't apologize," she reassured him, going to his side. Ashur came, too, and nuzzled her shoulder. Kimon and Onokratos crept close. The children slept unaware in their arms. "What was that?" Kimon asked, appalled wonder coloring his voice.

"One of our foes, I would guess," Onokratos replied warily, his eyes sweeping around for other dangers.

A numbing chill descended over the arena. A cloud of vapor rolled from the crater's northernmost lip, blotting out the stars. Then, as they watched, the cloud shaped itself into a familiar visage, a nebulous face that grinned down at them.

Well done, daughter! The lord of worms laughed, and the sky shook with the sound of it. She heard his voice deep in her head. From the looks on her comrades' faces, they heard him, too. *First round to thee, or rather, to thy Korkyran friend.* Orchos laughed again. *Stout, for such an old fellow, is he not?*

Chapter Seventeen

Tras Sur'tian shook a defiant fist. "Not *too* old, corpse-monger!"

The wispy image of Orchos's face dissolved. "Thee honors me with such familiarity." The god of death wore human form as he appeared before them, clad in midnight garments that shimmered like moonlight on black waters. A slight breeze stirred the iron-gray of his hair. He looked altogether like a man, but for his eyes. They shone with a wisdom and knowledge that made his gaze impossible to meet.

Even his voice was almost human. "I have waited for thee."

Frost imitated the god's aggressive stance. "We had some difficulty on the way," she announced. "One of our number is missing."

His face crinkled in amusement. "Oh, he is not missing." He made a small gesture.

In the center of the arena a pale, mystical light suddenly radiated up from the ground, illuminating a tall wooden cross, the demon crucified. A low moan bubbled in Gel's throat as he raised his head and saw them.

Her eyes narrowed angrily, recalling what the demon had done to her. Gel groaned again, and the sound brought nothing but sweet pleasure.

"If it consoles thee," Orchos said amiably, "that moment of ecstasy expended the last of his power."

He knew of the rape! She cursed silently, then stopped, biting her lip. Her worst fear was now reality. Much as she loathed the demon, she had counted on his power. How would they fight Orchos now?

"Renegotiate," she said, inadvertently speaking aloud.

The death god shook his head. "Thee has made a bargain." His tone was chiding, almost fatherly. "Gel's corruption is complete, as I knew it would be." He turned toward the cross, and his voice raised in volume. "Demons are not gods. Thee could not dwell indefinitely on this plane and remain unchanged. Thee were a fool, Gel. I elevated thee, made thee a captain over the hordes of hell. But thee rebelled. Now, thee are no more than human." He nodded sadly. "Almost, I pity thee. But I do not forgive thee." He turned back to Frost, and she shivered. There was no more mirth in the maker of widows. "Thee has already defeated my servant, Kahlis, with thy magic water. So, it shall be five of thee against four of my demons."

The air shimmered. "Let none flee," the god declared.

A peculiar glow filled the arena. On the crater's lip a towering pillar of flame crackled up toward the heavens. Then, at astounding speed it began to widen. It raced around the rim until it met itself, forming a roaring wall of fire that sealed them from the outside world.

She glanced at her comrades in the strange orange-yellow brightness. Tras appeared outwardly unimpressed. Kimon, however, was not so unaffected. With Aki's weight shifted into one arm, he had bared his sword. Onokratos hugged Kalynda to his breast with both arms; his eyes reflected a hardness she could not fathom.

She turned back to the dread lord. "I don't see anybody running."

"So, let it begin," he proclaimed. He raised an arm to the sky and called, "Chaldee!"

Beside Orchos the earth heaved and split open. A terrible thrashing tossed dust and clouds. Up from the gaping fissure rose the demon named Chaldee. It drew itself erect, flexed muscles, shrugging off a cascade of dirt. Twice a man's height, he stood on powerful, bovine legs; a massive bellows-chest glittered with serpentine scales, rose and fell with each blustering breath. It curled its three-fingered hands into fists, and scimitar-shaped talons unsheathed from slits between its knuckles. Shaggy hair hid most of its head and face, but Frost could see the crooked yellow teeth as it grinned and the single huge eye that shone with festered intelligence.

Orchos's voice boomed. "Kiowye!"

A thunderclap shattered the sky. A piece of the night sky itself appeared to melt and flow to earth. As it touched the arena floor it suddenly hardened, forming a column of faceted obsidian. Another thunderclap sounded, and a webwork of cracks raced down the column's length. A third burst of thunder, so loud that Frost covered her ears. As the sound rolled away, the column collapsed in an almost musical tinkling of black crystal.

Kiowye stepped from the ruins, a creature of shining ice. Man-sized, its fingers long, razor-edged shards. It had no features, not eyes or nose or mouth. Where it stood the ground began to whiten with a fine layer of icy mist.

"Feel the cold?" Tras Sur'tian whispered. She nodded, said nothing.

"Dogon!" The death god's cry rose like a wind on the night air.

A chorus of high-pitched whines suddenly drowned all other sound. Out of nothingness, streamers of vibrant colors appeared and bolted crazily around the arena as if possessed with a wild life of their own. Round and around the streamers darted, creating an ever-tightening spiral, a dazzling vortex of scintillant hues. Mad harmonies crescendoed and abruptly ceased. The vortex whirled only a heartbeat longer. The colors dissipated, unveiling a hideous bat-winged, bat-faced monster with a man's body and the claws of a lion. Wings fluttered; a mouth opened to emit a shrill, challenging note.

Orchos's eyes flickered with anticipatory fire. Clearly,

he expected to enjoy this dark contest. "Thee has defeated the demon Kahlis," he acknowledged. "That leaves but one more participant. She is not yet arrived. But she comes, she comes."

He turned his gaze to the sky; his lips curled back to speak a name. "Ouijah!"

Frost knew what to watch for. She gazed up at the sky. A shooting star, barely visible against the fiery barrier on the crater's rim, plummeted from the velvet night. She guessed its trajectory, followed its descent, threw her arms up against the expected explosion.

Instead, the shooting star dissolved suddenly in a shower of resplendent droplets. The drops fell on the arena wall, and for a moment, nothing more happened. All was stillness. Then, Ouijah rose, dripping, born of that sparkling rain.

Orchos had called her "she." Indeed, her femaleness was obvious. Golden-skinned, proud, and tall, Ouijah was beyond the measure of any human woman. Snow-white hair cascaded in heavy curls down her back and over full, perfectly formed breasts. Frost could distinguish few other features over the distance. The demoness stared haughtily down at them from her perch atop Skull Gate's wall. The bow and the quiver of arrows Ouijah wore only enhanced her wild, alien beauty.

"The human children will be safe over there," Orchos instructed. A throne carved from gleaming onyx stood on a low dais against the opposite wall. Two small cots lay empty at the throne's foot. She was sure none of it had been there before.

Kimon carried Aki toward one of the cots. Onokratos seemed reluctant. Taking notice, Tras Sur'tian whispered some words and gently pried Kalynda from the wizard's arms. He started after Kimon.

Frost kept a careful eye on their foes. It was a perfect time for an attack with Kimon and Tras on one side of the arena, she and Onokratos on the other. Her hands drifted to her weapons, rested on the hilts. The children were placed on the cots; her friends started back across the arena.

A black shape flitted on the edge of her vision, and she jerked her sword free. It was only Ashur. Somehow, she had forgotten the unicorn. He pranced around the wall, passing under Ouijah's steady gaze, and took up guard between the sleeping girls.

"Now, I believe they are safe," she said with pointed satisfaction. She let out a slow breath and studied her opponents. It was almost a surprise to discover that fear had left her. She was resigned to what could not be avoided. "And I'm growing bored," she added. "Allow Gel to join us, and let's get on with it."

Kimon whispered, "What good is he to us now?" His sword was in his hand. She had not heard him draw it. The short sword remained in his belt.

"Fodder, if nothing else," she answered. To Orchos: "Since his magic is gone, will you give him a weapon?"

Orchos shrugged. The ropes that bound the powerless demon to the cross wondrously untied themselves. Gel tumbled to the ground in a heap. "Get up, rebel," Orchos commanded.

Gel struggled to his feet.

"Pick up thy weapon." The lord of hell pointed. "It is more than thee deserves."

Gel shook his head to clear it, bent, and lifted from the dust a huge, two-handed mace whose steel head was fashioned into eight razored edges. Had it been at the foot of the cross all the time? Frost doubted it. Orchos was taking an almost childish delight in these trivial displays of conjuration.

Gel moved sluggishly at first, then more boldly as he passed, not around, but through their opponents' line. He took a place at Frost's left hand and glared from one demon to the next. "Such as these are not worthy of me," he spat. He faced his former master. "Give me back my true form and see how quickly this farce ends."

Orchos's grim visage darkened. His anger radiated like a tangible force through the arena. "Nevermore shall thee wear thy raven form. Nevermore shall thee fly or ride the winds." The death god shook a fist, and the earth itself trembled. "Thee rebelled, broke pact with me. Now, thee are justly rewarded." He gestured to Chaldee, Kiowye, Dogon, and Ouijah. "Not worthy of thee? Foolish once-demon!" He spat, and a wisp of smoke curled up from the dust where the spittle fell. "True, they have not the magic thee once commanded. But they keep their faith and serve well the master to whom they swore allegiance. So, they are greater in value than ever thee were." A slender god-finger stabbed at Gel's heart. "Thee has forsaken much to become so little."

Gel scowled but said nothing.

Orchos turned to Frost. "Daughter, in fairness to thy frailty I have chosen warriors from the lower order of powers. These can be harmed and defeated if thee are skillful and clever. Yet, to be frank, I doubt thee can win. Still, thee made the bargain, and as thee has reason to know, I put much value in the keeping of oaths."

Frost drew herself proudly erect. The point of her sword rested on the ground; her hands rested, folded, on the pommel. "There was more to that bargain, corpse-eater," she reminded him.

"I will fulfill the terms and challenge the chaos god if thee wins."

She nodded, trying her best to meet his gaze. "Then," she said, "get out of the way."

He regarded her for an instant and the bare shadow of a smile turned up the corners of his mouth. Then, with a curt nod, he turned, strode to his throne on the arena's far side. Ashur snorted a low warning and his eye-flames flared with brief violence as the god passed near the children.

Kimon waved toward Onokratos. "What about him?" he said to Frost. "Without his demon familiar, he'll be no help."

The wizard bristled. "But I have the demon back!"

Gel growled deep in his throat. "Go chew a bone, human! My powers are gone; I am bound to no master now." He swung his mace experimentally, getting the feel of it. "I fight only because the lord of the nine hells will destroy me if I do not. I fight for a chance to live." He glanced sidelong at Frost and added, "A chance to see my son succeed where I have failed."

Frost felt her belly and the life within but refrained from any retort. Kimon did not yet know of the seed that grew in her womb, and this was not the time to worry him with that news.

"I am a man!" Onokratos insisted, balling his fists. "As much as you! I can fight!"

"You're a wizard," Kimon corrected calmly. "You *were* a wizard."

Frost put aside her own problems to deal with the old man's anger and frustration. Yet what should she do? Onokratos had no weapon, and he was too old for her kind of combat. He had some skill at sorcery, he claimed, but by his admission, that was small and weak.

Tras Sur'tian took the decision out of her hands. He moved to the other man's side and touched his arm. "Stand by the gate, friend," he said. Frost started at that. Had they, in fact, become friends? They had talked a great deal along the trail and had apparently come to an understanding of each other. Tras was not much younger than Onokratos. He was warrior-trained, though, and that made all the difference now.

Tras's voice conveyed sympathy and respect. He passed the older man his personal dagger. "If you see a way to help, do what you think best."

Onokratos hesitated, then wrapped his fingers around the blade's hilt. "My thanks, friend," he acknowledged. He shot a withering look at Gel. "You've won nothing," he said with quiet dignity to the once-demon. "You will win nothing." He turned and took up position in Yahwei's very mouth.

Orchos's voice thundered across the arena. "It shall be one on one, human and demon in separate contest."

Frost did not bother to raise her voice. She knew the lord of death would hear. "Free-for-all. When I defeat my foe I help my nearest man."

The god acquiesced. "As you wish, daughter." He raised a hand. "So, the dark contest begins." The hand came down to rest on the arm of the onyx throne.

Frost brought up her sword, crouched in a defensive posture. Chaldee yawned, grinned with wicked glee. He clenched fists, exposing his claws, and closed with her. She leaped away, taking note of the soft, powdery ground.

The demon's single eye gleamed redly, similar to the eye of the creature named Kahlis who was already dispatched. That brought her hope. Orchos had said these demons could be hurt, and they had proved that.

Chaldee blinked, then struck with viper swiftness, lashing out with his right hand. Barely faster, she ducked, sidestepped, swung her weapon in a tight arc. The blade rattled uselessly off the monster's talons. She danced away to catch her breath. Her foe was fast, maybe too fast. She was formulating a plan, but would she get a chance to use it?

She risked a glance around to see how her comrades fared. Close by, Tras Sur'tian flailed the air with his sword, thwarting an aerial attack by the bat-winged Dogon. Where were Kimon and Gel? She had no time to find out.

Soundlessly, Chaldee charged. She stood her ground until the last possible moment, then dodged, brought her sword around with all her strength, and sliced deeply into the back of the demon's thigh. But her surge of triumph was quickly smothered. No blood, no fluid of any color stained her weapon. Chaldee spun around, grinned through his shaggy beard.

She cursed, cheated of victory. *Not men,* she reminded herself bitterly. *Demons. But they still have weaknesses.* She steeled herself for protracted battle.

A piercing scream ripped through her concentration, but Chaldee moved before she could see the source. His right hand raked air, aimed for her face; his left swept upward to slash out her entrails. Her blade whistled, scoring twin gashes in her opponent's arms. Neither wound bled. Aside from diverting his attack, she had achieved nothing.

Sweat beaded on her forehead and arms. She sucked

breath and licked her lips. The veins throbbed in her
temples. She gripped her weapon with both hands, swayed,
crouched, waited for the next engagement. Dimly, she
perceived sounds of the combat around her, but she dared
not take her eyes from her foe.

Chaldee thrust twice with both sets of claws, driving her
backward. The great reach of his hirsute arms prevented
her from escaping left or right. He pushed her toward the
wall. That lone orb shone with amusement and anticipation. He opened one fist, and a set of talons retracted. He
reached for her.

With a fierce shout she rushed him, carving a trio of
cuts on his ribs. He backstepped, taken off-balance. She
lunged, seeking soft belly with her point. Too late, she
saw the hoof flash up. Pain exploded in her chest; the wind
*whoosh*ed from her lungs. She crashed to the earth, main-
taining a weak grip on her weapon.

The hoof rose again to stomp her into the dirt. Desperately, she rolled. The ground reverberated where her head
had been an instant before. Chaldee tried again, and again
she rolled, choking on the fine dust that clouded the air.
Her sword banged once on his ankle.

Suddenly, he stopped. His grin returned, and he unsheathed his claws. He bent over her, paused as if to savor
the moment, then a fist plummeted, preceded by razor
death.

With a cry, she forced muscles into action. Almost on
its own, her sword came up, pommel braced against the
ground at her side. A sickening rasp: her point slid up
between the unsheathed talons, impaling Chaldee's fist.

She gasped, drenched in fear-sweat. An uncontrollable
tremor racked her. Still, the demon's grin did not fade.

He leaned forward. Slowly, the pierced extremity forced
its way down her blade. Chaldee was oblivious to pain.
The claws descended, and she felt the strain of his weight
bearing down. He would pin her like an insect. Her muscles bunched, arteries bulged in her neck. It was no use.
Chaldee leaned upon the sword.

Gritting her teeth, she rolled again, abandoning her

sword. She scrambled to her feet. Calmly, the demon plucked the steel splinter from his flesh and tossed it away. She noticed where it fell, too far to hope of retrieving it.

He came for her then, scything the night with great, sweeping blows. She dodged, leaped, ran. It took all her skill and luck to avoid being carved like a holiday game fowl or stomped into the dirt like a worm on a wet day.

Her original plan was worthless. Chaldee kept her on the defensive. It was all she could do to stay alive. She had hoped to wound him badly enough to slow him down; then she could take time to find his vital points. Though he did not bleed, there was a way to stop him. Orchos had said so. Now she had lost her sword. That left her but one weapon.

Demonfang.

She must allow Chaldee to close with her. A single quick thrust would be her only chance. She didn't know if this demon possessed Gel's ability to control the arcane dagger. He was supposed to be a weaker, lower order of power. She could not count on that. It must be swift.

She leaped, rolled on her shoulder to avoid the demon's lightning attack. She got to her feet and glanced down. Three rips showed in the poor tunic she wore. A red scratch appeared livid through one tear. She panted for breath, ignored the mild stinging sensation and the thin line of blood that rose moments later.

She licked her lips, tasting the bitter dust that caked them. Her fingers curled around Demonfang's hilt. *All or nothing*, she resolved. She had known from the beginning it would be so, from the hour she had made her pact with the caller of souls.

She waited, tensed, for Chaldee's next rush. He opened his arms to embrace her, talons glittering in the firelight from the crater's rim, red eye shining.

"For thee, good and faithful servant!" she shouted, imitating Orchos's archaic speech. In a single swift motion she drew and hurled the dagger. A short, ear-shattering wail shivered the air before Demonfang embedded itself in Chaldee's eye.

The monster stumbled backward, fell, clutching his face. A horrible mouth opened, twisted in mute shrieks of fear and agony. Rolling, thrashing up thick clouds of dust, he tried to dislodge the cruel splinter. A pink froth began to bubble from the wound. It spilled over his scaly chest, oozed into the matted hair of his groin and legs. He struggled up, groped blindly, and fell again. Legs kicked the air; hands clenched and unclenched convulsively; claws sheathed and unsheathed.

She stared in relief and terror. No moan escaped the demon's lips, no word or curse or plea for help. His chest stopped heaving, fists suddenly relaxed, limbs spasmed once and no more.

Well done, daughter! Orchos's voice touched her mind. *A pity thy comrades fare not so well.*

Chaldee's body began to smoke and fume. The flesh cracked, split open. More of the pink froth poured out, engulfing the hidous bulk.

"Get out of my head, lord of worms!" Her triumphant shout rang with defiance and pride. "I've the weapon to beat your children. I've had it all the time. I gambled on it!"

Look again, daughter, Orchos warned.

Nothing remained of Chaldee but a rapidly congealing ichor from which the hilt of Demonfang protruded. She seized it, drew it free, and cried out in despair. Half the blade was gone, dissolved with the monster's body. What remained was a misshapen ruin bearing no resemblance to the silver metal it had once been. Nor did she sense its familiar tingle, the aura of its magic. The screaming dagger remained silent. *Dead,* she despaired, though she had never before thought of it as living.

"Damn you!" she raged. "Damn you! Damn you!"

Daughter, the death god chastised, *how can thee damn the lord of nine damnations?*

In a fury, she threw the useless scrap at him, more a gesture of angry contempt than of honest intent. It fell at his feet between the two enchanted children. Ashur trum-

peted a long, eerie note and stamped the broken blade with
his hooves.

The contest is not yet ended, he reminded her. *Attend
thy comrades.*

A new outcry caught her attention. She whirled. Onokratos
wrestled with a mighty serpent. Its coils wrapped around
his throat and upper chest. Its fanged mouth sought his
face. With one straining hand he held it off. It spat venom
at his eyes, and he barely averted his face. Then Onokratos
struck with the blade Tras Sur'tian had given him. The
first blow bit deeply, and the second sent the serpent's
head flying. The headless coils lashed him, constricted,
whipped him. Yet he managed to shrug free.

At his feet, Frost spied the corpse of another snake. The
old man was holding his own, then. She felt a flash of
pride for him.

But she was weaponless in the midst of danger. She
looked for her sword lying where Chaldee had cast it, ran,
and snatched it up.

Gel and Tras Sur'tian fought side by side against the
creature called Dogon. The Korkyran's left sleeve was
ripped away; blood streamed down that arm from a series
of deep scratches that ran from shoulder to elbow. Nor had
the once-demon gotten by unscathed. Dogon had raked
flesh from his back and upper chest. Gel bled as redly as
any human and wielded his mace with admirable determination. Unfortunately, he lacked skill and training. The
brunt of combat fell to Tras Sur'tian.

Dogon climbed the sky, let out a piercing screech,
folded his bat-wings, and dived, claws extended. Tras
dodged and thrust with his long sword, scoring a small
rent in the creature's pinion, not enough to seriously slow
it. Stupidly, Gel held his ground. His great mace arced
high, catching the orange light. But before he could bring
it down, Dogon's wings unfolded and the demon banked
sharply, smashing Gel to the earth with the hard, leathery
ridge.

She started to their aid, then stopped. The sounds of
battle had noticeably lessened. Yet there was no smell of

decaying demon-flesh, no outcry of human victory. Suddenly, she missed Kimon.

Kiowye's icy fingers were closed on his face, and he was bent backward like a child's cloth doll. His sword hung loosely in a limp grasp. The tide of fighting had carried them toward the northern wall. Even over that distance, she could see the hoary rime frosting his skin.

Red rage pumped strength through her veins. She ran at the ice-demon, jumped, kicked with both feet, spilling them all in the dust. She tumbled lithely and came up swinging. Her blade struck Kiowye at the base of the neck as he rose. The demon staggered; she spun to build momentum and slammed the keen edge against his belly with all the power she could muster. A third came down on his shoulder, intended to cleave him. Kiowye fell, and the earth whitened with a fine mist around his body.

Then he got up, unharmed. No more than a few deep chips marked the places where her blows had landed. She could not guess from his featureless face if she had even caused him pain.

Kimon staggered to her side. Bluish, mottled marks showed where Kiowye had gripped him. She could smell her lover's sweat, hear his ragged breathing, but he held his sword firmly once more. "He just won't die!" he shouted harshly.

"Fight!" was all she could say.

Together, they began to hack at the demon. She put her back into every stroke, grunting, straining. Kiowye just stood there. *I'll chip you to ice slivers*, she swore, and attacked with renewed, unreasoning fury until her arms were half-numb from the reverberating impacts.

Suddenly, Kiowye's hands shot out, caught both swords. A white wave rushed down the metal. Frost felt her hilt grow cold, the flesh of her palm start to freeze. Still, she clung to her weapon. She pulled, seeking to wrench it from the demon's grasp. Kimon tried the same, planting a booted foot in the monster's stomach for leverage.

Kiowye gave a twist, and the steel, made brittle by his touch, snapped.

She stared, dismayed, at the broken half she held. First the waterskins, then Demonfang, now her sword: what was left for her to fight with?

Kimon still had his short sword. Drawing it from his belt, he rushed Kiowye, stabbing downward with all his might. Straight through the eyeless face it plunged, and the point protruded from the back of its head.

Too late, she saw his danger. The thrust was no matter to the demon. It reached out before Kimon's hands left the hilt. Again, its frigid grip closed around his face.

His cry of pain froze the blood in her veins as surely as her lover's flesh began to freeze. She ran at the demon with the stub of her weapon.

Before she could strike, something hissed through the air. Slick, dark coils looped around her throat; twin eyes gleamed, small and red before hers. An oily, reptilian smell filled her nostrils. A wide mouth opened, fangs dripped.

Her hand darted. Fear-strengthened fingers locked around the ophidian horror close to its flat, scale-shimmering head. It writhed furiously; its coils squeezed. A throbbing drummed in her head. A red haze settled over her vision. The serpent hissed and spat, and she snapped her eyes shut to avoid the shower of its venom. No matter; the strangely cold liquid splashed her skin, and moments later, it began to burn.

An anguished scream bubbled on her blue-coloring lips, and she fell, tripping in the thick dust. The sword stub tumbled from her grasp.

A weird, warming calm wrapped around her then, and she knew she was dying. Fear lost meaning. Pain meant nothing even as more venom burned her cheeks and bare arms, as rippling muscles crushed her throat and the blood beat tempestuously in her brain. She was no longer aware of the arena. The world seemed to float around her. Only two tiny eyes remained fixed like crimson stars in a swirling cosmos.

Her empty hand rose of its own volition and gripped the serpent just below her other hand. Her fingers squeezed.

She twisted, and the scaly foe squirmed in sudden desperation. She twisted, and the muscles in her arms and shoulders and back bunched. She twisted, then jerked with a power she never knew she possessed, and her hands flew in opposite directions.

A new fluid spurted over her arms, soothing the venom burns. The coils suddenly loosened around her neck and chest. She gasped as sweet, fresh air surged into her lungs, stared at the separated pieces of the monster that had tried to strangle her. Even in death, those tiny, malicious eyes gleamed.

She cast the parts away and tried to stand, but her legs would not support her. She collapsed, lifted her head, striving to see around.

Her heart sank.

Kiowye bent over Kimon, the butt of the short sword jutting ridiculously from the demon's face. Both of its gelid hands were locked on her lover's head, and a glittering frost had turned his flesh a startling white. Forced to his knees, Kimon tore weakly at the creature's arms. A muffled, hopeless moan issued from his rimed lips.

"No!" She tried to get up, failed. Tears of frustrated anger welled in her eyes. She crawled toward the demon. "Let him go. Orchos!"

The death god was silent.

Kimon sagged unconscious as she watched. Cursing, crying, she managed to get one foot under her, then the other. She stumbled forward, weaponless, thinking only of the man who had once tried to take her life.

Kiowye batted her aside with a casual backhanded gesture. She landed hard, stunned, ears ringing. "Help him, somebody!" she sobbed. "Help him!"

But she knew there was no help.

Even as she called, Gel fell to Dogon's sweeping attack. The tip of one wing struck him at the base of his skull, and the boastful once-demon lay still.

Tras Sur'tian braced himself, weaving a halfhearted defense with his sword, unable to take the attack to his opponent, who climbed back into the sky with a shrill, victorious screeching.

Then, from the corner of her eye she saw the demoness Ouijah lift her bow. Straight for her Korkyran comrade the shaft flew. But strange transformation! In midflight the arrow elongated, thickened, took on a scaly sheen.

With a superb effort, Tras Sur'tian clove the serpent still in the air. The pieces fell lifeless and bleeding in the dust. But in that instant of distraction, Dogon plunged. His shrill cry ululated as lion claws flashed. Frost knew her friend could not react in time.

Then another sound answered the demon.

Trumpeting his challenge, streaming eye-flame, Ashur thundered into the arena, knocked Tras Sur'tian out of harm's way with a massive shoulder. The old warrior fell hard as the unicorn reared, spearing the flying demon before it could alter the path of its flight.

Dogon's inhuman cry of pain nearly split her ears. It rose into the night, spilling a dark substance from its belly.

That small victory gave her strength to move again. She struggled against her own wounds and bruises to rise. The unicorn was magic, and he had hurt the demon. Holy water and Demonfang had hurt them. Magic, then, was the only effective weapon.

And Kimon had something.

She took three swift steps and leaped, feet first, repeating a move she had used once before to topple Kiowye. She kicked hard and fell hard, but the ice-demon went sprawling.

She had only instants before the creature would be on her.

Kimon lay unmoving. She scrambled to his side. His flesh felt so cold as she listened for his heartbeat. She couldn't be sure. Maybe it was there, or maybe it was her own wishful thinking. She called his name. She slapped him twice. But his eyes did not open and he didn't move.

A hasty glance over her shoulder let her know time was up. Kiowye took the first step toward her, his hand reaching.

She tore frantically at Kimon's tunic, ripping it open

from the collar. The pouch was there, tied around his neck
with her knots. She jerked, snapping the thongs, and the
ruby talisman rolled into her palm.

She made a fist around it and anxiously turned to confront the ice-demon. A crimson nimbus radiated around
her hand; the jewel glowed with a light that revealed the
delicate bones of her fingers. She raised it over her head,
hoping its protective power could save her from Ouijah's
arrows as well.

Kiowye took another step and stopped.

A voice spoke inside her head. *Daughter, it is not
enough to hold my servants at bay. Thee must win the
contest.*

"Get out of my head, corpse-eater!"

He ignored her shout. *The odds are too much for thee.
They always were. I have not even allowed Ouijah to
unleash her full power.* She didn't want to take her eyes
from Kiowye, who stood motionless before her; yet she
felt compelled to look to the wall where the demoness
stood. *Behold,* Orchos said.

Ouijah drew a shaft from her quiver, set it to the string,
and released it straight at the earth.

The ground erupted in a huge, rolling cloud of madness.
Out of the dust rose a serpent of incredible size. Uncoiled,
its length would have stretched from head to tip of tail
completely around the arena. It showed fangs as long as
war spears. The ring of hellfire that burned on the crater's
rim glinted in a thousand places on the creature's squamous
hide and in the scarlet beacons of its eyes.

Those eyes sought hers, mesmerizing. She lifted her fist
slowly in response. The jewel's glow intensified; its light
cast shimmering rays between her fingers.

Thy pitiful talisman cannot save thee. Orchos's voice
was a pitted steel edge that sawed at her brain. *The field
shall be mine, and our pact settled as agreed. I shall cart
your souls to the fiery lake.*

The serpent slithered out toward the center of the arena,
its girth making a dry, raspy noise as it shifted the dust.
Tras Sur'tian backed away uncertainly, on guard for an-

other attack from Dogon, who still fluttered just beyond sword reach.

The serpent undulated; its great, flat head rose; its mouth opened and venom dripped. It loomed over the Korkyran.

Again, Ashur reared, bellowing, stomped the earth. The unicorn shook its wild and tangled mane and charged.

She screamed. "No! My beautiful! No!" With all her might she threw the ruby, praying its power would drive the serpent back and save her unicorn, who, she feared, had little chance against such a monster. It bounced off the oily scales with a red flash and lay in the dust.

Then, the world tilted.

Frost was thrown backward. The ground bucked and heaved beneath her. She threw her arms and legs wide in a spread-eagle, her fingers clawing, seeking purchase in the soft powder. But the earth rose and fell, wild as a raging ocean, alive with rolling, tempestuous waves of choking dirt and dust. She rode them helplessly, trying to catch glimpses about her.

Ashur's four legs pawed the air, and he trumpeted fearfully, impotently. Tras Sur'tian bounced about like a child's ball. Kimon's and Gel's bodies were tossed about like broken driftwood. Even the serpent thrashed helplessly, its sinuous bulk no advantage as great waves of earth buffeted the monster.

Suddenly, an explosion rocked the arena. On the crater rim a blinding prominence of flame leaped up from the ring of fire. It arced high across the sky and licked the earth, turning the giant snake to charred and smoking meat.

Another tremor shook the ground, evoking a sharp cry from the arena wall. Ouijah lost her footing and fell, spilling her quiver. As each shaft touched the ground it was transformed into a wriggling, angry snake.

Another explosion and a second prominence. Ouijah and serpents vanished in a shimmer of flame and smoke.

Dogon flapped around the arena like a trapped insect; leathery pinions frantically beat the air. He wailed his weird, shrill cry, a sound of purest terror. A third blast,

and a scarlet tongue of flame ended his fear. He plummeted earthward, a sparkling cinder.

An ominous quiet settled over the arena. Frost felt the
heart pounding in her chest, felt the ground tensing, gathering itself for something more.

An immense fissure suddenly opened in the arena floor,
sending a column of dust racing upward. A deep rumbling
drowned all other sound. New cracks split open, speeding
every direction, turning the floor into an unpredictable
lacework.

She had forgotten Kiowye. She glanced over her shoulder, searching for the demon. He stood not far away, as he
had when she'd used the ruby talisman against him. She
wondered if he had ever lost his balance during all the
turmoil. He stood, a frozen sculpture, while the world
fragmented. He made no effort to save himself. The earth
parted beneath his feet; he tumbled in with a surreal com-
placency that was all the more horrifying for its silence.

Kimon's body was not far away. She feared that he
might also be swallowed by the unnatural crevices that
fractured the landscape. Choking on the dust that filled the
air, she crawled toward him. If this was death, then she
would go at his side, and Orchos be damned. She reached
him, cradled his head in the crook of her arm, pressed her
face to his, and waited for it to happen.

Thunder rippled the sky. Great racking bolts streaked
the night with crackling fury. Strange colors swam in the
air, whirled in dizzying vortices, birthing winds that wailed
and made stinging darts of the finest particles.

An intense azure glow suffused the arena, and Frost
looked up to seek its source. Her voice was a small, weak
thing in the whistling gale as she called out in disbelief.

"Onokratos!"

Framed in Yahwei's mouth, the great Skull Gate, saffire-
colored energy coruscated madly around and through him.
Writhing lines of magical force whipped in all directions,
warping weather, splitting the earth, bringing the arena's
ancient walls crumbling down. On the crater's rim the ring

of hellfire swelled and raged, launching impossible blazing
streamers heavenward.

"Onokratos!" she shouted again, uselessly. "Stop! It's
over!"

But he could not stop. She saw through the scintillant
aura that surrounded him, watched him convulse in the
arcane flow. His face was a mask of terror and pain; his
mouth gaped in a noiseless scream.

He had told her.

Before Gel's enslavement made him a wizard, he had
dabbled in sorcery, learned to tap into the natural magic of
words and objects. He had never been very skilled, he
said. Yet to save their lives he had tapped into the raw,
wild power of Skodulac, magic so potent that she, too,
stripped of her witch-powers, could feel it like an unrelenting itch.

A movement caught her eye. Tras Sur'tian fought to
keep his balance as he worked his way through the rubble
that had been the wall. Winds blasted him, the heaving
earth tried to topple him. Sword in hand, he fought to
reach Onokratos.

"Don't hurt him!" she cried, swallowing dust. "He
can't control it!"

She knew the Korkyran didn't hear. He leaped a fissure
that opened in his path, tripped, recovered. His gaze fixed
on the wizard with determined intensity.

Too late, she shouted a warning. Another section of the
wall collapsed. Tras Sur'tian threw himself aside, but
battle and fatigue had taken a toll, and he moved too
slowly. Bone and mortar engulfed him, and he went down
in a cloud of obscuring dust.

She waited hopefully for something to stir in the ruins.
The dust quickly dissipated. She spied an arm. It didn't
move.

She cursed bitterly, and fresh, angry tears scalded her
cheeks. They had challenged hell and won. The dark
contest was finished. Orchos and his servants were beaten.

But her comrades were dead. And the last of their

fellowship would soon join them, slain by the same power that gave them victory.

She wiped at the tears, rose uncertainly to her knees only to be blown over by the screaming winds. She got up again, crawled on all fours toward Onokratos. Particles of dust and bone and mortar stung her eyes; a chunk of wind-driven rubble ripped a bloody gash along her right cheek. Lightning and thunder shivered the night as she made her way over and around jagged rents and cracks.

Onokratos saw her. He reached out, imploring. The pitiful look on his face spurred her on. The wizard begged for help, for release. She struggled to her feet, leaning against the rising maelstrom. She took a cautious step; another. Onokratos moved his mouth in an eerie, soundless plea.

A familiar sound rose over the wind's howling. Ashur trumpeted in fearful confusion. Someone called her name, she thought. But who lived? She dared not look behind her but focused all her will on reaching Onokratos before the power he had summoned consumed them all.

A blinding radiance surrounded him, grew brighter with each beat of her heart. He had tapped into the island's magic and could not break the link. She had to do that for him.

She was nearly there. The energy that poured through him sieved through her, now. She tingled all over; her muscles twitched and spasmed. She could not hesitate, she knew. In moments she would be as convulsive as he.

She sought forgiveness in the old man's eyes, found there a blessing. Calling up the last of her strength, she smashed her fist into his jaw.

Chapter Eighteen

All manifestations ceased. The earth stilled its rumbling. A final blast of thunder rolled away in a clear, solemn sky. On the crater's rim, Orchos's ring of fire flickered and died, leaving only pale stars to light the arena.

Frost blinked in the sudden darkness. The crumpled form of Onokratos lay at her feet. He moaned as she ran a hand over his face, and his eyelids peeled slowly back. He looked up at her, too weak to do more than nod.

She heard her name again and turned, searching the gloom. "Where?" she answered, recognizing the voice.

"I'm pinned," Tras Sur'tian called back.

She made her way carefully. With the ring of fire extinguished she could no longer see the fissures that latticed the arena floor. "I can't see you in the dark!" she shouted. "Keep talking."

A string of Korkyran curses guided her.

She had thought him buried in the rubble, but smoke and dust had deceived her. The arm she saw had been real enough; it was trapped at a peculiar angle beneath a pile of bone and mortar. His legs were also buried.

"I think it's broken," he told her as she set to work to free his arm. "I can't feel my fingers." She didn't answer but strained to move a particularly large, wedge-shaped segment that rested against his elbow. He groaned and

cursed as she shifted it. "Sorry," she said sincerely. He
shook his head, biting his lip against the pain.

"Let me help."

She whirled, seizing up a chunk of mortar to throw.

"Thee are victorious."

She knew that voice. A cold hand closed over her heart.
"Gel?" He emerged from the darkness. She stepped away
from him, and he bent to lift the piece of wall she had
been unable to move. "I thought you were dead," she told
him. Then, running a hand over her stomach, feeling the
life that grew within, life he had planted there, she added
hatefully, "I prayed you were dead."

Nearby, Ashur paced back and forth. At first, only his
eye-flames were visible in the night. But as Gel moved
closer to his mistress, the unicorn came closer. He stamped
and kicked up dust. He shook his horn threateningly. Frost
called to him. He came toward her, then stopped, backed
off a little, ran, and jumped a wide fissure. He trotted to
her side and nuzzled her shoulder.

She stroked his mane, feeling safer with him near. "We
have to free Tras," she whispered in the unicorn's ear as
she rumpled his forelock.

With Gel's help it didn't take long. A knee was badly
twisted, swollen and painful. But Tras was lucky. Bone
and mortar weighed far less than stone and mortar, or even
brick, might have. He could stand with help.

"We should get him over to the gate," she said to Gel.
"Will you carry him?"

Tras Sur'tian shunned the once-demon. "I don't need
your help. I saw the blow that knocked you down. It
wasn't so great. You feigned unconsciousness, hoping
Dogon would ignore you. You let me fight him alone."
He looked to Frost, then at Ashur. "Don't think I can
walk," he said. "Would you let me ride?"

She pursed her lips. To her knowledge, no one else had
ever ridden the unicorn. She didn't know how Ashur
would react if Tras tried to mount him, and the old warrior
was in no shape for any rough action. "Maybe, you'd
better ask him," she advised doubtfully.

But to her surprise, the unicorn went to Tras Sur'tian without another word exchanged. Tras looked questioningly at Frost. She could only shrug. "I've never figured him out," she said truthfully. She turned to Gel. "At least help me get him up."

"No." Tras Sur'tian was adamant. "I don't want his help for anything. He has shown me his mettle." Before she could argue, the stubborn Korkyran tensed his good leg and jumped, clapping his good left arm around Ashur's neck. Frost moved quickly and boosted him with a hand on the rump.

"Should have been my foot," she grumbled.

Tras lay across the unicorn's back in dead-man fashion. "No, this will do," he said, grimacing when she tried to swing his leg across. "Please, let's go."

Onokratos was sitting up by the gate. When he saw them coming, he scrambled to his feet and helped Tras Sur'tian dismount. Together, he and Frost eased the Korkyran down and propped him against a solid portion of the wall. Frost found the ruptured waterskins where her old friend had discarded them earlier. She squeezed out a few precious drops to wet his dry lips. Then she rolled them into a bundle to cushion his head.

"You seem to have recovered quickly," she said to Onokratos when Tras was comfortable.

"I feel fantastic!" the wizard answered, clipping his words. "Perhaps some residual effect of the energies that channeled through my body."

"It won't last," she warned him.

Gel thrust a finger at the sky. "Look."

The stars no longer held their fixed places but tumbled randomly around the heavens. Familiar constellations broke up and re-formed in other parts of the sky. Here and there, a star winked momentarily brighter, icy blue or smoldering red, before it vanished. New stars formed.

"What's happening?" Tras Sur'tian whispered.

Onokratos answered, awed. "Chaos."

"And death," Gel added, unmoved.

Frost could only nod. "Orchos has kept his pact. He challenges Gath for the souls of our children."

They watched the silent spectacle overhead. Frost thought she should hear explosions, thunder, crashes, and crackles, but there was only supernatural quiet. Even their breathing was muted.

"What can we do?" Onokratos said when he could stand the silence no longer.

"Wait," Gel told him dispassionately.

"We should get to Aki and Kalynda," Frost said, slapping her forehead. "Make sure they're still all right."

"They're fine," Tras Sur'tian reassured her. "The earth did not rise, nor fissure open where they lay. As if a barrier prevented any harm from reaching them."

"What about Kimon?" said Onokratos.

She stopped short, bit her lip, looked out over the dark field toward the place where she had left him. "I don't think we can help him," she answered, and blinked back tears. She had shed too many already; there would be no more. "I held him, but his flesh was so cold."

"Bring him anyway," Tras Sur'tian said. "Bring everyone here, together. We are . . ." He hesitated, shook his head, seeming at a loss for words. "I don't know. More than a family, now." He turned a scornful gaze on Gel. "Most of us, anyway. We have to care for our dead."

Frost bent down beside him. She could read the pain in his expression, in the thickness of his speech. She ran a hand along his face. His skin was very warm. "You're not well," she said.

He caught her hand, squeezed it. "Hang on, woman," he urged, returning her concern. "It's almost over."

She glanced up at the tumultuous sky and the insanely swirling stars. "Yes," she agreed. "One way or the other."

"Bring them," he whispered, patting the ground at his side. "Bring them all."

She promised him.

There was no way to measure the time that passed, but it crept by with agonizing slowness.

The stars stopped moving.

A while after that, Orchos appeared to them, man-sized. There was a different look to him. His shoulders slumped. The light in his eyes seemed weaker, almost bearable. Deep lines creased his brow. *Worn,* she decided. The god looked tired. She did not bother to rise from where she sat between the still forms of Aki and Kimon. She, too, was tired.

"I cannot win." The lord of hell spoke with a human voice, not trading thoughts.

"And you cannot lose," she responded with a shrug. She knew that for truth. There had been time to think about it while the gods battled. "Death and chaos are equally matched."

"Thee has failed!" Gel smugly accused.

Orchos raised a cautioning finger. The gleam returned once more to those dreadful eyes. "I will deal with thee soon, cursed rebel. Thee are to blame for much that has happened. For now, hold your tongue while honorable beings counsel."

Gel pressed into the deep shadows of the wall and said no more.

"Are you giving up?" Frost asked, too weary to pursue a passionate interrogation. She gazed on the gentle, composed features of the child-queen she had fought so hard to save. A lock of hair had strayed over Aki's face; she brushed it back in place.

She had come so far, struggled so hard. Now, none of it was in her hands.

"Daughter, I am bound by pact with thee," the death god said, "to fight to a conclusion, even though there can be none." He indicated the stars. They twinkled now in calm serenity, as if nothing had transpired. But they were not the old stars she knew. "Our conflict is not without consequences, however. We ravage the very fabric of destiny with our contest. Gods and mortals alike will suffer for this."

She cut him off. "Are you asking me to release you from your freely given vow?"

The god looked askance. "Daughter, thee has fought bravely with good friends when other mortals would have shriveled in fear. Thee has dared hell, defeated demons, and bargained with gods—"

"The point," she insisted dryly, "get to the point."

He fixed her with his gaze. For an unsettling moment, she feared she might have pushed him too far. But he let out a long sigh, an oddly human thing for one such as he. "Very well. In the short of it, thee has impressed even the lord of spiders with thy deeds."

That brought her to her feet. "What?"

"He offers solution." His gaze shifted to include Onokratos, who sat with Kalynda's head cradled in his lap, her fine hair spilling over his knees into the dust. Orchos pointed to the child. "The soul of that one belongs to Gath; he will not surrender what is rightfully his. She died of the spider's venom, and he will not be deprived."

He pointed to Aki. "That one, however, did not die. Her soul was unnaturally stripped from her body. Gath has no legitimate claim to it."

Now the god looked at each of them, one by one, long and lingering looks that chilled her to the marrow. "The chaos lord offers generous terms. He will give up her soul if another soul willingly takes her place."

The silence thundered in her ears. Then, she looked down on Kimon's sweet face. There was no warmth left in him. He was lost to her forever. She could think that, now, without a little knife turning in her heart. How easy it was to accept death when she had lived with it so long.

And Aki. She bent and touched the smooth ivory of her cheeks. That day seemed so distant when the little queen had named her champion and made her royal guardian. Over the days and nights they had shared, the formality between them had faded, replaced by casual hours of storytelling and secret sharing.

She had been *changed* by the child. Transformed by a special kind of magic. Aki had taught her to love and let herself be loved. Why hadn't she realized that before?

She owed Aki for that. She owed her the chance to grow up and find her own Kimon.

"I'll go," she said, meeting the death god's gaze. She had not been able to do that until now.

"No, you won't." Tras Sur'tian's eyes batted open. She had thought him asleep. "I'm old. These bones will never heal properly enough to let me bear steel again. I'll be no good to Aki or anyone else as a cripple. Let me go."

Onokratos looked slowly up. When he spoke, Frost saw the sheen of tears on his lashes. "Neither of you may go," he said. "I'm to blame for this sorry affair." He smoothed Kalynda's hair, lifted her head, and let it softly down to the ground. He folded her hands in the traditional manner. "She was the only child of an old man's body. When she was born, I thought it a miracle. Her mother died in childbirth, and I raised her alone." He turned to Frost, pleading for understanding. "She was the only thing I had to love!" he cried. "I have to be the one to go. She'll be so alone without me." He hung his head; his tears fell on Kalynda's bosom. His next words were a barely audible whisper. "And I would be so alone without her."

Frost knelt beside him, took his head in her hands, touched her forehead to his in sympathy. "It won't be any of the known nine hells," she said. "You don't know what it will be like."

His eyes, suddenly lucid, penetrated to her very heart. "Whatever horrible thing awaits, could I let my daughter face it alone?" He clasped her wrists and pressed her palms together. "Could you let Aki face it alone?"

She hung her head.

"It is right and fitting thee should come," Orchos approved. "Thee fought surprisingly well and nearly to self-destruction. I admit I never thought thee skilled enough in the sorcerous arts to shape the power of this sacred place."

Frost answered with unexpected pride, mocking the death god's speech. "Thee knows well enough: magic is seldom a matter of skill, but of courage and desire."

Orchos took no offense. "Well said, daughter. Onokratos desired to save his Kalynda-child. And he had courage to act on what he thought must be done to achieve that. Such qualities are human-rare.''

''You speak in eulogies already!'' Tras Sur'tian shouted angrily. ''You so-called gods! You disgust me!''

The merest trace of amusement lifted the corners of Orchos's mouth. ''To be honest, thee humans are often equally mysterious to the gods. We made thee, but we do not understand thee. Thee are not like us. This *love* for instance. Where did thee get it? It comes not from us. Yet it pervades you creatures, dictating much of what you do, determining much of who you are.'' He spread his arms, a gesture meant to include them all. ''Everything you have done here, you have done for love.'' He indicated Onokratos. ''He began this for love of his daughter.'' He pointed to Frost. ''She hunted the wizard for love of the Aki-child; and she came to love a man who meant to kill her for money.'' He pointed to Kimon, then to Tras Sur'tian. ''She allied herself to one she loves as a father, one who loves the Aki-child as much as she does.'' Lastly, he returned to Onokratos. ''And now, she even begins to feel love for the man who began it all.''

The god rolled his eyes. ''All of you are bound to each other by expressions of love.'' He looked back at Tras Sur'tian. ''You find us disgusting?'' He shook his head. ''We find you unfathomable.''

''You've slipped into human speech patterns,'' Frost pointed out.

Orchos shrugged again. ''Such as thee may corrupt even the gods.''

He turned to Gel in the shadows. ''Come out, rebel. There is no love here for thee.'' There was no movement by the wall, and Orchos called out again, darkly. ''Face me, miserable creature. Show at least as much courage as these humans who stand in my presence!''

Gel drew himself stiffly erect and strode up to his former lord. A damp sweat-shine gleamed on his dark skin, though his outward manner betrayed nothing but arrogance. ''Thee cannot order me about, worm-eater. I am no longer yours, nor shall I serve that human miscreant. My powers are gone and all pacts made meaningless.''

The death god spat in the once-demon's face. ''Thee are less than the vilest beast. Had thee any honor, thee would recall thy pact with the Onokratos-human was binding until his daughter's soul was returned to her body.

''But thee has no honor! Thee are a rebel, rebellious to the human and to me. Thee wished to be free of the nine hells.'' Orchos's eyes burned with a strange glow. Suddenly, slender bolts of white fire leaped from his black pupils to lick at Gel's face. The once-demon screamed and stumbled back, clutching his cheeks. ''Then, by my name, thee shall be free. But by those cruel brands shall all know thee and shun thy treachery.''

Gel shot back a look of purest hatred and anger. He lowered his hands as if to deny the pain, but they clenched into fists at his sides. On his right cheek, Frost saw the charred, smoking glyph, the sign that meant rebel, that Orchos had seared into his flesh. She knew there was a similar brand on his other cheek.

''Free, then,'' Gel bellowed triumphantly. ''I'm free!'' He turned his back on Orchos to show his contempt. A hideous grin split his face. ''These little marks,'' he said, ''such a small price for freedom! Now, your kingdoms will be mine.'' He clapped his hands together for joy. ''Rebel is not a bad name. I shall gather men, the corrupt, the greedy, men you would call evil, and many others. They will flock to me, all seeking the one thing I still possess.'' He turned back to his former master. ''Tell them, you great butcher! Tell them!''

Frost waited for the death god's answer. Gel was too self-assured in his boasts. What was it she still did not know? She ran a hand over her belly, feeling for the life within. Did he mean that?

Orchos met her gaze evenly. ''He cannot die by normal means,'' he told her. ''Though he is powerless, he is still born of magic. Only magic can harm him.''

''And I have more to look forward to in this brave new life!'' Gel raved. ''See how she rubs her belly? Soon

I shall have a son bestowed of all my powers, demon-spawned on mortal flesh.'' His eyes burned with an insane light. At least, it would have been insane in a human. "Through him, my power will live!"

Tras Sur'tian struggled up on one leg. Onokratos moved to her side, caught her elbow. "Is it true?" the wizard insisted.

"How?" shouted the Korkyran. "When? Was it in the woods? That night you both disappeared?"

She separated herself from her friends and closed the distance between herself and the once-demon. He towered over her, grinning. "And it was not so bad, either, was it, woman?" he said.

She smiled a broad, false smile. Her bare foot lashed out, smashing his groin. He doubled in excruciating pain and his chin met her knee. She pounded the back of his skull, sent him crashing nose to the ground. She kicked him twice in the ribs with a cold, relentless fury. Then, spying a chunk of rubble near at hand, she paused long enough to fetch and hurl it with all her strength down upon his upturning face.

Gel lay unmoving for only a moment. Then his eyes peeled slowly open above a crushed nose and ruined mouth. A large bruise quickly purpled his forehead. Yet only a few drops of blood trickled from any of the wounds. Swaying uncertainly, he got up.

"Thee can hurt me," he said thickly, and his grin returned, an evil mockery of a smile through torn and swollen lips and shattered teeth. "But I will never die. Go where thee will, woman, and remember to look over thy shoulder. I will be behind thee until the day I take my child from thy helpless arms. On that day, look no more for anything."

Frost was numb to fear and to threats, numb to every-thing but her anger. Bending, she scooped up another fist-sized piece of mortar. "I'll never have it!" she swore defiantly. "I'll never let your abomination be born! Not to my body! Follow me, if you dare. I'll find a sword, cut off your legs so you can't follow far, cut off your arms so you can't even drag your pathetic husk along in my trail. So you can't die? Live, then. Live, and suffer as mortals suffer. I can make you suffer!'' As she had seen the death god do, she spat full in his face. ''How new you are to this world. How naïve!''

Orchos broke in before her fury was fully vented. ''There will be no child, rebel. I deny you that, or any progeny.'' Again, white fire erupted from his eyes. Frost recoiled, an uncomprehending scream rising in her throat, a scream that died unvoiced. There was no pain where the flames touched her, only a sensation of emptiness. She touched her belly and rejoiced.

Gel's seed grew no more, nor would it ever grow.

''Curse thee!'' Gel howled, shaking his fist at the lord of the nine hells. ''Thee has killed my child, my son! But not all my hopes. I am yet free from hell!''

A strange smile parted the god's lips, an expression that suddenly made Frost shudder for the cruelty behind it. ''Are thee?'' he taunted. ''Or have thee entered another, more subtle hell?''

Gel squinted, stricken by those words; fear and doubt twisted his broken features. ''Play no games with me!'' he shouted. But Orchos only smiled. Gel peered long into that godly face, then let go a horrified wail, turned, and fled, shoving Tras Sur'tian aside as he disappeared through Skull Gate and into darkness.

''Good riddance!'' Tras Sur'tian barked, hauling himself up on his good leg, trying not to bump his arm.

Frost stared through Yahwei's mouth into the impenetrable gloom. Over her shoulder, she said to Orchos, ''Where will he go in this world?''

Came a sibilant whisper in her mind: *Not far, daughter. The scales always seem to balance.*

A cry sounded in the distant stillness; a hoarse shout was cut brutally short.

Moments later, a measured, casual clip-clop echoed on the smoothly worn path just beyond the gate. All turned to watch the flickering pair of flames that descended the road, passed beneath Yahwei's rotten teeth.

"Such eyes," Orchos said. "In all the vast cosmos I have never seen their like."

The unicorn emerged from the night, went straight to Frost, and nuzzled her shoulder. The ebony spike that jutted from his brow glistened with a slick wetness.

She stroked his mane from crest to withers. "I didn't see him leave," she said.

Onokratos also stroked the unicorn. "Born of magic," he mumbled. "Slain by magic."

Orchos glanced upward at the stars. "Balance is almost restored," he said. "Gel is justly rewarded, as I knew he would be." His gaze fell heavily on Onokratos. "Now, it is time for thee to show that a mortal's honor has greater value."

Onokratos moved off from the others. He looked steadfastly on the lord of the nine hells. "I am ready to join my daughter," he said. "For Kalynda's sake and for Aki's, do what must be done."

Orchos gestured. "Look thee on the sky."

They followed his upward gaze. The stars shifted again; constellations took on their familiar shapes and claimed their proper positions in the heavens. Then a tenuous web woven of soft saffron light segued over the firmament. Tangled in the strands was Kalynda. She did not struggle. Indeed, she smiled and beckoned to her father.

But in the center of the sky-spanning web, Frost spied something else, an amorphous black thing, limbless, eyeless. She had the sensation of being scrutinized and knew that the thing looked back. The hairs stood up on her neck.

"Gath?" Tras Sur'tian whispered.

She could only nod.

Father? Kalynda's voice touched their minds. *Do you love me, Father?*

Onokratos gave a small, choking cry and nearly collapsed. Tras Sur'tian moved with surprising speed, considering his twisted knee, and caught the old man. He gasped from pain as he took part of the weight on his broken arm. But he did not let go.

"The chaos lord waits," Orchos said.

Onokratos recovered himself. His gaze drifted up to Kalynda's image. "She needs me to be with her," he told everyone. To Orchos: "What must I do?"

"Give yourself willingly."

His eyes never left Kalynda, never wandered to the yawning blackness that was Gath. "I've already said I would."

Orchos answered, "Then, there is no more."

With a serene grace, the wizard fell back into Tras Sur'tian's arms. The Korkyran made not a sound but lowered him gently to the dusty floor, peered deeply into the open eyes, which even in death seemed fixed on his daughter. Tras's shoulders drooped, and he hung his head, unable to give voice to his feelings. Finally, he looked up. "He's gone," he said.

"So is Gath," Frost informed him, "and Kalynda and Orchos."

They gathered him up between them and placed his lifeless corpse beside his daughter. Frost touched the cheeks of the silken-haired child. It was no longer enchantment that kept her so still, but cold, icy death.

"What about Aki?" she asked of Tras Sur'tian when he bent over the little queen.

"She breathes," he said, though all joy seemed drained from him. "See, her chest rises and falls in an easy rhythm."

She leaned over and felt Aki's face. It was warm with life. Two small eyes fluttered open, then closed again. A faint smile lighted her innocent face. "Let her sleep a while longer," Frost decided. "Maybe we can carry her away before she has to see any of this."

Tras sat back wearily and covered his eyes with a hand. The pain of his injuries was present once more in his demeanor. She sat down beside him, wishing she could lean her head on his shoulder as she had done once before, wishing for the comfort of arms around her. But that would cause him greater discomfort. She would have to get up soon and find something to splint his broken arm.

"I want out of this business," she confided quietly. "A farm, maybe, like Oona's. Or maybe an inn where I could dance and drink until dawn and never have to report to a barracks." Tras didn't respond. He had passed out or fallen asleep.

She looked at the stars, at the blackened crater rim, at the bodies of Onokratos, Kalynda, and Kimon. Somewhere, upon the road, was Gel's body.

"Thank you, Ashur," she said to the unicorn standing patiently close at hand. He tossed his mane, whickered, and was quiet again. "Thank you for killing him."

Her gaze fell on Kimon, lingered. A wistful memory stole upon her of a day in the woods and soft breath on her face. That little knife began to turn in her heart again, and she waited for the pain to pass. She had tamed bitter memories before. If only she could cry; but she was too exhausted.

I know thee has no tears . . .

She started as the thought touched her mind. "Orchos!" She sat up. There was no sight of the master of men's souls.

. . . or thee might rouse him from this sleep as thee did once before.

In an instant she scuffled through the dust on hands and knees to lean over Kimon. Her tears *had* awakened him once before from a spell Onokratos had called the doom-sleep. How many days, weeks ago? Would it work now? Was that all Kiowye had done? If only she could cry! She had to cry!

Do not, daughter. He is my gift to thee. Unlike the chaos lord, I am not so pinching with a soul. I get so many, and I shall have him again someday. But there is one more matter . . .

A piercing shriek from the far side of the arena brought her to her feet. "No!" she wailed. "I saw it destroyed!" She clutched the empty silver sheath on her hip. "I haven't the will to fight it. I'm too tired!"

It was not destroyed, Orchos told her. *It can never be destroyed. It was Ouijah's illusion that made thee think it ruined, and my power that kept it under control when thee cast it away.*

The tortured sound reached a higher, insistent note. "It wants blood!" she said. "And I am sick of blood!"

The image of the lord of nine hells took shape before her. In his hand, he held Demonfang. He studied it curiously, turned it so the blade caught and reflected starlight. The dagger screamed its hunger.

Be silent, she heard the death god say, and Demonfang obeyed. He tossed it at her feet. *Now, sheathe it.*

She hesitated, reluctant to reclaim the cursed weapon. "No, I want no more from it. I have fed you souls long enough, corpse-eater. I am done with killing."

Sheathe it, daughter. Then bury it, if thee likes, or drop it in a well. But it belongs to thee for as long as thee walks this earth.

She bent, picked up Demonfang from the dust, slammed it into the sheath. Then she unbuckled its belt and held it out to the death god. "Take this burden from me," she begged. "I can't bear it any longer. I'm too weary."

Orchos was no longer there.

"Samidar?"

She turned at the sound of her name. Kimon stirred, raised himself up. His eyes opened slowly, beautiful eyes that smiled and made her forget Demonfang's evil, eyes that filled her with joy. She flung herself down beside him and kissed him, pressed her face to his.

Then the tears came, grateful, happy tears.

And a voice in her head said: *Farewell, daughter, until we meet forever.*